Wild Rose

MARY CANON

D044587

A SIGNET BOOK

NEW AMERICAN LIBRARY

For Brenda and Randy Autrey, beautiful friends

NAL BOOKS ARE AVAILABLE AT QUANTITY DISCOUNTS WHEN USED
TO PROMOTE PRODUCTS OR SERVICES. FOR INFORMATION PLEASE
WRITE TO PREMIUM MARKETING DIVISION, NEW AMERICAN LIBRARY,
1633 BROADWAY, NEW YORK, NEW YORK 10019.

Copyright © 1984 by Mary Canon

SIGNET TRADEMARK REG. U.S. PAT. OFF. AND FOREIGN COUNTRIES
REGISTERED TRADEMARK—MARCA REGISTRADA
HECHO EN CHICAGO, U.S.A.

SIGNET, SIGNET CLASSIC, MENTOR, PLUME, MERIDIAN AND NAL BOOKS
are published by
New American Library,
1633 Broadway,
New York, New York 10019

First Printing, August, 1984

1 2 3 4 5 6 7 8 9

PRINTED IN THE UNITED STATES OF AMERICA

CHAPTER ONE

BELLE ERIN.

Just the plantation's name made Rose Marie's hands pack faster.

"September is upon us, little ones," Andre Jacquard had proclaimed just two days earlier. " 'Tis time we thought of Belle Erin!"

It was the way of the Carolina low country. All the planters fled the swampy rice lands of the plantations in early May because of the danger of malaria.

Andre Jacquard was even more punctual than his fellow planters about moving his family to Charleston for the summer months. The dread disease had claimed his beautiful wife, Nelia, five summers before.

Unlike her younger sister. Catherine, Rose

could not wait to return to Belle Erin in the fall. It wasn't that she didn't enjoy the summers in Charleston. She did. It was a town of elegance and gaiety, and she would not think of missing racing day, or the St. Cecilia Ball, or the cotillions beneath the giant oaks and magnolias in the gardens of Johnson House on the Cooper River.

But always, come the first of September, Rose's thoughts would turn to Belle Erin. There she could ride in the early morning, and shoot with her father in the afternoons. And in the evenings she could sit rocking on Belle Erin's wide, white-columned veranda and smell the scents of her beloved South Carolina nights. The peace and tranquillity of those evenings with her father, the muted singing wafting up from the Darkies quarters near the river, were the stuff of life for Rose.

"Miz Rose, why yo take all dese clothes ta Belle Erin? Ain't no way in de worl one gal can wear so much in de country!"

The puzzled frown on Arleta's face brought a chuckle to Rose's lips. Her maid's words had been the same each September for as far back as Rose could remember.

"Because, Arleta, if I didn't take five brimming trunks of finery, what would you have to do at Belle Erin?"

"Hawmf! I takes care of you, *dat's* wha ah do!

10

No self-respectin' Southern lady be wit'out a maid. Lor', Lor', what would peoples think?"

This Arleta truly believed, for, like Catherine and Rose herself, the black girl had been raised on tradition. No self-respecting Southern lady would be without a maid, any more than a Southern gentleman would be without a manservant.

It was just the way things were.

"Rose . . . Rose?"

It was Cat's voice from the foot of the stairs.

"We're nearly finished," Rose called. "Come help us sit on the lids!"

Rose heard her sister's slippered feet on the stairs, and seconds later Catherine burst into the room.

Cat was, to the day, three years younger than Rose. Every October 10 at Belle Erin, Andre Jacquard would invite the neighboring planters up and down the Ashley River to a birthday party for his "little Cat" and his "wild Rose."

It was Rose who had shortened her sister's name. Catherine had arrived on Rose's third birthday, and no matter how she had tried, she could never get beyond "Cath." Eventually the *h* was dropped and Catherine had become "Cat."

"Your beau is here to say good-bye," Cat said, a sly smile spreading across her cameo-perfect features.

"I have no idea *which* beau you mean," Rose said, assuming the haughtiest air she could manage while bouncing on top of a chest. "Come, sit on the other end. Arleta, see to the catch."

"Yes'm."

"Your *best* beau," Cat replied, adding her diminutive weight to the lid, "Hollis Johnson. He's come to bid you a fond adieu, and he's brought news of the abolitionists!"

The "fond adieu" brought a piercing laugh from Rose's full lips. It was a product of the romantic French novels they had purloined from one of their mother's trunks months before. In the novels, the hero was always bidding "fond adieu" to his lady before going off to die in some horrible war.

"I think you shall miss Hollis, Rose. He truly loves you."

"Does he, now?" Rose replied, bouncing on the trunk lid. "Well, maybe he will appreciate me more after he has been around the Yankee girls at West Point for a while."

"I think, dear sister, you have the coldest heart in the world. Poor Hollis, going away to Yankeeland! I daresay he'll be converted and return to us a Northerner!"

Rose moved to a second chest with a shake of her head. Cat was overdramatic. Rose was fairly sure that when she was twelve, no such thoughts had ever entered her head.

They didn't now, a month short of her sixteenth birthday.

But then, there were few things alike about the Jacquard sisters.

Rose had her father's wine-dark hair, olive skin, and raven-black eyes. And like Andre Jacquard, Rose was romantic, had an eloquent wit and a profound zest for life.

Cat, on the other hand, was the picture of their Irish mother, Nelia O'Rourke. Her hair was auburn, her skin alabaster, and her eyes a pale blue that turned to gray when a mood was upon her, which was often.

Her mood now was one of mischief as she refused to let the matter of Hollis Johnson die.

Hollis was almost twenty, four years Rose's senior. His father, Cory, was Andre Jacquard's law partner and dearest friend. Their children had practically grown up together, and Charleston society had long ago decided that a match between Hollis and Rose was made in heaven.

In the past year Hollis had made it all too plain to Rose that he agreed.

She didn't.

"He is with Father now in the piazza."

"Who is?" Rose said, moving to yet another trunk.

"Hollis, of course," Cat replied, exasperation in her voice until she saw the faint smile on Rose's lips. "Oh, you're teasing!"

"Am I? Arleta. . . ."

"Comin' . . . comin'."

"I think Hollis is so handsome, and I'm sure he'll be even more so in West Point gray."

"I agree. By the time he gets his commission he will have grown into a fine man."

"Rose," Cat cried, "Hollis is nineteen. He *is* a man!"

"Perhaps to you, darling sister, but . . ." Rose saw the perplexed look on her sister's elfin face and thought better of finishing the statement. Instead, she changed the subject. "What of the abolitionists?"

"They caught two of them before they could get off Hilton Head Island. The third got away, and they say he's headed inland."

Talk of the three abolitionists from Boston had been sweeping the low country for the past week.

The year before, a slave—Toby Garrett—had run to freedom in the North. He had managed to reach Boston, but once there he had been apprehended and returned to his South Carolina owner under the Fugitive Slave Law.

His deportation back to the South had caused riots in Boston, and a federal marshal had been killed. Boston abolitionists had held meetings, marched in the streets, and started huge fires to protest the law.

Three of the more radical abolitionists had decided to take the matter into their own hands. Secretly they had come south to Hilton Head Island and attempted to start a slave rebellion on the Brownhill Plantation and once again free Toby Garrett.

In the ensuing melee, two slaves and the plantation's white overseer had been killed.

A shiver of fear ran up Rose's spine at the words "Slave rebellion."

In 1831, a Virginia slave named Nat Turner had led Virginia slaves in a rebellion that had left fifty five whites dead.

Rose had heard the tale of this rampage over and over again when she was a little girl. Even now the thought of it made her cast a furtive glance at her buxom black maid, Arleta.

"Wha's wrong, Miz Rose?"

"Nothing, nothing, Arleta," Rose replied, forcing the thoughts of rebellions and abolitionists into the back of her mind. "Only one left. Hurry, Father surely thinks I've dawdled away the day!"

As if this were his very thought, Andre Jacquard's rich baritone reached her from the foot of the polished mahogany staircase. "Ladies, if you would, please? We'll never reach the Jacksonboro ferry by nightfall!"

"Yes, Father," Rose called out as she bounced from the lid of the last trunk.

"And, Rose, you have a visitor on the piazza!"

"Yes, Father. Arleta?"

"Yes'm?"

"Fetch Otis and Luther to bring the trunks."

"Yes'm."

Rose paused in her own flight in front of the

full-length mirror near the door. Carefully she smoothed the flounces on the full skirt of her carriage dress, then frowned. Really, two instead of three crinolines beneath it would have been enough. The dress was one of her favorites, of a deep indigo-blue silk. It was close-fitting in the bodice, with soft folds crisscrossing and outlining her breasts. It nipped in at her tiny waist, then fell in swirling folds to her ankles.

All in all, not too distressing a sight, she thought. But I must remember not to lean over too abruptly, or I shall show a bit too much bosom.

She snatched a pelerine mantlet of a light blue edged in white lace from a hook on the mirror and draped it around her shoulders, then placed a matching ruched silk bonnet on her head.

She was arranging her raven ringlets to fall just so on each side of the bonnet when she saw Cat's face in the mirror beside her split into an impish grin. "Must your dress and hair be so perfect for Papa?"

"Of course not," Rose said, matching the mischievous gleam in Catherine's eyes with one of her own. "I wouldn't have Hollis going off into the clutches of those Yankee belles without remembering how pretty a Southern girl can be!"

"Why, of course," Cat said, curtsying slightly with a rosebud pout at her lips, "especially when that girl is the next belle of Charleston."

"Next?"

"Of course," Cat slyly replied, edging toward the door. "When Camilla Boyd abdicates—"

"Imp!" Rose cried, and lunged.

With a shriek of laughter, Cat leaped through the door and in seconds Rose heard her scampering down the carpeted stairs.

Camilla Boyd, indeed! Rose thought, choosing a dark blue parasol from a nearby stand and moving into the hall.

Camilla was Rose's chief rival for the attention of Charleston's beaus. But, unlike Rose, who enjoyed the adulation, Camilla craved it. Her every waking moment was spent with her mother discussing the problem of choosing Camilla's future husband.

Until the blossoming of Rose Marie Jacquard this past year, the petite blond Camilla had enjoyed a clear field with the wealthy merchants' and planters' sons, including Hollis Johnson.

But Rose had changed all that when she appeared at this year's St. Cecilia Ball. Within minutes after her arrival Rose's dance card was filled, and during her moments of rest between dances she was attended by all but a few of the available beaus.

Rose had enjoyed the attention, but thought little of it until later, when she heard how angry Camilla Boyd had been. From then on, at every gathering, Rose had nurtured the flames in the

17

young men's eyes—not because she coveted one of them for a husband, but because Camilla did.

Rose had disliked Camilla for as long as she could remember. Not only had Camilla gone to a seminary in the North, but she had traveled with her parents to England and France. And she hadn't failed to tell Rose and the other planters' daughters about her travels, as well as impress upon them how "mature travel makes one."

In a pique one afternoon, Rose had informed Camilla that Charleston, Belle Erin, and eastern South Carolina were as "mature" as she wanted to be.

And there were other things. Camilla could be merely spiteful and haughty to her friends, but she was downright cruel to her slaves. Unlike Camilla's father, Rafe Boyd, and a few of the other planters, Andre Jacquard had never beaten a slave. But what if some hellfire abolitionists from the North were to fill their ears with tales of freedom and lies about the promised land north of the Mason-Dixon line? Would they, too, run riot and rebel?

Rose shivered.

She hoped they would catch that third abolitionist soon.

A gentle breeze rolled from the sea, filling Meeting Street and wafting across the piazza of the Jacquard town house. Though the sun was

and quickly moved to make light of it. "Oh, Hollis, must you be so formal?" She laughed and threw her arms about his neck.

Before the young man realized it, he had been soundly kissed, and felt a tremor run through his body from the contact with hers.

"There, that's how two old playmates should greet one another!"

"Rose . . ." Hollis' stocky, well-built body now looked awkward as he stood before her, shifting his weight from one foot to the other. A crimson flush had already crept up from his collar to his cheeks.

Behind the couple, a rumbling laugh erupted from Andre Jacquard. "Pay her no mind, lad, she is baiting you."

"I'm not!" Rose said, allowing Hollis to lift her arms from his neck. "That would be flirting, and one doesn't flirt with old friends."

"Doesn't one? Your mother and I were fast friends for five years before we wed."

"And did Mother flirt?"

"Outlandishly," Andre said with another laugh, and extended his hand to Hollis. "I must see to the carriages. Do well at the Point, my boy. Show the Yankees!"

"I will, sir. But then, it should be easy. There's not a Yankee alive who can outride or outshoot a Southerner."

A slight cloud passed over Andre Jacquard's face as he released the younger man's hand.

"More than riding and shooting will be needed in the days ahead, son. Show the Yankees you can outthink them as well."

As soon as the tall figure had disappeared around the corner of the house, Hollis gripped Rose's elbow and spun her to face him. "Must you act so in front of your father?"

"How so, Hollis?"

"You were flirting."

"Was I? Perhaps a bit, but then, I'm fifteen and ready to begin. Besides, Papa knows it means nothing."

"You can be the most exasperating and . . . and . . ."

Rose moved her fan over the bottom half of her face to hide the sudden smile on her lips. Hollis was biting his lower lip, and one eyebrow was arched in frustration as he searched for the right word.

"And . . . ?"

He swallowed. "The most beautiful creature in Charleston."

"Merci, mon gallant," she quipped. "And you are the handsomest."

Hollis flushed red again. "Then all the more reason, Rose . . ." His hands came up to find her waist and pull her to him. Deftly Rose eluded his grasp, and Hollis found himself turned toward the stairs.

She knew what he was about to say, and she

didn't want to hear it. She didn't want to say no to Hollis, because she didn't want to hurt him.

And there was another reason: Rose didn't know herself how she felt.

She adored Hollis, but was adoration love? She loved her father, her sister, and perhaps even Hollis, but all in different ways.

Was love the romance of being swept off one's feet, as Cat dreamed of?

If it was, Rose didn't love Hollis.

"Come along, we'll say our good-byes in the garden."

"There you go again," he hissed, allowing himself to be guided down the steps to an oyster-shell path that led to the gardens.

"What do you mean?"

"You're teasing me!"

Rose tugged his arm, halting him. At the same time, she took one more step and turned so that she faced him directly, blocking the way. "No, dear Hollis, I'm not," she whispered, running a finger over his cheek and along his strong jaw to press the tip against his lips. "I swear I am not."

"Then let me speak seriously."

"Seriously? Of what? Betrothal . . . marriage? I'm fifteen and you're only nineteen."

"I'm nearly twenty."

"And you're going off to Yankeeland."

"That I am, and I want to know you'll be waiting as my betrothed when I return."

There were anxiety, need, love, desire, and only God knew what else in Hollis' eyes as he stared balefully down at her.

It wrenched Rose's heart, but she knew she could give him no answer. Hope, perhaps, but no definitive answer.

At night, in her dreams, or even awake staring at the French blue of her ceiling in the moonlight, she often thought about being a woman, a wife, a mother. Her awakening body had already told her many times over that she was ready; often more than ready, ripe and yearning.

But the blurred image of the lover that filled her thoughts was never Hollis.

"I'll be here, Hollis."

"As my betrothed?"

Rose's long-lashed eyes blinked only once. "I'll not be wed, Hollis. That must be enough, for now."

His shoulders sagged and something of the fierce light left his eyes as he shrugged and nodded.

"Good," she said, again pressing his arm to her side. "Besides, Hollis, we are so young. And if it is heirs you're thinking about, don't worry."

"What . . .?"

"I have a good strong body and my hipbones are wide. I'll wager I can safely birth babies clear into my thirties."

"Ye gods!" he murmured in shock.

Rose smiled and tightened the pressure on his

arm. Out of the corner of her eye she could see that, for the third time that morning, a bright red flush had filled his cheeks.

For the next half-hour they strolled in the formal gardens in the rear of Jacquard House. Even though the summer lilies had faded and the blossom was gone from the wisteria draping the walls and gates, the air was still filled with scent. Rose breathed deeply, filling her nostrils with the aroma of honeysuckle, lantana, and magnolia.

The sun was higher now, but a soft breeze ruffled the broad leaves of the palmetto trees and now and then lifted a white magnolia blossom and wafted it across the garden to lodge in the dark foliage of the oleanders.

"How I do love the South."

"Charleston and the low country are not all of the South," he replied.

"They are to me. Though I've never been anywhere else, not even to Atlanta, I know there is nowhere but Delle Erin any prettier than this."

"And there is no way of life more genteel or charming than the way we live."

Something in his voice, a note of sadness as well as of longing, made Rose stop and gaze up into his brooding face.

It was there again, the same hard stare and clamped jaw she had seen when she first stepped onto the porch that morning.

"It will always be here, Hollis—our beloved

Charleston, our plantations, our life-style. Not even God would change anything so perfect."

Hollis returned her gaze, his own image swirling in the bright pupils of her eyes.

He thought then that she had never been more beautiful. Her dark, flawless skin had taken on a rosy glow in the sun, making her features as innocent as her words.

Rose knew he was going to kiss her, but this time she made no objection.

He caressed her cheeks with his fingers, and then her hair. And then his lips found hers and a gentle rush leapt through her body as his arms wound possessively about her, drawing her to him.

Rose went limp against him, enjoying the feel of his body, the caress of his lips, but not thrilling to it. Somehow, deep within her soul, she knew that, as lusty as Hollis was, he hadn't the expertise of a man knowledgeable in the ways of women. He was kissing her, holding her in his short, powerful arms, but he was not possessing her.

His lips suddenly left hers and began to rain kisses on her cheeks and neck. His mouth, between kisses, whispered endearments as his hands snaked up her back.

"Rose, Papa says you must come along. The carriages are ready."

Hollis leapt back, his face now in full flush.

Rose, too, blushed as she watched Cat approach, then cross the garden.

Boldly the young girl came up to Hollis, grasped his hands, and went to her tiptoes. "Won't you kiss me good-bye as well, Hollis?"

Cat's innocent request seemed to calm the air in the garden and the people in it. Over Cat's head, Hollis' broad face beamed a smile at Rose. "Of course I'll kiss you good-bye, little one." Lightly he pecked her forehead.

"That's the way Papa kisses me!" Cat cried.

"Is it, now?" Hollis tried to keep a straight face.

"Yes!"

"Then how should I kiss you?"

"Like this," Cat replied, and tugged his face downward until her bowed lips met his.

In one brief second it was over and Cat was scampering back across the garden. At the gate she paused, snapped open her parasol, and assumed an imperious pose not unlike Camilla Boyd at her haughtiest. "I think you make a perfectly beautiful couple." She smiled. "But don't worry, Hollis . . . If my sister won't have you when you get back, I shall!"

And then she was gone, leaving behind her a dumbfounded Hollis staring at Rose, who was holding her sides with laughter.

"The little imp!" Hollis moaned. "She heard every word we said."

"It would seem so . . . and seen all we've done."

Rose's laughter was infectious, and soon Hollis found himself chuckling along with her.

"Well, at least she's on my side. Rose. . . ."

Suddenly the laughter had stopped. Rose could see that special look creeping back into his eyes.

Hurriedly she pecked him on the lips and scurried to the garden gate. "I must be off, Hollis, if we are to make the ferry by nightfall!"

"Rose. . . ."

She stopped just beyond the gate, forcing herself not to turn and face him. "Yes?"

"I love you, Rose."

"I know, Hollis, and I can only tell you how flattered I am that you do."

Hollow words, she thought as she raced toward the waiting carriages, but what else could I say?

He was going to be gone a long time. A lot could happen in the meantime.

CHAPTER TWO

THE JOURNEY SOUTH from Charleston and across the Edisto River by ferry was accomplished by dusk of the first day. A short distance from the river, near Jacksonboro, Andre Jacquard halted the carriages at Bromley Inn for the night.

The inn was named after an Englishman, Alfred Bromley. He had long since sold off his plantation acres, freed or sold his slaves, and moved back to England. But before his departure he had converted the plantation house into an inn and leased it to a freeman of color, Jason Alberta, and his wife, Althea.

It was rumored that Jason was old Mr. Bromley's illegitimate son and this was the old man's way of providing for his offspring without openly proclaiming to the world Jason's parentage.

Under Jason's firm guidance, Bromley Inn had become the main stop between Savannah and Charleston on the overland route. On any night, in the inn's huge dining room, laughter and good conversation abounded between weary travelers.

Not so this year. There was little laughter, and all talk was shaded by the near-rebellion on Hilton Head Island. So irate were the men concerning the Yankee abolitionists that Andre had to quietly remind those present that there were ladies within earshot of their oaths.

Even their host, the tall, kindly, aging Jason, and his frail, diminutive wife were not spared from the uneasy fear of the wary travelers.

It was muttered by more than one man around the long dining table that free blacks like Jason, even though they owned slaves themselves, were a dangerous influence on the slaves. Rose heard one man go so far as to suggest that Jason's property should be confiscated, and, for the safety of all, he and his wife returned to bondage.

Later that evening, as they mounted the stairs to their rooms, Rose brought the subject up with her father.

"Why would they say such things? Jason has earned all he has gained, and if there is disagreement between the North and South, Jason would always side with the South. I know he would!"

"Yes, I daresay he would, Rose," Andre replied, a wan smile on his lips as he tried to find an answer to his daughter's probing question. At last a light came into his eyes. At the top of the stairs he paused and knelt by her side. "Do you remember, years ago, when we planted only rice at Belle Erin?"

"Vaguely," she replied.

"In those days we had little need of slaves. The rice grew almost by itself, so few slaves were needed."

Rose carefully followed his every word. "And then you switched many of the fields to cotton and we needed many slaves for the harvest."

He nodded. "Not all the planters are like me, Rose, with a good law practice besides their plantation income. To retain this style of life they love, they need the cotton—"

"And so they need slaves."

Again Andre nodded. "Our life here in the low country is racing, shooting, riding, lavish dinners, the Cecilia Society—"

"And cotillions and balls!"

"Yes"—he smiled—"those, too. And cotton gives us all those."

The answer was suddenly crystal clear in Rose's mind. "Then let us all go back to raising rice, and, like the emancipators say, send the slaves back to Africa!"

Her words were answered with a low chuckle and a shake of her father's head. "Bless me, girl, if all Southerners were as to the point in their thought as you, we wouldn't need the Congress in Washington City to argue out our differences! But it will never be. The making of money occupies us all, and when it comes to making money, cotton is king."

Rose slept uneasily that night. She knew that her father was trying to tell her something important. But she didn't understand.

And so the overnight stop at Bromley Inn, in this fall of 1855, was not a pleasant diversion. Both Andre Jacquard and his daughters were relieved the following morning when again they stepped into their carriage to continue their journey.

The morning was crisp, with a sweet breeze blowing inland from the sea and offshore islands. By the midday pause, the previous evening was forgotten and spirits were again soaring.

All thought and talk turned to Belle Erin.

Would the fall cotton crop be good? Would the rice be plentiful and strong? How frisky were the spring colts, born all legs and wobbly heads just before their departure earlier in the year? How many more pounds had dear Mammy Loka gained since last they saw her?

Even Cat, who much preferred Charleston to life on the banks of the blue Cambalee, became more fidgety in her seat as familiar landmarks were sighted.

"De ribah, Massa Jacquard!"

The coachman's rumbling bass announcing the Cambalee brought squeals of delight from both girls. As one, they squeezed to the far right of the carriage and peered toward the sound of the rushing water. Suddenly, through the thick lines of cypress and gum trees, they saw the river.

"Two miles," Andre said, watching the delight on his daughters' faces. "Only two miles to Belle Erin!"

Rose breathed deeply and sighed. *Two miles.* She followed the rushing waters as far as she could see, and then tightly shut her eyes to imagine the sight as the river passed their beloved plantation.

She could visualize the wide green lawn sloping up to the double stairs and the rear veranda. She could see beyond the pilastered doorway into the great hall, with its sweeping double staircase. Her hands tingled from the imagined feel of the richly carved mahogany banisters, and her nostrils flared with the delectable aromas that surely would be wafting from the huge kitchen.

"You do love it, don't you, Rose?" Her father's voice was accompanied by the gentleness of his big hand smoothing her dark hair.

"I do, more than anything," she replied, opening her eyes to see him staring back at her in an odd, brooding way. "There is no place on earth quite like Belle Erin."

And then they were there, the carriages rumbling through the tall brick pillars of the gate and up the circular drive. Above them, giant oaks festooned with Spanish moss dappled the sunlight. Rose's face glowed and her heart seemed to expand in her chest as the lane widened and suddenly the huge old house burst into view from between the trees.

She saw the steeped gables first, and then the four tall white Doric columns. Scarlet cassena berries glowed on the hedges before the wide veranda, and white tufts of mockingbird flowers were just coming out beneath them.

"Home," she sighed, squeezing Cat's hand tightly in her own and glancing at her father's smiling face through misty eyes.

"Always think of this land as home," he whispered.

In the first rush of arrival, Rose hadn't noticed the almost total absence of house servants. Always upon their return to Belle Erin the veranda was full of shining black faces smiling their greetings.

Now the veranda was nearly empty. Only a few small children stood staring, their eyes wide and white in their chocolate-brown faces. The only adults in sight were a few field hands gathered in small groups in the distance toward the stables and slave quarters.

"Father, what is it?" Rose asked as Andre handed her down from the carriage.

"I don't know," he replied, and then raised his voice to the house. "Seymour ... Mammy Loka!"

Neither of the familiar faces appeared.

"Father . . .?" Cat rose in the carriage and squinted toward the far-off cotton sheds.

They all followed the line of Cat's raised arm. In the distance, beyond the quarters and the cotton sheds, all the slaves, house servants, and field hands were assembled in a giant horseshoe.

Something was definitely wrong. The sun was still in the sky, way too early for the field hands to have stopped work for the day. And even though smoke rose from the kitchen chimneys and the back cookhouse, there was no bustle of activity around either place, no fragrant aromas in the air announcing the evening meal.

"Father, what could it be?" Rose quaked, moving unconsciously closer to the safety of his tall figure.

"I don't know."

A small boy of about ten suddenly scooted around the edge of the veranda and came to a sudden wide-eyed halt when he saw the carriages. So abruptly had he stopped that his bare feet had raised a cloud of dust from the path.

He was about to bolt in retreat when Andre's booming voice halted him again. "Boy! Come over here!"

"Yessuh."

The boy approached, his eyes to the ground, until he stopped, the top of his dark head barely coming to the tall man's waist.

"What's going on out there in the cotton sheds, boy?"

Silence.

"Look up here at me, boy! What's happening out there in the fields!"

Again silence, suddenly broken by the coachman, old Lucas, banging the heavy handle of his whip on the carriage seat. "Speak up, boy, an' tell yo massuh what's de trouble out dere."

"White man in de cotton shed," the boy said, his voice barely a whisper.

"White man? What white man?" Andre roared, leaning forward to better hear the boy's words.

"Come from de North."

"Speak up, boy!"

"Come from de North," the lad said in a much louder voice, lifting his head until his wide eyes stared directly into the tall man's. "Come ta burn down de plantation and free all us niggers."

"Oh, dear God," Rose gasped, grasping the side of the carriage for support.

"Papa," Cat cried, curling fearfully into the seat, "are they gonna rebel and kill us all?"

"Hush up, girl!" Andre cried, brushing the boy from his path and speaking over his shoulder as he moved across the drive in long strides. "Lukas, Otis, Luther, see to the ladies!"

A chorus of "yessuhs" followed his hurrying figure, and Rose suddenly found herself between two of the young Charleston house servants. She watched her father for a full two minutes, and then she could stand it no longer. "Cat, you stay here!"

"Rose . . ."

"Here, Miz Rose. . . ."

But Rose had already eluded their grasping hands, and with her skirts and crinolines held high, was loping after her father. She raced around the big house and down a long avenue of pride-of-India trees. She passed the carpenter's shop, the smokehouse, and the big enclosure that held the stables, the barns, and the overseer's house. And then she was gaining on her father even as he picked up his pace through the long rows of the houses in the slave settlement.

The only sound, other than the tread of their feet on the hard-packed earth, was the whimpering of the babies arrayed in baskets in front of the nursery.

As they passed, neither the older children who sat near the baskets tending their charges, nor old Charlotte, the nurse who sat like a huge calico-clad stone in the nursery doorway, looked up or spoke.

Something is wrong, Rose told herself. Frightfully wrong. After a full summer's absence, there should have been a shouted chorus of greetings as they passed.

Instead, there was only cold, ominous silence.

They passed through the last line of shrubbery that separated the fields and cotton sheds from the settlement, and crossed toward the assembled hands.

The black faces and homespun-clad bodies parted like a wave before the tall, stern-faced figure of their master. Rose barely managed to ease in behind him before the circle closed again behind her.

Muttered comments as she passed brought a clammy sweat to Rose's skin and a chill of dread up her spine.

"Abolitionists gonna free us all."

"Ain't no more dis nigger's burr-head gwine tote de cotton basket."

"Why fo you talk like dat, field nigger? Who feed you if you free?"

"De massa come shoot dat boy."

Inside the circle, Rose spotted four men in the gray-and-green militia uniforms of the Palmetto Guard. Their faces were cold and hard as they crouched on the dusty ground with their muskets cocked and ready.

The only white man in the circle was Belle Erin's overseer, Joshua Kincaid. He was tall, bone-thin, with a hawk's eyes and a beaked nose that had been broken several times. A crude, tobacco-chewing man, Kincaid was as pious as he was profane. He was both feared and respected for his fairness by the slaves, and Rose had often heard her father say that was why he was a good overseer.

Now Kincaid looked like a man who had seen

hell and was about to fight it back. A raging storm brewed in his black eyes.

Andre Jacquard made directly for his overseer, and stood shoulder to shoulder with the man, staring at the big cotton shed. "Tell me, Joshua, all of it, and quickly."

"Abolitionist, suh," Kincaid drawled with a back-country twang. "They done hung his pappy and uncle over at Hilton Head."

"I've heard about that. What's he doing here at Belle Erin?"

One of the militiamen disengaged himself from his fellows and joined them. "Lieutenant Harrison, suh, Third Carolina Volunteers."

"How do you do, Lieutenant ... Andre Jacquard."

The men shook hands, and the young lieutenant slowly explained. "We been chasin' this boy for near on to a week. Damn near had him twice't, but he slipped away."

"To here," Jacquard said in a low voice.

"He was holed up at the Orkney place downriver, Mistuh Jacquard," Kincaid offered, "when they spotted and flushed him again."

"Only trouble is, by that time he'd talked three of Cyrus Orkney's niggers into joinin' up with him." The lieutenant paused here and spit derisively before he continued. "They stole some guns and fired the big house before they run."

"Cyrus' place? Burned?"

"Yessuh, to the ground."

"Dear God, what fools," Jacquard moaned. "What do they want here?"

"Man's crazy," Kincaid rasped. "He wants all our guns, a boat with enough niggers to row it back downriver, and safe conduct north on the first paddle-wheel up the coast."

"And if he doesn't get it?" Jacquard asked.

"He'll fire the cotton shed and shoot my boy," Kincaid replied.

"What?"

The overseer nodded and loosed a stream of tobacco juice toward the shed. "Tha's right. He grabbed my boy fer a hostage when these fellers here got close. They been in there since jest afore dawn."

Rose stifled a gasp and moved slightly back from the group of men. She noticed a mixture of emotions on the black faces around her. Most were solemn and stern, waiting. But a few of the hardened field hands were openly smiling.

She spotted Seymour, oldest of the house servants, and moved sideways toward him, keeping one ear cocked toward the conversation before her.

"Have you a plan?" her father was asking the lieutenant.

"Only one way, as I see it," came the reply. "They's in the loft up there. Find some way to get him to show hisself, then blow his damn head off. Reckon then the niggers'll give up yer overseer's boy an' quit."

"Seymour?"

"Yessum, Miz Rose ... turrible things heah today."

"Where's Mammy Loka?"

"She dead."

"What? Dead?"

"Yessum. July. Fever done got her."

The shock was like an arrow in the heart. It had never occurred to Rose that the blacks weren't entirely immune to the dreaded malaria.

And of all the blacks, her beloved Mammy Loka. The old black woman had raised her and Cat. It was on her pendulous breasts that Rose and her little sister had cried out their grief when their mother had died of the fever.

It can't be true, it can't! Rose thought, and was about to say as much to the bent, impassive Negro beside her, when her father's stern voice split the air.

"No! There's already been enough killing. I'm to understand this is only a lad ... fourteen, fifteen!"

"That might be, suh," the lieutenant drawled, "but he cusses like a man, shoots like a man, and he's a wild-eyed radical jest like his daddy and his uncle."

"I'll talk to him."

"Ya'll suit yerself, Mr. Jacquard, but I don't think you can give him any sense. This boy's crazier than a loon. He's been teched. Thinks he's down here doin' the Lord's work rilin' up our niggers."

"We'll see. What's his name?"

"Donne, suh. Clay Donne."

Rose stood like a statue, watching her father through mist-clouded eyes as he walked across the clearing with long, even strides.

She wanted to cry out to him to stop, to let the militiamen do it their way. She wanted to put her arms around him and lay her head on his chest and tell him that Mammy Loka was gone and in the ground.

But she couldn't move or speak. Her throat was constricted as if there were iron bands around her chest. She could only watch, and pray: *Oh, dear Lord, let this and all these other sudden troubles pass from us. Let the Yankee go back from whence he came and leave us in peace with our homes, our fields, our darkies, and our peaceful life. . . .*

"Donne . . . Clay Donne?"

"Yeah."

"My name is Andre Jacquard. I own this plantation, and I—"

"You're a slaver and you killed my daddy . . . hung him fer doin' God's work!"

"Listen to me! You can have everything you ask, just don't harm the boy."

"Iffin I killed him, it would be jest one less that'd grow up ta be a slave driver!"

Rose moaned aloud and wrapped her arms

42

tightly beneath her breasts. The boy *was* crazy. He wasn't hearing anything her father was saying.

"I'll have a boat ready for you in twenty minutes. You can leave as soon as you release the boy."

"An eye for an eye, saith the Lord! You killed my daddy an' my uncle. Now two of you must go to hell for it!"

Suddenly a figure stepped into the open loft doors, a musket to his shoulder, a wild, red-rimmed eye sighting down the barrel.

He is only a boy, Rose thought, seeing the bedraggled figure suddenly emerge from the shed's darkness in frayed breeches and a torn cotton shirt. He's no older than I am!

Somehow that thought, that all this was being caused by a mere youth, stilled the fearful pounding of her heart.

"I came south ta do my duty as a Christian man."

"Listen to me, son." Andre Jacquard took three measured paces forward, lifting his arms and spreading his hands to show that he wasn't armed.

"Don't come no further, slaver!"

"All I ask is that you release my overseer's boy."

"Overseers is white trash—darky beaters!"

"Not on this plantation."

Her father was almost directly below the boy

now, staring straight upward, his arms raised in supplication.

"Son, you know nothing of our life here, other than what you've been told. There's been enough blood—"

Suddenly the loft door around the side of the shed burst open and two men leapt to the ground.

"It's the Orkeny niggers!" someone shouted.

Rose never knew, and she was never told, who fired first, the two blacks or the militiamen.

But it made no difference. Someone did fire, and pandemonium reigned.

The field hands and servants shouted in fear and scattered in every direction, adding to the chaos. She saw one of the black runaways fall, and then the musket in the boy's hand spewed flame and smoke.

Rose screamed and lurched forward as her father cried out, clutching his chest and staggering backward.

Another musket went off, so close and so loud that the sound staggered her and the smoke burned her eyes.

The abolitionist in the loft fell outward in space. He seemed to pause for seconds in midair, and then his body hit the hard-packed earth with a dull, sickening thud.

"Papa! Papa!" Rose cried, grinding the powder smoke and tears from her eyes.

Then she saw him staggering toward her, his eyes wide in shock and astonishment. Just before they collided, his arms left his chest to reach for her. His hands dripped blood, and an ugly crimson stain spread across his white linen shirt.

A garbled moan from his fluttering lips, one word that sounded like her name, and then he fell into the dust at her feet.

All was silence for several seconds. And then, from somewhere far, far off, Rose heard a keening, piercing scream.

Just before she fell across her father's lifeless body, Rose knew that the scream was her own.

CHAPTER THREE

Rose lay for two days and nights between wakefulness and a deeply troubled sleep. Only once, when she saw Seymour's kindly old black face swimming above her, did she speak a few words.

"Cat . . . ?"

"De little missus is fine."

"Does she know?"

"She do. She cryin' a lot an' sleepin', but she be all right."

Rose nodded, closed her eyes, and let the peaceful darkness overtake her once more.

On the morning of the third day she was awakened by Joshua Kincaid. "Miz Rose, we got to have the funeral today. The darkies, they got everything ready."

Rose nodded numbly, and with Arleta's help

she managed to pull herself from bed. Hot water had already been poured in her old wooden tub, and while she bathed, her trunks were searched for something suitable to wear.

Nothing could be found.

"Miz Rose? Yo got no black, Miz Rose."

"No. I've had no need ..." Again the tears poured from her eyes.

"Iffin yo don't mind wearin' black folks' clothes, Miz Rose, my Sunday meetin' dress is fittin' black."

"That will be fine, Arleta."

"I'll take a quick tuck here and dere."

"Thank you, Arleta. That's very thoughtful."

Wearily she settled back in the bath, her father's image floating on her inner lids.

The kindest, wisest, most generous man was gone from her, taken away from her forever by the people he had loved and cared for, his slaves.

No, it was the abolitionist's ball that had killed him

But was there any difference, really?

Abolitionists gwine free us all. ...

Why fo you talk like dat, field nigger? Who feed yo if yo free?

Rose wondered if the darkies were glad that their old massuh was dead and gone.

Her father's words: *Son, you know nothing of our life here other than what you've been told. There's been enough blood—*

The image of her father's face disappeared, to

be replaced by the gleaming red eye of the boy sighting down the musket barrel.

And then even that disappeared in more tears.

Why did they come south? Why didn't they stay in Yankeeland and leave us alone?

And why her father? He had been first among the planters in the low country to recognize the slaves' rights as human beings. He had stopped the ritual of jumping over a broom as the consummation of marriage on his land. Now, on Belle Erin, slave marriages were Christian and recognized by law. And all up and down the Cambalee, other planters ridiculed him for giving his slaves meat twice a week and real coffee instead of the brew made from okra seed. Her father didn't even employ a whipping boss on Belle Erin. Many of the other planters had thought him naive and foolish for that, too.

And now the abolitionists had killed him.

Rose tried to push it all from her mind, and let her weary body sink lower in the warm water.

"Miz Rose . . .?"

"Yes, Arleta?"

"Is time, Miz Rose."

"All right. Arleta?"

"Yessum."

"Do you like it here at Belle Erin?"

"Yessum."

"And in the great house at Charleston?"

"Oh, yessum."

"Are you sorry that Massuh Andre is dead?"

"Miz Rose, how dare you say dat to Arleta?"

The harsh tone of the woman's voice popped Rose's eyes open. Arleta stood at the foot of the tub wringing her hands, her face a mask of contorted pain. "Dat's a turrible bad thing to say, Miz Rose. Massa Andre a good man. He treat his nigras good. It was no-quality white trash killed de massa, not one o' his nigras. We takes care of our white folks."

"I'm sorry, Arleta." Again the tears had misted Rose's eyes, and it was all she could do to keep them from becoming sobs that would choke her throat.

Arleta had taken tucks in the long black dress so that it fit Rose perfectly. From somewhere she had found black gloves and a black bonnet.

"You look fine, Miz Rose, jest fine. Yo momma be proud the way you look."

"Cat . . . ?"

"I go see to her now." Arleta was nearly out the door when Rose whirled and called to her.

"Yessum?"

"Arleta, you said you loved us, that you loved our Charleston house and Belle Erin . . . and many times you've said you've got all you want. Do you, Arleta? . . . do you have all you want?"

"What you mean, Miz Rose?"

"Don't you want your freedom, Arleta?"

The pause was long; it seemed as though it would go on forever. The two women stared deeply into one another's eyes across the room.

Finally Arleta sighed. She straightened her spine, bringing her bulk to its greatest height and lifting her chin. "Yessum. Iffin I had my choice, I'd choose to be free."

"But why, Arleta, why? You said—"

"I know what I said, Miz Rose. Yessum, I gots everything I needs, and more'n likely everything my bones would ever want. But, Miz Rose, I still gots to stand in front of de white man wit ma hat in ma hand and call him massa."

Rose sat, outwardly calm, in the Charleston house parlor. Beneath the robe across her lap, her hands nervously worried an Irish linen kerchief. Minutes before, the fine lace at its edges had shredded, and now the linen itself threatened to tear under her manipulations.

Outside, unseasonably chill December winds rattled the windowpanes and added to the gloom of the moment.

To her left, Cat sat like a stone, her elfin face pale and drawn. Her eyes were vacant and unblinking as she stared into the crackling cedar-log fire.

They had stayed nearly three months at Belle Erin after their father's funeral. Valiantly Rose had tried to keep the bustling plantation together. But almost hourly the fabric of daily life was pulled further asunder.

Runaways became a weekly occurrence. Work slowdowns were common, and thievery became the order of the day. Before, Joshua Kincaid had rarely sought out Andre Jacquard with his troubles. Now he was at the big house morning and night, in consultation with Rose about the plantation's problems.

"Miz Rose, I do believe I'm an honest and efficient overseer. I've always tried to run Belle Erin as if yer daddy was at my shoulder. But now . . ."

"Now he's gone."

"That's right, Miz Rose, and the darkies are testin' us—both of us."

It was clear, even to Rose, that a sixteen-year-old girl couldn't run a plantation.

"Like yer daddy, I always said the whip should be used sparingly. But it can't be done away with entirely, I fear."

"Is that the only way, Joshua?"

"Miz Rose, no matter what we'd all like to believe, here in the South it's always been the only way."

But Rose couldn't bear the responsibility. If whipping the slaves back into order and submission was the only way, she couldn't give the order to do it.

Andre Jacquard's friend and law partner, Cory Johnson, was the executor of her father's will. He had arrived at Belle Erin shortly after the funeral and tried to convince Rose to go back to Charleston and leave the running of Belle Erin to Kincaid.

She had been defiant and refused. But two months later she had had no alternative but to summon Cory Johnson back to Belle Erin for his advice and counsel. In just two days the situation was clear to the wise old barrister. "Without you on the land, Rose, Kincaid *is* the master. Long ago your father chose him wisely. Unlike most overseers, Kincaid has schooling. He knows the land and farming, and he knows the nigras. He can run them, if they can't run to you."

The message was all too clear. Within the week, she and Cat returned to Charleston with Cory Johnson.

But even in town, things had changed. There were more militia patrols hunting runaways trying to escape to the North. A curfew was on. No black person could be on the streets after dusk. When one was caught out after dark, violence often ensued. Abolitionist literature was pouring into the city, and every householder held his breath, waiting for an insurrection.

Now Cory Johnson had come to tell them that even Charleston was not safe. "You and Cat are alone here, Rose, no matter how many friends you have nearby."

Rose listened to his words and watched him pace the parlor floor through misty eyes.

He was an attractive man, like his son Hollis, short and stocky with a barrel chest and powerful, muscular arms. His hands, holding a sheaf of papers, seemed too large for his body. And his broad, bearded face with its heavy features made him look more like a blacksmith than a barrister.

"So you want us to go north—to Washington City?"

"I do, Rose. Your aunt has written weekly that she wants you to join her."

Rose closed her eyes and conjured up a picture of her mother's sister, Mrs. Glynis O'Rourke. Her aunt had fallen in love with a Yankee trader and gone north when Rose was just a little girl. The love affair had not worked out, it was rumored that the Yankee had jilted her, left her at the altar and disappeared. Rather than return to Charleston with her shame, the woman had remained in the North.

It had been five years now since Rose had seen her. When her mother was alive, Aunt Glynis had visited every year. After Nelia's death, she had stopped coming.

"She runs a prosperous boardinghouse for Southern gentlemen in Washington City, Rose. There you can further your education, and Cat can attend seminary school. I think it best—"

"To leave the South?"

"Yes, Rose, at least for now." Cory Johnson stopped his pacing and stood directly in front of the two girls. "Your aunt loves you, Rose . . . both of you. And more than anything else, she wishes to take care of you."

Here he paused, a huge pawlike hand reaching out and tilting Rose's face upward. "You're both very wealthy young heiresses now. I honestly believe that two proper young ladies in your position will fare far better in Washington City during these trying times than—"

"Than here in the South!"

The sudden harsh tone in Rose's voice shocked even herself, and brought Cat out of her lethargy to stare at her sister.

"It will only be for a while, Rose," the lawyer continued. "As your father's friend and your attorney, I promise you I shall watch over your property as I do my own. And, who knows, when you return, you might bring with you a new master to Belle Erin."

There it was, all too clear in his eyes if not in his words. If Rose were married, if there were a *man*, then there would be no problem.

She could almost finish Johnson's thoughts in her own mind: *In four years Hollis will finish at West Point. By that time you will be ready, and the two of you can return to Charleston together.*

Rose didn't mind Cory Johnson's hope that one day she would marry his son. In many ways, Rose herself had planted that thought in the old man's mind. But she did mind that she couldn't run her own life, her own property, without the help of a man.

"Stay independent, Rose," her father had often told her. "The world is a cruel place. You and Cat are lucky that you have been born to wealth and position, but don't believe that alone will be enough to give you happiness and security."

Cory Johnson was speaking again, breaking into her jumbled thoughts. "I think you will be surprised in Washington, Rose. It is really a Southern town in many ways. It is Southern ladies who have made Washington society. Because of that, you may be pleasantly surprised to discover that Washington is not too far separated from our own Charleston."

But Washington City was not *in* the South, Rose thought grimly, feeling the linen handerkerchief split in half at last.

"Cat . . .?"

Slowly the younger girl turned and gazed steadily into her sister's face. Rose was shocked by the look in Cat's eyes. Gone was the vacantness, and in its place was a burning flame. Her tiny jaw was set, and there was a resolute defiance in the tilt of her head. "I'll be happy to go to Washington City. I hate the South and the nigras and the plantation. At least in Washington we can sleep in our beds at night and be fairly sure we will awaken in the morning."

On Christmas Day, the Jacquard sisters boarded the packet steamer *Southern Light* for the trip to Baltimore. From there they would travel overland by carriage to join their aunt in Washington.

It was a crisp day, but clear and sunny, with

only a few fluffy white clouds scudding across a blue sky. But Rose saw no beauty in the day as the ship made its way past Fort Sumpter toward the mouth of Charleston Bay. The sun never reached the cold marrow of her bones as she thought of the weeks and months—perhaps years—ahead in the cold, inhospitable North.

She vowed that no matter how long it took, she would return to the South she loved. No matter what she learned or saw or whom she met, she would never change. She had been born and raised a Southerner, and a Southerner she would remain.

PART TWO

1859

CHAPTER FOUR

GAILY COLORED BUNTING adorned the raw wooden poles of the West Point dock. As the Hudson River sloop from New York eased into its mooring, a small segment of the Academy band struck up rousing march songs and interspersed them with popular airs like "Jeannie with the Light Brown Hair."

Cadets in gray tailcoats with gleaming brass buttons milled on the dock. Their white summer trousers and shiny leather shakos gaudily trimmed with gold tassles and pom-poms shone in the summer sun. Most yelled or waved their greetings to the boat as they spotted the particular belle they would escort to the graduation ball the following evening. Others cast an appraising eye at the young ladies who had been invited as guests but not yet matched with an escort.

On the sloop, the ladies lined the rail, scarcely able to conceal their exuberance and excitement. They looked not unlike brightly colored bells in their multicolored frocks, hoop skirts billowing from their tiny, cinched-in waists.

The gowns made a rainbow of color, and many were garlanded with live flowers, the scent of roses, white clematis, water lilies, violets, and scarlet honeysuckle wafting delightfully from the ship's deck to greet their waiting suitors. Their flounced bonnets and parasols matched their gowns, and were garlanded with the same blossoms that swelled at their bosoms and trailed down over the distended skirts.

During the last hour of the five-hour trip up the Hudson, all the ladies had dashed below. They had made a madhouse of the sloop's lower deck as they discarded their drab traveling clothes and donned the silks and satins they now wore for their arrival at West Point.

And shining brightest among the beautiful belles were the Jacquard sisters. Rose wore a sky-blue satin patterned with her namesake flower and overshot with soft pink tulle. Her glossy blue-black hair was pulled back into a bun beneath her bonnet, with finger curls left exposed to dance at each side of her handsome features.

Beside her, Cat stood demurely, her eyes scanning the cadets' upturned faces. In short white silk, with a pink sash and pink love ribbons on her bonnet and parasol, she looked like a honey-blond Dresden doll.

"Oh, look, Rose, there he is . . . Hollis!"

"Hollis . . . Hollis!" Rose shouted, waving her spread fan toward the dock.

Hollis Johnson spotted them, and his wide, still-boyish face broke into a toothy grin. He waved and shouted in return, but the music and the other shouting voices smothered his words.

Seconds later, the long, low sloop bumped into its place at the dock, and the gangway was barely set before the chattering, laughing ladies were streaming down its length.

"Hollis!" Rose cried, running forward with her skirts clutched nearly to her knees.

"Rose, you're more beautiful than ever," Hollis said, his voice raised above the din. Gallantly he locked one of her hands in his and bowed stiffly from the waist to brush it with his lips.

"Oh, Hollis, you're such a prig!" Abruptly Rose threw herself into his arms and soundly kissed him on both cheeks.

"Good Lord, girl," Hollis sputtered, "you haven't changed a bit!"

"Oh, but I have," Rose replied in a husky voice, appraising him from beneath lowered lids. "Indeed I have."

Hollis was about to comment further when

Rose stepped slightly to the side and his eyes fell upon Cat.

"Catherine. . . ."

"Hollis," she replied in a silky voice, and offered both her white-gloved hands to him.

Gently Hollis took them and brushed his lips from one to the other.

As they stood gazing deeply into each other's eyes, Rose watched. A knowing smile curled her full lips, but she quickly masked it with her fan. If she had ever seen two people falling in love, it was her sister and Hollis Johnson.

Since they had arrived in Washington City, Hollis had returned five times to South Carolina, and each time, going and coming, he had stopped overnight to see his childhood sweetheart. But by the third visit it was no longer Rose he stopped to see. Cat had quickly blossomed in the capital city. It was evident to Rose, to the many gallants of Washington, and to Hollis.

Rose had become a leader, sought after for her beauty, her biting wit and brilliant conversation, and her knowledge of the capital. In Washington Rose had grown from a lively young Southern belle into a woman of charm, substance, and character.

There were other changes as well. There was a bitterness in her breast that she hid from everyone, including her sister. Beneath her vivacious manner were moods that swung from gentle to furious. Rose considered her stay in

Washington a time of exile, no matter how long its length.

All this while Catherine blossomed into a soft, feminine young lady. Unlike Rose, she cared little for politics, but she had the knack of listening, and, most often, demurely agreeing with those she listened to. She never took sides on any issue, and, more often than not served as peacemaker when her older sister provoked uncomfortable arguments with men and women of more than twice her age and experience.

For this reason Catherine was truly loved, while Rose was admired—and sometimes feared—for her too-quick caustic tongue.

Watching them now—Hollis staring with unabashed love, and Cat returning his gaze coyly beneath lowered lashes—Rose could only smile and remember: *"But don't worry, Hollis. If my sister won't have you when you get back, I shall!"*

Well, Rose thought, the little imp had truly succeeded in capturing Hollis' heart. Suddenly an uncontrollable laugh bubbled from her throat. Hollis and Cat stared at her. "Forgive me," Rose said. "I was just thinking how fickle men are!"

Hollis' reaction was the blush that he still hadn't conquered. Catherine only smiled and chided her sister with her eyes for being her usual out-spoken self at Hollis' expense.

A quiet cough at Rose's shoulder made her turn. Until then the three of them had had eyes only for each other. Now Rose found herself looking at a young man with wild red hair trailing from beneath his leather shako.

"Ye gods, forgive me," Hollis said, jumping forward. "Rose, your escort to the ball. May I present Chauncy Flynn. Chauncy, Rose Marie Jacquard!"

"Mr. Flynn." Rose nodded, flashing the young man a wide smile and curtsying as she offered her hand.

"Miss Jacquard," he replied with a melodic lilt, taking her hand in his and examining it closely.

"Is something wrong?" Rose asked. His lean, freckled face was drawn in a frown. "Is my glove soiled?"

"Not at all ... spotless it is."

"Then ...?"

"I was just hoping," he said, pausing to flash her a mischievous look with his deep blue eyes, "that I'd get the same greeting as Hollis."

Rose cocked an eyebrow in mock dismay. "Mr. Flynn, I do believe you're forward!"

"Aye, that I am"—he grinned—"but only with the prettiest of ladies."

"And of course I fall into that category."

"Of course."

"Then you're forgiven."

"I knew I would be," he said, throwing back his head and erupting in a clear tenor burst of laughter. " 'Tis my Irish charm!"

Rose liked him immediately. There was an

awkward gentleness in his tall, lanky form, and laughter seemed constantly to bubble from his eyes as well as his lips.

"Hollis calls me by the name me mother gave me, because he knows I hate it. Would ya mind calling me Chance?"

"Not at all ... Chance. Let's forget Queen Victoria's stiffness. I'm Rose."

"Rose it is." He kissed the back of her hand at last. "And may I say, you glow like the radiant flower for which you're named."

"Chance, I do believe you've kissed the Blarney stone."

"Of course I have," he replied, startling her by dropping the rough brogue in his speech and continuing in cultured British tone. "Is there an Irishman who hasn't?"

"Don't let him fool you, Rose," Hollis said, linking his own arm with Catherine's. "His grandfather fought with Washington in the Revolution and he's never seen Ireland. Worse yet, he's a Yankee from Ohio! But all in all, a good chap."

"Hush, Hollis!" Flynn waved his free hand while his eye twinkled at Rose. "You've said the lady's mother was an O'Rourke. What better way to make her mine than lead her to believe I'm 'bourne ta the ould sod'?"

Rose laughed all the way to the carriage the two cadets had hired. Hollis sent a plebe scurrying off for their luggage, and by the time he had returned, the four of them were in the carriage ready to go.

They were barely across the West Point plain and on the bumpy road toward Cozzens Hotel, where Rose and Cat would stay, when Flynn produced a bottle of claret and four glasses from a satchel at his feet.

"Isn't this against Academy regulations?" Cat asked, staring at her glass.

"Of course it is," Flynn replied. "But we're of the Brotherhood of Nine, and follow the example of our leader."

"Your leader?" Rose asked, now totally immersed in the carefree mood Chance had created.

"His name is Custer," Hollis explained. "George Armstrong Custer. He's only recently arrived at the Point, but already he's charmed us all with his leadership."

"And what leadership it is!" Flynn added. "The man flouts authority with real style, and he's already acquired more demerits than any ten cadets. You'll meet him at the ball." Here Flynn paused, and raising his glass, stared directly into Rose's eyes. "To beauty, and a charming weekend."

Rose lightly touched her glass to his and thought: Yes, it is going to be quite a weekend after all.

They sipped the wine and Rose matched Flynn's bold stare with her own until it was he who averted his eyes.

"Rose?"

"Yes, Hollis?"

"How is Washington City?"

"Washington? It's not different. Still gay, exciting, wonderful . . . and muddy."

Again the carriage erupted with laughter, arrested only when Hollis said, "Then you no longer miss Charleston and the South?"

Rose looked at him quickly. "I'll always miss the South, Hollis," she replied, the smile fading from her lips.

Her sharp tone quickly stilled the laughter and brought a quizzical look to the uninitiated Flynn's features.

Catherine quickly jumped in. "What Rose means is that we have found Washington almost a Southern city . . . much larger, of course, but not without the charm and gentility of Charleston."

"Yes . . . yes, of course." Rose nodded, and then added, "The great difference is that it is in the North."

"Your tone, dear lady," Flynn said, "when you speak of the North, puts a bit of a chill in my blood."

"Does it, Chance Flynn?" Rose replied, again smiling. "Perhaps that's because I speak of the North with such a Southern accent."

Rose's heart had sunk at her first sight of Washington City. The much-talked-about Pennsylvania Avenue was no more than a very wide, muddy lane. The gleaming monument to President Washington was merely an abandoned nub of stone with debris littering its base, and near it the Potomac had overflowed to create a swampy mire that, come spring, would breed mosquitoes and malaria.

Few of the government buildings were finished, and those that were seemed to sprout directly out of the thick forests, with great distances between them. One statesman of the time called the city "a rude colony camped in a forest, with unfinished Greek temples for workrooms and sloughs for roads."

Rose agreed.

As the rented carriage made its way through the seamier parts of the city, Rose and Cat clutched each other's hands and stared in awe. There were narrow alleys of ramshackle houses and poverty-stricken faces. Painted women with worn features and bearded men with savage eyes stared at them as they passed through English Hill and the Irish colony of Swampoodle.

"And Cory Johnson thought we would be safer in this?" Rose murmured, just loud enough for her sister to hear.

Catherine swallowed deeply, clutched her sister's hand harder, and stared straight ahead at the driver's back. It will be better, she thought. It has to be!

The bleak four-story house on H Street was

little better. It too seemed unfinished and impermanent, with jutting chimneys and different-sized windows. A rough clapboard extension had been tacked onto the side and rear of the building as if it were an afterthought.

Glynis O'Rourke however, made up for the city's coldness with cheerfulness and warmth. Unlike her sister Nelia, who had been soft, quiet, and petite to the point of fragility, their aunt was a tall woman with broad, beaming features and a booming laugh that could be heard—and often was—all over the city.

She had grown stout since Rose had last seen her, and though her eyes were bright and her mood gay, lines of age now showed in her face.

Tearfully she embraced Rose until the girl thought her ribs would crack. And then she turned misty eyes on Catherine. "You look more like her every day. Oh, Catherine, you're the spittin' image of your dear mother!"

If the outside of the boardinghouse was bleak and dreary, the inside was just the opposite. Glynis O'Rourke had spared no expense to make the place warm and cheerful for her guests. The downstairs main rooms were high-ceilinged and spacious. All the tall windows were swagged in heavy damask with fine white lace curtains beneath. Each room was done in a different motif, from the Chinese parlor to the French dining room.

"Come, you must see your rooms!" their aunt

said, taking each of them by the hand and tugging them up a narrow stairwell. "I set them
aside for you and had them completely redone
when I was sure you were coming!"

They were side by side on the very top floor,
with a connecting door between.

If Rose had misgivings about life in Washington, many of them were overcome when she
saw the room that was to be her home. The
white wallpaper was patterned with hand-paint-
ed red roses, the furniture was dark mahogany,
and a pale blue Aubusson carpet covered the
floor. A large four-poster with a canopy and
spread of a darker blue dominated the room,
and matching velvet draperies were at the
windows.

Catherine's bedroom was almost identical,
done in pink and white.

"It's beautiful, Aunt Glynis!"

"Oh, yes," Catherine echoed, "I feel at home
already!"

"And you'll see, Washington City is not so bad
as it looks. Underneath, there is gaiety and excitement . . . and much of the South."

Rose soon found out that her aunt's words
were very true. It was 1856, and Franklin Pierce
occupied the President's mansion. He was a New
Englander, but a man with Southern leanings.
Washington society was ruled by Southern
women; levees at the White House, diplomatic
receptions in Georgetown, and dances and soi-

rees at the big hotels were all dominated by Southerners.

Glynis O'Rourke was wise in the ways of Washington City. Deftly she steered her charges through not only the mud of the capital but also its political and social life.

Powerful men of all persuasions often assembled in Mrs. O'Rourke's parlor to discuss the day's events on the Hill. Rose met and became friendly with President Pierce's Secretary of War, Jefferson Davis. Through Davis she became fast friends with his Natchez-born wife, the former Verina Howell. They spent many an afternoon in Verina's parlor over madeira and iced fruitcake, reminiscing about the South.

Rose also endeared herself to Pierce's former ambassador to England, James Buchanan. Even then it was rumored that Buchanan might well be Pierce's successor, and, like Pierce Buchanan was a friend to the South.

In her aunt's parlor, Rose equally charmed the political giants who favored the North, such as William Seward, Charles Sumner, and Henry Wilson.

Seward was particularly attentive to Rose. He was always ready to listen and comment on her views concerning the merits of Southern life. Their conversation often grew into heated debates, but Seward, always the diplomat, managed to change course before unforgivable words could be said. "Enough, Rose," he would say.

"Be done with the South. Play ... play some soothing music and still this savage beast that seems to straddle the Mason-Dixon line!"

So Rose would sit at the spinet and play with the same savage determination with which she had debated. And in her stirring mezzo voice she would sing, and Seward would smile.

With her aunt, she took tea many afternoons at the houses of important Washington hostesses. She became a favorite of Mrs. Slidell, wife of the governor of Louisiana, and a confidante of Mrs. Greenhow, who believed more than anyone else in the rights of the South.

When word of Rose's beauty and wit got around, there was no shortage of escorts and suitors. She became quite at home, dancing quadrilles and waltzes with foreign ministers resplendent in court costume. Almost nightly, in season, Rose could be seen dancing in the ballroom of the Kirkwood, the Metropolitan, or Willard's Hotel.

There were minstrel shows and operas to attend at the Washington Theater. On the arm of an admiring officer or doting diplomat, she laughed and cried at the drama of Joseph Jefferson and Charlotte Cushman.

Because of her inheritance and Cory Johnson's able management of the Southern property, money was no problem. Rose was able to buy jewels at Maureen's, and almost daily shopped at Madame Delarue's for dress bonnets and ordered Jouvin gloves and boots direct from Paris.

She bought horses and had them stabled across the long bridge in Virginia. Weekly, in good weather, Rose and her beau of the hour would ride in the nearby Virginia countryside.

Sometimes she would make the longer pilgrimage by coach past the Navy yard and the government insane asylum on the eastern branch, to a picnic in the rolling hills of Maryland.

On rainy days she would bundle herself in a velvet cloak and climb the Hill. There she would listen raptly to the fiery debates of the political warriors she had grown to admire: the fierce buckskin-clad men of the West; the stiff, darkly dressed men of New England; and the men of the South with their large colored cravats and bright brocade waistcoats. It was to these last, the firebrands of the South, she listened most closely. These men had strong passions and didn't temper their speech when airing them.

"Read Calhoun," they said when they learned of Rose's love and admiration for the land of her birth, "and learn how a real Southerner looked at the South!" Rose did, and became enthralled.

When James Buchanan replaced Pierce in the White House, Rose's future in Capital society was secure. Not only did Buchanan favor the South, but also he favored gaiety, champagne, and beautiful women in the White House.

Buchanan was a bachelor, so the duties of host-

ess in the mansion fell to his vivacious niece,
Harriet Lane. Rose had met Harriet shortly after her arrival in Washington, and they became
fast friends. So when the tall, rather foppish
man with the easy grace and courtly manners
became the nation's fifteenth President, Rose
Marie Jacquard became a White House favorite.

By the summer of 1859, with secession cock-
ades blazing on the lapels of almost every government clerk, and talk of states' rights domi-
nating every soiree, Rose was in the thick of it.

CHAPTER FIVE

FEW OF THE GUESTS, least of all Rose and Catherine, would guess that the long narrow room they entered had only hours before been the drab cadet mess hall.

The raw wood benches and tables had been removed, and in their place were damask-covered chairs and upholstered settees. The bare beams of the ceilings were disguised with a huge multi-colored drape that gave the room the intimacy of an Arab's tent. Borrowed or purloined tapestries covered the walls, and the refreshment tables were layered with cloth of fine cotton.

Adding even more brilliance were the people themselves, nearly six hundred cadets, their ladies, the West Point officers, and visiting dignitaries from Washington and New York.

Beneath the candlelight from three enormous chandeliers and the dancing yellow glow of over a hundred oil lamps, the room was a rainbow of color.

Ladies glided on their escorts' arms in enormous dresses of every imaginable color. Rose received looks of open admiration as she entered the hall on the arm of Chance Flynn.

"You are already the belle of the ball," he whispered. "I may have to fight a dozen duels to reclaim you by evening's end!"

Rose only smiled. She knew how she looked, and she reveled in it. She had spent hours in her room at The Cozzens Hotel preparing for this moment.

With extreme care she had added blue to her already darkly smoldering eyelids, and smoothed a faint pink blush over her finely structured cheekbones. She had brushed her hair for an hour until the light danced on its raven gloss, and then carefully coiled it atop her head, leaving a row of finger curls dancing at the sides.

Her dress was yards of white satin, draped and flounced over hooped crinolines. There had been a moment of reticence standing in front of the hotel-room mirror to study the daring cut. Her breasts seemed to pour from the top of the bodice. In Washington she would never have given a second thought. But here, at staid West Point?

She needn't have worried. Many of the other women wore dresses even more daringly cut.

"Hurry, Rose," Flynn said. "The first dance must be mine. And from the hungry eyes of my classmates, I feel I'll not claim many more. They will all fall madly in love with you!"

"Best clip Rose's tongue, then," Cat laughed from beside them. "For they'll soon forget her enchanting eyes and her dazzling curls once she begins to flay them!"

Sixteen fiddlers and a piano provided the music as they glided across the floor in a waltz.

Flynn's prophecy quickly proved true. Rose's dances were quickly claimed by a dozen gentlemen. She met all of Hollis' friends. There were Wade Hampton Gibbs from South Carolina, Charles Ball of Alabama, a tall, swarthy Texan named Tom Rosser, and countless more.

At last, dizzy with it all, she was again claimed by Chance Flynn.

"Tired?"

"Never," she laughed, her dark eyes glowing in the candlelight.

"But you *could* rest . . ."

"I *could*."

"Then come along. I want you to meet someone."

Arm in arm, they moved across the room toward a small cluster of cadets. In their center was a tall, broad-shouldered man with golden hair falling well below his ears, sporting a huge mustache that flowed from his upper lip to frame a strong, jutting jaw.

As they moved into the group, the blond man was just finishing doctoring his glass of punch from a flask.

"I say, gentlemen, damn the Republicans and damn the abolitionists!"

"Hear, hear," came agreement from several of the men around him.

"George . . . ?" Flynn said, guiding Rose into the center of the circle.

"Chance, old chap! Dear God, what have we here? I didn't know they made angels with dark hair!" Without further introduction, the man took both of Rose's hands in his and brought them to his lips. "Custer, ma'am, George Armstrong Custer, at your service. Shall we dance?"

Rose couldn't suppress a tinkling laugh. "I don't wish to intrude on such weighty man talk, Mr. Custer. And besides, do you always ask a lady to dance before being introduced?"

"Always. Angels don't have names, do they?"

"This one does."

"All right, then, dammit . . . excuse me. Cadet Flynn?"

"Rose Marie Jacquard," Chance said, smiling and shrugging at Rose.

"French?" Custer asked, narrowing his eyes as if he mistrusted anything foreign.

"American," Rose countered. "My grandparents came to Charleston from Burgundy."

"And do you speak the language?"

"I do—fluently."

78

"Good!" he roared, tossing his blond mane and waving open a path for them through the circle of cadets. "I do, as well. Come along, we can have a private conversation in French while we waltz!"

"They are playing a quadrille," Rose said, only slightly awed by the man's charming bluster.

"No matter, we'll waltz. I live by one axiom, Mademoiselle Jacquard: *don't* do what the other fellow does!"

Onto the floor they went, and for the next two quadrilles they waltzed. Rose could hardly believe it. Somehow the man made it work, and though it was difficult, she was able to follow him.

"Must we?" she asked finally, sensing the stares from the other dancers. "Must we waltz while they play a quadrille?"

"I told you, I never do what the other fellow does."

"And is that the only reason?"

Again he threw back his handsome blond head in a roaring laugh. "Of course not. The truth is, the waltz is the only dance I know."

Rose laughed with him. "First I meet Chance Flynn, and now you. Are you all insane here at West Point?"

"Of course we are," Custer replied, barely noticing the fact that he had practically crushed her toe. "Have to be a bit balmy to keep our sanity in these times."

The next dance was a waltz. During it, Rose learned that George Armstrong Custer was twenty years old, born in New Rumley, Ohio, thought study was a waste of time, and by the time he was thirty he fully intended to be the best damn general in the army.

By the time the dance ended, Rose was foot-sore and out of breath. But as they moved back toward Chance and the waiting group of cadets, she remembered his earlier statements. "You damned the Republicans and the abolitionists before, Mr. Custer."

"I did."

"But, being from the North . . ."

"I am a Yankee," he replied without hesitation.

"Yes?"

"A Yankee who damns the abolitionists and the Republicans. They will go too far one day, and deprive a portion of our fellow citizens of their just rights or cause the dissolution of the Union. Southerners have had insult after insult heaped upon them, until they are determined to no longer submit to such aggression."

Rose warmed to his words, even if they were spoken with the somewhat shallow boisterousness of youth. "Then, Mr. Custer, I assume you approve of secession."

"Yes, Mr. Custer, the lady's question is well taken. Do you approve of secession?"

The voice was a low, rumbling bass, and it came from just a few feet behind Rose. So commanding was it that she whirled in mid-step to seek its owner.

He was tall, even inches taller than the lanky Flynn, and broader in the shoulders and chest than Custer. A strong forehead and classic Roman nose with flared nostrils dominated his powerful features. His jet-black hair was unruly, with several locks hanging carelessly over his forehead. But it was his eyes, as raven-black and as intense as her own, that made a tremor pass through Rose's body. Never had she felt so strange. Looking into those eyes, she felt that she was staring into his mind ... or into his very soul.

"Well, Custer? We are all waiting your answer."

The voice was low, slightly mocking in its brittle intensity.

"I, sir, am sworn to uphold the Union," Custer replied, much of the boyish bluster gone now from his tone.

"Then, Mr. Custer, you agree with the gentleman from Illinois that a house divided against itself cannot stand?"

"I didn't say that, sir."

"I don't believe you know for sure what you're saying, Mr. Custer. Therefore, I think you should limit your political discussions to the barracks rather than this ball, where no one beyond a few Southern ladies is impressed."

Rose heard a low growl hiss from Custer's throat. Out of the corner of her eye she saw a flush begin at his neck and crawl up over his chin.

She suddenly heard her own voice enter the exchange. "Is there a law, here at West Point, that prohibits free speech?"

The black marbles of his eyes shifted to her. They met her own gaze and then traveled brazenly down her body. The intensity was both frightening and thrilling at the same time.

"I haven't had the pleasure, ma'am." Even his pronouncement of the word "pleasure" seemed to have a ribald connotation.

"Rose Marie Jacquard . . . of Charleston."

The full, sensual lips curved into a smile that Rose could only call condescending. "I might have known."

"Known?" she replied, locking her suddenly watery knees beneath the flounces of her dress.

"That Mr. Custer's anti-Republican wrath would be directed toward the ears of a Southern belle."

Beside her, Custer stepped forward, his fists clenched at his sides so tightly that the knuckles gleamed white. "By God, Darcy, first captain or not . . ." His voice was choked with anger and his whole body was shaking. In contrast, the man named Darcy was frighteningly calm. His stance was almost a casual slouch, but beneath his gray jacket Rose could see the powerful muscles of his chest and shoulders gathering. When he spoke, the mocking smile was still spread across his lips.

"Or not *what* . . . Mr. Custer?"

Suddenly Chance Flynn had slid his gangly body between the two giants. "Gentlemen, I suggest we remember that this is no place for our differences of opinion. There are ladies present."

"Quite right, Mr. Flynn." Darcy again turned to Rose and bowed slightly at the waist. "My apologies, ma'am, for all of us. Ladies are meant for pleasure, not politics. I believe this dance is mine."

Without waiting for a response from Rose, he whirled her onto the floor, leaving a cursing and flustered Custer and a scowling Chance Flynn staring after them.

Rose had already witnessed such unabashed arrogance from Chance and George Custer, and accepted it as part of their boyish exuberance. But this was no boy who now held her so cavalierly in his powerful arms and swung her so fast in a reel that her feet barely touched the floor.

Much against her will, Rose had been impressed by his forthright manner and his calm self-assurance, but she refused to let him know it. "Are you always so sure of yourself, Captain Darcy?" she said haughtily.

"Always. Particularly when there is a beautiful woman involved." He stared down at her with a relentlessness that brought an uncomfortable flush to her cheeks. "Are you always so outspoken on matters of war and politics?"

"Always," she said, matching his even gaze with great difficulty, willing her heart to stop its incessant pounding. "Particularly when I know I'm right."

He threw back his head as laughter rumbled from his throat. *"Touché,* Rose Marie Jacquard from Charleston," he said, and then his eyes leveled on hers once more.

Rose shivered with an excitement that was completely foreign to her. It took all her will to return his gaze, feeling as she did that she was being drawn into a vast, swirling whirlpool that had no bottom to its depths.

"It is unusual," he said, a throaty huskiness entering his voice, "to find such beauty matched with wit."

He drew her closer in his arms, and Rose could feel the strength emanating from him. It made her slightly dizzy, and she closed her eyes as he swung them skillfully through the other couples on the floor. He was an excellent dancer, his hand at her waist at once light and commanding in its touch. Rose felt like a feather in his arms as they swayed to the music.

Now and then she ventured a sidelong glance at him, and felt her breath catch in her throat at the strong, firm cut of his jaw, the determined set of his full lips, the way his tousled black hair fell over his high, intelligent forehead. She felt intoxicated with the masculine scent and feel of his body moving against hers. *I wish this dance would last forever.*

"You are very quiet," he said suddenly, his voice a whisper at her ear.

Startled, Rose struggled to regain some measure of composure. "I ... The music is very lovely," she stammered.

"As are you, Rose Marie Jacquard," he said softly.

Rose thought surely her knees would buckle beneath her as she felt his warm breath so close to her lips. She wanted to feel those lips on hers, claiming her, branding her with their fire.

What was wrong with her? What was happening to her? Moments ago this man had come from nowhere to strip her naked with his eyes, to claim a dance which he had no right to claim, and to make her feel like an inexperienced girl with the silken velvet of his voice.

How dare he! And how *could* such a brief encounter possibly have such an effect on her!

"You blush." His voice held a tinge of amusement.

"It ... it's the heat," Rose said lamely. "It's very close in here, don't you think?"

"Is it?" His eyes never left hers. "Or are you still so innocent you don't recognize the appreciation a man may have for a woman?"

The room spun around Rose as she gazed into the burning pools of his eyes, feeling herself drawn deeper, deeper into their glistening depths. Summoning all her inner strength, she determined to put the conversation on a less personal footing. "You do not seem to care much for George Custer," she ventured.

His body stiffened against hers, and when he spoke his voice was controlled, detached. "Custer is brusque and bold, often too much so. In the last year, his rantings have brought him three times within a hairsbreadth of expulsion from the Point. That would be a pity. He will make a good cavalry officer."

Now on safer ground, Rose pressed her point. "You do not agree with his feelings about the Republicans and abolitionists?"

His eyes dropped to hers, and for an instant she felt afraid of the anger she saw flashing in their depths. "Do you honestly believe that war will resolve any differences?"

Rose bristled. "I, *sir*, believe that the South has a right to preserve its rights. And besides, there will be no war, surely."

His eyesbrows arched sharply. "Oh? Then you agree with Senator Hammond from South Carolina." His mouth took a downturn at the corners, his eyes drooped, and his face seemed to age and change as a chameleon changes color. His voice, when he spoke again, was raspy and contained much of the puffery she had heard so often on Capitol Hill. " 'I say, gentlemen, that Cotton is king! You dare not make war upon

Cotton! No power on earth dares make war upon it. Cotton is king, I say?' "

He had meant it in jest, but Rose saw nothing humorous. He was mocking the very world she had been raised in. "You are a very good mimic," she replied coolly, nearly biting her lip to withhold her anger. "Perhaps you would make a better actor than soldier."

"Perhaps. But you haven't answered my question. Do you agree with this fool, Hammond?"

"Damn your arrogance, sir! Senator Hammond is a respected gentleman—"

"In the *South*, dear lady," he countered calmly, infuriatingly. "But do *you* agree with him?"

"I most certainly do," Rose replied firmly. "The North would be foolish to declare war on its largest colony. For that is what we are. The North sells all its goods to the South—why cut off the hand that feeds you?"

"My dear child, you have much to learn. Do not identify rebellion with independence."

"Why, you pompous . . ." Rose's cheeks burned with anger. Even as worldly as she had become in Washington City, this man's sophistication was intimidating and infuriating.

"Ass?" he supplied, suddenly smiling. "You are too kind. I've been called much, much worse." And then the smile disappeared and he was holding her tightly against him, his eyes riveted to hers. She could feel his heart beating through his uniform, and it sent shivers through her entire body. "But it does pain me to hear it come from your lovely lips, Rose Marie Jacquard. I had hoped that perhaps we could at least be friends. It would seem that is impossible. The dance is over, and I shall return you to your escort."

With that he released her, and guiding her by the arm, led her briskly back to where Custer, Flynn, and Hollis were standing.

"I thank you for the dance, mademoiselle," he said with a low bow. "It was very . . . interesting." Then, with another riveting look and a curt nod in George Custer's direction, he turned on his heel and was gone.

"One day, I swear," Custer growled, "one day. . . ."

"Stow it, George," Flynn whirled on the other man, his demeanor totally altered now from the cavalier jokester Rose had seen previously. "We both know that day will never come."

Custer glared at Flynn, his crystal blue eyes sparkling with unconcealed fury, and for a moment Rose was afraid the two would come to blows.

But then Custer regained his self-control, and with a curt "Pardon" whirled and moved away into the crowd.

Rose sighed with relief, but Chance seemed unaffected by the confrontation, dismissing it with a shrug as he turned to Rose. "Dance with me, darlin'. I do believe my feet have gone to sleep!''

Try as she might, Rose found it impossible to concentrate on Chance's glib patter as they whirled around the floor. Her eyes constantly scanned the room, searching for a tall figure in a first captain's uniform.

She was consumed with curiosity about this irritating yet magnetic man who was so different from all the other cadets. He was impossible, of course; his pride, his arrogance, his contempt for anyone's opinions but his own were more than obvious. And yet he was the most handsome, fascinating man Rose had ever met, and she was furious with herself for being unable to get him out of her mind.

She determined to find out more about him— discreetly, of course. She opened her mouth to question Chance about this Captain Darcy, then quickly thought better of it. She didn't want to risk rousing Flynn's suspicions or his Irish temper.

Chance was chatting on about something or other, when Rose interrupted. ''By the way, my question was never answered—about speaking one's mind here.''

The raffish smile again faded from Flynn's lips as he looked down into her questioning eyes. She could tell from the frown that made his brows meet that Chance was carefully weighing his answer. "Robert E. Lee once said that the West Point corps was a band of brothers."

"Yes?"

"Well, that's not quite so true these days. Because of all this talk of secession and the rights of the South as opposed to the sanctity of the Union, the band of brothers is breaking off into two camps."

"The North and the South," Rose said, feeling a tug in her breast as she realized that the camaraderie and good fellowship she had seen since her arrival were not what they appeared.

Flynn nodded. "There have been fights, several of them pretty vicious. Only last week, Wade Gibbs and a cadet from New York had a rather bloody brawl in the barracks over the admitting of Kansas as a free or slave state. We managed to keep it quiet, but others haven't been so lucky. Many cadets have been expelled for brawling, and even dueling. Darcy probably did Custer a favor just now by shutting him up."

Rose's head was spinning. "But you and Mr. Custer are Yankees, and you are friends with Hollis, who is most assuredly a Southerner."

"True, but George and I agree somewhat with Hollis. The Southern states *do* have rights. It's just . . ."

Rose's eyes, like her mind, had been wandering, as if she could see the truth of Flynn's words in the faces around her. Now, at his sudden pause, her gaze swung back to his frowning face. "Yes?"

she whispered, sensing that what he was about to say would greatly affect her.

"I, like George, may sympathize with the South, but we both agree that the Union must stay intact."

Suddenly Rose stiffened in his arms. It was as in his hand in the small of her back had become a block of ice.

"Then ..." she stammered, "if war should follow secession, you and Custer ..."

"Would fight for the North, Rose. We would have no choice."

"But you said Hollis was like a brother!"

"If war comes, Rose, it will be brother against brother."

Suddenly the lanky redhead with the smiling face and the ready quip didn't seem so amusing to Rose.

Her lower lip was quivering as she raised her eyes and looked deeply into Flynn's. She suddenly felt that she was gazing into the eyes of the enemy.

For the next hour Rose was uneasy. Dissension in Washington was rife, but here among these young men of West Point she suddenly felt the intense heat of animosity. In the Capital, war talk was dismissed; it was felt that war would be foolishness and would gain nothing for either side. But here at West Point among the military youth—many of them hotheads hungering for a fight—war was suddenly a possibility. And it frightened her.

If all of this didn't unsettle Rose enough, Captain Darcy did. She lost count of the times she turned to find his jet-black eyes staring at her. The longer he stared, the more Rose felt her will drain away.

Who was he, this ruggedly handsome man with the aristocratic features and the rapt eyes that seemed to mesmerize her?

She was thankful when, at last, Hollis claimed her for a dance. She felt that with Hollis she could satisfy her curiosity without arousing his.

She was wrong.

"So he's captivated you, too?"

"Captivated me? Why, Hollis, whatever do you mean?"

"I mean, dear girl, that if you look around you, you will see every woman in the room, young and old alike, casting furtive glances at Bramfield Darcy."

"I'm merely curious."

"Of course you are *merely* curious," he agreed skeptically, "so I'll tell you all I know about Bramfield Ashworth Darcy."

CHAPTER SIX

THE SUNDAY DEPARTURE from the West Point dock, unlike the arrival two days before, was not a festive occasion. A wind-driven rain early that morning had turned the gaily colored bunting into limp tatters.

Even now, as the crowd moved toward the waiting sloop, thunderclouds hovered overhead, blocking out the setting sun. The dreary weather worsened Rose's dreary mood. Also, she was bone-tired. The revelries had lasted until the wee hours, and it had been nearly dawn when she and Cat returned to their hotel beds.

Cat had mumbled a few words about Hollis and what a grand time it had been, and promptly fell asleep. But Rose remained staring at the cracks in the ceiling above her and listening to the distant thunder. The faces of all the cadets she had met rolled like waves of heat across her eyes.

She thought of the brash, rather boyish protestations of George Armstrong Custer, and how his words extolling about the South meant nothing when he was faced with a choice between his words and his duty.

And Chance—gay, charming, witty Chance Flynn. Until he had made his damning statement that should war come he would fight for the North no matter what, Rose had thought him devoid of any allegiance. Indeed, until then she wouldn't have given him credit for having a serious thought in his head.

How wrong she had been.

By the time the last waltz played, Rose was all too aware that West Point's "band of brothers" had indeed disbanded.

And there were other thoughts that kept her eyes wide that morning, refusing to let blissful sleep overtake her—thoughts of Bram Darcy. She saw every tiny line at the corners of his piercing eyes, visualized the premature flecks of gray at his temples that suggested what Hollis had confirmed while they danced: Bram Darcy was considerably older than his fellow cadets.

As quietly as possible, Rose had slipped from the bed. Cat slumbered on as Rose donned a robe and moved out onto the balcony. Now she could see flashes of lightning to the east across the river.

Bram Darcy was like that lightning: powerful, slightly mysterious, and almost terrifying.

She had felt chilled the first time she stared into those eyes that could look so cold and brooding one second, and then flash with mockery in the next. In both figure and face he exuded power, authority, and an aura of brute force—a maleness that, no matter how much Rose tried to deny it, excited and stirred her.

According to Hollis, Bram Darcy was almost thirty years old, and he had already lived a thrilling and adventurous life. His family were the Darcys of Baltimore, traders, shipbuilders, and landowners. Bram was one of three children, having an older brother and sister. While the sister married an English lord and the brother went on to a distinguished military career after graduating with honors from the Point, Bram had seemingly concentrated on becoming the black sheep of the Darcy family.

No school could hold him, and he shunned his father's businesses. Even in his youth he had gained a scandalous reputation as a great fascinator of women. He indulged himself to the full in all the pleasures available to a young man of his class and wealth: fox hunting, cockfights, the racing of blooded horses. It was said that a duel over a woman finally decided the elder Darcy to send his wayward son abroad.

What escapes or scandalous affairs he had in Europe, Hollis didn't know. Darcy never mentioned that part of his life. What he did speak of was the love and respect he had for his older brother, Steven.

Steven had risen quickly in the military. When the Mexican War broke out, he was a major and an aide to General Zachary Taylor. He distinguished himself at the battles of Matamoros and Palo Alto. At Resaca de la Palma, the Mexicans were soundly defeated, but Steven Darcy was captured and eventually executed.

When word reached Bram in Europe, he rushed home. Through his father's influence, the young man's enlistment was approved, and off to Mexico he went.

He fought at Cerro Gordo, Contreras, Churubusco, and was decorated for bravery during the siege of Mexico City. Along the way he was wounded three times, once seriously, which caused him to spend nearly a year following the war in a military hospital.

Here Hollis was interrupted in his story, but during a dance with West Point's handsome and dashing commandant, General Pierce Beauregard, Rose obliquely inquired about the past of several cadets, idly slipping in the name of First Captain Bramfield Darcy.

Unwittingly, General Beauregard obliged, filling in more bits and pieces of Darcy's checkered past.

Evidently the war and the time he spent in the hospital made a radical change in Bram. He returned home to find that his father had died and the family's business affairs had degenerated into chaos.

Like a man possessed, he threw himself into the family business and, at the same time, cared for his ailing mother. Then when his mother went to her reward, Bram put the bulk of his business holdings in the hands of his solicitors and followed in his brother's steps at West Point.

At the Point, he had excelled as both scholar and military leader. In his junior year he attained the highest cadet rank, first captain, and would soon graduate at the top of his class.

For the answer to Rose's last question, she returned to Hollis.

"Women? Dear God, Rose, who knows? He furloughs off to New York, Boston, and Baltimore quite often, and I've heard that more than one daughter of those cities' fine families has set her cap for him, but as far as I've heard, he pays them no mind."

"And here at West Point?"

"The same." Hollis shrugged. "He beguiles them, but they get little more than a smile or a passing word."

A smile, Rose thought, and a passing word. She herself had already received more than that—looks from his brooding black eyes that had sent her blood racing.

But she knew she was a fool to think that Bram Darcy considered her anything other than a passing diversion at a West Point ball. Women found him irresistible, and although he feigned coolness and detachment, he had undoubtedly had more than his share of them.

Rose bit her lip at the thought of him holding another woman in his arms, gazing at her with those eyes burning with fire, his lips whispering words of love as he trailed kisses over her throat and neck. And then . . . and then . . .

Rose blinked rapidly, refusing to think of him making love to anyone else. Her body ached to touch him, to feel him, to see him standing naked before her, ready to take her, body and soul, and drown her with the force of his love.

Never had she felt like this before, so willing— yes, *eager*—to give herself completely. She remembered the thrill that had surged through her when, for a brief instant, she thought his eyes were actually piercing her clothing and examining the naked flesh of her arching breasts and firm white hips. But what, exactly, did such a feeling imply. Surely not love. Perhaps Bram Darcy was simply so different from the other men she had known that she had become merely infatuated.

A bolt of lightning pierced the sky, its jagged white light driving her back against the rough brick wall.

It was then that Rose realized with a start

that her hands had been moving over the muted round of her belly and the sleek firmness of her thighs. Her nipples had grown hard and taut so that they now strained against the thin material of her robe and nightdress. Surely they've become so because of the cold, she thought.

"Rose, whatever is wrong with you? You're soaked to the skin!"

Cat was standing white-faced just inside the French doors.

"I . . . I didn't realize it was raining."

But now she did. Her robe was glued to her body, outlining every curve, every sensuous hollow. Her breasts seemed swollen much beyond their normal size. They ached and threatened to burst through the material.

"You didn't realize . . ."

"No. I couldn't sleep. I . . . Never mind. I'll dry off and change."

Cat shrugged, shook her head at such lunacy, and staggered back to bed.

Hurriedly Rose peeled off the robe and nightdress from her body. There was but one towel in the room, and it was soaked through by the time she had dried herself. With her hair still wet, she slipped naked into bed beside the sleeping Catherine.

Just as she drifted off to sleep, she realized that her body was burning up.

Had she caught a fever?

Or had she caught something else?

* * *

"I'll be graduating in ten days, Rose. I'm to visit my parents in Ohio, but I would like to stop off in Washington on the way. Rose, did you hear me?"

"What? Oh, yes, Chance, of course."

"Then you'll see me?"

"When?"

"When I'm in Washington. You haven't been listening."

"I have," she replied, trying to match his smile. "I'm just a bit weary, that's all. I didn't sleep well this morning, and then you and Hollis insisted on luncheon before we came to the dock, and—"

"And I'm a downright cad and I admit it. After last night I just couldn't wait to see you again, Rose. I didn't sleep a wink myself."

"I believe that's more of your blarney, Chance Flynn."

"Not a bit of it, you're the first girl I've been daft about this year . . . and something tells me you'll be the last."

As idle as his tone was, Rose could tell from his calf-eyed look that she had made a conquest, one that she didn't want to make.

Suddenly she had to get away, away from the adoring eyes of Chauncey Flynn. She had to be alone to think.

"You will see me, then, Rose, in Washington City?"

"Yes, yes, of course, Chance. We must get aboard now. We're the last ones on the dock. Cat—"

"Rose . . ."

Suddenly she was in his arms, pinned to his chest. The front of her hoops was against his ankles, and she thought how ridiculous she must look with the back bell of her skirt lifted nearly to the back of her knees.

"Chance—"

But there was no stopping him. She saw his grinning lips descending and, barely in time, turned her face to the side. Nevertheless, his lips were pleasingly soft against her cheek, and she was surprised at the strength of his slender arms. For the briefest of moments she enjoyed the feel of her breasts pressed tightly to his chest and the coil of his arms around her body. But behind her half-closed lids, it wasn't Chance Flynn holding her. It was Bram Darcy.

"Ah, Rose, I can feel the fire of ya, just in a touch. Ye're a wild one, ye are, but I'll tame ya."

Her body went stiff, frozen. She knew Flynn was only being himself, half-jesting with his brogue, teasing her in schoolboy style. But she had long ago outgrown schoolboys, and no man was going to "tame" her. When the time came—if it ever did—for her to be domesticated, it would be done by a far more mature man than Chance Flynn.

But his freckled, beaming face wouldn't let her tell him the truth. Instead, she went to her toes and, untangling herself from his arms, kissed him lightly on the cheek. "Write to me before you arrive in Washington," she called over her shoulder as she scampered toward the sloop's gangway. "Cat . . . hurry along."

"I'll do more than that—I'll to write you each and every day!"

He said more, but it was lost in the eerie blast of the ship's whistle.

Rose and Cat moved up the gangway, and their slippers had barely found the sloop's hard deck when the chains were rattling and the gangway was hoisted.

"There's a place!" Rose shouted to Cat over the din. "We can wave good-bye from there!"

"No, I'm going below."

Cat started off, but Rose managed to grab one elbow and gently turn her around. Her small chest was heaving with silent sobs and tears were streaming down both cheeks.

"Cat, what is it?"

"Nothing."

"You're crying—is that nothing?"

"Yes."

"Don't be a ninny. What is it? . . . Hollis?"

"Yes."

"You argued."

"Yes."

"Oh, Cat," Rose exclaimed, folding the smaller

girl in her arms. "That's all right. We all fight with our beaus. If we didn't we would miss the fun of making up."

Cat wriggled from her grasp and stepped back to face Rose. The tears still erupted from her eyes, but her body no longer shook and now her fine-boned jaw jutted defiantly. "I doubt that this argument will be settled so easily. All this talk of war and secession, of saving the Confederacy and retaining the Union . . ."

"What of it, Cat?"

"I asked Hollis what he would do if there was war."

"And he told you?"

"Yes. He said he would resign his commission, that he would be faithful to his state. He said if there was war he would return to the South at once."

"And what did you tell him?"

"I told him he would go without me." Cat whirled and, with her skirts raised, bounded for the ladder that led below to the ladies' quarters.

Dear God, Rose thought, watching until her sister's fragile figure and honey-blond head had disappeared from view, if there is war, it will be even worse than brother against brother.

The slow roll of the sloop as it glided through the Hudson River darkness brought a nauseous feeling to Rose that made sleep impossible. Through the tiny porthole she could see that the threatening clouds had disappeared and now the river was bathed in pale moonlight.

Gently she rolled her feet to the deck and stood. In the upper bunk Cat slept fitfully, rolling from side to side. Now and then a barely audible moan escaped her lips.

Rose was amazed that the girl could sleep at all in the stifling closeness of the cabin. Her own chemise stuck clammily to her skin and her pantalets felt like weights on her legs.

After carefully blotting beads of perspiration from Cat's forehead and cheeks with her kerchief, Rose pulled a beige travelling dress of sashed muslin over her head. She picked a heavy petticoat and a hooped crinoline from her chest, but quickly discarded them.

Damn propriety in this heat, she thought. Besides, it's dark, and there were likely to be few people on deck.

She draped a light saffron cotton shawl about her shoulders and, armed with a fan, mounted the narrow ladder to the main deck.

The few deck chairs in the bow were occupied by other ladies who were obviously suffering the same insomnia as Rose, their fans vainly trying to stir some coolness in the air.

Rose turned aft toward the fantail. In her present mood, she preferred to be alone.

Rounding the superstructure, she came up short as she realized that this area, too, was occupied. A tall, bareheaded man in a black cutaway and trousers stood at the rail, his highly polished Wellington boots reflecting the moonlight. She saw a flash of ruffled lace at his cuff as his hand came to his face. Then the glowing ember of a slender cigar outlined his chiseled profile against the night sky, and Rose's stomach caught in a knot.

It was Bram Darcy.

She was about to turn and flee, when the now familiar rumbling bass voice broke the stillness between them. "Good evening, Miss Jacquard."

He turned to face her, and the moonlight fell full upon his face. Like a thudding blow to the center of her chest, Rose again realized how handsome he was.

As they stood staring at each other, he smiled. His teeth gleamed starkly white in the deeply tanned face, but his eyes remained cold. Even smiling, the firm mouth had a line of cruelty about it.

"I saw you emerge from the hatch," he said, as if Rose's wide-eyed look were asking him how he had known it was she even before he turned to face her.

"Good evening, Captain Darcy. I . . . I didn't know you were aboard."

"A last-minute summons from my solicitors in New York—a bit of business."

"I see."

Rose willed steadiness into her hand as she flipped open her fan and moved it back and forth in front of her face. For just a second she had allowed herself to hope that Bram had followed her aboard so they could meet again, alone, as they were doing now.

But just as quickly she cast the thought aside as preposterous. As much as it pained her to admit it, she was sure that their brief meeting at the ball the previous evening had not affected Bram Darcy as it had her.

"Forgive me," he said, extending his hand. "May I fetch you a deck chair?"

"No, thank you." Rose evaded the proffered hand and glided to the rail. "I'd really rather stand. The breeze, however light, feels good."

"Yes, it does. I was wondering how long you would stay below before coming on deck for some air."

Rose swung her head around. "You wondered . . . then you knew I was aboard?"

"All the visitors took the Sunday-night boat."

Quickly Rose returned her gaze to the sloop's frothing water. Of course he knew you were aboard, you ninny, she told herself, hiding the quiver of her lower lip with her fan.

"I would like to apologize for last night."

"Apologize? Whatever for?"

He had moved closer, until his lapel was brushing her shoulder. Even turned away from him, Rose was awed by his size, his sheer presence seemed to envelop her.

"For my abruptness and rudeness at the ball

last evening. More often than not lately, I have found myself playing mediator between our young gentlemen of the North and their counterparts from the South. Sometimes it has embarrassingly involved a third party, such as yourself."

"I . . . I'm afraid I involved myself, Captain," Rose replied a little too quickly. "For that *I* apologize."

"Then we have a truce?"

Rose turned, her shoulder brushing his chest. The touch sent yet another unfamiliar shudder through her. She covered it with a throaty laugh and stared directly into his eyes. "Truce? I wasn't aware that the animosities between us had grown to such an extent that a truce was required to end them."

His dark eyes narrowed. "Miss Jacquard, I think you would make a better diplomat than most of the oafs playing that dubious trade in Washington City."

"Perhaps I would. We Southerners in Washington are treading a narrow path. A ready tongue and quick wit are often necessary to soothe the savage Northern beast."

Rose faced him squarely now, and for the first time she noticed that he wore no cravat. His fine linen shirt was open in the front, and try as she might she could not tear her eyes from the dark, curly hair covering his muscular chest.

"You sound like an old and dear friend of mine, an Irish planter in the Mississippi delta."

"You have Southern friends?" Rose blurted, realizing as soon as the words left her mouth that it was a stupid question.

There was more cynicism than humor in his answering laughter. "Nearly all of my friends —my dearest friends—are in the South." There was a wistfulness in his voice as he paused and his eyes drifted from hers.

His silhouette was sharp in the bright moonlight and Rose fought an impulse to reach up and trace the line of his jaw with a fingertip. As she continued to study him, it was as if he had forgotten her presence and retreated completely into his own thoughts. The silence grew awkward between them.

"What of the Southern planter?" she prompted.

"What? . . . Oh, yes. Forgive me, I fear my mind wanders at times." He sighed. "His name is Ian. He's a big, brawling, hard-drinking, wonderful man. He's half Irish and all Southerner, to the tips of his toes. We've had many a discussion about secession, and what would come of it."

Bram at last brought his gaze back to meet hers. His black eyes still glittered like brooding coals, but now there was a warmth in them that she had not seen before. A muscle tensed in his cheek as he continued.

"Ian has often told me that the South is like

Ireland in her troubles with England. 'We are freemen,' he said, 'and as such we are damned if a brood of Washington politicians in their dotage will tell us how to run our land!' "

"And what did you reply, Captain Darcy?" Rose asked softly, almost afraid of receiving an answer, should it be one that didn't agree with her own thoughts.

"I cautioned him as I've done others who speak as he does. The South fighting the North is like the Irish peasant fighting the English lion."

The contempt in his voice rankled Rose. She was about to reply that in no way could the Irish peasant be compared to the Southern planter, when a sudden gust of wind lifted her shawl from her shoulders. It poised in the air like a saffron butterfly and threatened to glide over the rail into the river.

Darcy's movement was as lithe and swift as a cat's as he leaned far over and speared the garment with a deft hand. And just as deftly he returned to her side, lifting the shawl in his hands to drape it around her shoulders. His fingers lightly caressed her neck, and Rose was hard put to stop the electric sensation from showing on her face.

She started to turn away, but his strong hands gripped her, the fingers moving up to find her chin. She had not pinned her hair, so now it streamed below her shoulders, rippling in harmony with the breeze like a black cloud about her upturned face.

"Must we be always discussing politics or war when we are alone together?" he murmured, his voice a low growl. "Surely there are other things we have to say to each other."

"I . . . I don't know what you mean," she stammered, unable to move her eyes from his.

"There is a wildness in you, Rose—in your eyes, in the tilt of your chin . . ."

Now there was something else in his eyes: passion, the hungry passion of a man for a woman.

It erased all else from Rose's mind, all sound from her ears. The whole world had ebbed away, leaving only the two of them suspended in moon-lit space.

One of his arms slipped around her waist and, like a feather, she was brought to the tips of her toes. The fingers of his other hand curled in her hair as his face lowered and his mouth took possession of hers.

His lips were almost cruel, but Rose welcomed them and went limp in his arms. His tongue darted over her mouth, seeking entrance between her lips.

Rose felt drugged. He was taking possession of not only her lips but also her mind and body. She knew that she was being almost wanton as her arms slipped about his neck and her body surged forward to mold against his.

But she didn't care. It was as though his mouth was commanding her surrender, and her body was giving it.

His hand moved up and down the length of her back, building a fire everywhere it touched. The fingers in her tresses became velvet claws as they drew her more tightly to him, holding their lips together.

Her own fingers curled in the thick hair above his collar, and then tightened as something wild and primitive burst inside her. Her breasts swelled and throbbed against his chest as his lips left hers to move across her cheek until they found the slight hollow of her neck. Her body arched as his mouth branded that sensitive area with a kiss of fire.

She had never been kissed like this. No man's lips had ever felt as stirring or as sweet. And never had she felt so helpless against the overwhelming desire that now consumed her.

And then she felt his hard maleness pressing against her belly, turning her whole being to a burning ember.

"Rose . . ." His breath was warm and ragged against her ear. "I knew . . ."

The rest of his words were drowned in the swelling tide of desire that engulfed her. There was no denying it. Her body had been awakened beyond her wildest dreams by this dark, brooding giant.

Rose knew that the pounding ache in her breast

was love, and she was eager for it. She wanted to give herself totally, completely, to this man who held her so tightly against him she could feel the blood pulsating wildly through his body.

And then suddenly his lips left hers and he released her. When he spoke, his words were like a sudden frost, shocking her back to reality. "I'm sorry, Rose."

"Sorry ... ?" she managed to gasp, placing her hands on his chest to steady herself.

"I had no right—"

"Stop," she cried, her fingers pressing against his lips to stop their movement. "It was as much my doing as yours. I ... *wanted* you to kiss me, Bram."

"I know ... at least, I hoped as much. But I still shouldn't have taken advantage of it."

Advantage?

Oh, Bram, she thought, if only you knew how much of an advantage you could have pressed, had this happened in a more private place than this.

She longed to take the strong, firm hands that now rested on her shoulders and press them to her breasts so he could feel the throb of desire he had aroused there. She wanted to throw herself back into his arms and again have his lips devour hers. But the spell was broken.

The world came back into focus, and the sound of the sloop's paddle wheel broke the stillness of the night around them.

And then Bram's fingertips gently tilted her chin upward, and his black eyes fixed on hers as he spoke. "After graduation I've been assigned to General McClellan's staff in Washington. I should be there in six weeks' time. We'll meet again."

Oh, yes, Rose agreed silently, indeed we will meet again.

CHAPTER SEVEN

Rose returned to a Washington seething in the miasma of summer heat and political unrest. Harriet Lane had moved President Buchanan and his entourage to the summer White House in the Soldier's Park north of Washington. Most of the city's Southern contingent had already left for their annual trek north to Saratoga Springs.

Even though the underbelly of Washington society still seethed with secessionist talk and hints of war, the lounges and ballrooms of the big hotels were nearly devoid of revelers and debaters.

Rose was bored, but she was also apprehensive. Exactly when would Bram Darcy be assigned to Washington? Would he indeed call upon her when he arrived?

She spent many sleepless nights pondering these questions and others.

Darcy was a son of Maryland wealth. Rose had learned that most of the Darcy family's business dealings were in the South. Bram himself had said as much. Maryland itself was a border state, but strongly Southern. She had even heard many say that, should war come, Washington City might well be the first to fall, resting as it did between Virginia and Maryland.

Wouldn't it then follow, she mused, that Bram Darcy would opt for the South when the last card in this impending crisis was finally dealt? Rose vowed that when again they met, she would somehow force an answer from him on this all-important question.

But what if, like Chance Flynn and George Custer, Bram believed in the preservation of the Union and chose to be an enemy of the South—*Rose's* enemy?

Could she bear it? For she had little doubt now that Bram Darcy was the man among men that she had been waiting for her whole life.

The steamy days of June passed, and the first week of July proved even hotter and more frustrating.

And still no word from Bram.

She did receive a message from Chance. Critical sickness in his family had forced him to bypass Washington on the way to Ohio, but he was counting the days until this crisis was over and he could see her again.

Rose was relieved. From experience she knew that once Chance arrived in Washington he meant to court her, and she wanted to put off that embarrassment as long as possible.

Added to her own problems were Catherine's. Since the graduation ball at West Point, letters had arrived almost daily from Hollis. Every one implored Cat to reconsider the finality of her statement.

"Hollis loves you, Cat."

"Perhaps. But as a woman, I think I have the right to disagree as much as Hollis has to insist."

Rose was somewhat taken aback by Cat's defiance. *As a woman.* Potent words for a blossoming girl. Or were they? Hadn't Rose herself felt the same maturity at Cat's age? She began to realize that even though there were vast differences between herself and Catherine, there were many similarities as well.

"Do you love Hollis, Cat?"

The petite body stiffened and for just a second Rose thought she saw the beginnings of misty tears in the large almond eyes. But quickly the angelic features hardened and the jaw steadied as it jutted toward Rose. "I do. Yes, I'm sure of it."

Rose's mind whirled. She thought of Hollis' wide, smiling face, the tender warmth and the devotion in his eyes when he stared at Cat. "But,

Cat, if you're sure of it, if Hollis is indeed the man you love, how can you deny that love?"

"I don't deny it. I just told you, I do love him."

Rose felt the beginnings of anger. "Then how can you fight his wishes? Hollis is a Southerner, born to live in the South. If you would be his wife, it is your duty to—"

"*Duty?*" Cat's loud retort coupled with the sudden stony coldness in her pale blue eyes shocked Rose into silence. "What is good for the goose is good for the gander, dear sister. I see the look in your eyes when Bram Darcy's name is mentioned. What will *you* do, Rose, when Bram Darcy tells you that he is—and will remain, no matter what—an officer of the Union and the North?"

The thought of such a thing had troubled Rose for weeks. Now, having Cat actually verbalize it, made her frustration surface.

Where was Bram—New York, Baltimore? The final ceremonies of West Point's fifty-third graduation class had long since passed, and still he had not arrived in Washington.

Should she write to him?

No, Rose told herself, she had already been too forward in their relationship. Now, viewed from a distance, the memory of how she had wantonly pressed her body to his that night on the sloop brought a deep blush to her cheeks.

Perhaps Bram's chivalry that night in apologizing for his ardor was only an act. Perhaps he was only toying with her, preserving her for an idle tryst when he did arrive at last in the capital city.

She cursed her own weakness at letting her emotions show so clearly. But at the same time, Rose had to admit to herself that she could not wait until she saw him again.

To make that time fly faster, she threw herself into what social life there was during the hot July and August days. Since returning from West Point, Rose had been drawn more and more to the house of Mrs. Greenhow, a widow in her forties, who was originally from Maryland. When Rose wasn't prying information from her friend about Bram and the Darcy family, she was inquiring about Maryland and its largest city, Baltimore.

"Baltimore City," Mrs. Greenhow told her, "is seething with secession. Yet many powerful families sympathize with the North and the Union. I would say, Rose, that the state is evenly split between North and South. There is no way to tell which way it will go."

This perplexed Mrs. Greenhow as much as it did Rose, for the famous Washington widow was herself a staunch supporter of the South.

Together with Mrs. Clement Clay and Mrs. Greenhow, Rose made the rounds of afternoon teas, White House and Georgetown gatherings, and fashionable dinner parties. These women assured Rose that there would be no war, that the Southern way of life that she missed so was as solid as marble.

In the evenings there were the never-ending dances in hotel ballrooms or beneath a hastily constructed tent in the rear of a private residence.

If anything, Rose was courted with even greater fervor than she had been the previous year. The son of the French ambassador asked for her hand in marriage the first evening he met her. He was crushed when Rose refused, and two days later returned to France.

There were many to take his place, but no number of compliments, smiles, or amorous glances from the scores of handsome and fascinating men she met blurred her memory of Bram Darcy.

The heat of August gave way at last to the crispness of September, and the President and his entourage returned to the White House. Rose was delighted to have her old friend Harriet Lane nearby again.

Fashion had changed swiftly that summer, and so, with the new social season beginning, the two young women scoured Washington for the newest materials after consulting *Godey's Lady's Book* for the latest modes.

Frail gossamer tulle and flounces had given way to heavier materials. Newly fashionable accoutrements included rosetted slippers and wrist-length white gloves. Lilies, violets, and other flowers were still popular adornments for gowns and hair, and hoops, if anything, were getting wider. Harriet herself set the style by popularizing the new wide, lace-embroidered bertha neck.

As close as Rose was to the President's niece, Mrs. Greenhow was even closer to James Buchanan himself. It was said in many circles that Buchanan often queried Mrs. Greenhow about affairs of state, and that many of his administration's Southern leanings originated with that venerable lady. Because Mrs. Greenhow had all but taken Rose under her wing, the Charleston beauty became as informed as anyone in the day-to-day affairs of the Capital.

So it was that, when Harriet Lane was not able to secure an invitation for Rose to the season's first gala event, Mrs. Greenhow, through the President himself, was. The event was a costume ball honoring the British ambassador, Lord Lyons. The ball's sponsor was Kate Chase, the brilliant daughter of Northerner Salmon Portland Chase, its purpose primarily to woo British sympathies away from the South. Attendance by Rose or Mrs. Greenhow, or both, would certainly send sparks flying and tongues wagging.

Rose looked forward to it with eager anticipation.

She chose materials two weeks before the ball and commissioned Madame Foshay, the best dressmaker in Washington, to make her costume.

The gown would be made with cream silk, broken with an indigo sash at Rose's wasplike waist. Matching flutes of indigo satin would flow from waist to hem. The wide bertha neck was designed to flow into a daringly low-cut square bodice, also fluted to accentuate Rose's stunning bosom. Frothy cream-colored lace was to be added at the neckline to partially disguise her décolletage and yet make it more demurely inviting.

Rose arrived at the little shop on Fourteenth Street promptly at noon on the day of the ball. She had already undergone four fittings as the dress took shape, and now could barely wait to see the final results.

"Ah, mademoiselle, you will be enchanting!" chirped the tiny Frenchwoman, hopping about Rose like a mother bird.

Rose's eyes glowed as Madame Foshay removed the protective wrapper from the gown. "It is lovely, madame."

"*Merci, merci, ma chérie* ... but of course I have a lovely subject with which to work!"

"Exquisite," Rose breathed, loving the sensual feel of the silk sliding down across her shoulders and over her body. "You have outdone yourself."

"You are too kind, mademoiselle. *Ici, ici*, move in front of the mirrors!"

Rose positioned herself in front of three mirrors, all angled perfectly to expose every facet of the gown. Slowly she pirouetted in a full circle, carefully examining her image. There was a flash of triumph in her dark eyes when she at last faced the mirror full front. This should certainly do the trick, she thought.

Mrs. Greenhow had been slightly mysterious when she asked Rose to be at her most beautiful and charming for this occasion. "You have expressed your desire many times, Rose, to do something constructive here in Washington for our Southern cause. Well, at Kate Chase's ball you will have your chance."

Rose had been surprised. What on earth could she do for the Southern cause at a ball?

"It rests with you, my dear, with your youth and beauty and wit, to turn the eye and ear of Queen Victoria's minister. You will take away much of Kate Chase's glitter, and in so doing wean Lord Lyons away from the Northern camp."

Rose had met Lord Lyons before. He was a handsome bachelor with an eye for the ladies. Because of this, many of his ambassadorial decisions recently had been influenced by the beautiful and haughty Kate Chase.

At first, flirting with the Britisher had seemed slightly distasteful to Rose. Besides, when she had first mentioned to Mrs. Greenhow doing something for the Southern cause, she had had in mind something slightly more weighty. But then, at a recent dinner party she had crossed swords with Kate Chase, and suddenly the challenge given by Mrs. Greenhow was too much to be denied.

Now Rose sighed and smiled with satisfaction at the picture she made in the mirror. The color set off her dark skin to perfection, and the fit of the gown was perfect. Her breasts swelled over the frothy lace edging the neckline, and the snug bodice accented her tiny waist.

Yes, she thought, Mrs. Greenhow had made a good choice in Rose Marie Jacquard to counter the influence of Kate Chase with the British Empire.

"Ah, zee bell! *Excusez moi, mademoiselle!*"

The little woman scampered through a set of curtains into the shop's outer alcove while Rose replaced her street shoes with indigo satin slippers. She was just tugging on a pair of short white gloves when the muffled voices of Madame Foshay and her newly arrived client reached her ears.

"Ah, Lady Fontaine, your appointment is not until two. I fear your gown will not be—"

"Surely, my dear woman, your seamstresses do not wait until the last minute."

"Of course not, but I have another—"

"I'll wait," came the curt reply, quickly followed by more harsh words spoken too low to reach Rose's ears.

Odd, Rose thought, the voice of the unseen Lady Fontaine was strangely familiar. The woman's speech patterns were clipped in the English style, yet there was almost a Southern lilt to many of the words.

Rose racked her brain, but could not remember ever meeting a Lady Fontaine. She dismissed the angry voices and began to remove the gown.

"Please, Lady Fontaine, you will have to wait ..."

Rose heard the curtains part behind her and the rustle of skirts as the two women entered the fitting room.

Rose turned to speak some sort of greeting, but the imposing stature and beauty of the woman before her made the words catch in her throat.

"Well, my, my, ah declare, if it isn't little Rose Marie Jacquard!"

There was no remnant of British now. The accent was pure Southern low country, and the face was all too familiar. She still had the pale cameo skin and the slanting catlike green eyes that were always full of mocking laughter. Her lips, always a shade too full, were even more sensuous than Rose remembered them. She was not quite as tall as Rose, but the elegant pile of her perfectly coiffed golden hair atop her head made her seem so.

"Hello, Camilla."

"My, my, Rose Marie, how you have changed! Ah declare, you look absolutely beautiful!"

Rose felt an instant flush creep up her cheeks.

Camilla Boyd had matured, obviously changed in many ways, but her acid tongue hadn't.

"I'm happy to see, Camilla, that you haven't changed a bit."

"You two ladies know each other?" Madame Foshay asked, her eyes flitting from one to the other.

"Oh, yes," Camilla said, her lips pouting in the semblance of a smile. "We're old ... *friends*. Madame Foshay, would you please fetch my gown? I'm sure the alterations are finished ... by now."

The little woman cast a sparrowlike look at Rose, who nodded. "Yes, go ahead, madame," she said. "If you'll just bring a box, I'll take the dress with me."

The dressmaker scurried away, obviously relieved to be away from these two women whose eyes devoured one another. She had been in business too long not to recognize what lay behind the looks being exchanged between the two. And she had no desire to become arbitrator in what could become a war of wills.

"Here, Rose, let me help you with those!"

"I can manage."

"Nonsense. It really takes three or four people to get out of one of Madame Foshay's creations!"

"Thank you."

As the woman's hands deftly worked at the gown's snaps, Rose studied Camilla Boyd in the mirrors.

Her face was a perfect ivory oval, emphasized by winged brows. Her nose was thin, aristocratic, and somewhat turned up at the tip. Her gown was elegant copper silk cut in the latest of Parisian styles, yet its severe quality didn't diminish the full, curvaceous figure of its wearer.

There was little doubt of it. Camilla was every inch a thoroughbred. She was like a beautiful statuette chiseled from marble, breathtaking to look at, but every bit as cold as stone.

"I didn't know that you were still in Washington City."

Rose suppressed a smile. For all the range of the Capital, it would be nearly impossible for someone of Camilla Boyd's obvious station not to know that Rose Jacquard of Charleston was in Washington.

"You must have just arrived then, Camilla."

"Oh no, I've been at Brown's Hotel for a full week, however indisposed with a cough. And a horrid place it is, a hotbed of Southern secessionist activity!"

The disdain in Camilla's voice instantly drew Rose's attention. "You don't approve of secessionist activity, Camilla?"

"Good Lord, no. I see them as a group of maniacal hotheads who would tear the country apart! There, you're undone."

Rose weighed the woman's words as she stepped from the gown and carefully hung it on a satin hanger before donning the dress she had worn to Madame Foshay's shop.

For all of Camilla's faults and, in Rose's eyes, shallowness of character, the woman had been born to the South. It was difficult for Rose to imagine that, whatever had transpired in her life since leaving Charleston, Camilla had lost the love of her Southern heritage.

And what exactly *had* transpired since Rose had last seen Camilla Boyd?

"Madame Foshay addressed you as Lady Fontaine . . ."

"Yes," Camilla said, a slight smile curving her lips. "Mama made quite a good marriage for me—Lord Geoffrey Fontaine."

"How wonderful," Rose commented with little enthusiasm. "And did Lord Fontaine accompany you to Washington?"

"Hardly," Camilla replied. "The poor dear died a few months ago—May, I think it was."

A chill went through Rose at the other woman's callous indifference to her husband's demise. She tried to hide the shudder from registering on her face, but Camilla's keen eye detected it.

"Oh, Rose, I know what you're thinking. Don't! Lord Fontaine was much older than I. In fact, he was positively ancient. It was not a marriage of love, simply one of convenience. I daresay I gave the poor man two of the most thrilling years in bed he ever had, and an heir, which was the one thing he really wanted from me."

Rose's mouth dropped open at Camilla's bold words, but she quickly recovered. "Then you have a son?"

"Yes." Camilla shrugged. "He's in London with his nanny."

Before Rose could reply, Madame Foshay returned with Camilla's dress, already packaged, and an empty box for Rose's gown.

Accounts were settled, and as the women were leaving the shop, Camilla asked Rose where she was staying.

"With my aunt, Glynis O'Rourke. She has a house on H Street."

"Indeed, then allow me to drop you there. It's right on the way to Brown's, I believe."

The carriage was highly polished, fine-grain wood, upholstered with soft leather and amber velvet. Two blooded matched bays were at its head, and the black driver was dressed in a fawn-colored coat and black breeches tucked into highly polished leather boots. A black silk top hat adorned with rust-colored feathers sat atop his head.

Rose was impressed, and she said so.

"It's been made available to me during my stay. Perhaps you know the owner—Kate Chase?"

Rose swallowed. "Yes, I've made the lady's acquaintance."

Camilla chattered away for the first few blocks about her new wealth, her life in London, and her travels. Finally, Charleston came up in the rapid stream of one-sided conversations.

"Do you plan on visiting Charleston while you're in the country?" Rose ventured.

"Oh, hardly. There's really nothing to visit anymore. I've sold much of the land, and I fear what's left has gone to seed."

"But your parents . . ."

"Mama is with me, and of course you know about Papa."

"No, I don't."

"Killed. Yes, while punishing one of the field hands. The darky turned on him and stabbed him to death."

Rose felt instant revulsion, not only for the manner in which Rafe Boyd had met his end but also for the casual way his daughter now accepted it.

"We all knew it would probably happen someday. I mean, it was no secret about how my father mistreated the poor nigras. Mama, of course, took it quite hard, but I for one was not sure that justice wasn't served."

Rose knew she should feel something for the woman, something like kinship, but she couldn't. Instead she felt the bile of anger rise up in her throat. "Camilla, I am shocked."

"Shocked? How so?"

"For all your father's faults, he was your blood . . . and a white man."

"True, but he was also a slave owner and slave trader. By owning another man's soul, he was taking the risk of rebellion."

"Dear God, Camilla, I know you for a Southerner, and yet you sound like an abolitionist!"

"And well I should," the blond replied haughtily without a breath of hesitation. "I believe, at heart, that all Southern women are abolitionists. And if they're not, they should be."

"What a stupid observation," Rose cried hotly, her eyes flashing undisguised anger.

"Is it? Do you think Southern wives just ignore the darky wenches their husbands bed right under their noses?"

Rose's face flushed. She remembered Rafe Boyd and others of his ilk who made no secret of their lust for the black women in the slave quarters. But still she felt she had to reply to Camilla's statements. "Some men are basically weak, Camilla, it's their nature. But there are just as many who are faithful."

"Oh, I see. In other words, you're saying each and every Southern wife believes in the depravity of men, with one noble exception—her own husband . . . or father."

Rose seethed, but she managed to remain outwardly calm. "It sounds to me, Camilla, as if you no longer believe in our Southern way of life."

Camilla glanced sharply at Rose. "What you

call 'our Southern way of life' has been doomed for a long time."

Rose knew that the anger that had been rampant in her bosom was now clearly evident on her face. "I take it then that your sentiments no longer rest with the South."

"I am British, Rose, so I am neutral."

"But if you weren't British?"

"With the North, of course," came the calm reply, "and the Union."

Not another word passed between them during the remainder of the ride.

Rose, on her side of the carriage, mused that it was indeed going to be a very interesting ball.

Rose stormed through the door of the house on H Street and made directly for the stairs. She was halfway up when her aunt's ringing voice halted her. "Rose, Rose, you've had a caller!"

"A caller?" She whirled to face her aunt, her heart leaping in her breast.

"A gentleman caller."

Bram! It had to be. Instantly an image of him materialized before her eyes. He stood tall on the landing beneath her, striking in his uniform. Desire flashed from his dark eyes. *Rose, there hasn't been a moment that I haven't thought of you, not a second, waking or sleeping, that I haven't wanted to hold you in my arms.*

All the ire she had felt each day because he hadn't written melted away like mist in bright sunlight. She raced down the stairs and felt herself whisked into the air by his powerful arms.

"Bram . . . oh, Bram, my dearest . . ."

"Rose, what on earth is the matter with you?"

The words shocked her back to reality, and Rose found herself clutching her aunt's shoulders.

"Nothing. I . . . Nothing is the matter. I just . . . Oh, never mind. Did he say he would return?"

"Yes, tomorrow afternoon. He said he had been assigned to General McClellan's staff at the armory, and his duties would keep him busy until then."

Bram. It *is* Bram! *I've been assigned to General McClellan's staff in Washington. I'll call you when I arrive.*

"He left you this note."

Rose snatched the note from her aunt's hand and raced up the stairs with her skirts flying. Closeted in her room with the door locked behind her, she threw herself across the bed and unfolded the paper:

My dearest Rose,

There hasn't been a moment that I haven't thought of you, not a second, waking or sleeping, that I haven't wanted to hold you in my arms.

At last I am here, and I shall count the seconds, each an eternity, until I can say how I feel in person.

Until tomorrow at three, I remain

Your servant,
Chance Flynn

Rose's fingers curled into talons, crumpling the paper as she rolled to her back and stared at the ceiling through misty eyes.

Again she had made a fool of herself, to herself.

It wasn't Bram. Where was he? Would he ever come?

General McClellan will be at the ball tonight, she thought. I'll swallow my pride and some way find out if Bram Darcy is going to be assigned to Washington at all.

And then she thought of Chance Flynn.

"Oh, dear God," she moaned aloud. "Whatever shall I do with him?"

CHAPTER EIGHT

From the moment of her arrival it was clear to Rose that this first gala social event of the season was to be dominated by political maneuvering.

Conspicuous by their absence were Mrs. Slidell and Mrs. Clay, as well as Mrs. James Chestnut, the wife of one of South Carolina's largest slaveholders and plantation owners.

Mrs. Greenhow, with Rose at her side, had barely stepped through the massive double doors into the ballroom of Willard's Hotel when Kate Chase appeared before them. She was regal in a gown of deep lilac watered silk that complemented her violet eyes and translucent skin.

"Mrs. Greenhow, how wonderful that you could attend my little affair," she said in the husky tones that had made her voice famous throughout the Capital. "And, Rose, you look divine."

Rose accepted the woman's proffered hand and acknowledged Kate's warm smile with one of her own.

"So nice of you to invite us, Kate," Mrs. Greenhow said.

"Ah, but, Mrs. Greenhow," Kate replied, staring directly into the older woman's eyes, "what would any Capital gala be without the presence of Washington's leading hostess? I do hope the President will attend . . . now."

"I'm sure I don't know, Kate," Mrs. Greenhow replied. "I really have little knowledge of President Buchanan's social calendar."

"Of course not," Kate Chase replied with a chuckle, unable to keep a tinge of sarcasm from her voice. "You must excuse me . . . new arrivals and all. There is a buffet along the north wall, and waiters are everywhere with liquid refreshments. Please make yourselves comfortable."

As quickly as she had come, she was gone, the voluminous dress floating like a lilac cloud from her hips.

"Damn the woman," Mrs. Greenhow said without rancor. "She is very charming, brilliant, and absolutely beautiful."

"I know," Rose replied with a nod and a smile of her own. "It's a pity we're on opposite sides. I truly like and admire her."

"I agree. What a shame it is that our differences are making such bitches of us all. Come along, Rose, Lord Lyons has already spotted you. He'll be panting for a dance, I'm sure. I shall flatter our senator from New York, Mr. Seward, to see what the enemy camp on the Hill has in store for us this session!"

For the next half-hour Rose was monopolized by the erudite and handsome Britisher. His conversation was charming and witty on every subject, but in spite of Rose's subtle questioning, he made great pains to shy away from making any comments about his government's stand on Southern secession.

Then Kate Chase appeared to "rescue" Lord Lyons, although it was obvious to Rose that the gentleman had no desire to be rescued from his present company. Kate had a fat and balding artillery colonel in tow, whom she introduced to Rose as she whisked Lord Lyons away.

His name was Rufus Starling, and to Rose he had the unfortunate appearance of an English bulldog. She guessed his surface personality immediately: uncompromising, unquestioning— a man who would blindly obey orders with uncaring tenacity.

As the colonel led her awkwardly through a waltz, Rose quickly realized that he was also a pompous and lecherous ass. She tried not to show her discomfort, even when his beady eyes refused to leave her bosom and his hand at her back kept forcing their bodies together.

At last she could take it no longer. "Colonel, if you will forgive me, I fear the whirling of the waltz has made me light-headed," she said, backing away and attempting to extract herself from his clutches.

The corners of his mouth descended, only to be followed by a leering smile. "But of course. I will take you out for some air, a walk in the garden—"

"No! I mean, no, thank you, I'll just rest here for a moment."

With noticeable irritation, he bowed stiffly and left her.

Relieved, Rose moved toward the refreshment table. Then, a glass of punch in hand, she surveyed the room. A few people were dancing, but many more stood in small, solemn groups. Rose could guess at the content of most of the conversations. The assemblage was made up of Northern senators, their wives, and their constituents from Northern states. Most of the uniformed officers present were also from the North.

President Buchanan, with Harriet Lane on his arm, had already made his promised appearance. He had stayed as long as necessary for protocol, and then, claiming early-morning affairs of state, had left.

Rose observed Mrs. Greenhow moving from group to group with her usual verve and ability to insinuate herself into any conversation.

Suddenly Rose felt alone. Many of the men

and women in the room had become her friends
when she first arrived in Washington. Now she
was here to spy on them. Yes, spy, she thought,
no matter what Mrs. Greenhow called it: "It's
not spying, Rose. Better to call it good-natured
inquisitiveness. It's merely good politics to find
out what the other fellow is doing."

But Rose still called it spying, and she had
the feeling, from the stares she had received,
that others felt the same way.

She was halfway across the room to Kate Chase
to plead a sudden headache, when she suddenly
stopped short. Lady Camilla Fontaine had just
entered the room, her tall, voluptuous figure
swathed in billowing cascades of azure satin
and tulle, her golden hair held in place atop her
head with a dazzling sapphire-and-pearl clip. A
matching necklace gleamed at her slender neck.
But it wasn't Camilla's beauty that had robbed
Rose of her breath.

It was the man who stood next to her.

At Lady Fontaine's side, his hand protectively
holding her elbow, was Bram Darcy.

His words uttered that night on the sloop thundered in Rose's ears: *I'll call upon my arrival. . . .*

But he hadn't called. He hadn't even made his
presence known.

Now, seeing him here, standing tall in his
crisp new dark blue uniform, wearing the self-
confident, arrogant smile she remembered so
well, Rose was torn between anger and frus-

tration. Anger because he had obviously deceived her. Frustration because she had let down her defenses and allowed him to so fully enter her life.

Well, he had made a fool of her for the last time!

She was about to turn and flee, when his eyes flickered across the room and met hers. There was an instant spark of recognition, but no more.

If anything, this bare recognition added fuel to the fires of torment in Rose's bosom. She couldn't just stand there like a ninny. She had to escape.

She whirled and strode to the man standing nearest her. "Why, Senator Seward, how nice to see you again!"

"Good evening, Miss Jacquard," the senator replied, slightly surprised at her friendliness. At a recent dinner party Rose had openly debated Seward on his antislavery stand on the Hill.

"I haven't had the pleasure of a dance with you yet, Senator!" she said, turning on her brightest smile and gliding into his arms even as he stepped back in shock.

Before the poor man realized it, he was moving awkwardly across the room to the strains of a waltz.

"Miss Jacquard . . ."

"Yes?" Rose replied brightly, keeping Bram Darcy in sight out of the corner of her eye.

"Miss Jacquard, I don't dance. I would think that is fairly obvious."

"Ah, Senator Seward, how can you say that? I think you dance divinely!"

"And, Miss Jacquard, I think you prevaricate charmingly. But can we stop after the next turn at the refreshment table?"

For the first time, Rose looked directly at the senator. His keen yet impish eyes were studying hers as if they could read there the very reason she had suddenly thrust herself upon him.

"Of course. I'm sorry."

"It's not that I don't enjoy the proximity of such a beautiful and youthful lady, but I am prone to a shortness of breath and—"

"Here we are," Rose said, snatching two glasses of punch from the table and practically pushing one of them into the senator's hand.

"Who *is* that couple?" he asked, a smile curling his lips beneath his heavy mustache.

"Couple?" Rose's eyes were wide with what she hoped was innocence rather than alarm.

"That handsome young captain and the woman in the blue satin gown. They're very attractive."

"Oh? I hadn't noticed before. Yes, I suppose they are."

"I thought you might know them, since you seem to glance at them every few seconds."

Rose could feel the color blooming in her cheeks, but she still made the attempt at innocence. "No, I . . . I don't know them."

"I see. Well, Miss Jacquard, if you'll excuse me . . ."

"Of course. Oh, Senator . . . ?"

"Yes?"

"Thank you." She smiled.

"Think nothing of it." Then he leaned forward until his whiskers tickled her ear. "Would you like to escape further—perhaps the veranda?"

"Thank you again," Rose sighed, curling her arm through his. "No wonder they call you our most diplomatic legislator."

Once safely alone on the hotel veranda, with the night sounds from the garden around her and the cool evening air bathing her face, Rose was able to think more clearly.

If her flustered countenance had been so obvious to Senator Seward, then surely it had been so to Bram Darcy.

"Damn the man," she hissed under her breath.

How did he know Camilla Fontaine? And just what was their relationship? She thought of the possessive way Camilla had held Bram's arm, the way she had looked up into his face with those green, catlike eyes.

Suddenly Rose's head throbbed with it all.

Darcy had been so attentive at West Point, so compelling when he had held her in his arms on the sloop. Had he only been amusing himself at her expense? Why hadn't he come to call when he arrived in Washington, as he said he would?

Two couples emerged from the ballroom, chatting and laughing gaily. Rose quickly descended the wooden stairs and moved into the garden. She wished that she had her wrap, so she could just leave and send a note of apology to Kate Chase later, pleading sudden illness as the reason for her departure.

"Rose . . ."

She had been walking with her head lowered, her eyes to the ground. So intent had she been on the sound of her own footsteps that she hadn't heard anyone approach. Now she whirled, nearly crashing into his chest. His hand caught her elbow to steady her, and Rose recoiled instinctively—not because she didn't welcome his touch but because she feared that it would wash away her anger and put her back under his spell.

"Good evening, Captain Darcy."

"I saw you come out for some air and—"

"Yes, I abhor the smell of cigars."

What did the slight smile and cocked eyebrow mean? Was he mocking her? Had he already seen through her facade of calm to her anger and jealousy?

"It's a rather boring affair, don't you think?" she asked, opening her fan with a snap and rapidly moving it back and forth in front of her face.

Bram shrugged and let his eyes travel slowly down over her body. Their intensity sent a shiver through Rose that lasted until he was again looking directly into her eyes.

Damn the man! she thought. Why do I have the feeling each time he looks at me that I am naked? Men always stared at her—she was used to it. But no man's stare had ever before made her feel like a wanton.

"You should always wear light colors, Rose. They show off your beautiful skin to perfection. I saw every man in the room following you with his eyes."

Yes, she thought, every man but you. "Did you?" She shrugged. "I admit I am flattered when men look at me in a certain way."

"Flattered, Rose . . . or amused?"

She was without a ready response, and Bram saw it. Again he grasped her arm, this time turning her toward a nearby stone bench.

"Come, let's sit."

"I'd rather stand."

"Very well. But I prefer to sit."

And sit he did, leaving Rose to stare down at the casual way he crossed his legs and leaned back to smile arrogantly up at her.

"It is a pity," she said, fanning her face with much more agitation than she meant to show, "about your manners."

Suddenly a deep bass laugh erupted from his chest. He was on his feet like a cat and lifting Rose from hers like a feather. Gently but firmly he deposited her on the bench and then sat beside her. When she tried to regain her feet, he curled her arm in his and held her like a vise.

"How dare you—"

"I dare a great deal when the stakes are to my taste. Now, settle down and let's have a sensible conversation."

"Settle? . . . Let me go!"

"I will—when I'm ready."

"I'll scream."

"Please do. I've never been accused of molesting a lady, but I'm sure such an accusation would further enhance my reputation as a rake and a scoundrel. I've heard that in Washington a man with such a reputation is quite sought after."

"Damn you, you are the most arrogant, self-centered, ill-mannered—"

"—man who has ever made you tremble to the very depths of your soul with a single kiss."

Again the full lips curved into a smile of pure mockery.

"You're insufferable," Rose spat, even as her emotions screamed the truth of his words. "I repeat, it's a pity your manners do not match your position as an officer and a gentleman!"

"And that your deportment," he countered, "does not equal your beauty."

His words completely unleashed Rose's anger. Again she tongue-lashed him, this time in vituperative French, using many phrases that were decidedly unladylike.

"Excellent," he said when at last she had exhausted herself. "But as coarse as French can be,

I find that Spanish is even more descriptive and often far more satisfying in venting one's wrath."

Suddenly he began to swear in perfectly accented Spanish, loosing a stream of lovely-sounding oaths that soon had Rose's sides aching with laughter.

"You must admit," he said, breaking off suddenly, "that I have you beaten." His smile, no longer sardonic but disarming, had Rose beaten as well.

She felt the anger flow from her body like the ebb of an outgoing tide. His viselike grip on her arm eased, but Rose made no move to withdraw it.

"I concede . . . for the moment."

"Good. I consider that a a major triumph." He stood, pulling her to her feet beside him. "Let's stroll . . . it's a beautiful evening."

Rose allowed herself to relax as he guided her down the cobbled path through the garden, her flesh tingling where his fingertips lightly touched her arm. She forced herself to maintain her composure, determined to keep their conversation on neutral ground if possible. "Did you learn your Spanish in the Mexican War?"

"That . . . and other things," he replied grimly.

"Yes, I know about your brother."

He turned sharply. "You seem to know a great deal about me."

"I . . . Well, Hollis Johnson mentioned you served in the Mexican campaign under General

Taylor and that your brother had been captured and executed."

"I know."

"What?"

Darcy chuckled. "Hollis told me that you extracted from him every bit of information you could about me."

"I didn't! I . . . I just asked a few questions."

He looked down at her, unsmiling now, and lightly brushed her silken hair with his hand. "And the next time you see Hollis, Rose, I'm sure he'll tell you that I asked him many more questions about you."

"You . . . you did?"

"Of course I did."

Rose's eyes widened, and she could hold back the question no longer. "Then, if you wanted so much to know about me, why didn't you call on me when you arrived in Washington!"

"Aha!" he laughed, his dark head rearing back in the moonlight. "So that is the reason for your belligerence!"

"I'm not belligerent!"

"Of course you are—it's a great part of your charm."

"Damn you!" Rose said, but couldn't stop a laugh from her own lips.

"My dear lady, you have damned me so many times this evening that if you have the ear of our Maker I'm sure I'm bound for hell."

youthful dream could match. The tingling in the tips of her breasts and the heat that seethed at the base of her belly and leapt upward could never be imagined.

No, Rose thought, holding hungrily to his powerful body, this was no dream. This wild craving that was burning her inner core was real, and it demanded satisfaction.

Again his lips lifted from hers. Rose opened her eyes. She saw him staring down at her, his look a thrilling blend of tenderness and desire.

"Tomorrow, Rose . . ."

No, Rose thought, *now*! She wanted to shout her desires to him, but suddenly she knew there was no need. Their eyes and the melding of their bodies spoke far more than mere words.

"Yes," she sighed. "Tomorrow."

CHAPTER NINE

THE MINUTES of the morning inched by.

Glynis O'Rourke had taken to her bed with what she called, "a spring cold—I always get them in the fall!" Cat was playing nurse to her aunt one moment and cautioning Rose about Bram Darcy the next.

"I am afraid of him, Rose."

"Afraid? Oh, Cat, whatever is there to be afraid of? He is handsome, witty, and charming. He comes from the best of families, and his wealth has been properly earned. What is so fearful about him? And you have met him only once, briefly at that! How can you come to such conclusions?"

"And you have seen him only three times, Rose. How can you be so in love with him?"

Rose had been standing at her closet in pantalets and chemise, trying to choose a frock for the day's outing. Now she whirled and quickly crossed the room to where her sister sat on the large canopied four-poster. "Love?" she said, dropping to her knees and placing her folded arms across Cat's lap. "I've never told you I was in love with Bram Darcy!"

"You didn't have to, Rose, any more than I have to tell you how much I am in love with Hollis. I've seen it in your eyes these past weeks every time his name is mentioned. I've heard it in your voice when you speak of him. And last night, when you came home from the ball and told me that you had seen him, that you were going on an outing with him today—never have I seen your eyes sparkle so."

Rose sighed. "Is it so very plain?"

"To me it is."

Rose stared into Cat's eyes. So pale they were, and so strained was the face that held them. Oddly, as she knelt before Cat, it was Rose who felt like the younger sister. Cat's eyes seemed to hold a sagacity and maturity far beyond her years, and her tiny shoulders seemed stooped with the weight of the world.

"I don't know, Cat, if it is love," she said, and then her chin lifted. "But I mean to find out."

"And if it is, Rose, what will you do?"

Suddenly Rose felt the need to laugh, to lighten the somber mood Cat had brought into the room with her. She grasped her sister's hands and tugged her from the bed. "I will do, little one, whatever it is that women do when they are in love!" She smiled, swinging Cat in circles at the end of her arms.

Cat slid to a sudden halt, her eyes wide and her mouth gaping. "Rose, you wouldn't!"

"Wouldn't what?" Rose said with mock sternness.

"You . . . you know what!"

Rose erupted with a high, tinkling laugh. "Oh, my darling Cat, must you be so serious? I know it's how you are, but do try to smile a little. It somehow seems to soften things when you do. And today of all days, I want to be happy!"

"But, Rose, how can you even think of . . . a man you hardly know . . . and he's so *old*!"

Rose erupted in another burst of laughter. "Oh, Cat, that is exactly the reason I *could* love him. For all of your deep thought, you cannot see the difference between my situation with Bram and yours with Hollis."

"No, I can't," the girl solemnly intoned. "Have you asked him, Rose?"

So stern was Cat's tone and so accusing her stare that Rose felt a knot begin to form in her breast. She knew what Cat meant, for it had come up more and more in the past few days.

"No, I haven't. But I will—today."

"Do that, Rose," Cat said. "And don't scowl at me so. I just don't want you to give yourself to

Bram and then someday make the choice that I've had to make!"

Rose wanted to tell her, to scream at her, that her choice was foolish. If Cat truly loved Hollis as much as she said she did, she would agree to return to Charleston with him.

But her aunt's voice calling to Cat from a nearby room interrupted her.

"I must see to Aunt Glynis."

"Cat?" Rose's voice stopped the younger girl just before she had stepped into the hall. "You will tell Chance when he arrives that—"

"That you are sorry you missed him, but you've had this appointment for days. Yes, I'll tell him, Rose."

Then she was gone, her slippered feet moving down the hall. "Coming, Aunt Glynis, coming!"

Troubled, Rose moved back to her closet. This time there was little thought or hesitation. She chose a sashed primrose muslin and quickly scoured her drawers for gloves, bonnet, and reticule to match.

The muslin was heavy, but Rose attached only one crinoline about her waist beneath the skirt. The dress was meant for travel, so it was slightly shorter than an everyday skirt, and revealed her underpetticoat and riding boots.

There, she thought, staring at her costume in the mirror, I'm ready for whatever may strike his fancy—a carriage ride and picnic, an afternoon on horseback in the Virginia countryside, or . . . whatever.

Rose quickly turned from the mirror to avoid seeing the scarlet that had crept into her face at her own thoughts.

It's right, she told herself, fastening the taupe bonnet beneath her chin, I know it is!

The rap of a stick on the door below sent Rose flying to the window. She couldn't see the stoop, but a beige open buggy sat behind two prancing white horses at the gate. The fawn-colored leather seat gleamed beneath a yellow-fringed canopy, and the polished sheen of the mahogany dashboard reflected the noonday sun.

"Miz Rose?"

Rose whirled from the window. Her aunt's free colored maid stood in the doorway, a card on a silver tray extended.

"Yes, Retha?"

"They's a gen'amin come to call, Miz Rose."

Forcing herself to remain calm, Rose picked the card from the tray and barely glanced at it. "Oh, yes, Mr. Darcy. Tell him I'll be a few minutes, Retha."

The maid swept Rose with a look and shrugged as she moved away. Rose was obviously ready to meet her caller. She had already put on her gloves and tied her bonnet. But if Retha was instructed to tell the gentleman that the lady was not yet ready, that's what she would tell him.

Rose paced, forcing herself to wait a full five minutes before lifting her skirts and racing to the head of the stairs.

He stood, wide-brimmed hat and cane in hand, in the center of the foyer. Tan breeches hugged his long, powerful legs like a second skin and ended in high chocolate leather boots. A frilled white linen shirt gleamed from beneath a maroon frock coat, and a matching maroon cravat was perfectly tied at his throat.

From the corner of her eye Rose could see Retha lurking in the darker recesses of the rear hall. From the awed look on her dark face, Rose could tell that Bram Darcy had already charmed her.

"Good afternoon, Captain Darcy." Rose glided off the last step with her hand extended.

"Miss Jacquard," he said, bowing slightly and brushing the back of her gloved hand with his lips. "I had the chef at Willard's prepare us a picnic lunch. It's in the buggy. I thought perhaps a ride over into Virginia, if that meets with your approval?"

"Fine."

Together they moved toward the door. As Darcy leaned forward to open it, his lips found her ear. "You're ravishing," he whispered.

"Shhh!"

"It's good that your maid was watching us. If she wasn't, I would have been sorely tempted to carry you right back up to your bedroom."

"Shhh!" Rose hissed again. "Dear God, how forward can you be?"

"I haven't decided yet." He handed her into the buggy and gained the seat beside her with an easy, lithe grace amazing for a man his size.

He drove skillfully, as he seemed to do everything else, guiding the prancing horses with an easy hand, and now and then speaking to them quietly in his low voice.

They rode in silence to the end of Maryland Avenue and crossed the Long Bridge to Virginia. In minutes they had left the city and gained the mail road that linked the North and the South.

The fall colors were not yet in their full glory, but already a few trees sported russet, crimson, and yellow coats. There was a quiet yet steady breeze that softened the heat of a midday sun shining down from an almost cloudless sky.

To their left the Potomac flowed steadily by, and to their right the rolling green countryside seemed to stretch forever, broken occasionally by a gleaming white mansion.

"Where are we going?" Rose asked at last.

"There is a place overlooking the river a few miles farther on. It's very lovely. I thought we could stop there for lunch."

Rose relaxed back into the soft leather and breathed deeply of the crisp, clean air. She felt Bram's eyes on her and was further exalted.

"Tell me," he said, "about your home."

"Charleston?"

"No, Belle Erin."

She began slowly telling him of the plantation life she remembered as a little girl, how she had learned to ride and to shoot at her father's side. How she had grown up in the genteel atmosphere of Charleston but longed each September to return to the country life of Belle Erin. Because it was only at Belle Erin that she had felt secure and free.

Then she began to speak faster, her words trembling one over the other as she related her mother's death and the years leading up to her father's murder.

"You loved your father very much."

"I did." Rose blinked back the tears that suddenly threatened to squeeze from her eyes. "He was my friend, a friend to all who knew him."

"What would he do now, Rose?"

Something in his voice, a crispness in its tone, made her turn slightly in the seat to stare at him. His eyes were straight forward and his profile was fixed with a clenched jaw, as if his face had suddenly turned to stone.

"What do you mean?"

"I mean, if he were alive today and he could see the direction the South is taking, what would he do?"

"Do? . . . I don't know. What *could* he do?"

"Would he free his slaves voluntarily . . . if that became the law?"

"Of course not."

"Why?"

"Why? Why are you asking me these things?"

"I am asking. *Why*, Rose?"

Suddenly Rose didn't want to talk about the South, or Belle Erin, or slavery. She didn't even want to talk about her father. She wanted to talk about the two of them. She wanted to find out how he felt about her, if he loved her. And she wanted to find out, in her heart, if she loved him.

But the scowl on his face and the burning intensity in his eyes when he turned to her seemed to demand answers.

"No, he wouldn't free them. Where would they go? Who would take care of them?"

"They would learn to take care of themselves. Slavery is wrong, Rose."

"Then you are an abolitionist." She felt a hard knot begin to grow deep inside her.

"Not a bit of it. The fire-breathing abolitionists would sacrifice the very Union itself if necessary to free the Southern slaves."

Rose's spirits lifted. "And you don't agree with that?"

"Of course I don't. And I don't agree with secession either. I think if the Southern states secede, there will be war."

"How can there be war?" Rose cried. "The South has the best horsemen, the best marksmen, the most officers, and the only trained militia.

No, it would be foolish, suicide, for the North not to acquiesce to the South's demands!"

Darcy's eyes, if possible, became even darker and more brooding as he let them stray over her face. "You have a good education, Rose, but little grasp of reality."

Her first reaction was retaliation, but there was something in his voice, a sudden sadness in his eyes, that made her hold her tongue. Now, she thought, now would be the time to ask him just where his sympathies would lie if, as he suggested, there were to be war.

But before she could speak, Darcy's strong hands were reining the horses in and the buggy rocked to a halt. "Here we are."

Rose's throat constricted with the sheer beauty of the panorama before her. They sat at the very top of a hill, with densely foliaged trees at their backs shielding them from the distant road. The grassland before them sloped gently down to the wide, sun-drenched river. Directly beside the buggy was an area of grass so soft it resembled a green carpet.

"It's beautiful."

"Not nearly as beautiful as you, Rose." His fingertips lightly caressed her jawline, gently turning her face to his.

"Bram ..." Her cheek burned beneath his touch, and her lower lip would not stop quivering.

"Yes?"

"Nothing," she whispered, and turned from him. Lightly she jumped to the ground and then forced her lips into a broad smile as she looked back up to where he sat. "I'm famished. Come along, I'll spread the cloth."

"Your moods, my wild Rose, are like those of nature—constantly changing."

She laughed. "It's much more interesting that way, don't you think?"

Together they spread blankets, and over them a white linen cloth. Bram crouched on one knee, watching Rose as she removed covered dishes from the picnic basket and arranged them on the linen.

How utterly lovely she was, with her glossy raven hair spilling in soft curls from the slats of her bonnet. His groin throbbed as his gaze swept lower, down into the shadowed sweetness beneath her bodice. He had desired this woman from the moment he first met her, weeks before. Since then, without even seeing her, that desire had grown into a passion that threatened to run out of control.

There had been many women in Bram Darcy's life, but none had affected him as this dark-skinned, dark-eyed beauty who knelt before him now. He knew that with a touch, with a single embrace, he could take her now. He could possess the wonders and mysteries of her perfect body here in the tall, sweet-smelling grass. She had said as much with her tantalizing eyes. Bram

160

knew that she desired him as much as he wanted her.

But what of the aftermath? What if the same fate that threw them together in a maelstrom of passion chose to tear them apart? Could he bear to part with her after tasting the sweetness of what he knew would be an ultimate love?

And what of Rose? Could the love he saw shining in her eyes wash away any obstacles that might come between them?

So many questions, and so few answers, Bram thought, sighing aloud and massaging his temples with his fingertips.

"You have a headache?"

"No"—he smiled—"just a touch of the vapors. Isn't that the ailment women usually use when they can't reach a decision?"

"I wouldn't know," Rose replied, passing him a well-filled plate. "I pride myself on making quick decisions."

"I'm sure you do, Miss Rose."

Their hands touched briefly as he accepted the plate. It was as if a charge passed between them, jolting their eyes upward to meet and lock.

In that second, they both knew what would happen before the day was out.

The food was just right for two, and perfectly prepared. Rose was surprised to find that she was ravenously hungry.

Bram had also thought of wine, a hearty French red, which he poured with a flourish. "To peace and beauty."

"To life and happiness," Rose replied with no hesitation.

They ate and spoke about meaningless things in their past and noncontroversial things in the present. Only once did Lady Fontaine's name come up. When it did, and Rose saw the now familiar dark curtain fall over Bram's eyes, she quickly shifted the subject. "I dearly love my sister, but I think she will one day be sorry if she persists in rejecting Hollis."

"I wonder. Is she rejecting Hollis ... or the South?"

Rose dropped her eyes to her lap. "Both, one because of the other. Hollis has written to me that he is trying to obtain duty in the North when his commission is final. I think it's very sad."

"You do?"

"Yes. Hollis' roots are deeply in the South. If Cat forces him to remain in the North, I think it will eventually destroy their love."

"That's very wise. Did you tell Hollis as much?"

"I did," Rose replied, straightening her shoulders and meeting his eyes with her own. "I wrote to him just yesterday."

"You don't have to defend your advice to Hollis, Rose."

"I wasn't defending it, I ..."

Darcy uncoiled to his full height. Effortlessly he caught her beneath her arms and tugged her to her feet.

For a moment Rose was sure he was going to ask her the very question she had been so reluctant to ask him.

What would she, Rose, do if she were Cat and the situations were reversed—if Hollis were a Northerner?

They stood for several moments, their eyes colliding. The unasked question hung between them like a gray cloud, with neither one of them willing to break the spell by asking.

"Shall we walk by the river?" Darcy said at last.

"Yes."

His hands had slid up her arms and now held her shoulders. A force as powerful as life itself seemed to flow from his hands to infuse every inch of her body. His eyes seemed almost demonic, and Rose felt swallowed into their dark, bottomless depths.

He had already revealed to her a part of her nature that Rose only suspected existed until now. And he had done it with a kiss.

How much further would he take her, with his whole body? Was it love she was feeling . . . or was it lust?

There was only one way she could understand the feelings he had aroused within her and truly deal with them as a woman.

"Yes, Bram, let us walk by the river," she whispered. "And bring the blankets."

They followed the river for some distance, saying nothing, for no words were needed.

By mutual consent they stopped at a grassy depression sheltered on three sides by tall grass and trees. Bram carefully spread the blankets, and then turned to face her.

Rose removed her bonnet and the pins from her hair. With a single shake of her head, the coils of lustrous ebony cascaded over her shoulders and down her back. A few strands framed her face and delicately touched the rounded swells of her breasts.

Deftly, with no hesitation, Rose began unbuttoning her dress. It fell to her hips, exposing the lacy chemise she wore. Above the bodice of the chemise she could sense her breasts swelling to be free.

With two fingers she opened the snap on her crinoline, and the heavy muslin of the dress took both garments to her ankles.

With a quivering smile of surrender, Rose stepped from the garments and opened her arms to him.

Bram stepped forward, and she glided into his embrace. His arms felt like iron bands wrapped in soft velvet as they coiled about her, bringing her body up to his.

His fingers curled in her hair before he bent

his head and kissed her with a hunger that took Rose's breath away.

His tongue found hers and became a darting flame, sending searing heat down through her breasts and quivering belly to the seat of her desire.

"Rose, Rose," he moaned, showering her face and neck with kisses and then returning his mouth to hers.

With their lips still locked, their hands moved between them. As Rose worked the buttons of his shirt, he unfastened her chemise. At last they were flesh to flesh, her full breasts and passion-hardened nipples spilling across the hard muscles of his chest.

Still kissing her, he lifted her from her feet and laid her gently on the blankets. Her breasts shimmered in the sunlight, inviting first his eyes and then the soft fire of his hungry lips.

Rose could not keep her body still. She rocked from side to side, curling her fingers in his hair to keep his lips where they were.

There was a nervous, gasping sigh from somewhere above her, and then Rose realized it was her own voice telling him how much he was satisfying the wild craving in her body.

With his impassioned lips still at her swollen breasts, he slid his hand under the waistband of her pantalets. Her belly shivered under his fingertips and then her thighs opened wide to his touch.

His fingers probed gently, bringing wrenching cries from Rose's throat. When she could stand it no more, she covered his hand with hers and arched her hips, seeking to send his loving fingers deep inside her.

"Calmly, my sweet," he whispered from her breast. "Slowly and calmly."

He could say that, Rose thought, while she spun in a maelstrom of need. Never had her body felt so alive. It was as if she were going against the current in a powerful river and had given up at last. Now she was spinning and swirling, letting the sweeping current take her where it would.

She felt cool air between her legs and knew that he had removed her pantalets. Then his lips found her inner thigh and spread more fire as they moved upward.

What was he doing? Rose thought, fright along with ecstasy momentarily freezing her body.

She felt his gently probing fingers, gasped at the caressing envelopment of his lips, and screamed aloud as his darting tongue convulsed her body. Liquid fire raced through her every vein until she thought her pounding heart would explode in her chest.

It seemed to go on forever, almost too long, until the pleasure bordered on pain. Bram seemed to sense this. He left her and she was in immediate agony for his touch.

Sounds of movement floated through her jumbled brain, and at last she was able to open her eyes. "Bram . . ."

"Here, my sweet."

Rose shielded the sun from her eyes and turned her head until his body blotted out the painful rays.

He stood like a sinewy god above her. His long, heavily muscled legs seemed to go up forever, to end in narrow, taut hips. Slowly he slid to his knees beside her. His chest, bared, was even more massive than she had imagined, and the muscles of his flat belly were taut.

He was a beautiful man.

And then she saw it, a wide, ugly scar running from his left nipple down his side and ending in the thick hair above his manhood.

Rose couldn't resist. With a single fingertip she traced the scar. "How . . . ?"

"A Mexican saber. It doesn't sicken you?" he said softly.

"No. Somehow I don't find it ugly. It . . . it's just a part of you."

"You are the most beautiful and exciting woman in the world, Rose. Under that composed, ladylike veneer you show the world, there is a creature that is all passion. You are every man's dream, my darling."

She managed a wan smile as she moved her fingertips along his flesh. "I've wanted you, Bram, since that first night I danced with you."

"And I you."

"Will you make love to me again, now ... completely?"

"Are you sure?"

"I've never been more sure of anything in my life," she sighed, pulling him down beside her.

His hands and lips explored every hollow and curve of her body. She gloried in his touch and sought his lips with hers. With a low moan of desire, she pressed the full length of her body against his, thrilling to the throb of his manhood when she captured him between her thighs.

They kissed, moving and exploring together, until the wild anticipation built to the point that Rose thought she surely would explode.

"Bram ... oh, Bram!" she choked, her voice as taut as a drawn bowstring.

"Yes, my darling," he sighed, moving between her open thighs.

She thrilled to his weight upon her and curled her arms and legs about him in welcome. Her desire was at fever pitch now, and she whimpered pleadingly for him to wait no longer.

His hands found her buttocks and kneaded lovingly as he drew her sex closer to his. Rose instinctively raised her hips and opened herself to the sudden pain of his first thrust.

In seconds the pain was gone, swallowed by the desire he was creating by his entry. More and more of him filled her until she was sure there could be no more and she would burst.

And then they were together, one with the other, and he was moving inside her with a rhythm that built and built until it consumed them both.

Rose clung to him, clutching his back and buttocks with her hands and whimpering her joy in his ear.

When he answered her need by moving more forcefully, Rose began to writhe and arch upward. So pure was the tempo of their joined bodies that Rose felt as if she had been loving him her whole life.

Her half-cries and gasps of ecstasy echoed his low moans until, at last, they peaked together. Their bodies jolted against each other in a wrenching explosion of love.

Then the wild fire of passion slowly ebbed until there was only a tingling, satiated feeling flowing through her. Bram rolled to his side, pulling her with him and coming to rest with her legs still entwined about his waist.

He kissed the tears that had coursed down her cheeks, and then found her eyes with his lips. "You were wonderful," he whispered.

She held his face with her hands and gently brushed the tip of his nose with her lips. "It was all I ever dreamed it would be. Thank you."

His arms tightened at her back, bringing her

head in to rest at the hollow between his neck and shoulder.

"I am so happy," she sighed. "We do go well together, don't we?"

"Rose," he said, an odd choke in his voice, "we go perfectly together."

CHAPTER TEN

Rose barely noticed the chill winds of autumn that arrived to spear the capital city. For a month following Kate Chase's ball and the afternoon on the riverbank in Virginia, Rose moved through the hours and the days in a euphoric cloud.

The tensions in Washington that had preyed upon her mind for so long faded at the mere mention of Bram Darcy's name. Partly because of his past military experience, and because of his family's connections in business and government—not to mention his own—Bram was expected to go very far, very fast.

It seemed that at every afternoon tea, every dinner party, at almost any social function, his name inevitably came up. And quite often, Capital gossips linked his name with Lady Camilla Fontaine's. At those times Rose would sit silently, her hands folded in her lap, a tiny smile curling the corners of her mouth.

"Believe me, Rose, when I tell you that all interest in Lady Fontaine is purely political," Bram had told her. "My family and the Fontaine family have had very close business connections for years. Lady Fontaine can be a powerful ally one day. That is my only interest in the lady."

Rose believed him.

His work took up much of his time and often took him away from Washington City for days at a time. But always, on his return, the message would come. And soon after, Bram himself would appear in the large front parlor of the house on H Street.

During these times, Cat would discreetly slip away to leave them alone. Her Aunt Glynis' slight cold had turned out to be much more serious than her other yearly colds, so she was spending more and more time in bed. Consequently, during Bram's visits there was no one to chaperon them.

Bram and Rose took full advantage of it, losing themselves in each other's embrace, thrilling to the secret caresses that became more and more intimate, at least as much as propriety and the confines of the red velvet settee would allow.

But those stolen moments weren't enough for either of them. A touch, a kiss, only served to drive them both wild with frustration.

It was unspoken, but they both knew that somehow they would have to recapture the magic of that first afternoon or they would both go mad.

"Rose, I've taken a house."

"Here in Washington?"

"Yes, on Seventh Street, near the post office. Can you come to tea Friday next?"

"Tea?"

"We must appear *somewhat* proper," he replied with a raffish smile.

Rose gazed at him, breathtakingly handsome as he stood before her. He was wearing a wasp-waisted sky-blue swallowtail coat, and the ruffles of his crisp white linen shirt came to just beneath his chin, contrasting with the deep tan of his complexion. His cravat was cream-colored, matching the tight trousers that hugged his muscular thighs like a second skin before disappearing into high-topped Spanish leather boots.

Rose felt her breath catch in her throat. There was nothing she could deny this man—absolutely nothing. She wanted to be with him every second of every day, watching him move and eat and laugh, sharing with him his every mood.

Well, there is a way, she thought, mulling over his words and studying the look in his dark eyes, that we could observe *all* the proprieties.

Marriage.

Love had not been mentioned between them, nor had marriage.

Rose had already admitted to herself that she was hopelessly in love with Bram. But she had never voiced it. Even in his arms, with her heart beating wildly against his chest and the words racing toward her lips, she had never spoken them.

And what were his real thoughts? Did he love her with the same all-consuming fury she felt? Or was he just toying with her, as she had once feared?

"Will you come, Rose . . . Friday?"

She was about to speak, to blurt out the question that hung between them like a cloud, when his powerful arms wound about her tiny waist and crushed her to him.

It was as if he had read her mind and was saying with the touch of his hands and lips: No, not yet. Don't let's think of tomorrow. Tomorrow is a dangerous thought. Let us live the here and now, today, while we can.

At the touch of his lips, all thoughts of possible differences between them vanished. Only the full-blown passion that had raged between them remained.

Her lips parted eagerly, hungrily accepting his. A shudder raced through her as his body caressed her, then crushed her body to his.

"God, oh God, Rose, how I want you." His

voice was a harsh rasp in his chest as he pulled back from her. "But not here, not like this."

"Friday," she moaned. "Let the days fly till then!"

It was Cat who forced her back to earth.

"People will talk, Rose. I have heard the gossip start already."

"Let them!"

"Has he spoken yet of marriage?"

Her younger sister's words stung Rose to the core of her being. Thankfully, the knot of her hair covered the back of her neck. If it hadn't, Rose knew the hot flush she felt there would be only too evident.

"Rose . . . ?"

"Damn, Catherine, must you be my conscience?"

"Yes—because I think you've lost your own."

Rose turned and faced her sister, lifting her chin defiantly. "I love him. That's all that matters."

Cat's eyes were gentle, unaccusing, as she returned Rose's gaze. "But does he love you?"

"He must!"

"Why must he, Rose?"

Because of the way he looks at me, touches me, possesses me when we make love. . . . That was what Rose wanted to say. But she didn't. Instead, she counted the moments until Friday afternoon, willing her mind and body to be patient.

*   *   *

Chance Flynn came several times to call. And each time, Rose was civil, even talkative, but no more. She rebuffed his advances and made light of his obvious affection for her, afraid that any encouragement would be misinterpreted.

Eventually his visits ceased altogether.

So euphoric was the haze of love around Rose now that she didn't realize, didn't see the hurt in Flynn's eyes or hear the harsh tone in his voice when he uttered his last good-bye.

It would be months later, over a year, before Rose would realize that she had turned an admirer into an enemy.

"Chance loves you, Rose," Cat declared.

"I've not encouraged it, and you know it," Rose retorted. "Besides, it is puppy love."

Cat smiled, but there was little humor in her eyes. "The kind of puppy love Hollis once felt for you?"

"Yes," Rose barked, and then saw the pain in her younger sister's eyes.

The love between Cat and Hollis wasn't puppy love. It was real, and each day, with each new letter that arrived from West Point, Rose saw a new line of pain and worry seam Cat's elfin, angelic face.

Hollis was in his last year at the Point. He had already requested and gotten duty at Fort Sumpter, in Charleston Bay. Soon, very soon, the final decision between them would have to be made.

"Do you answer his letters, Cat?"

"Yes."

"And what do you tell him?"

She shrugged. "About the weather, you, Aunt Glynis, Washington gossip."

"Nothing of love?"

"I tell him in each letter how much he means to me. He wants to spend Christmas with us, here in the Capital."

"*Wants* to?"

"He won't, if I don't wish it."

"Dear God, Cat, how can you *not* wish it?"

Cat remained silent, but Rose knew the answer to her own question.

Neither Cat nor Hollis would bend in his determination—one to remain in the North, the other in the South—no matter how strong their love for each other.

Rose herself had pushed that one great question between her and Bram Darcy into the farthest part of her mind.

She wasn't sure she could deal with the answer.

Friday came at last, and when the carriage arrived to fetch her, Rose had been ready for over an hour, impatiently pacing the floor of the sitting room. When she heard the driver's heels clicking on the front porch, she quickly scooped up the folds of her saffron-yellow dress and dashed to meet him at the door.

As the carriage pulled up to the brownstone on Seventh Street, Rose alighted and as calmly as possible moved up the stone steps.

She didn't have a chance to knock. The door opened immediately. "Rose."

Rose flew into the arms of Bram Darcy. "Bram," she whispered, turning slightly in his arms and searching the large foyer with her eyes.

"What is it, my love?"

"Your servants."

His laugh was like soft thunder near her ear. "I haven't engaged any."

For a moment neither of them spoke. They stood, each of their bodies savoring the closeness of the other.

No servants.

They were alone, an entire afternoon before them in the large, rambling house.

"Come," he suddenly exclaimed, his face breaking into a wide grin, "let me show you what I've done so far!"

What he had done in less than a week was just short of a miracle. Rose exclaimed her approval with each new room she saw. The magnificent oak floors were burnished to a sheen and covered with the finest of hand-woven Persian carpets. The walls and wainscoting were freshly painted and hung with rich tapestries and fine oil paintings. The tasteful furniture, most of it lovely antiques, was arranged comfortably.

"But how on earth," Rose cried, "have you accomplished all this in less than a week?"

"I've practically robbed my Baltimore house."

Rose cast a quick sidelong glance in his direction. Could she dare hope that she was the sole reason for this? "Bram," she ventured, "does this mean you'll be in Washington indefinitely?"

His eyes clouded briefly. "There's never a certainty in the military, Rose, especially . . ." His voice trailed off, leaving the sentence unfinished.

"Especially if there is war," she said, barely able to suppress a choke in her voice.

Again there was silence, the dread of the days to come, and what they might bring, hanging heavily between them.

Do it now! her mind screamed. Tell him how you feel, and ask him where his allegiance will fall if there is war. Tell him you must know.

But before she could speak, he had again whisked her into his arms. "Let's not dwell on such unhappy thoughts today," he murmured, brushing her forehead with his warm lips. "Come along, there is one room that is completely finished. I've saved it till last to show you."

Before they stepped through the massive carved oak doors, Rose knew it would be the bedroom. Her heart began pounding like a triphammer. "Oh, Bram . . ."

The room was exquisite, with no expense

spared. A giant four-poster dominated the room, its lace canopy matching the fragile lace coverlet and delicate pillows on the bed. A rose-colored velvet chaise was placed before the large bay window, a silver tea service on an antique chest by its side. On the near wall, a mirror-topped vanity was spread with combs, brushes, and an array of perfumes and creams.

"Do you like it?" Bram murmured at her side. "Does it please you?"

Rose felt a flush rise to her cheeks. The room had obviously been furnished and decorated for her, with care and attention given to her every need.

But was it as a *mistress* she would be expected to enjoy the room . . . or as a *wife*?

Rose longed to ask the question, and opened her mouth to speak, then forced the thought aside. It didn't really matter. Not now.

She was aware of nothing but his nearness, of her longing to touch and to be touched in return. "It pleases me very much," she whispered.

His hand slid up her arm until it reached her waist. Then it moved across her back, pulling her forward. She felt herself pressed against the rough wool of his frock coat, her face buried in its intoxicating masculinity.

"Rose . . . my darling Rose," he said huskily. He lowered his head until their lips met. Never, even on the riverbank, could she remember being so overcome. Her knees grew weak, and she knew she would fall if Bram were to loosen his hold on her.

"Oh, Rose, my love, I want you so very much." His voice was a whisper, his breath hot against her cheek.

"And I want you, my darling," Rose cried, "more than life itself!" Her arms encircled his neck, and once more his lips met hers.

His arms tightened around her, and Rose, almost in a trance, felt herself being lifted and carried like a feather across the room. Gently he laid her on the bed. Then his lips left hers and he quickly shrugged out of his frock coat and tossed it carelessly on the velvet chaise, then unbuttoned his linen shirt, opening it to the waist. With a growl of impatience he was back on the bed beside Rose. His mouth covered hers with liquid fire as his fingers nimbly worked at the buttons of her dress.

Rose writhed beneath him, urging him to work faster, helping him until she was, at last, naked.

Bram gazed at her, his eyes filled with undisguised adoration. "God, you are so lovely."

Quickly he shed the rest of his clothes. Rose trembled as her eyes traveled the length of his magnificent body, drinking in the muscles that rippled beneath the burnished flesh, the trim leanness that exuded such pure masculinity. She raised her arms to him. "Come to me, my darling," she whispered. "Love me!"

With a cry of desire, Bram eased himself down

beside her, and Rose gasped as she felt her cool skin touch his hot body. She pressed closer to him and brushed her fingertips over the mat of black hair on his chest, trailing them across his collarbone and down a lean, muscular shoulder.

Bram wrapped one arm around her waist, drawing her against the hard length of his body. Then his mouth closed over hers.

Rose was swept by a dizzying tide of desire. She responded wildly to his kiss. Then his mouth left hers and his lips and teeth began tracing teasing patterns over her throat and the soft curve of her shoulder. Rose shivered, writhed in ecstasy as he explored every inch of her sensitive flesh with skillful fingers and mouth.

He moved over her, kissing her lips, neck, sucking her tender breasts with tantalizing skill. Rose trembled in exquisite torment, caressing Bram's body.

There was a sweet, wild throb in her belly that grew more intense with every touch. At last his fingers touched her aching desire, flickering through the downy soft curls, and Rose cried out, opening her slender legs to him.

"Oh, my love, my darling, please," she gasped. "I want . . . I want . . ."

"Yes, yes," Bram whispered. "I cannot bear another moment of such torment."

His mouth was on hers again, one hard-muscled arm clasping her back, his other hand cupping her buttocks, pressing her to his flat, hard belly and his maleness.

Then he moved over her, and with one last searing kiss knelt to enter her.

Rose, feeling tiny and fragile beneath him, gasped at the momentary stab of pain as she felt the hardness of his throbbing flesh merge with the softness of her own. And then she was lost in ecstasy.

Her hips sought his, driven by an instinct as old as mankind. Clinging to him, her nails digging into his back, she gave herself completely to him, wrapping her legs around his body, as, again and again, they fused and became one.

Bram's breath was harsh against her ear as his own passion mounted, moving within her with exquisite deftness.

Straining against the mattress, she moved beneath him, arching against him and then dropping away, her arms encircling his shoulders, pulling him to her. And then she felt a rhythmic pulsating sensation deep inside her body, plunging to the deepest core of her, building and growing.

She lost track of time and space. She was immersed in a whirlwind she was powerless to control. The whirlwind grew and grew, arching and cresting.

The rhythm of her motions increased, matched by his own as he moved above her. His lips rained kisses over her lips, her eyes, her ears, the sensitive skin at the side of her neck, his breath mingling with her own as they drove each other to the peak of passion.

And then her body exploded, and Rose screamed with the sweetness and pain of it as she felt Bram's simultaneous release deep inside her.

For a long moment they seemed suspended in time and space, and then, with a long, deep sigh, Bram eased his body down beside hers, his skin covered with a sheen of perspiration. For long moments they lay silent, struggling to regain their normal breath.

Sometime later—perhaps minutes, perhaps hours—Bram got up from the bed and slipped into his breeches.

"Where . . . where are you going?" Rose asked as he reached the door.

He turned. "I invited you for tea, remember?" He grinned and disappeared out the door.

He returned a few minutes later with a pot of hot tea and a tray of sandwiches and sweets, and proceeded to serve Rose as if she were royalty and he her manservant.

Never could she remember feeling such joy, as they talked and laughed, and demolished the tray of food as if they hadn't eaten in months.

And then Bram took Rose's teacup from her hand. "My God, what a woman you are," he murmured, and from the look in his eyes Rose knew they were about to make love again.

He pressed her gently down into the soft

pillows, and Rose wound her arms around his neck, eager to feel his magical touch once more.

"Yes, my darling, yes . . ." she whispered.

Her flesh tingled as his fingertips again began touching her in those secret places. Rose could not suppress the moans of delight erupting from her throat.

Just as his lips descended to hers, however, they heard a loud, incessant pounding on the front door of the brownstone.

"Damn!" Bram gently slid her arms from about his neck and stalked to the window.

"Who is it?" Rose asked, pulling the sheets over her naked breasts as she sat up in the bed.

"My sergeant," Bram replied, throwing the window wide and leaning out. "Yes, Sergeant, what is it?" he called impatiently.

"Orders, sir . . . at once."

"I'll be right down!"

Closing the window, he hurriedly shrugged into a shirt. The frown on his face deepened when Rose's tinkling laughter reached his ears from the bed. "You find this much more amusing than I do," he growled, but allowed a tight grin to soften his scowl.

"Not so. I was just wondering how you were going to explain *that* to your sergeant."

Bram followed her eyes downward, to the obvious bulge in his trousers. "Damn!" He laughed, and tugged on a dressing gown as he made for the door.

His steps had barely faded from the stairs when the mood of lightness fled. A chill replaced it, making Rose gather the covers tighter about her suddenly trembling body.

What could be so great an emergency that Bram was rousted in his off-duty hours?

She could hear the drone of voices from below, but she couldn't distinguish the words. She was about to slide from the bed and dress when Bram reentered the room.

The storm clouds in his eyes were ominous now, and there was a rippling beneath the skin of his tightly clenched jaw. Without a word, he sat on the bed and began pulling on his heavy riding boots.

"What is it?" Rose whispered, alarmed by the thunder in his mood.

"You've heard of the abolitionist from Kansas, John Brown?"

"I know of him, yes."

"The damn fool and some of his insane follow-ers have staged a raid on the armory at Harpers Ferry. Several men have been killed already."

"On the armory? Dear God, what for?"

"Guns, Rose, to arm his Negro army and free all the Negroes in the South."

"But . . . but that's impossible!"

"Of course it is," Bram replied, standing and stomping into his boots. "And dangerous. If John Brown and others like him succeed, there could be a slave rebellion throughout the South that could cost thousands of lives."

Rose was struck dumb. She said nothing as she watched Bram finish dressing. And then he was kneeling beside the bed, tenderly holding her face in his hands.

"Colonel Lee is commanding a company of marines to put down the rebellion. I'm to ride with them, Rose. We leave at once."

Several men have been killed already.

Suddenly those words struck her like a fist. She cried out and threw her arms about his neck.

"Easy, girl, easy. It's not war, only an insane, harebrained scheme. I'll be back in a matter of days."

"But you said several were killed—"

"They were, but all but one of them were the raiders themselves. Shall I order you a carriage?"

"No, it's a short walk. Don't worry about me."

He brushed her lips with his, and for the first time since he had entered the room, a smile returned to his lips. "It's ironic, you know."

"What?"

"I've worked my fool head off on this house to make this afternoon perfect, and politics rears its ugly head to spoil it."

"It's not spoiled," Rose whispered, holding him tighter. "It *was* perfect. And there will be many Fridays when you return."

Again their lips met. This time the kiss was

bruising, and for the briefest of moments Rose had the wild feeling that it would be the last time she would ever feel his lips on hers.

Then he was gone. Only when she heard his booted feet on the stairs did her eyes snap open. And out of her jumbled thoughts came his angry words: . . . *there could be a slave rebellion throughout the South that could cost thousands of lives.* . . .

He cared, she thought, he cared about the South and its plight!

Gripping the coverlet about her body, Rose flew from the bed to the window and threw it wide. Her intention was to damn propriety and the gossips. She would shout her love to Bram.

But he was already out of earshot, his broad back almost obscured by the mist and fog rolling off the Potomac to shroud the city.

"I love you," she whispered. "I love you, Bram."

The raid on Harpers Ferry was bloodily suppressed and John Brown was captured. But the nation, particularly the South, was electrified and alarmed. Now the people of the South feared internal rebellion as much as they feared the Republicans and the abolitionists in the North. Washington itself became a hotbed of further secessionist activity on one hand and abolitionist rhetoric on the other.

And through it all, Rose yearned for word from Bram.

She knew he was safe, for no military men had been killed or wounded in the raid's suppression. But he hadn't returned, and no amount of discreet questioning around the Capital gave her the reasons why.

Not so news of John Brown and his trial. It had begun at Charles Town, Virginia, ten days after the raid, and daily the Washington papers were filled with the proceedings. Rose, like everyone else, followed every word, no matter how chilling.

In the North, Brown was hailed as a martyr. In the South, he was dismissed as a madman.

Brown himself, at his sentencing, made a speech that was the most chilling of all: "If it is deemed necessary that I should forfeit my life for the furtherance of the ends of justice, and mingle my blood further with the blood of my children and with the blood of millions in this slave country whose rights are disregarded by wicked, cruel, and unjust enactments, I say, let it be done."

It was the first time Rose fully realized that men were not just willing to fight over the issue of slavery, but also were fully prepared to die.

It was near the end of November when Cory Johnson arrived in the Capital. Sitting in the parlor of their aunt's house, Rose was shocked at his appearance. It had been almost four years since last they had met face to face, but Hollis' father had aged more than a decade. Layers had dropped away from the powerful, stocky body. Now his finely tailored clothes hung on his frame as if it were a rack. His hair was a murky gray, and that same grayness seemed to cloud his eyes.

His hands, holding the papers he had brought for Rose and Cat's signatures, constantly shook. Throughout the amenities of greeting, small talk of old friends, and the serving of tea, Rose watched him and squirmed.

At last she could stand it no longer. "Cory, are you ill?"

The wan smile in answer was a stab to Rose's breast. He set the papers before him, removed his spectacles, and gingerly rubbed his eyes. When he looked at the girls again, his eyes were red-rimmed, and, if anything, the whites around his irises was grayer than before.

"Sick? Yes, I suppose I am sick . . . at heart."

"Because of the war?" Cat intoned.

"Cat," Rose cried, "there is no war! Must you—?"

"There will be," Cory Johnson said, his voice almost a whisper. "As sure as there will be a tomorrow, there will be war. Our own people in Charleston have already decided that should Mr. Lincoln be elected, they will secede. I do believe many states will follow their lead."

"So?" Rose said with a shake of her head. "The South should have already seceded. We are like two different countries already. That doesn't mean there will be war."

Cory Johnson and Catherine exchanged knowing glances. There were several seconds of awkward silence before Cat leaned forward and, like a matron rather than a young girl, patted the old man's hand. "What is it you've come to see us about, Mr. Johnson?"

With a sigh he again filled his quivering hands with the papers. "Just this. I have received a good offer—in fact, a quite spectacular offer—for both the Charleston house and Belle Erin."

Rose shrugged. "We've received many offers, at least one each year since we arrived in Washington."

"Yes, but none so large as this, and none coming at such a time."

"What do you propose, Mr. Johnson?" Cat asked.

"As your attorney and your business adviser, I can propose only one thing. Sell."

"Never!" Rose cried, leaping to her feet and balling her hands into fists at her hips. "Belle Erin is the only link we have to the South. We will never sell!"

"Rose," Cat said, rising and placing her hands on her older sister's trembling shoulders, "if there is war, we might lose everything."

"No! Belle Erin is all we have."

"Precisely, and if it goes, we have nothing. You enjoy our wealth, Rose. What would we live like without it? Sit down and listen to what Mr. Johnson is telling us."

"No!" Rose cried, squirming from Cat's grasp and facing her sister squarely, fury flashing in her eyes. "You hate the South, Catherine! You're a traitor, do you know that? You're a traitor to the South, to our people, and to me!"

With her skirts flying, Rose ran to the door, only to stop and whirl back to face them. Tears ran down her cheeks in streams now, and her face was flushed a bright red. "One day I'll have children, Catherine. And I swear to you they'll be raised on Belle Erin!"

Then she was gone, her feet pounding up the stairs.

When Catherine heard the door of Rose's bedroom slam, she turned and calmly regained her seat. "Explain it to me, Mr. Johnson, explain everything to me in detail. I'll talk to Rose."

John Brown was hung on December 2. On the scaffold, before the noose was placed around his neck, he handed his executioner a note. It was published in Washington two days later. Rose and Catherine read it together: "I, John Brown, am now quite certain that the crimes of this guilty land will never be purged away but with blood."

"Rose . . ."

"Yes."

"There will be war, Rose. As surely as there is a God in heaven, there will be war."

"Yes, I know."

That afternoon they sent a message to Cory Johnson in Charleston. The text contained only one word: "Sell."

CHAPTER TEN

ONLY BRAM'S RETURN to Washington brought some relief to Rose's troubled mind. The moment he stepped into her aunt's parlor, the hunger she felt for him returned.

"Rose—"

"Shhh." She curled her arms about his neck. Catching his lips with hers, she slipped her tongue nimbly between his teeth.

His groan of pleasure was like music in her ears. His hands slid up to cup the swell of her breasts, and her own moans of pleasure mingled with his.

The kiss ended abruptly when the sound of swishing skirts reached their ears from the nearby hall. Seconds later, Cat entered the room. She paused in the doorway for a brief second, then moved forward, her right arm extended. "Captain Darcy."

"Catherine," Bram replied, the stiffness in his voice matching hers.

Bram's lips had barely touched Catherine's hand before she withdrew it and turned to Rose. "Aunt Glynis needs you for a moment."

"Of course," Rose replied, turning to Bram. "I'll only be a moment."

"Will you take tea, Captain Darcy . . . or perhaps some brandy?"

"Brandy would be fine, Miss Jacquard."

The overly formal tone of their voices brought Rose to a halt halfway up the stairs. She and Cat had hardly spoken this past week, since the decision to sell Belle Erin had been made. Now the cold calm in Cat's voice as she spoke to Bram jarred Rose. It was like a danger signal telling her not to leave Cat alone with him.

Rose was about to retrace her steps to the parlor, when she heard her aunt weakly call her name. Quickly she lifted her skirts and ran up the remaining steps and down the long hall to her aunt's room.

Glynis O'Rourke was a shell of her once energetic self. It seemed as though overnight the skin had become like parchment on her hands and face. Her hair, freshly brushed, now framed what seemed to Rose only a masklike reproduction of the face she had known.

Glynis was being treated by two of the best

doctors in Washington, but she continued to fail.

"Your aunt is tired, Rose. That is the only diagnosis I can give."

Rose knew that Glynis O'Rourke was dying. So did Cat. Neither of them spoke of it. It was just an accepted fact, and both of them tended to her needs . . . and waited.

"Rose, come closer."

"What is it, Aunt?"

There were droplets of perspiration on her forehead. Rose dampened the corner of a towel and patted them away.

"You have guests?" Rose nodded. "I won't keep you long, then. A little water."

Gently Rose lifted the woman's head and placed the rim of a cup to her lips. After only two swallows, her aunt lifted a bony finger signaling that it was enough.

"Sit, Rose, for a moment . . . here on the bed."

Rose sat, and again ran the damp towel over her aunt's forehead.

"Your caller . . . it's Captain Darcy?"

"Yes."

"Do you love him, Rose?" Rose couldn't suppress the surprise that leapt into her face. Her aunt smiled and covered one of Rose's hands with both of her own. "Catherine and I have had some very long talks."

"Yes," Rose mumbled, "I love him."

"Will you marry him . . . one day?"

"Yes, if he asks."

"Good. Then I will tell you something. When I was young, younger even than you are now, I made some very bad choices in my life. I fear Catherine will do the same."

"Catherine?"

"Did you know she used to have dreams—nightmares, really—about your father's death, about being murdered in her bed?"

"I . . ."

Suddenly bile rushed to her throat. She and Cat had been so close, yet her sister had never confided these things to her. And then she remembered her own lack of fear. She had never feared anyone or anything. Now she felt guilty because she had been blind to the fear in someone she loved so much. Had she seen it, she could have been more of a comfort to Cat.

"Since she has been here in this house," Glynis continued, "she no longer has those fearful dreams."

"And that's why she won't marry Hollis?"

The old woman nodded. "And it's foolish. Wait, let me finish. Foolish, because love—real love—is a precious and rare thing. If Catherine thinks she can ignore it and still find happiness in this world, then she is a fool."

"Have you . . . have you told her this?"

"Yes, and she agrees."

"She agrees?" Rose exclaimed, her head spinning now with the import of her aunt's words.

"You are so different, the two of you. You, Rose, are like your father—strong, self-reliant, in many ways fearless. Catherine is like my sister, a fragile soul who faces the realities of this world but fears them."

"I don't understand. Why are you telling me . . . ?"

"Don't make Catherine's mistake, Rose." Suddenly the old woman's eyes closed and her head rolled listlessly to the side. "Go see your Captain Darcy now, Rose. I need to rest."

Rose wanted to say more, ask more, but obediently she stood and left the room.

She had the feeling that her Aunt Glynis knew something she was not telling her. The answer to the riddle nibbled on the fringe of her mind, but like so many things that threatened to annoy her, Rose pushed it away.

At the foot of the stairs she heard no voices, and until she stepped into the parlor, she feared that Bram had left.

He hadn't. He was seated in a large velvet chair directly in front of the fire. Slowly he swirled the liquid in his glass as his dark eyes stared broodingly into the saffron glow.

Catherine stood near the mantel, as stiff as a statue, her eyes staring with equal intensity at Bram Darcy.

So heavy was the mood between them that it washed over Rose like a surging tide. Neither of them was even aware of her entrance until she was directly beside the chair where Bram sat. And then only Cat looked up. "Rose, how is Aunt Glynis?"

"Resting." Rose slid her hand to Bram's shoulder. "But perhaps you had best look in on her."

"Yes, perhaps I should." Without another word, Cat left the room.

Rose knelt in the bell of her skirt and leaned forward until Bram could no longer ignore her. Slowly his eyes shifted from the fire until they met hers.

Rose's hand tightened on his arm. There was a weariness, even a trace of pain in his eyes that she hadn't noticed when he first arrived.

And then she wondered: had it been there when he first arrived, or had it crept in while he and Cat talked?

"I think, Rose, that your little sister doesn't care very much for me."

"What do you mean—what did she tell you?"

"About Belle Erin. I'm sorry."

The hair on the back of Rose's neck seemed to curl. If the wool of his uniform coat had not been so thick, her nails would have dug into his arm. "What has Belle Erin to do with Cat not approving of you?"

"Perhaps a great deal," he replied, a smile of sadness curving the corners of his mouth downward as he stood.

"Bram . . ."

He lifted her gently to her feet and brushed the tip of her nose with his lips. "Can you come tonight?"

"Yes, but—"

He brushed by her into the hall. Rose followed and grasped his arm as he lifted his hat from the rack.

"What did Cat say, Bram? What did she tell you?"

"Nothing that I didn't already know—that you're a woman full of fire, with a mind of your own. Until tonight, my love." Quickly his lips touched hers, and he was out the door before Rose could say more.

For the next hour she occupied herself with household chores and instructed the cook on the evening meal. At last she could stand it no more, and rushed upstairs. Her aunt was alone, sleeping and breathing evenly.

Cat was in her room, at her desk, writing, as she always did, in the daily journal she had kept since their arrival in Washington.

"What did you tell him?"

Cat turned slightly. "Captain Darcy?"

"Of course, Captain Darcy! What did you say to him?"

"I told him we had sold Belle Erin."

"I know that," Rose replied, struggling to keep a calm tone in her voice. "What else?"

"He told me of the horror of watching an old

gray-haired fool die on the gallows. We talked of war, and how it will affect all our lives."

"And me, Catherine—what did you tell him about me?"

"I told him that you love him, Rose. You do, don't you?"

"You know that I do."

Taking a letter from her desktop, Cat moved around Rose and into the hall. Rose caught up with her at the bottom of the stairs just as she was shrugging into her coat.

"Where are you going, Catherine? I want to talk to you."

"I can't talk now, Rose. I must make the last post with this letter." In the doorway she turned, tears brimming from her eyes. "It's to Hollis, telling him that I don't want him to come for Christmas."

She was on the bottom step and turning down the narrow walk when Rose called to her. "Why didn't you tell me about your nightmares?"

"Because you never asked."

Light flakes of snow swirled in Rose's face as she watched her sister slosh through the mud of Washington City.

They lay naked, side by side, with only a sheet over their bodies. Their breathing was even now, but there was still a slight tremor where their bodies touched.

They had joined together almost wildly, with

unbridled passion, moments after Rose had arrived.

Without a word, Bram had swept her into his arms and carried her to the bedroom.

"No, Bram ... a moment," Rose had cried, pushing vainly against his chest.

"No," he had replied gruffly, "now!"

And seconds later, Rose was helping him free her body of her dress, the bulky crinolines, and her underthings.

He was like a man gone wild as he coaxed her nipples erect with his tongue. "Help me," he urged, tugging at his own clothes, and Rose did, eagerly.

In seconds his body was naked, already burnished with a light sheen of perspiration. Effortlessly he lifted her until her legs were around his waist and he was striding toward the bed.

Rose clung to his powerful back as she felt her own caress the cool sheets. She sensed him moving along her inner thigh, and then she cried out as he entered her.

The wildness of his passion quickly enveloped her like a warm cocoon. His thrusts were rhythmic, meant to please, yet there was a need to them that she had never experienced from him before. His voice was a guttural roar as he cried out her name over and over. And then there were other words, not just her name—a phrase, a question, that echoed through the room: "Do you love me, Rose ... love me ... do you love me?"

"Yes ... dear God, yes, I love you," she cried out. "I love you!"

His manhood seemed to grow inside her, filling her whole body with desire. His thrusts became a pounding delight until she grew dizzy and thought she would swoon.

She felt her mind whirl until she felt herself go beyond the bounds of passion to indescribable ecstasy.

The final thrill was greater than any he had given her before. It grew, deep in her being, until, like a bubble that had swollen too large, it burst in satiated fury.

His insistent desire answered hers, and as his warmth filled her, he again cried out his love for her.

Now they lay silently, hand in hand, both prisoners of the voluptuous passion they had just shared. But there was more. Rose could sense it—a tenseness between them that had nothing to do with their sated bodies.

"Rose, did you mean it?" he whispered finally.

"Yes."

"Do you mean it now—after?"

Rose nodded. "Yes. I think I loved you the first moment we met at West Point." Then she turned to face him. "Have you ever doubted it?"

He rolled to his elbow until his face was above hers. "No, not really." Gently his lips kissed her eyes, brushed the tip of her nose, and then caressed her lips. "And I love you, Rose. I always will."

A tiny laugh escaped her lips as the fingers of one hand ran like a butterfly over the taut muscles of his back. "Why have we been so long telling each other?"

"Maybe we were both afraid that—"

Her fingers left his back and closed his lips. "Maybe . . . but no longer. Kiss me!"

He did, gently, and then rolled to his back, tugging her with him until her head rested against his neck.

"How sad it is that we've feared these times so much that it was Cat who had to voice it first," she said.

"She told you?"

"Yes, after you left. I went to her room. She had written a letter to Hollis, telling him not to come to Washington City for Christmas."

"Then she has made her decision," Bram said, his voice barely a whisper. "She won't marry him. Foolish."

"That's what my Aunt Glynis said. Now I know what she meant."

"Your little sister told me that if I loved you, I should marry you—now."

It was Rose's turn to raise herself to her elbow and stare down at him, unable to speak. The movement caused her breasts to cushion gently over his chest.

He curved his hand over one of them and lightly ran his thumb over the nipple. Rose's reaction was instant as a tremor of renewed desire rippled through her body.

"You have beautiful breasts."

"And you have beautiful, dark, brooding eyes."

With a groan he took one of her hands and moved it down across his belly. Her fingers found him swollen again with desire. Still gripping his hardness, she deftly moved her body over his. Slowly she lowered herself, guiding him with her hand, until he was there.

This time their desire was muted. Their lust was love, as he rose to meet her and she slid downward, taking him easily.

"I love you," he whispered, placing his hands on her hips and guiding her movements.

"And I love you," Rose replied, showering his darkly handsome face with tender kisses.

"Will you marry me, Rose?" His movement stopped, but his hands still gripped her hips, forcing them together until there was no space between them. His eyes were like bottomless pools that drew her forward as much as the hard life of him filled her and forced her toward the gentle demand of his desire.

There will be no war. The Southern states will peacefully secede, and in time the two new countries, North and South, will live side by side, each pursuing happiness in their separate ways.

And one day she and Bram and their children would create a new Belle Erin.

"Yes, my darling, I will be your wife."

Christmas was full of contradiction, conflict, and wild emotion for Rose.

She and Bram made no secret now of their love. Rose spent as much time at the house on Seventh Street as she could without openly flaunting their affair.

Bram pushed for a wedding date as soon as possible. Rose demurred. "I want to be traditional," she insisted. "Charleston belles marry in June!"

"I can't wait until June."

"And why not? Other than a few words and a piece of paper, we're married now."

She also toyed with the idea of marrying in Charleston. After all, she thought, all of her old friends—as well as many of Bram's from West Point—were in or around Charleston.

It was Cat who scotched that idea the moment Rose mentioned it. "Bram has responsibilities here, Rose. Even a honeymoon tour will be difficult. Think what a chore planning a Charleston wedding would be, in terms of time and travel."

Reluctantly Rose agreed.

Practical Cat.

She found that she was agreeing with Cat on almost everything now. Their differences seemed to be over. She also noticed that Cat no longer referred to Bram as "Captain Darcy." Now it was Bram. Indeed, it was Bram this, and Bram that, and Bram everything. There were times when Rose thought it was Cat, and not she, who was wedding Bram Darcy!

Christmas was the high point of Washington City's social whirl. Rose and Bram were in the thick of it. They met Lady Camilla Fontaine several times, and each time Rose was civil. In her opinion, Bram was far too charming to the woman. Rose was still hearing rumors that Bram had been seen dining at Brown's or Willard's with her.

Once she asked him about it.

He seemed amused. "I do believe your eyes are turning a bit green."

"Not a bit of it!" Rose bridled. "I just think it's a bit embarrassing to hear that your fiancé is lunching with another woman!"

"Not when no one except you, your aunt, and your sister know I'm your fiancé. When are you going to announce our engagement?"

"Soon," Rose replied vaguely. "I'm waiting for just the right time and the right place."

Silence.

"Are you?" she asked.

"What?"

"Lunching with Camilla Fontaine?"

The amusement in his eyes suddenly disappeared and his mood turned dark.

"Well?" she pressed.

"Yes, I do have an occasional lunch with Lady Fontaine, Rose. And I'm afraid I'll have to keep doing so. Now, I'll hear no more of it!"

Rose decided to drop the subject. But it came up again on Christmas Eve at a White House party. Each time Rose looked around, Bram seemed to be huddled with Camilla Fontaine. Furious, she mentioned it in the carriage on the way home.

"It's politics, Rose . . . please."

"Damn politics! You were practically kissing her neck."

"I was whispering in her ear."

"Like you whisper in mine?" Rose cried. "Do you say the same things? We're about to be married—"

"Are we?" he thundered, turning sideways in the seat and grasping her angrily by the shoulders. "Are we to be married, Rose?"

"Yes. Stop, Bram—you're hurting me."

"June—months from now! Rose, marry me now, *tonight*!"

"Tonight? You're mad."

"Yes," he growled, "or at least I sometimes think I am heading in that direction. Will you?"

"No, it's impossible. Really, all the plans . . ."

He slumped against the leather seat, and Rose's heart sank when she saw the sudden vacant expression in his eyes. The look in his eyes frightened her. It was the look of a wary, cornered animal, not the look of the Bram Darcy she knew.

At last the carriage pulled into H Street and then lurched to a halt.

The silence between them filled Rose with dread. Something was wrong. Was it just her jealousy that was unnerving him so? Rose thought not, but she couldn't stand to leave him in such a mood, and now was not the proper time to add curiosity to jealousy.

"Bram, I'm sorry. We'll announce our engagement right after Christmas, and I'll move the date up, I promise."

His only answer was a nod. His kiss on the stoop of her aunt's house was perfunctory, almost coolly polite, before he turned on his heel and regained the carriage.

Alone in bed that night, Rose promised herself that she would never let her jealousy interfere with her love or her future husband's duties, however odd they seemed to be.

Christmas morning dawned on a blizzard, but Rose was up early and determined to make it the happiest Yule ever. In the back of her mind was the thought that it might well be her aunt's last holiday. She was overseeing the preparation for the afternoon feast when Cat entered the kitchen, still dressed in her nightdress and robe. She looked haggard; there was an awful puffiness about her eyes, and they were red-rimmed from weeping.

"Cat, what is it—what's wrong?" Rose cried in alarm.

"Hollis was here last night."

"Oh, no!"

"Yes, and he insists on coming to dinner."

Rose moved to her sister and took her in her arms, holding her close and rocking her, almost like a child. "And did you agree? Will he be coming?" she asked softly.

Cat's shoulders began to shake with renewed weeping. "Yes," she sobbed, "he'll be here."

Hollis was changed. He was older, more self-assured, and, Rose thought, wiser. She quickly realized that no one else at the table agreed.

All through the meal, he talked of secession. None of the Southern senators on the Hill or the firebrands at Willard's were more caught up in this new religion of the South than Hollis Johnson. He went on at length about states' rights, the state of the country if this man Lincoln became President, and the plight of the Yankees if war was declared.

Rose found herself agreeing with him, but when she saw how miserable Cat was, she remained silent.

Bram seemed to listen, and even nodded once in a while, but Rose could tell that he, too, was upset.

Only Glynis O'Rourke—who was still deathly ill, but had insisted on joining the Christmas festivities—offered any words of reply to Hollis' diatribe. In her weak voice she asked, "Do you know how much I love the South?"

"Yes, ma'am."

"Do you know what city in this country has the biggest port?"

"Why, New Orleans, ma'am."

"New York, Hollis. And New York is in the North, along with most of the factories, all but a few of the railroads, and all of the shipyards. Have you ever been to Pittsburgh, Hollis?"

"No, ma'am," he replied, tight-lipped, a red flush creeping up from the high tight collar of his uniform blouse.

Glynis O'Rourke shook her head and bored into the younger man with all the steel left in her gaze. "The entire city sits under a heap of smoke and over a heap of coal. The coal goes into the furnaces, but more than smoke comes out. Cannon come out, Hollis, cannon that will turn the South red if there is war."

Silence, like a tomb, followed the old woman's words.

Hollis pushed his food around his plate. Bram and Catherine exchanged haunted glances, and Rose thought she would gag.

"But there will be no war," the old lady resolutely intoned, looking at everyone in turn, as if she dared them to doubt her statement. She clutched a bottle of wine with a quivering hand. "So let's eat! Who wants more wine?"

Hollis left abruptly at the conclusion of the meal, and Bram shortly thereafter.

Cat disappeared quietly into her room, and Rose helped her aunt upstairs. When she was tucked into bed, Rose began to read her to sleep. It didn't take long.

As Rose passed Cat's room on the way to her own, she heard muffled sobs. Gently she opened the door and peered in. "Are you all right?"

Cat was seated at her desk, her head in her arms. When she looked up, her eyes were too tear-filled to focus. "He won't give up, Rose. He just refuses to believe that I won't return to Charleston."

"Are you that afraid of the South, Cat?"

Instead of answering, Cat said, "Bram said you were thinking of moving the wedding date forward."

"Yes, perhaps January or February."

"Do it, Rose. For God's sake, do it!"

CHAPTER ELEVEN

JANUARY of the new year was blisteringly cold, with high winds, rain, and occasional flurries of snow turning the roads of Washington to mud. Rose often braved the weather and walked to the Capitol. There she sat and appraised the discussions that seemed to grow more heated every day. She was like a moth drawn to the flame of political debate. She knew that the conclusions her quick, agile mind might make could destroy her, and yet she found it impossible to stay away.

The courtly days of James Buchanan's term, presided over by the lovely Harriet Lane, were coming to a close now. That saddened Rose. The quiet dinners with Mrs. Greenhow, Harriet Lane, the President, and a bevy of Southern ladies and gentlemen were fewer and fewer. Soirees at the mansion and in the various embassies still occurred, but there was a marked difference in who attended what party.

Taking tea at Brown's Hotel, she heard "secession" on nearly every tongue. It was the same in the homes of her Southern friends. And in the evenings, in Bram's arms, she often prayed that it would be secession, and not war.

In February Bram was attached to the State Department and raised to the rank of major.

"Whatever do you do?" Rose queried during an idle moment. "It must be much more than drilling troops, for your name is on everyone's tongue."

"I talk to people."

"Is that all?"

"That's enough"—he smiled—"when you speak in enough tongues." So saying, he launched into the soliloquy from *Hamlet* in every accent imaginable, from Greek to Rose's own Southern drawl. Halfway through, she was holding her sides with laughter. It was only when she was alone, much later, that she realized that he had told her nothing.

At last, at a small dinner party, Rose announced their engagement and set the date— April 23. Bravos and applause met the announcement. All the women insisted that Bram kiss his bride-to-be, and the men insisted that they must kiss her as well.

"April?" Bram whispered into her ear.

"It will take that long for the arrangements, my darling. I want a beautiful wedding, one we can remember all our lives."

It was shortly after the announcement of their wedding that Rose found that she was no longer automatically on the guest list of many afternoon dances and teas. There were evening dinner parties at Mrs. Clay's and Mrs. Greenhow's that Rose only heard about the next day. She chose to ignore it rather than question it.

To herself, Rose used the excuse that her time should be used to prepare for her nuptials anyway. She would not admit it—to herself or anyone else—but she was becoming a chameleon in much of her thinking: if she was given a cold shoulder by some Southerners who had been her friends for years, she excused it as pure worry on their part about their own fate; if Mr. Lincoln's popularity was growing, she told herself that it was only in the North, and that had nothing to do with the South.

It was on a February afternoon, in the shop of Madame Foshay, that Rose again ran into Camilla Fontaine. As usual, the lady was regal in flounced gray satin, maroon ribbons, and an immaculate velvet cape. Rose could not fathom how the woman avoided the grime of the streets.

"Congratulations, Rose. You've snared the most eligible bachelor, and, I must say, the most charming man in this godforsaken place."

"Thank you, Camilla," Rose replied sweetly. "Have you taken a house?"

"A house?"

"Yes. You've been in Washington so long, I would assume that by now you would be bored with hotel living."

"No, quite the opposite," Camilla laughed. "I adore it, as do my lazy servants. The hotel staff does half their work!"

Madame Foshay bustled in, eyed the two women, and quickly retreated again. As soon as she was out of earshot, Camilla moved closer to Rose and gently grasped her arm. "I heard about Belle Erin, Rose. I am sorry, truly sorry. I know how much you loved the land."

Rose could hardly believe her ears. In that moment, the brittleness was gone from Camilla's voice and Rose could read nothing but sincerity in her eyes.

"Thank you, Camilla. Yes, it was a bitter blow."

"I wish . . . well, I wish I had known. If it was money, Rose . . ."

"No," Rose replied quickly, and then added, "Cat and I just found it impossible to carry on from such a distance."

"Oh?" Camilla's eyes arched, and her stare grew more intent, as if she were reading Rose's lie and demanded the truth. "With a good overseer and Cory Johnson, I would have thought—"

Before she could finish, Madame Foshay bustled back into the room with the sketches for

Rose's wedding gown. Abruptly Camilla excused herself and glided toward the door.

Rose had turned toward the sketches being laid out by Madame Foshay when Camilla suddenly spoke again. "I shall see you tomorrow evening, Rose."

Rose whirled. "Tomorrow evening?"

"Yes. Perhaps we can secure a moment alone and talk further."

"Tomorrow evening?" Rose questioned again, her eyes narrowing and her mind whirling, trying to remember her social calendar.

"Of course. Kate Chase's dinner party. I noticed Major Darcy's name on the guest list, and assumed—"

"Oh, yes, of course," Rose said, quickly plastering a smile on her face. "It had slipped my mind."

"Of course," Camilla replied, again the quizzical lift to her eyebrows. "I'll see you then."

And then she was gone, with Rose staring after her.

She had every moment of every day planned, both in her mind and on her calendar. It was impossible that she would forget a dinner party given by one of her old rivals.

For the next half-hour Rose listened to Madame Foshay with only half an ear as the woman explained the elaborate creation that was to be Rose's bridal gown. As her eye scanned the sketches, she vainly tried to equate the penciled lines and various shadings with cloth and substance on her body. Constantly her mind strayed.

A dinner gathering at Kate Chase's would be highly charged with politics. Senator Seward and the stalwart antislavery Henry Wilson from Massachusetts were bound to be there. In fact, because the dinner was being given by Kate Chase, it was bound to be a Northern affair.

Was that why she had not been invited?

But if Bram had been invited, surely she had been included in the invitation. Kate Chase would not commit the social blunder of inviting a gentleman and not his fiancée. But if that were true, if Rose had been invited, then it was Bram himself who had not told her of the invitation.

"You do not like the design, mademoiselle?"

"What?"

"You seem to be bored with the sketches."

"Oh, no, not at all, madame," Rose stammered. "It's just that my mind seems to be wandering these days."

"Ah, it is normal, mademoiselle," the petite Frenchwoman clucked, "to be a bit—how you say?—distracted at such a time. And Major Darcy is a very handsome man! Oo-la-la, when I was a young girl in Paris—"

"Yes, yes," Rose interrupted, barely able to disguise the impatience in her voice. "Tell me, madame, should the train be quite so long? I fear I shan't be able to walk."

Again Madame Foshay explained the design.

This time Rose forced herself to pay rapt attention. And, she had to admit, Madame Foshay had outdone herself. The gown was exquisite, snow-white satin cascading to the floor, with hundreds of tiny pearls adorning the bodice and sleeves of Irish lace. The train contained yards of satin, with delicate lace inserts, and the tiara holding the veil contained hundreds more of the tiny pearls.

Rose's eyes misted as she gazed at the sketches. Her wedding gown. The gown she would wear to become Mrs. Bramfield Darcy.

The happiest day of her life.

Oh, dear God, will that day ever come! she thought.

Convincing Madame Foshay that she was delighted with the sketches, Rose finally took her leave. Carriage cabs were scarce on the streets of Washington, but she managed to secure one. She gave the driver Bram's address on Seventh Street, and pulled the warming blanket over her legs as the carriage lurched forward. It was late afternoon, near five. Bram was usually at the house by four. But how could she explain an afternoon visit, when just the previous evening she had declined luncheon, pleading appointments all day?

And, once the visit was explained, how could she tactfully approach the subject of Kate Chase's dinner party?

"Here we are, miss."

Rose had one foot on the carriage step, when she quickly darted back inside. Just emerging from Bram's front door were Senator Seward and the wealthy merchant from Detroit, Zach Chandler. They were closely followed by five other men Rose recognized immediately as the core of the antislavery movement in the government.

She gasped.

"Anything wrong, miss?"

"No, nothing," Rose replied quickly. "Could we just wait a few moments, please?"

The driver shrugged and closed the peep trap above her.

Within minutes the men had dispersed in separate directions, and Rose alighted from the carriage. As was her wont these days, Rose had immediately rationalized the reason for these powerful men meeting in her fiancé's home instead of on the Hill or at the War Department. They were in the government, and Bram was in the government, and that was all.

" 'Afternoon, Miz Jacquard."

Bram had finally given in and hired a manservant, a tall, burly, free colored man who had worked for the Darcy family since his youth in Baltimore.

"Good afternoon, Joshua. Is Major Darcy in?"

"Yessum, he be in the study. I'll—"

"That won't be necessary, Joshua," Rose said,

piling his arms with her packages, cloak, and bonnet. "I'll just go on in."

Bram stood over his desk, a goblet of brandy in one hand and a thin cigar in the other. He was rarely in uniform these days, and this afternoon was no different. He was dressed in tight black breeches and a frilled linen shirt. He had discarded his waistcoat and cravat, and even partially unbuttoned his shirt. So intent was he on the papers before him that Rose was halfway across the room before he became aware of her presence.

"Rose!"

"Hello, darling! I've been shopping, bought oodles of beautiful things, and I just had to show them to you!" She glided easily between his arms and tilted her head upward to be kissed. "Is that the kiss of a man madly in love?" she teased, when his lips barely touched hers.

"That's the kiss of a man who has been surprised in the middle of his work."

"Work?" She laughed, tugging at the fingers of her white gloves. "Paperwork! Can't this be done in your office?"

"Hardly. I find it difficult to concentrate on certain matters there," Bram replied, catching her elbow in a grip much harder than she thought necessary.

"Ugh," Rose said, wrinkling her nose, "you must have been working for hours. The smoke in here is like a fog!"

"Yes, filthy things." He mashed his cigar out in a desktop ashtray and quickly grasped her elbow again. Rose stiffened, but allowed herself to be led away from the desk.

Why hadn't he just volunteered that the heavy smoke in the room had been caused by his recent visitors?

"Come, sit by the fire. There's a bit of a chill in the room."

"Yes, there is."

If he noticed the sudden chill in Rose's voice, he gave no indication of it. When she was seated by the fire, he visibly relaxed, his lips curving in an easy smile. "Sherry?" he asked, brushing her cheeks with his lips.

"Please."

"Now, tell me," he said, moving to a sideboard behind the desk, "how was your day? Will your gown be the most stunning of any bride that has ever said her vows in Washington City?"

"It will," Rose replied, trying to keep a lightness in her voice that she didn't feel. As she continued to speak, by rote reciting what now seemed the mundane events of her day, her mind buzzed with doubts.

Bram wasn't actually *lying* about anything to her, but she was sure he was keeping something from her.

And she hated it. Even now, with tensions at a fever pitch all around them and tempers flaring, there should be no secrets between them. With the entire city dividing itself into separate camps, it was madness for the two of them to do the same, no matter how many political maneuvers Bram might be involved in.

"... and I saw Camilla Fontaine at Madame Foshay's ..."

His back stiffened slightly; Rose was sure of it. And out of the corner of her eye she saw Bram turn over the papers on the desk as he passed.

"Here you are."

Rose accepted the glass and slid over, making room for him beside her on the settee.

But he didn't sit. Instead he stood towering above her like a glowering statue. She felt, rather than saw, the penetrating gaze in his dark eyes as he studied her over the rim of his glass. Her hand, raising the glass of sherry to her lips, was shaking.

"You are cold."

"No, I ... Bram?"

"Yes."

"Do you love me?"

His brow furrowed into a scowl. "How can you doubt it?"

"I don't doubt it," she said, unable to suppress the sudden choke in her throat.

"Then why do you ask?"

She almost blurted out the words, asking him why he was deceiving her, what he was hiding from her, but then thought better of it. "Because I am a woman." She shrugged, trying to make her lips curve into a smile. "And, as a woman, I must constantly be reminded of it."

Bram set his glass aside, and seemed to swoop down over her. His nearness was intoxicating, but the dark fire in his eyes was almost frightening. His powerful hands slid up over her shoulders to find her face and hold her eyes to his. "Know that I love you, Rose. No woman has ever bewitched me as you have."

Her own hand came up, one nail lightly tracing the strong line of his jaw. "My aunt once told me that love is the most important thing in the world. She said that nothing could take its place, that it should never be set aside for anything else. Do you believe that, Bram?"

If anything, his eyes grew even harder. He tried, but failed, to soften the look with a smile, but the corners of his mouth just wouldn't lift. "Like people, Rose, love must live in this world. And, like people, love must sometimes bend. Know that I love you, Rose, but each of us has to live with himself as much as we live with each other."

A fist of cold iron seemed to clamp over Rose's heart. Was he telling her that duty—his and hers—was more important than their love? Was he suggesting that, if and when the time came, one—perhaps both—of them would have to make a choice?

Of course that is what he is saying, you little fool, Rose told herself.

Face it!

But she could not; she refused.

With all the will in her mind and body, she held back the emotion boiling inside her. She knew that if she didn't, if she allowed the tears to spill forth, the time she had dreaded would be now.

"Oh, Bram, Bram, I love you." She threw her arms about his neck and felt him stand, carrying her effortlessly with him. "I love you so much that at times I think my heart will burst with it."

"I know," he whispered in her ear, his breath a hot flame on the tender skin of her throat. "I know, my darling, I know."

Rose felt the fear drain from her body. Again her mind played the chameleon, and she believed what she wanted to believe.

And then, suddenly, he ceased his caresses and stepped back from her. Rose opened her heavy-lidded eyes and saw his face, somber with desire, but with a new firmness in the line of his jaw and the way he stood.

"Why have you stopped?" she asked dreamily, her body full of need for him.

"As sad as it is, we haven't time to be lovers just now."

His clipped, precise words were cold water poured over her heated body.

"What do you mean? Does your *duty* prevent you?"

"As a matter of fact, yes." Slipping an arm about her slender waist, he turned her and they began walking toward the door. "I must catch the last train to Baltimore. I'll drop you at your aunt's on the way."

Rose waited while he dressed. Her body was still in turmoil from the instant need he seemed always able to arouse in her. But her mind was somewhat at ease. If he had planned to be in Baltimore, then he had never planned to be at Kate Chase's dinner.

In the carriage, she cuddled close to him, curling her body under his arm and pressing his leg beneath the blanket. "When will you return from Baltimore? The day after tomorrow?"

"No, I hope to be back in the late afternoon tomorrow."

Rose tensed. She raised her eyes to his, not bothering to hide the flash of anger in them she knew he would see. "Then you'll be able to attend Kate Chase's dinner party after all."

"Kate . . . ?"

"Yes. It must have slipped your mind and you forgot to tell me."

"No, Rose," he said, sudden steel in his voice. "I didn't forget to tell you."

"Oh? Then we're not going?"

"I shall probably drop in—just to make an appearance."

"Then I wasn't invited?"

"Yes," he growled, his anger now matching hers, "you were."

"Then you didn't forget to tell me?"

"No. I didn't think you would want to attend, knowing how you feel about Northerners these days."

"You thought my acid tongue would perhaps embarrass you, is that it?"

"That's part of it, yes. The other part of it is that I thought *you* might be embarrassed."

Rose flared. "Well, I won't! And I shall be on my best behavior, I promise!"

The carriage halted and Bram handed her down as if he were unloading flour. His grip on her elbow as he guided her up the walk was like iron.

"You're hurting my arm!"

"I'm sorry."

At the door he halted her abruptly and whirled her to face him. Roughly he gripped her shoulders, and for a second Rose thought he would shake her.

"Rose, I would prefer that you not go to Kate Chase's tomorrow evening."

"And I would prefer that I do."

And then he did shake her, hard enough that her head began to wag like a rag doll's. Thunder came into his eyes, and his lower lip began to quiver.

"Stop it!" she cried, striking his arms to throw his hands from her shoulders.

"Damn, if you're not the most exasperating woman!"

"And damn your secrecy!" she cried. "Oh, Bram, don't you see what is happening?"

"I see that I'm getting an interfering wife."

"You're not! You're getting a wife who wants to be a part of what you do. In the past few weeks, you've drawn a curtain between us. Even when we make love, you seem to be holding back something from me. Bram, please, I need to know what it is."

"Do you?" His voice was like a rasp on hard steel.

"I do. If we can't share our thoughts, Bram, how can we share our daily lives?"

He looked at her steadily for a long moment as he exhaled deeply. "Then, by God, it's on to Kate Chase's tomorrow night." Without kissing her, he stormed back down the walk to the carriage and viciously yanked the door open.

She started to run toward the carriage, but before she reached the gate, Bram had barked an order to Joshua to drive on.

CHAPTER TWELVE

ROSE was seated between Bram and Senator
Seward. As usual, the senator from New York
was charmed by Rose, and throughout the early
part of the meal directed his witty small talk to
her.

Kate Chase and Henry Wilson occupied opposite ends of the table. The wealthy Detroit merchant Zach Chandler was seated beside Lady
Valerie Bevins, with her husband, Lord Bevins,
between Kate and Seward. Camilla Fontaine sat
across from Bram, with a Frenchman, Jacques
Valery, between her and Lady Bevins.

Rose soon lost her fears that this was a political gathering. Lord Bevins and Valery were
wealthy industrialists in their respective countries. The conversation that reached her ears

was mostly concerned with money: the rise and fall of world prices, grain crops, the sudden surge in the building of railroads the world over, and myriad other comments concerning world trade.

Rose found herself relaxing and listening intently to the interesting exchange. But near the end of the main courses of wild turkey and snipe prepared in the English style, and just before the servants scurried in with the cherry cobbler, the conversation shifted.

It started with the casual mention of John Brown.

"It is a pity," Kate Chase declared, "that in every cause there must be martyrs. In John Brown's case, I think the man will one day be considered a saint."

Suddenly the cobbler stuck in the center of Rose's throat. Carefully, as Kate's comment was discussed around the table, she set down her fork and brought her napkin to her lips.

Most of the comments were in agreement with Kate's, which seemed to spark her to praise John Brown with even more vigor. As she spoke, her attitude became even more imperious, her tone more self-assured.

Rose's eyes fluttered shut. She saw her own father's bloody, lifeless body in her arms. She remembered the young boy who had killed him, fired with the religious zeal of the abolitionist. She again saw the crazed, red-rimmed eyes as they sighted over the barrel of his musket. And then she heard the explosion that sent the ball into her father's chest.

"Kate, excuse me . . ."

"Yes, Rose?"

"Have you ever even been in the South?"

"Why, no," Kate replied, filling the room with a haughty laugh. "As a matter of fact, I've never had the slightest desire to travel south of Washington!"

Rose felt the pressure of Bram's hand on her knee through her skirt and crinolines, but she ignored it. "I think it rather narrow for someone to comment on the Southern life-style when she knows very little about it," she said slowly.

"I'm not sure, my dear," Kate replied with another tinkling laugh, "what the Southern life-style has to do with the sainthood of John Brown." Here she paused, looking around the table as if for confirmation. "Unless, of course, by applying for sainthood, he should bury it forever—which it definitely deserves."

A red film formed over Rose's eyes. Her leg, beneath Bram's hand, began to shake.

There was a hush around the table.

"Mademoiselle . . ."

Rose opened her eyes and looked across the table into the Frenchman's smiling face. There was a quizzical bend to his brows, and the eyes themselves were narrowed, as if trying to fathom the sudden chill he felt in the room.

"Yes, Monsieur Valery?"

"You, mademoiselle, have lived in the South?"

"Monsieur, I was born in the South, near the city of Charleston, on a plantation. Several people call it the low country. I call it God's country."

Bram's hand was now like a vise on her knee. Rose removed it and turned to Camilla.

"Though she has removed every trace of her Southern speech, Lady Fontaine was also born in the South. Weren't you, Camilla?"

The beautiful blond returned Rose's stare with unwavering eyes. For the briefest of moments, Rose was sure she saw sadness in that gaze. But when she answered Rose, her eyes were slate-hard. "Yes, I was born in the South. But, like you, Rose, I was wise enough to leave."

"My leaving, Camilla, was not from choice. My return shall be."

Bram coughed and started to speak. But before he could utter a word, Rose had already turned back to Kate Chase.

"It is extremely difficult for me to have any sympathy for John Brown or any of his ilk. I think he was an extremist, a radical who used violence and was rewarded with violence. I also think he was a madman."

Again Kate laughed, but this time her laughter was far from light. "As a lady of the South, Rose, and a youthful one at that, you are naturally expected to hold somewhat callous views."

"Come, come, ladies," Henry Wilson said.

Suddenly a rumbling laugh filled the room, and all eyes turned to Lord Bevins. "Never mind, Henry, let the discussion continue! After all, isn't that why Monsieur Valery and I are here—to discuss the merits of the North *and* the South? Tell me, Senator Seward, what do *you* think?"

Rose turned with relief to Seward. He was a devout Northerner and an antislaver, but he had long railed against the radicalism of the abolitionists, both in the press and on the Hill. But Seward was squirming in his chair, his gaze wavering away from Rose's intent gaze, raptly studying the filigreed molding near the ceiling. "I met Brown only once. At that time, I thought him wild and visionary but singularly striking in appearance."

"Striking in appearance?" Rose repeated in dismay.

"That's what I said, Rose," Seward replied, giving her a look that she could only interpret as a warning.

She ignored it. "I heard you ... and it was said, Senator, like a true politician."

"Then perhaps," Seward replied through clenched teeth, "a better evaluation could be supplied by your fiancé." Here Seward paused and leaned around Rose. "I believe you represented the State Department at Brown's trial, Darcy. How did you find the man?"

Rose whirled on Bram. She had no idea he had attended the Brown trial. But then, she had very little idea just what Bram Darcy *did* do when he was pursuing his duties. He was the one man in Washington closest to her, yet the one man from whom she received no information.

Bram flashed a quick look at Rose before speaking. "I think Brown did indeed have an unsettled mind. But I also thought him a bold, truthful, and honest man. He saw the evils of slavery and in his own rather stupid way tried to rectify them."

"A stalemate!" Lord Bevins said, rising and patting his protruding paunch with satisfaction. "Shall we adjourn to brandy and cigars, gentlemen? I think it is time we got down to a serious discussion."

For Rose, it was not a stalemate. It was a betrayal.

As they moved into the hall, the men to the study, the women to a sitting room, Bram fell in step beside her. "Are you satisfied?" he whispered.

"Not completely," she replied in a tone of annoyance.

"You broke your promise to hold your tongue— but I must say, you did so with flair."

"Then you approve?"

"Of course not. You made an ass of yourself, and you did embarrass me."

"For that I apologize. But I made an even bigger ass out of Kate Chase."

"That you did, Rose, that you did."

He was chuckling as he turned into the study.

Rose hated the custom of men and women withdrawing to separate rooms after dinner. Within ten minutes she was totally bored with the talk of babies and embroidery and at the first opportunity asked several questions about the male dinner guests. She learned from Lady Bevins that her husband was one of the largest shipbuilders in England, and Camilla told her that Jacques Valery was a large munitions manufacturer and that Zack Chandler, who had been ominously quiet all through dinner, was a merchant trading worldwide in all sorts of commodities.

Slowly Rose began to piece things together. The dinner tonight—and the meeting taking place below in the study—was bringing together men of great wealth and strong beliefs. She ached to know what they were discussing.

Twice, Camilla had made subtle suggestions that Rose join her in the nearby dressing room, and Rose had ignored her.

The third time, she nodded in agreement.

They sat side by side in front of twin vanities, idly making repairs to their makeup and tucking stray strands of hair back into place. At last the idle chit-chat was over and Camilla came to the point. "From your words at the dinner table, Rose, I suspect that your heart is still in the South."

"I make no secret of it, Camilla. There are *some* of us who are still loyal Southerners."

In the mirror, Rose saw Camilla wince before speaking again. "What will you do when the war comes, Rose?"

"Do? I will have to do nothing. The Southern states will secede and there will be no war."

"Please, Rose, if there is one thing I have admired you for all these years, it is your intelligence. Mr. Lincoln will be elected, and he is committed to preserving the Union. Do not delude yourself. There *will* be war."

Rose could feel herself begin to perspire. "If there is war," she retorted, "the Yankees will run and hide. They're all cowards."

"Good God, you're talking like we talked when we were giggling girls parading our new bosoms in front of our first beaus at Cooper Plantation!"

Rose started to rise, but was immediately caught by Camilla's next words.

"Do you love Bram Darcy?"

"It's none of—"

"Do you?"

"Yes."

"And he loves you, Rose—enough to marry you, which is the supreme act for a man like Darcy."

"Listen, Camilla—"

"No, *you* listen. What are you going to do after you're married, when war burns like a grassfire over this country?"

Rose was shocked speechless by the sudden power of Camilla's words. With cold dread she realized where the conversation was going and where it would end. All she wanted to do was stop it.

But Camilla was now standing over her like a bird of prey. "What will you do, Rose? How will you live with yourself and a Yankee officer at the same time—a Yankee officer sworn to defeat the South, to bring it to its knees!"

Rose felt tears welling in her eyes. "Bram is from Baltimore," she babbled. "Maryland is a slave state. He'll go with the South."

"Maryland is a *border* state, and Bram will see to it that Maryland ultimately sides with the North."

"He won't!"

"He will. He has already started to do just that."

Rose looked up through the film that covered her eyes and tried to bring Camilla's face into focus. "He ... maybe he'll resign his commission."

"Never. If there is anyone in this country who believes in the sanctity of the Union, it is Bram Darcy. Even now, Rose, he is down there in the study preparing for war."

"*What?*"

"Yes. He is using the power of his family business, his personal charm and reputation, and his common sense to convince Lord Bevins and Jacques Valery not to aid the South when war comes. He has already convinced others in Europe and Canada, and he will convince more, that the South's cause is a hopeless one."

Rose thought that she would lose what dinner she had eaten. There was no stopping the flood of tears that welled from her eyes now, and she no longer cared.

All those fears she had pushed to the back of her mind, all those agonizing doubts, came rushing to the surface, forcing her to face them.

Bram would stay with the Union. As his wife, she would have to forget the South, forsake her childhood, her friends, deny her memories and her beliefs.

"I'm sorry, Rose." Camilla's hands were gentle on her shoulders. "I suppose he didn't tell you because he loves you so much, and he knows how you feel."

"We never talked. How would he know how I feel?"

"All Washington knows how you feel, Rose." Camilla gazed at Rose for a long moment before continuing. "You can believe me or not, Rose, but my own love for the South has not changed."

She paused, as if waiting for Rose to whirl on her. When she didn't, Camilla spoke again, her voice almost a whisper. "Any help I can give Bram and the North, here or in England, I give because I want to save the South from a long war. Because, Rose, if there is a long war, the destruction of our land will be terrifying. In the end, the South will lose. I would prefer the end be as quick and painless as possible."

Rose didn't know how long she sat staring at her own distorted image in the mirror after Camilla left the room.

He did lie, she thought, to himself and to me. Did he think he could change me, trap me, if I didn't learn all this until after our wedding?

Cat and Aunt Glynis knew. That was why Cat had urged her so vehemently to rush the wedding.

Bram had listened and nodded when she rambled on about her childhood at Belle Erin, about the deep love she felt for Charleston and the low country. He had calmed her with soothing words when she told him of the horrors of her father's death. And all the time he had been plotting the defeat of the South—before there was even a war.

Without repairing her tousled hair or her ruined face, Rose went downstairs. She easily found a servant—Kate Chase practically had them underfoot. "My things, please."

"It's powerful weather out there, Miz Jacquard. I gets the carriage."

"No, I'll walk."

"But, Miz—"

"I'll walk." She looked up into the handsome black face and smiled. "Are you free?"

"Yessum. I was borned right here in Washington—born free."

"So was I," Rose said, and walked out into the snow.

CHAPTER THIRTEEN

THE WASHINGTON DAILIES had announced the engagement and wedding plans of Rose Marie Jacquard and Major Bramfield Darcy on their society pages. There was no mention of the wedding's cancellation.

Word of the rift soon circulated through the parlors, the salons, and the hotel dining rooms of Washington. But reasons for the wedding's cancellation were only wild speculations. Only Rose, Bram, and, of course, Lady Camilla Fontaine knew the real story. And all three were tight-lipped, especially Rose, who tended to her aunt, but barely spoke to Catherine, who seemed to have crawled into a shell of her own.

Messages came daily from Bram Darcy. Rose returned them unopened. At least three times a week he came to call, pleading through Arleta or Catherine for an audience.

Rose refused to see him. Indeed, she not only withdrew from Bram and her close friends but also seemed totally unconcerned with the daily headlines and events of the world, even though all around her Washington was aflame with excitement.

Mr. Abraham Lincoln had accepted the Republican party's nomination for President, and his popularity was growing at an astonishing rate.

Secession became an all-too-real prospect to the Southerners in the Capital, but their Northern counterparts declared that "The Union of the North and the South is much like Adam and Eve—they cannot be separated."

Word came that soldiers were massing and drilling in the slave states.

But Rose paid attention to none of it. She now looked at the months past in the cold light of reason and reality. She realized her folly. Not for a second did she doubt her love for Bram Darcy, but neither could she deny the South. If war came—and she now knew that it would—she vowed that she would return to Charleston and do what she could for the Southern campaign.

The planned date of her and Bram's wedding arrived, and Rose stayed in her room, refusing to see even her sister.

"Rose . . . Rose . . . ?"

"Go away, Cat, I'm resting."

"But there is a message from Madame Foshay. She wants to know what she should do with the wedding dress."

There was silence from the room, and then the door was slightly opened and a coin purse thrust into Cat's hand. "Pay her, and thank her for her work. And tell her she can do whatever she likes with it." The door was abruptly shut again.

Late that afternoon, Cat knocked softly on the door once more.

"Go away!"

"Rose, there is a package for you from Madame Foshay," Cat said. "I'll leave it here." Quietly she stole back down the stairs.

For a long time Rose did not stir. Then, like an automaton, she moved to the door and retrieved the package. Carefully she lifted the lid and gazed at the contents of the box.

Her hands trembled as she slowly lifted the flounces of snow-white satin, her fingertips tracing the delicate pattern of pearls and lace that adorned the bodice and long, flowing train. She gathered her wedding gown around her, clutching it as if it were her lifeline to sanity, and then she crumpled to the floor and wept.

Glynis O'Rourke's health failed to the point that the determined old woman could no longer rally.

Her cough was constant, her body was racked with fever, and she was no longer able to eat.

Catherine and Rose prayed for a quick, painless end to her misery.

At last, during the first week of May, she was taken to Navy Hospital in a coma. For two days and nights, Rose and Cat remained at her side. She never regained consciousness, and during the evening of the third day she died.

Bram Darcy appeared at the funeral. He stood directly across the open grave from Rose and never took his eyes off her.

Rose found it impossible not to throw quick glances at him as the service was read. He had never looked so handsome in his crisply pressed uniform with its gold braid.

The uniform was blue.

Yankee blue.

In his eyes she could read his love, and it tore at her heart. She could also see sadness there, and knew it was caused by what he read in her own eyes.

How could you deceive me so?

At the conclusion of the service, she and Cat moved away quickly.

Bram caught them just before they reached their carriage. "Rose . . ."

"Good afternoon, Major," Rose said coolly. "Thank you for coming."

"My condolences, Rose. She was a wonderful woman."

"Yes, she was. Cat."

Catherine stepped into the carriage, but Bram continued to block Rose's way.

"Rose, I must talk to you."

"I think everything has been said, Major Darcy."

"Rose, I would have told you. The time just wasn't right."

"The time would never have been right. Excuse me."

"Rose, in a week's time I must go to London."

"I'm sure you must go where your *duty* takes you, Major."

"Must you be so—?"

"Yes, I must!" she cried in a voice loud enough to draw stares from the other departing mourners. Abruptly she moved around him, stepped into the carriage and slammed the door.

"Rose, I'll call on you tonight."

"I won't see you!" she hissed.

The carriage lurched forward and his face disappeared from the window.

Rose picked at a light supper with Cat and excused herself early.

Listlessly she undressed and donned her nightgown. She extinguished all but one wall sconce and lay down across her bed.

But she knew she would not be able to sleep—at least not until she knew that Bram Darcy would not come.

Try as she might, she could not still the desire that stirred in her. She closed her eyes and folded her arms beneath her aching breasts, her hands tightly clenched into fists.

Her skin suddenly felt feverish, and every pore cried out for the touch of his fingers, the feel of his lips.

Her body cried out for Bram Darcy, but her powerful mind denied him.

She heard a knock on the outside door, and then voices drifting up the stairs. A few moments later her own door opened a few inches.

"He's here, Rose," Cat said, her face barely lit in the shadows.

"I know. How many other times has he been here in the last few months, Cat?"

"More than I can count."

"And what did you tell him then?"

"That you were out, that you were indisposed, that you were sleeping and didn't want to be disturbed. Sometimes that you just never wanted to see him again."

"Then I'm sure tonight you'll not lack a reason to send him away."

Cat shook her head sadly. "I knew you could be hard, Rose, but I never realized just how hard you can be."

"If I had been harder in the beginning," Rose retorted, "I would have been wiser."

"He only wants to speak to you, Rose, to explain why he must do the things he does."

"I have all the explanation I need. Leave me alone, Cat."

Cat took a step into the room.

"Damn you," Rose hissed. "Leave me alone!"

The door closed quietly, and moments later Rose heard the carriage drive off.

She dozed, but was not able to let sleep completely overtake her. Her mind filled with the pained expression on Cat's face just before the door closed behind her.

Was she being fair to her sister? Catherine, she knew, was being torn apart by the same devils that plagued her. Soon Rose would return to Charleston and Cat would be left alone in this big house, for no amount of cajoling or pleading would make her sister return with her. With the storms that would one day soon engulf them, she might never see Catherine again.

Rose rolled from the bed and clutched her robe about her.

She would apologize.

Cat was not in her room. Rose went to the head of the stairs and called her name. When there was no answer, she called for Arleta. Still no answer. She was about to start down the stairs, when he stepped from the hall shadows onto the landing.

"They've gone out, Rose."

"Get out of here, Bram!"

"Not until I've had my say."

"We have nothing to say to each other!"

"I think we do." Deliberately he raised his foot to the first step and then began climbing the stairs.

Rose watched his catlike movements with both alarm and anticipation. Her first thought was to run, but her feet seemed rooted to the spot where she stood.

Her body cried out to him, but her mind screamed for reason; should she succumb to him now, all her days would be lived in doubt and remorse.

He was almost to the top of the stairs, his eyes and his hands reaching out to her, when her mind won.

"No!"

Whirling, she raced to her door. She could hear the heavy tread of his boots right behind her as she darted through the door and slammed it.

With trembling fingers she shot the bolt. As she backed away, a tiny scream bubbled to her lips. The hem of her nightgown and a good portion of her robe were caught in the door.

"Damn you, Rose, open this door or I'll make kindling out of it!"

"Dear God, can't you leave me alone?" Rose cried out.

In answer, his powerful shoulder smashed against the door.

Rose gasped and stepped backward. The material of her robe began to tear. She continued to retreat as his shoulder smashed again and again into the heavy door.

Slowly but surely, the bolt and the jamb began to give.

Rose lurched farther back into the room, and suddenly there was a rending tear and she stood naked as the bolt gave at last and the door flew inward.

"How dare you!" she screamed, tugging a coverlet from the bed and whirling it around her.

"I dare because I'll be damned if I'll leave Washington without forcing some sense into your stubborn head."

"Stubborn? Am I stubborn because I have my convictions? Are you the only one who is allowed convictions and the right to stand behind them?"

"No," Bram said levelly. "I say we should both hold to our convictions, but do it together."

"Impossible!"

Suddenly he swayed, both his hands coming up to massage his temples. "It's not impossible. There must be a way."

"They say it will be a war of brother against brother. Would you have it wife against husband?" she said, not trying now to hold back the tears that nearly blinded her.

Rose saw his eyes blaze with black fury. "Damn the North *and* the South!" he bellowed, starting toward her. "None of it has anything to do with us!"

"It has *everything* to do with us!" she retorted, and tried to run around him.

Bram made a grab for her, but his hand caught only the blanket. Rose's momentum carried her forward, right out of it.

Her shoulder struck the armoire and she whirled, her back to it, to face him stark naked.

They stood silently staring at each other.

Rose could do nothing to stop the gasping breath that caused her full breasts to rise and fall in a maddening rhythm. She was also powerless to stop his eyes from raking her, drinking in every inch of her trembling nakedness.

"Dear God, you are beautiful."

Rose could read only too clearly the intent in his eyes. If there was any doubt, it was dispelled when his coat slipped from his shoulders to the floor, quickly followed by his cravat and shirt.

"No."

"Yes."

"No, no, no, Bram . . . please."

There was a mixture of rage and lust in his eyes now that struck fear into the very core of her being.

"Don't, Bram, I beg of you."

"And I beg of you, Rose, don't fight it—don't fight us." He scooped her into his arms and carried her to the bed.

"Dear God, Bram, would you rape me?"

"Rape?" Bram tore at the remainder of his clothes. "If you think it rape now, my wild Rose,

I assure you you'll forget that it was an hour from now."

In a moment he was naked and on the bed beside her. Rose's mind was shot through with confusion, in turmoil with the burning flame that suddenly threatened to consume her body.

His hands cupped her breasts, and Rose shuddered as she felt her nipples instantly grow erect against his palms. She tried to protest, but all sound was muffled by his lips. The kiss was brutal, almost savage, but it grew tender as her struggling ceased.

One hand left her breast and moved over her belly, the fingertips playing across the soft, smooth skin, flicking lightly at the indentation of her navel.

Rose exerted all of her willpower to resist, but her body responded of its own accord to the exploring hand. Her heart was beating furiously, and her own hands began traveling over Bram's hard body, his muscles rippling beneath her caress.

Rose had not admitted to herself just how much she had missed him, physically as well as emotionally, in these past few agonizing months. Now she closed her eyes and gave herself up to the exquisite sensations he was causing in her hungry body, little cries and moans erupting from her constricted throat.

His lips joined his hands in exploring every inch of her heated skin, planting gentle kisses wherever they touched. And then his lips moved up the inside of her legs, and Rose cried out as he touched the soft hair between her thighs.

"I love you, my darling," Bram whispered, his voice a groan as he buried his face in the fragrance of her hair.

Rose's hips arched to meet his kiss, her brain reeling, on fire with the dizzying sensations his tongue was causing as it flicked and delved, again and again, into her honeyed sweetness.

Just when she was sure she could stand it no longer, that her body would explode, he lifted his face from between her thighs. "Love me, Rose. Please, love me," he whispered, his black eyes flashing as he lay back on the bed.

"Yes, my darling, yes!" she cried.

Without hesitation, she rolled atop him and pressed her mouth to his. She could feel his whole body tremble as he surged upward to meet her. His arms wound around her, clasping her to him in a fierce embrace that took her breath away.

Groaning with desire, she raised her body until she was kneeling astride him.

His cries matched her own as, with hunger driving her, she began to raise and lower herself around his hard, warm manhood. His hands cupped her breasts, teasing her nipples, increasing the hunger until she felt almost as much pain as pleasure.

She could feel his strong hands on her hips,

guiding her movements, his powerful thighs arching upward to meet her downward thrusts, driving himself into her again and again.

And then, as easily as a feather, he brought her body down beside his and rolled atop her, his thrusts never ceasing, but going deeper, faster, as they both desperately sought exquisite release.

Wrapping her arms around his back, Rose pulled him closer. She felt her heart thundering like a triphammer, fired to a response only the unleashing of her deep, suppressed emotion could bring. She could no longer deny the love she had fought so hard against.

Her skin burned like fire as it melded with his. And then she began to feel delicious shudders coursing all through her as they moved together in quickening rhythm until the fire in her loins consumed her entire being.

He felt it as well. He pulled her face to his and kissed her hungrily, allowing himself to give way to the tumult of emotion raging within his breast as he whispered soft endearments.

And then she locked her legs around him and urged him to thrust even deeper, as they were both seized in a tide of passion and swept toward the inevitable peak of ecstasy. She cried out as she felt a pleasure so intense it was almost torment—at the same time she felt the throb of Bram's warmth within her.

Slowly their rampant desire ebbed to a warm, satisfying glow, and she thought how wonderful it would be if they could stay like this forever. How delightful to lie in a quiet room and be fondled gently by the man you loved, protected from the ugly realities of the world by the circle of his embrace.

Her fingers combed through the dark hair on his chest.

"That's nice," she purred. "Have I ever told you what a magnificent body you have?"

"Kiss me."

She was almost startled by the intensity of his voice.

"Kiss me and tell me that you'll come with me to London."

Her body grew suddenly cold, as if some unseen hand had opened the windows and allowed the night air to enter the room.

Bram felt her tension and tightened his arms about her.

"If I were to go to London with you . . ."

"Yes."

"And marry you there—"

"You would make me the happiest man in the world."

"And, truthfully, it would make me the happiest woman."

"Then you'll go?"

For reasons only the darkest parts of her mind could fathom, Rose felt sudden modesty before his beseeching eyes. She slid from the bed and gathered what was left of her robe, covering as much of herself as she could. Then she walked to the window, parted the curtain, and looked out into the drab streets of Washington City.

"Rose . . ."

"There is a way, Bram," she replied quietly, "for us."

"Of course there is."

"We could go to London, be married, and stay there."

"What?"

"Stay there. Remove ourselves from this filthy war."

From the bed behind her there was an ominous silence. Rose used all her will not to turn and face him. She dreaded seeing what would now be in his eyes.

"Do you mean, Rose," he said at last, his voice soft, "that you want me to desert?"

"No. I want you to resign your commission, as I will turn my back on what I believe is my duty to the Southern cause."

There was a long silence, and then a deep sigh from the bed. "It's sad, but no man can live without honor . . . and, it seems, no woman."

"Then you refuse?"

"I cannot resign my commission, Rose."

She swallowed hard, and was amazed to see that her hand was not quivering at all on the curtain. "Then, Bram, my darling, my love, I shall not be going to London."

There was another long silence, and then she

heard the sound of his weight lifting from the bed. She heard him dress and pull on his boots.

It was then that she turned to face him.

He stood, ramrod straight, his jacket slung rakishly over one shoulder. His gaze was intent, and Rose felt that she saw a tiger lurking behind his eyes. "That is your final word?"

She nodded.

He moved to the door and, without turning, spoke again.

'We had a grand and glorious love, Rose Marie Jacquard. Good night, and good-bye."

A solitary tear squeezed from her eye and rolled down her cheek as Rose watched his broad back fade in the mist of the street.

A week later, Rose saw a notice that the ship *Algonquin* was sailing for England from New York. Among the passengers were Lady Camilla Fontaine and Major Bramfield Darcy.

She went to the closet, and from the rear of the top shelf retrieved the yards of white satin, lace, and pearls. In the downstairs sitting room she stoked the fire until the flames licked high into the chimney. When she was satisfied, she took two pairs of tongs and carefully laid her wedding dress in the flames.

It was only a few moments before a curious Catherine entered the room behind her. Rose heard her steps, but didn't turn. "Cat?"

"Yes, Rose."

"If Mr. Lincoln is elected, I shall be moving back to Charleston."

"I suspected as much."

"Will you be staying here?"

"Yes."

Rose only nodded, her gaze intent on the fire.

"Dear God, Rose," Cat exclaimed, gripping her arm, "what are you doing?"

Rose turned and took Cat into her arms. She held her sister's frail body to hers and returned her eyes to the fire. "Burning the past, Cat. I'm burning the past."

PART THREE

1860

CHAPTER FOURTEEN

Rose was slightly giddy from the champagne, and more than a little dizzy from whirling about the dance floor, but was glad she had finally succumbed to Hollis' pleading.

"Saratoga Springs is where everyone from back home will be for the month of August, Rose. We'll have a gay time. There will be horse racing and balls, and you can flirt with every man in sight. Please say you'll come. It may be the last fling for us all."

For most of the summer, Rose had said no. And then, the last week in July, Bram Darcy had returned to Washington from London. Rose couldn't bear to see him, and the fear that she might encounter him somewhere had become unbearable.

Now she was elated she had come. She had thoroughly enjoyed herself for three whole weeks, and this, the ball ending the last day of the racing season, was the grandest of all.

From the instant Rose had checked into the lavish United States Hotel, she promised herself that she would forget everything and have a good time.

Hollis had been right; many of the handsome officers she had already met at West Point, plus several others from the Citadel, who were now in the New Palmetto Guard, had come to Saratoga Springs for their last fling before pushing the Yankees into Canada.

Rose swam and dined and danced and flirted with them all. Perhaps, she thought, one would light her fires of fancy and extinguish the damnable flame burning inside her for Bram Darcy.

There had been, in the three weeks, only one solemn note. It came on the first morning of her arrival, when Hollis extricated her from a lively group and guided her into the hotel garden. "I've heard about you and Darcy, Rose. I am truly sorry. He's a fine officer, and a gentleman."

"And, Hollis, he is a Yankee."

"Is that why—?"

Rose placed a finger to his lips. "I don't wish to speak of it, Hollis."

But she quickly learned that it was not about her and Bram that Hollis wanted to talk. It was Cat.

"I'm afraid Cat will not change, Hollis. She fears the South. Sometimes I even think she hates it."

"Then she truly meant it when she told me that she would never return to Charleston."

"I'm afraid she did, Hollis. Can you don Yankee blue when this war comes down about our ears?"

"Never, Rose, you know that."

"Ah, Hollis, we all have our honor and our pride. And they will take second place to nothing—even love."

"Perhaps when all this is over . . ."

The sadness in his eyes and the pain suddenly etched across his face stabbed at Rose's heart. She hated to do it, but she felt it was best that he know. "Hollis, I truly believe that when all this is over, it will be too late."

"Too late? I don't understand."

"Catherine has been seeing Chance Flynn. At first it was just an occasional thing, but lately I think it has grown quite serious."

"Chance . . ." Hollis seemed unable to believe his ears. When he turned away rather than show Rose the further hurt in his eyes, she was tempted to tell him the rest of it, to reveal her own fears for Cat's well-being.

The day after Bram left Washington, Chance had called and asked for Rose. His intentions were only too clear, and Rose lost no time in relaying her own. To say that he was angry would have been a gross understatement. He was insanely furious. He had stomped from the house that day like a man possessed.

But he had returned, and this time it was to call on Cat.

At first Cat had merely tolerated him, but as he persisted, she had warmed to the relationship, enjoying Chance's intelligent wit and charming manner. In recent weeks she had seemed almost gay.

Rose couldn't bear to tell her sister that she thought Chance Flynn's pursuit of her was only spite toward Rose herself. She couldn't hurt Cat that way, any more than she could add more hurt to Hollis now.

"Brooding will not solve our problems, Hollis. You invited me to Saratoga Springs to forget and be gay, so let us do just that!"

He turned back to her with as much of a smile as he could muster. "I suppose you're right, Rose."

"Good. Now let's return to the party and I'll find you the prettiest girl there!"

"But that's you."

"Very well, then," Rose laughed, "you'll have to settle for the *second*-most-beautiful girl, and I shall flirt outrageously with the *second*-most-charming man."

It was toward the end of the first week when Rose met Clay Fulton. He was far from handsome, and his charm, Southern as it was, seemed almost calculating. He was tall, as tall as Bram, but lithe and thin. His face was gaunt, with a hook nose and ice-blue eyes that missed nothing. His voice when he spoke—which was not often—was reed-thin, as oddly arresting as it was grating on the ear.

For the first few days Rose couldn't understand what attracted her to Fulton beyond the fact that he was a rabid secessionist and a Southerner to the very marrow of his bones.

And then she began to understand. He was as self-assured and confident in everything he said and did as Bram. And, like Darcy, there was a devil that lurked somewhere deep inside him. He was surrounded by an aura of mystery, intrigue, even danger, that several of the women besides Rose sensed. Shortly after his arrival in Saratoga Springs, Clay Fulton became the center of feminine attention. But he gravitated toward Rose.

Rose was not so much at ease with Fulton's company and attention as she was intrigued by it. In keeping with the devil-may-care party atmosphere of August in Saratoga, Rose had missed no chance to flirt openly with Fulton. How far it would have gone, had he responded with more than a smile, and had Rose been able to submerge the image of Bram Darcy, she didn't know. But then, she hadn't been given the opportunity to find out: in the nearly three weeks they had been together, Fulton had not even tried to kiss her.

"You're frowning."

"Am I?" she said, forcing a light laugh. "Perhaps because tomorrow is the last day and we must all return to reality."

"Perhaps. Hollis tells me that you have made plans to return to Charleston."

"Yes, if Mr. Lincoln moves into the White House, and no one manages to burn it down around him, I'll be off for home."

"Home? You've lived for several years in Washington, Rose. Your Southern property has been sold, yet you still call the South home?"

"Haven't you heard?" Rose replied with a short laugh. "Home is where the heart is. And my heart has always been in Charleston."

"Ah, Rose, you have the traits of true Southern womanhood."

"And what might those be, Mr. Fulton?"

"Beauty, breeding, and intelligence."

"Thank you, sir." She smiled. "And I hope you have the two most endearing traits of a Southern gentleman."

He arched an eyebrow. "And what might those be?"

"An appreciation of a fine horse and a beautiful woman, of course."

"Oh, I do. Believe me, I do!"

"Then I find it odd . . ."

"What's that?"

"That in nearly three weeks, you have not once tried to kiss me."

Rose had expected her quip to elicit a roaring laugh or at least a chuckle from Fulton. It did neither. Instead, his icy eyes grew colder and a shroud of even greater intensity dropped over them. A tiny muscle rippled at the top of his jaw and then seemed to skitter down its length. "Perhaps I have an interest in you, Rose, that goes far beyond the appeal of your lips." His voice was almost cruel, and the grip of his arms about her matched his tone.

Then: "Come, let's stroll in the garden," he said quite coolly.

Rose was baffled by his sudden change in mood, but she let him lead her through the tall French doors and across the veranda.

Jasmine and honeysuckle scented the warm night air, and a huge moon bathed the hotel gardens as Fulton chose a path and tugged her along.

When they were some distance from the hotel, near a whispering fountain, he stopped. Grasping her shoulders, he turned her body to his and tilted her chin up with a finger. "You're very beautiful, Rose. But then, I'm sure you know that."

"I somehow get the feeling that you are still not going to kiss me," she murmured, the intense stare in his eyes threatening to mesmerize her.

"You are very popular in the capital. You have access to all the best homes of Northerners and Southerners alike."

"Yes," she stammered, both angry and curious at the same time.

"What will you do in the South if secession leads to war?"

"Do? I don't know. I—"

"There will be an abundance of nurses, of seamstresses. You will be one of many doing the same thing if you return to Charleston."

She shrugged from his grasp and, with a swirl of her skirts, placed the small fountain between them. "I dislike playing games, Clay. If you mean to say something, say it!"

His lips spread until Rose could see the even whiteness of his teeth in the moonlight. For some reason she couldn't fathom, his smile chilled her. Here, she thought, was truly a man like Bram Darcy, a man to be reckoned with, perhaps feared.

"Your sympathies are entirely with the South?" he asked.

"Yes."

"Unwaveringly?"

"Of course."

"Even though you nearly married one of the brightest lights in the Yankee officer corps?"

Why had he asked that? What did her relationship with Bram Darcy have to do with a walk on a moonlit garden path?

Fulton's voice was like the crack of a whip in the stillness. "Well, Rose?"

"Major Darcy *is* a Yankee—and that's why I only *nearly* married him."

Again the smile. "That he is, Rose. Here, let's sit."

Rose allowed herself to be guided to a stone bench. Fulton slowly and elaborately clipped a thin cigar. When it was lighted, he turned again to face her. "I am going to tell you, Rose, how one day you can be of more value to the South than you ever dreamed."

Rose's eyes grew wide and her heart beat faster, and then even faster, as Clay Fulton revealed his own part in the future Confederacy and the part he wanted her to play.

He was organizing a network of well-entrenched people in the North, men and women to gather and relay information to the South in the event war came. Already there was a swift-flowing stream carrying bits and pieces of intelligence southward under his direction. By the time war came—if Lincoln was elected—Clay Fulton and his Southern superiors wanted that stream to be a wide, rushing river.

"It won't be easy, Rose. In fact, it will be very, very dangerous. In the North, you'll be considered a traitor."

Rose licked her dry lips and nervously twisted the fan she held in her hands.

Spy!

For weeks she had tormented herself with questions. What would she do once she arrived in Charleston? To what use would she put her idle hands and brain to help drive the demon of Bram Darcy's memory from her heart?

Now Clay Fulton was practically paving a path for her.

Or was he?

Could she do the things he asked in a Washington that, for her, was filled with Bram?

"I know, Rose, that I ask a great deal. It will be difficult to remain in Washington and appear neutral, when your sympathies are for the South. You will have to be an actress, quick and adept, with those who will constantly question your status and your sincerity."

Rose smiled at the irony. She was sure she could be a very good actress indeed. And the danger didn't frighten her. Quite the opposite, in fact. The idea of spying for the South intrigued her. Already, as she turned her eyes to meet Clay Fulton's, adrenaline was shooting through her body.

Her thoughts returned to the vast, rolling fields of South Carolina she so loved. She conjured up in her mind's eye the sprawling, beautiful plantations and genteel people who populated them. She remembered the easy, gracious way of life she had known and loved as a young girl. The very idea of that life being trampled by the Union boot brought bile up into her throat.

As if that were not enough, Clay Fulton's next words sealed her decision: "And most of all, Rose, you can take pride in knowing that you will be bringing a quick end to this war, that you will be saving lives on both sides by helping us beat the Yankees as quickly as possible. Will you do it, Rose?"

Rose looked into his clear eyes for a long moment, her intensity matching his. "I will," she whispered. "With all my heart and soul, to the war's very conclusion—whatever it might be."

Rose's head was swimming by the time she returned to Washington, but from the hour of her arrival, she began to put into practice all of Clay Fulton's suggestions.

She used every minute of her time, every acquaintance, every invitation, to her best advantage. She concentrated on cultivating men of influence, from both the North and the South. She played her cards with the greatest care, keeping up all her Northern contacts and circulating freely on the social scene.

And as the drift of the South and the mood of the North took on unalterable shape, she hid her partisan feelings behind a bland yet radiant smile. She continued to consort with the men of the North when her Southern friends were cutting them dead. But she did it with a purpose, deliberately cultivating the strong antislavery element.

Rose hardly realized it herself, but in agreeing to help Clay Fulton she had, almost overnight, left her girlhood behind. Her eye was quick to see everything around her now, and her mind even quicker to weigh its worth.

In the weeks that followed, Hollis visited her several times, bringing instructions and returning South with information Rose had gleaned. During one of his visits, Rose was given a jolt that nearly tumbled her resolve.

"It has been rumored, Rose," Hollis told her, "that Darcy's duties as a military diplomat will soon end."

Rose kept a vacant expression on her face as she nodded in reply. "I've heard the same rumors."

"With his many contacts in the South, in Europe, and here in Washington City, he may well be placed in a high intelligence position."

Here Hollis paused. His features grew taut and a haunted look filled his eyes. It was obvious to Rose that her old friend hated what he was about to say.

"Clay has suggested that it might help a great deal if you were to recultivate your friendship with Darcy." He nearly choked on the words, and Rose's heart turned to ice as they reached her ears.

"Never, Hollis," she replied with all the resolution she could muster. "I would never betray Bram, as I know he would never betray me."

"I know," Hollis stammered, and then sighed in relief. "I have done my duty and relayed Clay's request. Now let's on to other things."

There was no further mention of Bram Darcy, but a tiny thought, a doubt, had been planted in the far recesses of Rose's mind. Would there, one day, after all, come the time when she would have to betray Bram in this dangerous game she played?

On two occasions, Fulton himself came stealthily by night. For hours, by candlelight, they pored over intricate ciphers he had devised. These, he told her, would be necessary when there was no longer any open travel between the North and the South.

Catherine, ignorant of Rose's intrigues, was elated at the sudden change in her sister's mood. Gratefully she threw herself into the redecorating of the house on H Street that Rose had planned.

"From top to bottom, Cat, we will make it new. But we must pay particular attention to the salon and the dining room, for I plan on doing a great deal of entertaining—a very great deal of entertaining."

Walls were removed to make the first-floor rooms more spacious. New carpets were ordered, and the newly installed windows were draped with the most expensive and tasteful fabrics available. Bone china and silver were acquired to augment their aunt's already large collection. A coach and a matched pair of fine horses were purchased to aid Rose in her afternoon and evening trips from house to house and hotel to hotel.

Only once did Catherine voice any alarm. "Rose, how extravagant we have become!"

"Pay no heed, little sister," was Rose's reply. "It is for a good cause."

"Cause?"

"Gaiety!" Rose replied with a short laugh. "We'll need much of it in the gloomy days ahead."

It was impossible to completely avoid Bram, even though the many hostesses in Washington did their best not to include the two of them on the same guest list. When meetings did occur between them, they were brief, consisting of little more than chill greetings and a mundane exchange of amenities.

Rose was proud of herself, in that after each of these encounters she was able to retain her facade of gaiety and outward calm. It was only later, alone in her own room, that she would sit at the window, slowly rocking, her arms tightly hugging her sides.

Her mood was like the city she saw through misty eyes: cold, dark, and lonely. Soon the glass would fog before her, the houses and dimly lit streets would recede, and the tall, erect figure of Bram would take their place. Black fire seemed to flow from his eyes. His nostrils were mere slits, and his lips were thinned into a cruel line. Try as Rose might, she could see no hint of regret in his demeanor. Quite the opposite; she saw resolution, accusation, and worst of all, cold dismissal.

By the time she turned away from this image to stumble to her bed, tears would be flowing down her cheeks.

Only once did Bram approach her alone. It was after an evening at the theater. Tired of waiting for her own carriage to arrive in the long line waiting on C Street, she lifted her skirts and began to trudge the rotting board sidewalk. She had gone the length of a few carriages, just beyond the pale light from the theater-front gaslamps, when his voice arrested her movement like a hand of iron.

"Rose."

She willed her legs to continue, but they turned to stone. Frantically her eyes pierced the semidarkness in search of her tan carriage and the pair of spirited bays.

And then he was before her, the dim illumination from the lamps behind her casting eerie shadows over his brooding face.

"Good evening, Major Darcy. I didn't notice you in the audience."

"I wasn't in the audience," he replied, his voice oddly tense and gruff. "I've been outside the theater for the last half-hour waiting for you."

"For me? Whatever for?"

"Don't be flip, Rose. I want to talk to you."

Suddenly there was a soft pleading in his voice. Rose forced her eyes upward to meet his gaze, and a knot formed in the pit of her stomach.

"We have nothing to say, Bram."

"We do, Rose, more than you know. May I walk you to your carriage?"

"If you wish," she replied with a shrug.

He fell into step beside her, and entwined his arm with hers. She found herself giddy at his closeness, and time seemed to stand still. She closed her eyes against the dizziness that threatened to overtake her, and felt her mind soar up into the dark night sky. She only returned to earth at the sound of his voice.

"You're redecorating your aunt's house."

"Yes," she replied instinctively, before realizing how unfitting to the situation his statement was. "It's almost finished."

"I find that rather odd."

"How so?"

"With all the Southern ladies in Washington shopping for trunks and valises, I thought you, too, would be packing. I mean, what with the coming election so near."

"Why should I think of moving? I don't know for sure that Mr. Lincoln will be elected."

"The hell you don't, Rose," Bram growled, his

head bent toward her ear until his voice sounded like thunder. "You, I, and everyone else in this country know that he will be elected. And we also know what will happen after he is."

"Yes, we do," she said, her voice almost a whisper. "Here's my carriage."

She started to step away, but Bram held her firmly by one arm and grasped the other to turn her to him.

"You're not going back to Charleston, are you?"

"It's none of your business where I go or don't go. But, no, I'm not."

"Why?"

"Because Washington is my home," she blurted, unable now to meet his penetrating stare.

"I don't think that's the only reason, Rose. I'm elated that you're staying in Washington, of course. It means that I can at least see you. But I'm worried about the real reasons you've elected to desert your beloved South."

He knows! she thought wildly. Oh, dear God, he knows! But how could he? She had done nothing yet—at least, not much.

She blinked, her mind a riot of confusion. She must say something quickly, something gay and flip. But before she could speak, Bram had moved them farther into the shadow of the carriage and his hands had slid to the small of her back.

"I love you, Rose. Even if we stand on different sides of this wall that every day grows higher and wider and won't let us touch, I love you."

"No! Don't, Bram, please!" Her body was pressed to his now, with only her hands between his chest and her throbbing breasts.

"My only hope is that one day this madness will end. And when that day comes, we can . . ."

Her legs were turning to water, and in another second she knew that her arms, of their own volition, would crawl up to encircle his neck and bring his lips down to hers.

She wanted to shout, to scream at him to stop it, to stop torturing her, to leave her in peace to do what she must do.

But no words would come.

"In a few months, this whole city will be a quagmire of intrigue, Rose. Please, promise me that you won't become a part of it."

"Let me go, Bram. We said our good-byes and went our separate ways months ago. Leave it at that. Please, let me go."

The last was a barely audible whisper, nearly silenced by a sobbing choke in her voice.

"Dammit, Rose, I love you, and you love me—"

"No."

"You do. I see it in your eyes across a room. I sense it in the little quiver of your lips when you speak. Even Cat has told me—"

Using all the strength in her arms, Rose pushed against his chest, freeing herself from his grip. She almost fell, but managed to right herself when her back struck the carriage door.

"Cat?"

"Yes, I—"

"You use my sister to spy on me?"

"Not spy, Rose. I only inquire of you when we meet."

"Oh? And where do you meet—shopping at Maureen's, or perhaps while she has a fitting at Madame Delarue's? Or perhaps you just run into each other at Lemmond's in the pursuit of ladies' boots, or at market when she does the weekly shopping! Cat is hardly a social butterfly these days, Bram. If you met in any of those places, I hardly think it was by chance."

Fury filled his face, but before he could speak, Rose whirled and stepped into the carriage. With a quick rap of her fist she caught the bored coachman's attention.

Bram's face appeared at the open window just as a whip cracked and the horses leapt forward. "Rose—"

"Good night, Major Darcy. And good-bye."

Her mind was in turmoil and her body felt sick with frustration during the short ride to H Street.

Dear God, she thought, I would spy on a city, an army, a whole government, without ever thinking that my own blood, my sister, could also be spying—on me. What will become of us when the rail-splitter comes to Washington?

* * *

A week later, November 6, election day dawned over Washington with bleak, gray clouds.

As had been her wont each morning for months, Arleta brought the morning papers, Northern and two-day-old Southern, along with Rose's morning tray. And as was Rose's habit, she read the Southern papers first.

The Charleston *Mercury* branded Lincoln a border ruffian, a vulgar mobocrat, and a South-hater. "And before the South will submit to such humiliation and degradation as the inauguration of Abraham Lincoln, the country will see the Potomac crimsoned in human gore and Pennsylvania Avenue paved ten fathoms deep with mangled bodies!"

Rose could read no further. Shuddering, she gathered the papers and padded to the fireplace, where they were added to the crackling early-morning log.

All through the day, word of secessionist activity in the South flowed into the Capital alongside the election returns.

Rose spent the day in a flurry of activity to keep her hands occupied and her mind from the inevitable. In odd moments, the image of Bram Darcy would flash before her eyes and she would lapse into a deep depression.

By nightfall there was no doubt. Abraham Lincoln had been elected the sixteenth President of the United States.

All over the Capital there were minor riots spawned by secessionists. But above the shouting and the sounds of pistols could be heard bands playing "The Old Gray Mare."

It was the new President's campaign song.

CHAPTER FIFTEEN

EARLY-MORNING torrents had turned the streets of
Washington City to ooze. So soft and bottomless
was the mud that carriages became mired hub-
deep within a few feet.

Now a light drizzle fell laconically from a
drab gray sky. But the rain, the chill air, and
the mud gripping their boots were not enough
to stop Rose and Cat and a hundred others from
trudging up Capitol Hill this January day.

Within days after the election, Palmetto ban-
ners had replaced the Stars and Stripes of the
Union in Charleston. Throughout the state, booming artillery had echoed above a shrill call to
arms.

South Carolina had seceded, and, one by one,
the other cotton states had followed. On this

day Mississippi would follow its neighbors, and the die would be cast.

Weeks before, Rose had made this same trek. Then the occasion had been President Buchanan's farewell address.

Now, clutching Cat's arm and moving steadily with the crowd toward the Senate chambers, Rose could vividly recall every dramatic moment of that morning.

Buchanan, always a vacillating man, had that day taken a stand at last. He had stood before the Senate, his aging face a mask of sadness, his eyes red-rimmed and weary. In a barely audible voice he had proclaimed his belief that the question of slavery had at last reached and passed its culminating point.

There was a low mumble of disapproval, mostly from the Southern side of the aisle. Cotton-state senators exchanged wary, knowing glances. For them, slavery was not the argument in question. It was states' rights, the rights they felt were due them as freemen.

The rumble of discontent seemed to put iron into the spine of the outgoing President. He stood straighter and his graying head came up so that his eyes could, almost accusingly, sway across the room.

"The fact is, our Union rests upon public opinion, and can never be cemented by the blood of its citizens shed in civil war. If it cannot live in the affections of the people, it must one day perish. Congress possesses many means of preserving it by conciliation. But the sword was not placed in their hand to preserve it by force."

Here he paused, again scanning the room with cloudy eyes.

From her seat in the gallery, Rose had looked down into the Senate chamber. On both sides of the aisle she saw cold, unyielding faces.

On the Northern side were men who hated slavery but loved power. Across the aisle were men of the Southern ideal. They believed in their gentility, their breeding, and, to a man, they retained a romantic conception of honor that no threat of death or war could diminish.

Buchanan knew this. He could read it on every upturned face. But to his credit, he continued his plea.

"May I be permitted to invoke my countrymen to pause and deliberate, before they determine to destroy this, the grandest temple which has ever been dedicated to human freedom since the world began. It is not every wrong—nay, it is not every grievous wrong—which can justify a resort to such a fearful alternative. This ought to be the last desperate remedy of a despairing people, after every other constitutional means of conciliation has been exhausted!"

The well of the chamber was as silent as a tomb as Buchanan made his way up the aisle and exited. But in the gallery there was muffled weeping.

The reaction that day to the President's plea for peace had been all too clear: there would be war.

In the days and weeks since, tension had mounted toward this day when the cotton-state senators themselves would proclaim officially, before Congress, their departure from the Union.

At the huge doors, Rose produced their pass. Cat suddenly held back. "Must we, Rose?"

"We must," Rose replied, determined to witness the day's events.

Cat chewed at her lower lip for a moment longer, sighed in resignation, and at last followed Rose as she made her way to the cloak room.

The small room was a crush of bodies, made worse by the ladies' huge hoops and crinolines. Several people spoke to the sisters in passing. Usually Cat replied, while Rose remained silent and withdrawn.

Her mind seethed with the reality of this day. Secession was no longer a word. In the next few hours it would be a fact, and she was determined to see it.

Late the previous evening, a messenger had appeared at the door of the H Street house with a letter:

My dearest Rose,

For all your outward neutrality and your sudden decision to stay in Washington, I know

*that in your heart you remain true to the South
that bore you. For that reason, I cannot claim
all of you.*

*Know this, dear Rose, that as an officer in
the Union Army and a man of reason, I am
and always will be as true to my beliefs as you
are to yours.*

*And I, like you, truly believe that our love
would wither and die if you, as my wife, were
forced to stand by silently while your husband
fought with all his heart and soul against the
South you so love.*

*I have been informed that tomorrow the sena-
tors from Florida and Alabama, as well as Mr.
Davis from Mississippi, will announce their
valedictories. By so doing, Rose, the Southern
Confederacy will be formed and, I am sure, the
gauntlet thrown.*

*If we must go our separate ways while this
catastrophe grips our nation, I pray that neither of us will hurt the other, so that when all is
calm once more, our paths may merge again.*

> *Your most obedient and loving,*
> *B. Darcy*

Dry-eyed, but with a churning in her breast
that left her gasping for breath, Rose had read
the letter over and over again.

Bram had seen through her facade. He knew
that no matter what happened, she would never
disavow the South.

What strange turns would their lives take if
one day he learned of her perfidy and intrigues?
What chance then would there ever be for their
"paths to merge" again?

Rose lay awake for hours, her head spinning. Near dawn, she had made her decision, and it did not change the vow she had made months before to Clay Fulton in a scented garden in Saratoga.

She would never love another man as she loved Bram Darcy. But in the days, weeks, months, even years ahead, she would suffer that love in silence.

And that afternoon she would attend the Senate chambers to hear the speeches that would prove to be the birth of the Confederate States of America.

Rose watched Varina Davis take her place in the gallery, her head held high. She wore a high-necked dress of pale blue velvet, lightly flounced and gathered tightly at her tiny waist. Woven through the skirt were indigo ribbons, and matching dark blue lace adorned her throat and wrists.

It was a dress that said much. No black of mourning for the sundering of the Union. Not for the wife of Jefferson Davis, even though in her large lustrous eyes Rose was sure she saw fear.

Like the senators in the chamber below, the ladies in the gallery had seated themselves on opposite sides of the aisle. To the right, the blue cockade lapel buttons of the secessionists gleamed as brightly on the bodices of the Southern ladies as the colors of the Union shone on the left.

Rose had wisely chosen to wear neither—she had dressed for the occasion in heavy pale green silk—and she guided Cat to a seat near the center, as if that alone would declare the neutrality she did not feel. As she sat, her gloved hands calmly folded in her lap, she heard the thin, demure voice she knew so well call her name.

She turned slightly. "Good day, Varina."

"I've saved a place for you, Rose. Come, sit here with us."

The moment had come, and Rose met it with a growing knot in her breast that threatened to choke the beating of her heart. Carefully she turned until her eyes met the other woman's. A lump formed in her throat and she had to swallow twice before she could speak. "No, thank you, Varina. I do think I will be much more comfortable here."

Varina Davis' face paled. Her eyes misted slightly and one hand went involuntarily to her throat.

It was a clear and open rebuke, and the woman took it as such. Rose quickly turned her face front, rather than see more of the hurt that was so evident in her old friend's eyes.

"My, oh my, will wonders never cease?"

The voice came from several spaces to Rose's left. She didn't have to turn to recognize its owner.

Kate Chase.

The deed was done. Rose Marie Jacquard was not exactly in the Northern camp, but she was definitely not in the Southern one, either.

With deaf ears, Rose waited through the brief speeches of the senators from Florida and Alabama.

And then, as a hush fell over the whole of the vast room, Rose, like everyone around her, leaned forward in anticipation.

Slowly, like an uncoiling spring, Jefferson Davis rose from his chair. His height and his thin-lipped, gaunt face dominated the very air they breathed.

Slowly, in a low, melodious tone, he began to speak.

He justified secession on the basis that all the states were sovereign. He declared officially the secession of his state, Mississippi, from the Union. And then he paused.

Around her, Rose could hear the unsnapping of reticules as handkerchiefs were found. Already she could hear a few choking sobs, and sensed that her own eyes had begun to tear.

Davis' voice had risen now until it was like a mellow trumpet sounding his words throughout the chamber: "I repeat, gentlemen, that secession is justified upon the basis that the states are sovereign. There was a time when none denied it. I am sure I feel no hostility to you, Senators from the North. I am sure there is not one of you, whatever sharp discussion there might have been between us, to whom I cannot now say, in the presence of God, I wish you well. . . . It only remains for me to bid you a final adieu."

With a regal bow, Davis turned and, accompanied by sobs, shouts, and applause, strode up the aisle and exited the Senate chamber for the last time.

He had barely disappeared when a deathly silence fell over the room. It was as if, in that instant in time, reality had commanded all sound to still and all movement to cease.

And in the gallery, Rose sat with steel in her back, her eyes suddenly dry.

It was done. Very soon the representatives of the cotton states would meet in Montgomery, Alabama, to draft their own constitution and elect their own president. Many of these men would urge caution, as Buchanan had. Others would damn the North and cry out that only the sword would determine the fate of the new nation and create a lasting peace.

Only God knew which voices would win out when the last word was finally uttered.

But for Rose it mattered little. She knew exactly what part she would now be playing in the strange drama to come.

Almost overnight, the sounds of the Old Tucker and the Virginia Reel faded from the great rooms of the fine old Southern-style mansions. And in

the great hotel ballrooms, satin-slippered feet
no longer flew through the steps of Fox and
Geese.

Even before Lincoln's inauguration, the mass
migration southward began. Each day, wagons
laden with furniture, linen, silver, and china—
all belonging to Washington City's Southern
aristocracy—rattled by the house on H Street,
headed for the Virginia Post Road, and Dixie.

Rose watched the exodus behind a mask of
indifference.

Once, while out walking, she paused to peer
between the boards covering a window of Mrs.
Benjamin Tayloe's glorious mansion, Octagon.
The interior, with its chandeliers and mirrors
draped, its paintings covered, and its elaborate
moldings gathering dust, looked ghost-haunted.

Rose returned home that day with shuffling
steps and a heavy heart. Suddenly she felt very
lonely. All her Southern friends had disappeared,
and the few that had remained would most probably shun her because of what she must do.

Cat met her in the parlor. "Rose, are you all
right? Are you ill?"

"They are gone, Cat. All of them are gone,
home to the South."

"Oh, Rose, I know how you feel. If you want
to go, you can. You need not fear for me. I shall
be fine here, truly I will."

Rose met her sister's innocent gaze for only a
moment before her conscience forced her to avert

her eyes and run for the stairs. She knew that in another moment she would blurt out the truth.

"Rose . . ."

"Yes?"

"I *will* be all right, you know."

"We both will, darling."

"No, Rose, what I mean is that Chance has asked me to marry him."

Rose halted at the top of the stairwell, her quivering hand grasping the banister for support. She didn't turn, fearful that Cat would see the anguish on her face.

"We would like your blessing, Rose."

"Are you sure, Cat, very sure?"

"Yes, I am. What is it, Rose?"

How could she tell Cat what she saw in Chance Flynn's eyes each time he entered their parlor? How could she explain to Cat how Chance's eyes roamed over her body like a man starved each time they met?

"Does he love you, Cat?"

"Oh yes, Rose, so very much."

"Then you have my blessing. When?"

"Soon—we hope."

"Don't be too rash. The days ahead could very well bend, even break, a marriage."

Cat was about to answer, but Rose had already run down the hall and entered her own room.

The rest of January and February matched the gray of Rose's mood. But she hid her true feelings behind disarming smiles and light banter. Each morning she made a new resolve to submerge all thoughts of her own safety, of Bram Darcy, of anything that did not further the Southern cause. She even forced doubts of Cat's impending marriage from her mind as she solidified her position as a neutral hostess in a Northern capital.

The refurbishing of the house was at last complete. The paint was barely dry before Rose sent out her cards.

At first they came slowly, these newcomers to Washington who would play a part in the Republican administration. After all, Rose Jacquard was a Southern belle—or at least she had been.

But Rose was witty and charming, and soon the new elite of Washington were clamoring for invitations to her teas and her small, select dinner parties.

Even though Senator Seward had campaigned bitterly against Lincoln for the Republican nomination, he backed him wholeheartedly for President. When Lincoln made Seward his chief adviser, Seward's appointment was celebrated at a dinner given by Rose Jacquard. The afternoon Simon Cameron of Pennsylvania was named Secretary of War, he received an invitation to dine that very evening at Rose Jacquard's.

By the time Mr. Lincoln arrived in Washington a week before the inauguration, Rose knew his entire cabinet.

It was soon evident, after Mrs. Lincoln's arrival, that Kate Chase would have a very high place in the new First Lady's "court," as it was soon called. Almost overnight, Rose became an intimate of Kate Chase.

Inauguration Day was sunny but cold. Neither of the Jacquard sisters attended, even though they had both received passes: Cat, because Chance Flynn was to be part of the cavalry guard that would escort Lincoln from Willard's to the Capitol, and she would be unescorted; Rose, because she had a sudden headache that had become so severe that it had caused a queasy stomach. Actually, she couldn't bear to watch the tall Westerner sworn in, believing as she did that he was the man who intended to crush the South.

For days, people had poured into the city from all over the North. There was not a hotel room to be had. Men slept uninvited on private porches, in market stalls along the streets, in piles of lumber, or in the streets themselves.

Assassination rumors had been flying from everyone's lips for days. Even Rose had speculated: Would the cotton states be left in peace if Lincoln was not sworn in? But, sitting at her window, with the strains of "Hail to the Chief" reaching her from Pennsylvania Avenue, she said a prayer that nothing would happen that day, for she knew that it was not one man who would bring about the dark days ahead; it was a great many men, and the killing of one would only inflame all the others.

It was early afternoon when Mrs. Greenhow came to call. Rose pleaded her headache, but the woman was insistent.

"Please have her come up here, Retha."

Rose received her in the tiny parlor off her bedroom.

When they were settled, Mrs. Greenhow wasted no time. "Well, it is done."

"Done?" Rose said innocently.

"Lincoln is President and it's only a matter of time until there is war. Soon the Capital will be sealed off, because Maryland and Virginia will opt for the South."

Mrs. Greenhow was smiling broadly as she said this. Her attitude and her manner gave Rose pause. She studied the woman carefully, as if seeing her for the first time. For years now, Rose had attended Washington functions with this woman. She considered her a friend, mostly because of her Southern leanings. But now, the very afternoon of Lincoln's inauguration, she realized that she knew almost nothing about this aristocratic widow sitting in her parlor.

The smile widened on Mrs. Greenhow's handsome face as she recognized the perplexed curiosity in Rose's wide eyes. "I admire you, Rose, in many ways. I'm sure it has taken a lot of grit for you to take a neutral stance in these months since you returned from Saratoga."

Truly alarmed now, Rose leapt to her feet. She was about to babble that neutrality was indeed her current attitude, when Mrs. Greenhow grasped her by the hands and gently returned her to the chair.

"I daresay that in the days to come I won't be able to do the same, Rose. No, even though I will serve the South every way I can, I will not be able to still my tongue from lashing the Yankees when my temper rises." She paused, her clear gray eyes locking with Rose's, and when she spoke again, her voice was barely more than a whisper. "Perhaps that is why Clay Fulton has given you the instructions he has."

"Dear God," Rose gasped, "do you mean. . . . ?"

"I mean, Rose, that by playing the part of the neutral, you may well gather more and better information than I. Of course, it will be through me that you will pass your information to Colonel Fulton and the Confederacy."

Rose was aghast. In her youthful and naive way, she hadn't dreamed that others, particularly other women, would also be carrying out Clay Fulton's orders.

At this, Mrs. Greenhow roared with laughter. "Ah, dear, sweet Rose, by the time war comes, Washington will be a hotbed of spies for the Southern cause!" She lapsed into silence when Retha entered with a silver tray of tea and cakes, but as soon as the servant was gone, she leaned forward and spoke again in a conspiratorial manner.

Rose realized for the first time just how deeply she was involved in intrigue.

Clay Fulton had become General Beauregard's adjutant general. As such, he now handled a vast network of spies recruited as far back as two years before.

With secessionist activity at a white-hot peak in Baltimore, and the Virginia Convention already meeting to decide which way that state would go, it was imperative that Fulton learn the Yankee plans for defending Washington City. If Washington could be taken in the first days of the fighting, the war might be ended then and there.

As Rose listened, excitement rippled along her spine. It was as if she were once again in the low country around Charleston, baiting danger by riding her spirited mare at breakneck speed over the plowed fields and down the narrow country lanes.

The two women spoke until light faded from the windows and the wall sconces cast eerie shadows over their rapt, intense faces.

At last Mrs. Greenhow stood and Rose helped her into her velvet walking cloak.

"Anything for the Confederacy, Rose—that must be our motto. Here in the North our deeds will be looked upon as cold treason. But in the South they will be considered patriotism." At the door she turned to face her new protégée one last time. "There is one more thing, Rose."

"Yes?"

"Do you still feel anything for Major Darcy? Indeed, I must be blunt—do you still love him?"

Try as she might, Rose could not summon a denial of her love for Bram, nor could she directly meet Mrs. Greenhow's stare.

"I see." The woman sighed and took Rose into her arms. Gently she kissed her on both cheeks. "It is a pity, my dear, and my heart goes out to you. But once again I admire your courage and your loyalty. Let us just hope that the future unpleasantness is over quickly."

"Yes," Rose replied over the lump that had risen in her throat, "very quickly."

News flowed from the South as swiftly as underground information from Washington flew into it.

The Confederacy was formed, with Jefferson Davis as its President. Demands came from Montgomery that Washington turn over all federal properties to the new nation. The South blazed with gold-fringed gray uniforms and glinting arms.

From Charleston to Texas could be heard the strains of "Dixie" and "The Last Waltz," telling

the world that the fires of Southern patriotism
burned to the skies.

In Washington there was the atmosphere of a
new era. Rose could see it, feel it, even smell and
touch it all around her on her daily forays around
the city. The accents were harsher, making her
own Southern speech stand out in company.
There was less grace and good manners in the
salons, and even the food seemed coarser. For
years, men had sported goatees and well-groomed
imperial beards. Now, with Lincoln in the White
House, full beards became the vogue. Creams
and unguents were hawked that assured men
they could sprout a full beard in six weeks. But
there was another mood, not so light, in the
Northern capital: fear. It stemmed from the question on everyone's lips: Would the Virginia Convention vote with the South?

Ultimately, the threat of war seemed to hinge
on the question of whether the last two federal
properties in the South—Fort Sumpter in Charleston Bay and Fort Dickens in Pensacola harbor—
would be turned over to the Confederacy.

Seward, in random conversation at Rose's
table, hinted that since Sumpter was of little
military value, the fort would most likely be
evacuated. "I dislike making an issue of it, and
perhaps providing the spark that could ignite
the flames of war," he murmured, his brows
furrowed with genuine concern.

Rose was relieved. If Lincoln's chief adviser was willing to go to such lengths to meet the South's demands, then perhaps there was a chance for peace after all.

What Rose didn't know was that the President not only disagreed with his chief adviser on most issues but also disagreed with most of his cabinet.

It was a warm Friday, April 12, when Rose set out in her carriage for what would be an eventful afternoon. The previous evening she had received a ciphered message from Hollis, who was staying at a tavern in nearby Alexandria.

The threat that Fort Sumpter might be held by the North and fired upon by the South had grown by leaps and bounds in the previous few days.

Lincoln had informed Seward that he, and not his chief adviser, would form policy. And the President considered that reinforcing, rather than abandoning, Fort Sumpter was part of his policy.

Hollis' message was cryptic: "We must know, Rose, what buildings in Washington are guarded, and how heavily. We also need to know the troop strength on all bridges and roads in and out of the city."

Rose had honed her powers of retention as well as her powers of flattery and flirtation. Young officers at the Long Bridge, the Navy

Yard, the Rock Creek Bridge, as well as other approaches to Washington, were only too happy to take a break in their duties to chat with the beautiful raven-haired woman who was so interested in their command.

By late afternoon Rose had a mountain of information stored in her brain. There was but one more stop, and this the most important: the Chain Bridge. It spanned the Potomac three miles above Georgetown, and connected the city with the Virginia turnpike. Its importance lay in the fact that it connected the army with the arsenal at Harpers Ferry by way of Leesburg.

Rose made a mental note that there were far more militiamen drilling near the bridge than normal, and swift riders thundering past her carriage were greater in number than when she had set out that day. She knew that something ominous was in the air when not only was she rudely turned back from the bridge but also all her attempts at conversation with the officers were rebuffed.

In a pique, she instructed her driver to turn about and return to the city, but they had gone no more than fifty yards when they were overtaken by a lone uniformed rider on a huge bay horse. Without a word to Rose's driver, he galloped by the carriage proper, grasped the bridle of the right-side horse, and sawed them to a halt.

"How dare you!" Rose cried, leaning from the open window. "What do you think you're doing!"

The words had barely left her lips when the rider turned and walked his horse back to where she sat. Slowly he pulled down the dust mask that hid most of his face.

It was Bram Darcy.

"I'm doing exactly as you are doing, mademoiselle. I'm making my rounds."

His eyes were cold and vacant, and his lips were curled into the same self-assured smile that had haunted so many of her dreams these past months.

"Whatever do you mean, Major?" Rose managed to reply, surprised at the calm in her voice. "Can't a person decide on a whim to ride in the countryside?"

"Of course a person can," he growled. "But it seems odd when that person can't seem to choose which road or bridge she would like to cross into the countryside."

Rose's face flushed, and she became even more flustered when he yanked open the door and effortlessly slid from his horse into the seat beside her. In one motion he closed the door and looped his horse's rein through the handle.

"What are you doing?" Rose cried, scooting to the far end of the leather seat.

"Begging your pardon, Miss Jacquard, but with

a storm threatening, surely your patriotism extends to giving an officer a ride?"

"Storm? There's not a cloud in the sky!"

"Odd," he replied with a chuckle, thrusting his hand through the window. "I could have sworn I felt a drop of rain."

"Major Darcy, you are an insufferable—"

"Romantic, just like you. Drive on!"

The carriage lurched forward and turned onto the Washington road, throwing Rose against him. Before she knew it, his arm was about her shoulder, and in the narrow seat there was no way to escape.

His touch, even the slightly horsey scent of him, sent a quiver through her.

"You have stayed."

"What . . . ?"

"In Washington. You've not run to the South with your Southern friends. You've stayed here."

Rose dared not look at him. She stared straight ahead. "I told you that was my plan."

"I know, but I thought it was only talk, that when it actually happened . . ."

"When what actually happened?"

Rose was only half-hearing his words. His nearness and her need had become overwhelming. With just his warm breath on the side of her face and the pressure of his hand on her shoulder he had created a wild, driving desire in her body.

When no reply was forthcoming, she turned her face up to his. The cocky, sardonic smile was gone now and his eyes were narrowed, the brows veed in perplexity.

"You mean you haven't heard?" And then he answered his own question. "But of course you haven't. Word came by telegraph only an hour ago, and you've been riding since noon."

Suddenly, without warning, her heart squeezed with fear. But before she could speak again, both his arms wound around her, crushing her body to his.

"Bram, what has happened?"

But he didn't answer. Instead, his arms wound tighter, clasping her in a fierce embrace that drove the breath from her lungs. His head lowered, and his lips claimed hers.

The thrill began deep within her, but before she could embrace him and return his kiss with her own burning ardor, his lips left hers.

Rose's eyes fluttered open in time to see the love melt from his eyes. She saw his face change. Sorrow replaced the desire in his dark eyes, and then turned quickly to anger.

"Leave, Rose. Go South before you destroy us both."

Her head was spinning and she tried vainly to understand what had brought about this radical change. "I . . . I've told you," she stammered, her head swaying slightly, "I want to stay in Washington."

"And now that it's upon us, I say you must leave." Abruptly he freed her and flung the door open. With one foot on the step, he freed his horse's rein and cried for the driver to halt.

"Why must I?" Rose hissed in a choking voice, the upper half of her body thrust through the open door. "When *what* is upon us?"

"War, Rose, dammit, *war*! Sumpter fell this morning to the rebel troops of Charleston. The Virginia Convention has opted for the South, and President Lincoln has called up seventy-five thousand militia."

"Oh, dear God!" Rose gasped, falling back to the cushion.

Darcy swung into the saddle and kicked the carriage door closed before leaning his face close to the window. "Go South, Rose, I beg of you."

And then he was gone, the thunder of his horse's hooves echoing like marching drums.

It had come at last, as they had all said it would.

War.

How could she have thought that Seward, or any of them, would come up with a last-minute solution? The South would settle for nothing less than complete freedom, and the North would at all costs preserve the Union.

Now, with war . . .

"Miss Jacquard? Ma'am . . . ?"

Rose looked up. Her driver's black face, the

huge eyes wide with what he had heard, stared down at her through the peephole.

"Home, ma'am . . . or to Mrs. Greenhow's?"

Rose took a deep breath and forced herself to relax, letting her mind drift back, before Bram's sudden arrival, to the rest of the day and what she had seen and heard.

"To Mrs. Greenhow's—and hurry!"

CHAPTER SIXTEEN

RUMORS were rife that Washington itself would be the first target of the Confederacy. Virginia, one-half of the vise around the Capital, had gone Southern. The other half, Maryland, was split in its allegiance.

With a spyglass from a high vantage point, the Stars and Bars Confederate flag could be plainly seen atop the Marshall House Tavern in nearby Alexandria.

It was rumored that a band of five hundred men, led by the Texas Ranger Ben McCulloch planned to raid the Capital from Richmond. Their object: to carry off the President and his cabinet.

Fear was the order of the day as, with every passing hour, Washington City was increasingly cut off from the rest of the North. And on everyone's mind was: *Where are the troops to defend the Capital?*

Colonel Robert E. Lee was one of the most respected military minds of his day. From his home in nearby Arlington Heights he was summoned to the Capital and offered the command of the Northern armies.

Rose learned of it from a smirking Chance Flynn, now a captain in the Washington regulars.

"Lee has arrived," Flynn announced smugly. "We've always had the men to lick the damn rebels, but not the generals. By tonight we will have a leader!"

Rose found it hard to believe. Lee was a devout Southerner and a Virginian. Could he turn his back on the South and lead the North to battle against his homeland?

The hours dragged by that afternoon, until the entire city was in a state of agitation. What would Lee's answer be?

At last Rose could stand it no longer. Taking her spyglass, she went to the roof and trained it on Blair House, blocks away, where Lee was closeted with General Scott and the cabinet. The bonnet she wore helped hardly at all to keep the sun off her worried face. But still she waited and watched.

At last she saw Lee's diminutive military figure emerge from the house and mount his horse. She knew from the stern, sad look on his lined face that his decision had been made. But what was the decision?

She held her breath, waiting for the President or members of the cabinet to emerge from Blair House. They did not.

And then she sighed deeply as she watched the lone figure of Robert E. Lee turn his mount toward the Long Bridge and Virginia.

But as Lee went South, others opted for the North.

No one, least of all Rose and her Southern comrades, dreamed that the same guns that had pounded Fort Sumpter into submission would also arouse the wrath and patriotism of the North. Men, money, and arms came from everywhere in support of the Union. The recruiting offices were clogged until President Lincoln's call for seventy-five thousand volunteers was far surpassed. And most of them seemed determined to reach Washington. Suddenly uniformed men were everywhere, their blue capes sailing in the wind behind them as they rode madly from one end of the city to the other.

And Rose took note of it all. Daily she haunted the train station, mentally recording the numbers of men arriving, their units, and their strength of arms.

Most were ragtag militia units or untrained volunteer vigilante groups. But then, one morning, news came that crack regular troops were arriving from Massachusetts.

Rose rushed to the station. The train had barely rolled to a halt before ambulances were backed up as close to the coaches as possible. Blue uniforms spilled from the open doors. Many of the men were wounded, with blood-soaked bandages around their heads and arms.

Rose clutched the arm of one young man, barely eighteen, whose head was swathed in bandages and who sported a splint on one leg. "What happened?" she cried over the noise and chaos around her. "Was there a battle?"

The wild-eyed boy barely looked at her as he spoke. "Yeah, battle. We was marchin' through Baltimore, when plain civilians up an' attacked us! I tell ya, ma'am, I ain't afraid to fight, but damned if I want to go through Baltimore again!"

Then he was gone, and Rose was pushed along by the milling crowd.

Steam hissed and swirled before her watery eyes, and her ears ached with the blaring sounds of the Marine Band on the platform behind her playing "Yankee Doodle."

She saw stretchers being handed down from the coaches. As she drew near them, she gasped. All of them were mere boys, barely ready for razors.

A woman bending over one stretcher suddenly looked up and grasped Rose's hand. "Are you here to help or gawk, girl!"

"What?" Rose stared into the narrow, pinched face of the tiny woman.

"There's but one doctor, and no bandages. If you're here to help, start tearing your crinolines and lend a hand!"

"Who are you?"

"Clara Barton. Usually I'm a clerk in the patent office, but today I'm a nurse. Come along!"

In a trance, Rose followed the woman toward another line of stretchers. This was far from her intent when she had left home that morning, but in no time she had removed her crinolines and ripped them to shreds. Blindly she assisted the spinsterish little woman with one wounded man, and then moved on to another stretcher.

Suddenly a short, barrel-chested man with huge side whiskers, blood staining the entire front of his uniform, and a caduceus on his collar, appeared by her side. "Don't bother with that one, ma'am."

"What? But, why not, doctor?"

"He's dead."

Then he was gone. Chilled, Rose looked down at the youthful, beardless face on the stretcher and began to weep. For several minutes she stood gazing at the lifeless face, tears running unchecked down her cheeks.

It had not even been a battle—not in the sense of a battle in a real war, or on a battlefield, where men died for their cause, for glory and honor. It had been a street fight between soldiers—who could not fire their weapons—and a civilian mob armed with bricks, pitchforks, and knives.

So what, she thought, had this boy really died for?

"On with it, dearie," Clara Barton said, tugging on Rose's arm. "There are lots more bleeding."

For the next two hours Rose did what she could. Out of habit, she stored in her mind that these men were the Sixth Massachusetts. They were but one of three regiments that had at last been sent to protect Washington. She also made note that there were over fifty seriously wounded and four dead.

At last all the wounded had been taken to the E Street infirmary and the crowd had begun to disperse. Wearily Rose plodded toward her carriage. There was dirt and soot covering her face and arms, and what was left of her skirt was bloody and ragged. Just as she stepped off the street side of the platform, three Union officers walked by.

One of them was Bram Darcy.

"Oh, dear God," she whispered under her breath, looking around for a place to conceal herself until he had passed. She had neither the desire nor the strength for a confrontation with him now.

But it was too late; he had already seen her.

He stopped as their eyes met, and waved the two officers on ahead of him.

"You've been treating Yankees, you know," he said, moving toward her.

"I've been bandaging boys," Rose replied.

He reached up with one hand and gently ran two fingers over her cheek, then held them before her eyes. They were stained with soot, dust, and dried blood.

"Welcome to war, Rose."

The death and heartbreak Rose had witnessed at the train station shook her, but it didn't alter her resolve. She knew that in other train stations her fellow Southerners would soon be suffering the same fate.

Troops continued to flow into the city until the Capital was fairly bursting. So fast did they come that there was no housing for them. Eventually, even the Capitol rotunda and the congressional chambers were turned over to them. Where once the laws of a great nation were decided, now fighting men sworn to preserve that nation lay down to sleep.

With the increased activity and influx of soldiers, Rose learned that she would have to be doubly careful in her clandestine activities. By now it was an accepted fact that Washington was full of Confederate spies. Rose even received a cryptic message from Mrs. Greenhow, telling her that they could no longer meet openly, even as casual acquaintances. Mrs. Greenhow's every move was being watched by Pinkerton detectives and officers from Army intelligence.

Rose was sure that she was not yet suspect, even though she knew in her heart that Bram Darcy believed her neutrality a sham.

Eventually, using names supplied by Clay Fulton and Hollis Johnson, Rose recruited her own coterie of couriers to pass information on to Richmond.

The whole city was now an armed camp, with drums matching the pounding tread of drilling boots everywhere.

And because of the soldiers, Washington also became a magnet for drifters looking for easy money. There were sharp-eyed gamblers, painted women with more of their bosoms exposed than covered, and rowdies who formed marauding gangs.

Cat became so fearful of the streets, even during daylight hours, that she rarely ventured forth from the house on H Street.

Not so Rose. She hired a Baltimore tough named Bennie McAdam to ride beside her driver or walk a few paces behind her everywhere she went.

Bennie was a short, broad-shouldered man with a seamed face and bright red hair. Besides a very shady past, a keen eye with a pistol, and two arms like logs, he brought to his new employment a deep love of the South.

"Ye'll not have to be fearful of any man, darlin',

least of all meself," he told her moments after
their first meeting, his grin wide and his eyes
twinkling. "The colonel told me ta mind after
ya, an' that I'll do till me blood runs cold."

Rose adored him immediately, even after she
learned that Bennie liked a "dram or two" now
and then. Later she found out that a "dram or
two" often turned to eight or ten, and more
often now than then.

But it didn't matter, for Bennie could make
her laugh, and under his watchful eye she felt
safe no matter where she was.

Rose duly recorded the arrival of the other
two regiments from Massachusetts, as well as
the Seventh New York and the First Rhode
Island.

The Rhode Islanders brought several women
with them, wives and lady friends who refused
to be left at home. One of these, a stern-faced
girl with long, flowing hair, was Kady Brownell.

So enamored of the military life and filled
with patriotism was the wife of Sergeant Brownell that she took to wearing a modified uniform.
It was of blue trousers covered to the knee by a
matching skirt, and augmented by a wide sash
with large curtain tassels and a sword.

The ladies of Washington were aghast when
Kady Brownell was made color-bearer for her
husband's company. It was Rose's first hint that
this would be just as much a woman's war as a
man's.

And still they came, by boat, by train, by forced march from every Northern state, until the sound of bugle, fife, and drum filled every daylight hour.

Rose, with Bennie McAdam in tow and a parasol twirling gaily in her gloved hands, daily toured the city. Then, by night, she encoded her findings and sent messages off to Richmond.

She relayed information on the city's fortifications, on troop strength and movement in and around the Capital, as well as the tent cities that had grown up just across the Potomac. She pinpointed with uncanny accuracy the amount of heavy artillery being gathered in the Union camp.

Because of her close social ties with members of foreign legations, Rose was able to predict other countries' drift toward or away from the Southern cause.

As much as she tried to avoid him, several times, at soirees or on the street, Rose met Major Darcy. Rarely did they speak, and when they did their words were charged with antagonism. With others, Rose steadfastly kept up her facade of neutrality. With Bram Darcy she knew it was useless and didn't bother.

These chance meetings with her old lover were painful. At times she wanted to throw duty and caution to the winds and tell him the truth. But she didn't. His scowls every time they met warned her that the gulf between them had widened too far to be spanned.

If seeing Darcy wrenched at Rose's heart, it became even worse when Lady Fontaine arrived back in the Capital from London. Ostensibly she was there to relate the woman's slant on the former colonies' civil war to the London *Times*. But Rose was sure that Camilla was actually in Washington to report to Bram and his superiors on her progress in England and France in stopping military aid to the South.

On the rare occasions when Rose met Lady Fontaine on the street, she would discreetly cross to the opposite walk rather than speak. She had a twofold reason for this. Like Bram, Camilla Fontaine knew the real Rose and where her sentiments lay. Rose also considered Camilla a traitor to the South, and knew that a chance meeting might erupt into a heated argument that would unmask her. And so she scrupulously avoided her whenever she could.

She also avoided listening to the rumors that Camilla Fontaine and Bram Darcy were seen frequently together, their intimate manner indicating that more than business was being discussed. Rose tried desperately to convince herself that, surely, Bram could not be taken in by such a shallow female as Camilla.

It was early in June, near the Fairfax courthoue in Virginia, when first blood was spilled in actual battle. Rebel prisoners were captured, and the following day the New York *Tribune* found its way to Washington with blaring headlines: ON TO RICHMOND!

"On to Richmond, indeed," Rose muttered as she read it.

The previous afternoon, she had received word from Hollis that a huge concentration of Confederate troops had gathered at Manassas, near Alexandria.

They were less than a two-day march from Washington.

It was only a matter of time.

CHAPTER SEVENTEEN

FIREWORKS, martial music blaring from myriad military bands, and the booming tread of twenty thousand booted feet filled the length of Pennsylvania Avenue. All along the route, gaily colored bunting, flags, and Chinese lanterns decorated the trees and hastily erected viewer platforms. Here and there, balloons drifted into a cloudless sky.

It was Independence Day, the Fourth of July, 1861, and all of Washington had turned out to review the army that would soon move south to crush the Southern rebels.

Normally on the Fourth, holidaymakers would flow across the Potomac for picnics and excursions in Virginia.

But this year, the groves and meadows of Co-

lumbia Spring on the Virginia side of the Long
Bridge were filled with tents, cannon, and caissons. The entire area now teemed with bored
soldiers, and was considered a place too dangerous for ladies and children. It had been dubbed
"Fort Runyan," and even the dancing pavilion
where Rose and Catherine Jacquard had spent
so many gay summer evenings in years gone by
was now a place to stable Union horses. So the
holiday celebration took place on Pennsylvania
Avenue.

Men, women, and children lined the street,
and special bleachers had been erected in Lafa-
yette Square to watch the bands and passing
troops.

High atop these bleachers sat Rose Jacquard,
a broad, absent smile on her rouged lips but a
keen, searching look in her dark eyes. The dress
she wore was slightly pretentious for the occasion, and she had picked it for that very reason.
It was of rich yellow silk embroidered with showy
flowers. The *point-de-Venise* collar and sleeves
were edged with pink ribbons. Her white bonnet was trimmed with live flowers, feathers, and
tinsel bells. The matching white parasol even
had a pink lining.

Few of the men and women lounging near the
bottom step of the bleachers or near the square
would have missed her arrival. And on this day,
that was exactly as Rose wanted it.

Across from the square, in front of the White

House, a canopied platform was gaudily draped with the Stars and Stripes and flags from the Northern states.

On the platform, amidst his cabinet, sat President Abraham Lincoln. Directly to his right sat his gouty and infirm General-of-the-Armies, Winfield Scott.

Rose had only recently met General Scott, and her first impression had been of a man sorely ill and living in glories of the past. If this, she mused, is the best that the Union can muster for leaders, the young lions of the South will run roughshod over the Union Army in a matter of days!

Rose's eyes drifted from the gray head and wrinkled, stern old face of Scott to the tall figure beside him. How odd it is, she thought, studying the gaunt, bearded face with the dark, hollow eyes beneath the tall stovepipe hat. Weeks before, men had massed their bodies closely around this man as he had made the brief trip from Willard's to the Capitol steps to be inaugurated. Every precaution had been taken to ensure that this tall man from Illinois would become President. Now, when he was in office, no one seemed to fear for his safety any longer. Many times Rose had passed him on the streets of Washington, alone, unguarded, out for a brief stroll or heading for a meeting in the Capitol building with members of Congress.

Idly Rose's eyes moved from the President to

the packed bodies along the avenue and in the square. Somewhere in that crowd was a man recently sent from Richmond by Clay Fulton.

What if that man's mission was not just to receive a ciphered message from Rose Jacquard?

What if he had a pistol?

It would be so easy to amble across the street, edge near the platform, even vault its low railing, and . . .

Rose paled at the thought.

"Is something wrong, my dear?"

Rose shook her head slightly to clear such thoughts and turned to face the portly, graying man seated at her right. His name was William Howard Russell, and he had been sent by his paper, the London *Times*, to report on this rift between the former colonies.

"Why, no, Mr. Russell," Rose replied quickly. "I just felt a pang of remorse for my dear friends in the South. How can they ever hope to defeat such stalwart lads as we see here today?"

Russell made a deprecating "Harumphh" that managed to come out in a dandified, British way, and scowled. "My dear lady, I fear that what you see before you is undisciplined, unofficered rabble. I have grave doubts as to their ability to fight as well as they march!"

Russell was a man of strong opinions, and he didn't care who was present or where he was when he voiced them.

"I am afraid I must agree with you, sir, at

least for the time being," replied the gentleman seated to Rose's left. He wore the blue uniform of the Union and was Rose's co-escort for the day's festivities. "But as more West Point graduates such as myself reenlist, the officer corps will turn the army around."

"Perhaps." Russell shrugged. "But by that time Jefferson Davis may well be cutting his meat in the White House."

Rose said nothing. In fact, she leaned slightly backward so the two men could better see each other to carry on their conversation. It was from verbal bouts such as this that she often obtained her best tidbits of information.

At Russell's words, the man to her left seemed to shrink into his newly acquired, ill-fitting uniform. He was, to Rose, an ineffectual man in both demeanor and looks. His scraggly beard was ill-kempt, and the shock of red hair on his head seemed to be in constant need of a brush. His body was rail-thin, and even though he had just passed his fortieth year, he looked hardly quipped with age or background to lead men into battle. Even his recent employment had brought a laugh to Rose's lips when she had heard it from his own lips two nights before during an intermission at the Washington Theater.

"For the last few years I have been employed by the street-railway company of St. Louis," he had explained.

"A remarkable feat," Rose had replied, "jumping so quickly from being a trolley conductor to a colonel."

His face had reddened, but he hastened to add that he was also a graduate of West Point—albeit some years before.

Rose thought little of him, but she had cultivated his company, even inviting him to tea and once to dine. He had been posted to General Irvin McDowell's headquarters in Arlington, and could well be privy to the Union Army's marching orders.

Even his name seemed commonplace to Rose. It was William Sherman.

Shrill bugles and thudding drums passing on the avenue before them drowned out Sherman's retort to Russell's words, and the argument seemed to be over.

Rose relaxed, warmed by Mr. Russell's words that if something were not done soon, Jeff Davis would be in the White House.

Russell had just returned from a tour of Richmond and the Southern encampments as a neutral foreign observer. The stories he had filed made it clear that he thought the current military superiority was tipped toward the South.

His reporting had made him very unpopular in Washington, but what she had read piqued Rose's curiosity enough to invite him several times to dine at the H Street house. There, in outward innocence, she had listened with a keen ear and a thundering heart to his stories about Southern readiness for war. Russell's light blue eyes had twinkled with amusement as he regaled Rose with tales of the comparative disorder in Washington as opposed to Richmond. "The Northerners drill, they arm, and they talk of running the rebel through. And the officers fret while they listen to the politicians and the press urge them on to Richmond."

"But surely," Rose had replied only the previous evening, "the Yankee officers will not march south before their men are ready."

Russell had laughed aloud. "You wouldn't think so, my dear. Why, only the other day I heard McDowell himself say that he didn't even have a decent map of Virginia! But march they will, I'm sure of it—and by the middle of the month, if I sniff the wind right."

"But Congress—"

Russell interrupted her with a wave of his hand. "Your Congress, my dear, indeed all your politicians, think that an army is like a cannon that can be fired off whenever the match is applied."

Thinking of Russell's words, and the added information she had overheard that morning from her future brother-in-law's lips, Rose squeezed her palm over the tiny silk-enclosed packet concealed in her glove. At the same time, her eyes strained over the sutlers' booths lining the square.

At last she saw him, a stocky little man with a rotund belly and a mane of wild gray hair. He stood behind the counter of a booth dispensing cakes and pies and drink, in a perspiration-stained calico shirt, its sleeves rolled to his elbows. Pinned to the collar of his shirt, on both sides, was a freshly picked bloodred rose.

"Gentlemen, if you will excuse me." Rose smiled, rising. "I fear the heat and the blaring bands have taken their toll."

Both men stood with her, offering to escort her back to her house through the crowds.

"Please, no, Mr. Russell. I know you have to put this great spectacle into words for your paper. I shall be fine."

Russell shrugged, but Sherman insisted that he be allowed to accompany her. "I must be across the Long Bridge and back in Arlington by dark in any event."

He would not take no for an answer.

Together they moved through the square until they were but a few paces from the booth.

"I've a mind for a pie, Mr. Sherman. And you?"

"No, thank you, ma'am, but I'd gladly purchase—"

"No! I mean, I know that a soldier's pay, even a colonel's, is given more in fame than in coin." She smiled. "I insist."

Sherman rather sheepishly shrugged in agreement and fell in behind Rose as she walked quickly toward the booth.

Carefully, she worked the tiny silk-encased packet from her glove and folded it inside a bill from her reticule. "I've a taste for berry pie, I think—that one there. A small slice, if you please!"

"Right you are, Ma'am," the sutler replied, not once meeting her eyes. He passed the slice of pie to her with one hand and accepted the bill with the other. Rose hardly saw him slip the packet from the bill into his shirt as he made change. "Yer change, ma'am . . . and we thank ya."

Rose felt a warm glow as she moved through the crowd, daintily tasting the berry pie, with a Union colonel at her elbow.

Inside the tiny swatch of silk was a ciphered message: *McDowell definitely moving south by middle of July. Will have date of marching orders and route by the tenth. R.*

Passes across the Long Bridge were increasingly difficult to get as more and more troops poured into the area near Arlington and Robert E. Lee's mansion, which was now General McDowell's headquarters.

But the absence of a pass did not daunt Rose.

The young, wide-eyes sentries were no match for her clever tongue, nor could they deny her fluttering lashes or her striking beauty.

"Why, Lieutenant, eggs and poultry are just so dear in the city now, and I know a farmer just down the road ..."

"Why, Captain, it's such a delicious day—I just wanted to pick a few flowers down there in Feldon grove. Thank you, I'll only be a bit!"

"Why, Sergeant, my poor ole' daddy lives just the other side of Arlington, off the Post Road. He's so ill, and I'm just bringin' him these jams ..."

Whether it was flowers, eggs, or her "ole daddy," Rose always drove very near the McDowell encampments. And she never failed to take note of new uniform insignia or the presence of new supply wagons.

Each of these times, she wore a simple calico dress that enhanced her figure but did nothing to disclose her social position.

Once, with daring audacity, she drove her buggy right up to the door of Lee's mansion and delivered two baskets of freshly baked buns to "our officers." As the young captains and lieutenants stumbled over each other to be near her, Rose coyly pursued the real reason for her "gift."

In the course of one afternoon, she learned that after July 9 further visits would be useless, "for we'll not be here, ma'am. It's Manassas for us, and then through the rebel lines and on to Richmond."

Rose had steadfastly refused to allow Bennie

McAdam to accompany her on these trips to Virginia. "How, Bennie," she told him, "can I flirt with all those young men with you scowling like a sphinx beside me?" She always dropped him off near the aqueduct, and picked him up again on the return trip.

On this particular afternoon, he wasn't in his usual place.

Rose fretted, waiting for almost an hour before continuing on into the city. Much to her surprise, Bennie awaited her in the stable behind the H Street house. His broad face was scowling and there was a cloud of worry in his usually mischievous eyes.

"Bennie, where were you? I waited . . ." Rose began, alighting from the buggy. And then she noticed his expression. "Bennie, what is it? You look as if you've seen a ghost."

"Not a ghost, Miz Rose. What I seen was all too real. When ye left me off, I watched ye go on and git yerself across the bridge as usual."

"Yes."

"Jest after you was over, two riders came up. They talked a long time to the sentries what let you over. I knew they was talkin' about you, 'cause they kept looking after yer buggy and wavin' and pointin' toward ya with their arms. Then pretty soon they lit out after ya."

Now Rose was herself scowling. In not a single one of her many trips to the Virginia side had she ever had a fear or given a thought to anyone following her. Now she tried to remember if she had unconsciously noticed two riders behind her that day.

She hadn't, and she told Bennie so.

"Nope, I don't reckon ya would, Miz Rose. I watched 'em fer a long time and they stayed a good space behind ya. I had my feelin's—little fingers runnin' up and down the back of me neck, so I took me glass and climbed me a tree."

Here he paused, rubbing his toe in the dirt and biting his lip as if he were afraid to tell Rose what he had seen.

He didn't have to. Rose could already guess. "They talked to everybody on the other side that I talked to after I left them."

Bennie nodded, his face twisted now with the worry that a moment before had only been in his eyes. "When you started to head back, they rode in a wide circle around you and got to the bridge first. They didn't even stop, they just rode right on across and kept goin'. It took me a few minutes to borrow me a horse, but I caught 'em jest inside the city."

Rose swallowed, sudden fear creeping up the back of her legs. "Where did they go, Bennie?"

"The building on Seventeenth Street, Miz Rose—the gray one across from the War Department."

Rose felt suddenly faint. She put out her hand and found one wheel of the buggy to steady her, but managed to keep her face a mask of calm.

The building across from the War Department on Seventeenth Street was called the Winder Building. It housed the offices of military intelligence.

Already, two of Mrs. Greenhow's couriers, one of Rose's own, and Howard Eagleton, the Shakespearean actor who had, like Rose and Mrs. Greenhow, been ferrying intelligence south for months, had been taken to the Winder Building.

For all of them it had been the first stop on the short path to trial and imprisonment as Confederate spies.

"Are you sure, Bennie, that they entered the Winder Building?"

"Yessum, I'm dead sure. I even went inside and hung around till they came back out. There's a kid there who sells papers on the steps every day. He knows one of 'em, called him E. J. Allan. Well, I shoots off down . . . well, down to some people I know to find out jest who this E.J. Allan is."

Even with fear filling her body, the sudden flush on Bennie's face brought a smile to Rose's lips. His "friends," she knew, were the underworld of Washington who hung around the notorious Marble Alley. Bennie knew them all, the bartenders and pug-uglies of the many taverns in the area, as well as all the girls who resided in the infamous Julia Deane's brothel.

"Go on, Bennie. What did your friends tell you?" Rose prompted.

"He's that detective from Chicago, Miz Rose—Allan Pinkerton."

Now Rose gripped the buggy wheel even harder. She knew that Pinkerton had been brought into Washington by the President himself to halt the flood of intelligence going south out of the capital. She had also heard that Bram Darcy was working closely with Pinkerton in the pursuit of Southern sympathizers in Washington.

How ironic it would be, Rose thought grimly, if it were Bram himself, through Pinkerton, who ran her to ground. She knew, and had known for a long time, that Bram suspected her, and in their meetings she had never concealed the fact that she still loved her homeland. It would have been pointless to deny it to Bram, for he, of all people, knew the dictates of her heart.

But on suspicion alone, would Bram send Pinkerton and his bloodhounds after her?

She thought not.

But Pinkerton himself, acting on his own, maybe without the knowledge of his superiors in the regular army?

Perhaps.

"They've been watchin' Mrs. Greenhow fer weeks now, Miz Rose. They could be watchin' you."

Rose nodded, then came to a decision. "If they are, Bennie, then so be it, for we've gone too far to stop now."

The broad, rugged face broke into a wide smile, the first since Rose had stepped down from the buggy. "Right ye are, Miz Rose. If we go down, it'll be with the Stars and Bars a-flyin'!"

"That we will, Bennie, that we will!"

But by the time she had crossed the yard and entered the rear door of the house, fear had once again made its way up her spine to curl the hair on the back of her neck.

That same evening brought an urgent summons from Mrs. Greenhow.

Rose wasted no time. She sent Bennie on a foray to all the streets nearby, while she donned a gay frock of amber satin and threw a half-shawl of black lace over her shoulders.

For several days, via messengers, she and Mrs. Greenhow had pooled their intelligence. They had both agreed that when they knew everything, they would meet and devise a way to get the information to Richmond.

"Your coachman's asleep, Miz Rose," Bennie proclaimed as he darted into the kitchen.

"Let him sleep," she replied. "It's better that you drive me yourself anyway, Bennie. Are they outside?"

"Aye, one at each end of the street, like hawks they are."

Rose smiled. "Have you sent word to the girl?"

"Aye, I have."

"Then the hawks will have some interesting

prey this night. Ready the buggy, Bennie, and we'll be off!''

"Off to where, Rose?''

Rose whirled at the sound of her sister's voice. Cat stood in the dimness of the doorway, her light brows veed quizzically.

"Why, to the theater,'' Rose said, motioning Bennie through the door. "I'm bored, and want Mr. Joseph Jefferson to make me laugh tonight.''

"But you've seen *Rip Van Winkle* already, Rose, at least twice.''

"Of course I have,'' Rose said, striding by her sister and searching the hall armoire for a bonnet. "But it's bound to be a classic one day, so one can't possibly see it enough.'' She selected one particular bonnet and moved toward the door.

"That's a sun bonnet, Rose. It's near eight at night. And it doesn't match your dress.''

Rose stopped and paused, then laughed lightly. "Of course it is, how silly of me,'' she tittered, replacing the wide-brimmed bonnet on a shelf and reaching for one trimmed in dark lace, with much narrower side brims and a longer tie. "Cat, would you fetch my gloves for me while I finish my hair? The plain black ones will do.''

She moved to a mirror and patted her dark hair until Cat had disappeared at the top of the stairs. Then she darted back to the armoire and retrieved the larger bonnet. Quickly she raised her skirts and tied the strings of the bonnet around her right leg just above the knee.

By the time Cat had descended the stairs, Rose was just fitting the small evening bonnet over her coif and tying it. "Thank you, darling," she said, accepting the gloves and tugging them on.

Cat followed her sister across the kitchen. "Be careful, Rose," she said suddenly, an odd heaviness in her voice.

"Of course I'll be careful, darling," Rose replied lightly. "And I have Bennie."

"I don't mean just be careful of the streets, Rose." Before Rose could reply, she recrossed the kitchen and, with sagging shoulders and lowered head, darted across the hall into the library.

Even though the night was warm, almost sticky hot, Rose felt a chill go through her as she climbed into the buggy. It was caused, she knew, by the almost ominous tone in Cat's voice.

Rose closed her eyes as the buggy moved down the drive, and whispered a barely audible prayer that, of all people, Cat would be the last to know the intrigues in which her sister was involved.

"Miz Rose?"

Bennie's low voice from the seat in front caught her attention. "Yes?"

"They're right behind us, they are, like plaster on a wall."

"Well, Bennie, let us hope they stay that way."

*   *   *

The buggy was barely under the cover of the lean-to shed when, unaided, Rose stepped to the ground. A few quick paces took her to the door, but before she could knock, it opened, bathing her in light.

" 'Evenin', ma'am."

"Mr. Higgins." Rose darted past him into the tiny kitchen.

The door closed quietly behind her, and the short, wiry man appeared at her side. He was about thirty, with full dark whiskers and hard eyes. "This way, ma'am."

He led her through a sparsely appointed parlor toward a narrow bare-board stairwell. An old couple sat rocking by dim candlelight. Rose knew them to be R. V. Higgins' aging mother and father. They were, like the son, rabid secessionists. The couple never so much as raised their eyes as Rose passed through the parlor.

At the top of the stairs, Higgins led Rose into a small bedchamber with homespun draperies pulled tightly over the windows. The room was lighted by a lone candle, and in its dim glow Rose saw a young girl sitting in a high-backed chair by the bed.

The girl stood as Rose approached, and extended her hand. "How do, Miz Rose, I'm Nettie Corcoran and I'm proud to meet ya."

"Thank you, Nettie," Rose replied, gauging the girl's coloring and height as she took her hand.

She had pale blond hair pulled back from a broad forehead and gathered in curls on one side of her neck. Her eyes were blue and wide, set above a wide nose and a tiny mouth. Her chin was firm, but now, as she squeezed Rose's hand, it trembled slightly.

"You're sure you want to do this, Nettie?"

"Yessum, I'm sure. It's no more dangerous than handlin' rowdies come Saturday night at Missus Deane's house."

Rose suppressed a smile and nodded. Nettie Corcoran was a prostitute, far from being a Southern belle, but just as true to the Confederacy as Rose herself.

"Good. We're about the same size, but we'll have to do something with your hair. We can pull it back into a tight roll. I have a wide bonnet here . . ."

Rose had pulled her skirts to her knees, when an embarrassed cough behind her made her drop them and turn.

She had forgotten that Higgins was still in the room.

"I'll be downstairs while you ladies change," he said. "Just call me when you're ready."

The door had barely closed behind him before the two women were unlacing and unbuttoning their frocks and exchanging them. Rose was right about the size. Nettie's summer-weight cachmerette riding habit fit Rose perfectly.

When they were both dressed, Rose applied a

brush to Nettie's blond hair, sweeping it back and curling it into a tight roll. When it was securely pinned, she tied the bonnet over the girl's head and tucked in a few stray strands. "There. In the moonlight they would have to be right beside you to know the difference."

The girl ran her hands lovingly over the bodice and down across the skirt. "It's a grand silk. I've never had anything so rich."

"Wear it well, Nettie," Rose said, impulsively taking the girl's bonneted cheeks in her hands. "Come tomorrow, I'll send it along to you as a present."

Rose called softly to Higgins from the door, and seconds later he was in the room.

"My father will watch to make sure the Pinkertons follow us. When they have, he'll fetch you."

Rose nodded, and Higgins and Nettie moved swiftly down the stairs. From a crack in the curtain she watched Bennie back the buggy from under the lean-to and then drive away toward the river. If he was able to follow the entire plan, he would drive all the way around Washington, and even go through the city itself before returning here to the house.

The ride would take about two hours.

Rose hoped that would be long enough.

"Ma'am . . . ?"

It was the old man at the foot of the stairs.

"Coming," Rose called.

As she sped down the stairs and followed the elder Higgins through the house, an odd thought struck her. What would Bram Darcy think when he learned that his near-bride had spent a romantic evening riding around Washington with a rough-and-tumble railroader from Baltimore? The thought brought a slight smile to her lips.

"Her horse is here, behind the shed," the old man said, guiding Rose by the hand in the dim moonlight.

Nettie's horse was a big roan mare, fitted with a man's saddle. Seeing the saddle, Rose carefully attached the sides of the riding-habit skirt to her wrists so she could mount astride. Then she fashioned a large dark kerchief over her head.

"Ready?"

Rose nodded and stepped from the old man's knee easily into the saddle.

"Ye sit a horse well, ma'am, even astride."

"I'm from Charleston, Mr. Higgins. I learned to ride like this when I was a baby."

The old man smiled, showing great gaps in his teeth. He whacked the mare on the rump and called out, "Bless ya, Miz Rose!"

Rose ground-tethered the mare in a stand of trees behind the house of Lily MacKall, a close friend of Mrs. Greenhow's. Lily was closely related to Adjutant General W. W. MacKall of the

Confederate forces, but as yet the woman was not as suspect as either Rose or Mrs. Greenhow.

Quietly Rose advanced along a graveled path through the trees and paused near the outbuildings. The rear of the house was dark, but she knew light would be blazing from the front windows. She only hoped that the Pinkertons who had surely followed Mrs. Greenhow this night had all stayed in the shadows of the street across from the front of the house.

With that thought in mind to bolster her courage, Rose ran across the rear yard as fast as her booted feet would carry her. Her heels barely touched the steps leading up to the veranda, and then she was tapping softly on the door.

It opened at once, and a candle was thrust in her face.

"Hurry, Rose!"

Rose slipped through the opening, and only when the door was closed and bolted behind her did she sag against the wall, breathless. Only then did she admit to the pounding of her heart and the sudden wateriness in her knees.

"Are you all right, Rose?"

She nodded, taking great gasps to regain her breath.

Lily MacKall was a short, stout woman with mouse-brown hair and a pinched face that, Rose noticed in the light of the candle between them, held more fear than her own.

"We thought you weren't coming."

"I lost my way," Rose managed at last, "twice . . . in the darkness. Are the Pinkertons in front?"

Lily nodded. "My boy's ill. Mrs. Greenhow has been bringing him broth for the last three nights. With any luck, they shan't suspect this night's visit is for any other reason."

"Where is she?"

"At the top of these stairs, the room on the right. Watch your footing, the steps are very narrow." With that, she thrust the candle into Rose's hand and scurried down the hall toward the front of the house. Rose knew that she would keep count of the Pinkertons from her front parlor until it was time for Rose to leave.

A muffled "Come in" answered Rose's knock, and seconds later the two women were in each other's arms.

"Thank God, child. I was afraid you hadn't made it!"

Rose explained the reason for her tardiness and allowed herself to be seated at a small table littered with papers and a silver tea service.

Mrs. Greenhow took the seat opposite. "Ah, these are trying, dangerous times," she murmured, and then forced a brightness to her manner. "But come, let us have a cup of tea!"

Rose accepted the proffered cup and met the older woman's warm gaze. "I'm sorry about Gertrude," she said in a quiet voice, saluting the other woman with her cup.

Mrs. Greenhow nodded and her eyes grew a

touch misty. "My daughter was ill a long time. I think she was spared much suffering from cold and heartless humanity by dying when she did. Unlike my second daughter, Gertrude loved the South as I do and believed in the work we do."

Rose hid her feelings behind her cup and saucer.

Mrs. Greenhow had lost one daughter to death, and another to a Yankee officer. The rest of her small family was split between the two sides, and her beloved Maryland had been forced into the Yankee camp. And if all that weren't enough, Rose knew that, as a result of risky investments, Mrs. Greenhow's financial situation was on very dangerous ground.

"You've done more than your share," Rose blurted. "Perhaps you should quit and go south."

"Never!" the woman cried. "I'll not stop until I can have tea in the White House with my dear friend General Beauregard!"

Rose chuckled, her own will strengthened by this courageous woman. "Nor will I."

"Good. Now, speaking of General Beauregard, I have informed him that the date of MacDowell's march has been delayed from the ninth to probably the sixteenth. I received his reply yesterday."

Rose took the slip of paper and moved it close to the candle: "Yours was received eight o'clock last night. Let them come. We are ready for them. We rely upon you and your friends for more precise information. Be particular as to the description and destination of force, quantity of artillery and men, and *most important*, line of march. Am sending courier known to you, Major Hollis Johnson, for your reply. Will arrive evening of the thirteenth and, as per your instructions, will contact Jacquard."

"Hollis?" Rose gasped.

"Yes. He knows Washington better than most, Rose, so it will be easier for him to slip through the lines."

"But if anything should happen, if he should be captured out of uniform in the North . . ."

Mrs. Greenhow covered Rose's hands with her own. "There is nothing to be done for it, Rose. Most of the couriers we have here in Washington are now known. And those that are not, I wouldn't trust with intelligence as important as we have to send."

Dumbly Rose nodded, and as Mrs. Greenhow spread maps and jotted notes between them, forced her mind back to the matters at hand.

Through a young clerk of the Senate Military Committee whom Mrs. Greenhow had befriended, she had learned MacDowell's marching orders and precisely where he intended to engage Beauregard. The plan was to overwhelm the Confederates in a surprise attack at Bull Run Creek. The advance would begin on July 16 from Arlington Heights and Alexandria, on to Manassas via Fairfax Court House and Centerville.

If Rose was surprised at the accuracy of Mrs.

Greenhow's information, she was overwhelmed when the woman produced a scaled map of Virginia with red-dotted lines indicating the marching progress of each of the Yankee regiments. "Dear God, Beauregard can practically time the arrival of the Union Army!"

Mrs. Greenhow's grin in reply was almost malevolent. "There is more."

A second, smaller map was produced.

"MacDowell plans to march a regiment—here —to cut the Manassas Gap railroad leading from western Virginia. If he does, General Johnston won't be able to reinforce General Beauregard."

"But if Beauregard has this in time . . ."

"Exactly."

The maps were set aside and, taking pen in hand, Rose put to paper all the numbers she had gathered on her many trips across the river.

She had learned to spot artillery, and the caliber of it. Dutifully she noted the size and number of cannon, as well as the number of caissons loaded with ball and shot. She estimated the strength of MacDowell's force at 55,000 men, and made note that a high percentage of them were undisciplined, untrained rabble.

There was little doubt in Rose's mind that the victory would be Beauregard's. Thus, if he wished to follow up with an immediate strike on Washington, she noted that the city's fortifications were rudimentary at best.

She wrote of the city's defenders, their lack of

morale, the filth of their camps, and their igno-
rance of drill and military decorum in general.

Finished at last, she passed the papers to
Mrs. Greenhow, who scanned them quickly but
thoroughly. By the time she had read the last
line, her head was nodding vigorously and her
smile was a beaming accolade for her apt pupil.
"Wonderful, Rose! You have trained your eye to
see and your mind to memorize."

The two women went over every tidbit of
information. A half-hour later, they had ciphered
the most relevant data into one message. This,
and the two maps, were folded into a tiny square
and sewn into a piece of black silk.

"This," Mrs. Greenhow said, holding the tiny
package between thumb and forefinger, "will be
easily hidden and match your hair color until
you can pass it on to Hollis. Remove your tucking combs and let down your hair!"

Rose complied, and then, using one of the
wide-toothed tucking combs, Mrs. Greenhow re-
did her coif, folding the black silk package deep
within its shimmering thickness. "There. Now,
you must hurry," she murmured, touching Rose's
cheek gently. "And be careful, my dear."

The two women embraced at the door, but
before Rose could fly down the stairs, the
older woman took her face in her hands. "You
know, Rose, that Bram Darcy has been given a
colonelcy."

"No, I didn't know."

"The promotion came directly from Mr. Simon Cameron, the Secretary of War. And the
reason for it will soon affect us both."

"Oh?" Rose tried to keep her face calm and
her eyes vacant. "How so?"

"Colonel Darcy is to the North what Clay Fulton is to the South. One of his major duties is to
advise Pinkerton on how to trap the likes of you
and me in Washington City. If he has suspected
you in the past, Rose, and overlooked his suspicions, after tonight . . ."

"I know. He can overlook them no longer."

Mrs. Greenhow's strong hands gripped her
shoulders tightly. "It is his duty, girl. He has his
duty and we have ours."

"I must go."

"Soon, Rose, soon it will be over."

Dear God, Rose thought, slipping into the
darkness, I hope so!

Rose accepted Bennie's hand as she stepped
from the buggy.

"A successful night, Miz Rose?" he asked.

"A very successful night, Mr. McAdam."

Gallantly he kissed her hand and passed her
through the door and into the yard. "I'll see to
the horse and watch for our visitor."

Rose moved to the darkened house. She had
an excuse ready, should Cat question the late-
ness of the hour: "Revels at Willard's after the
theater. It was a very gay group!"

Passing the parlor, Rose abruptly halted when she saw light beneath the door. Odd, she thought. Cat would never leave a bare candle burning. Gently she opened the door a crack, and then pushed it wide.

Cat sat in nightdress and robe, rocking by the hearth. The candle in her lap flickered with every movement of the chair, casting eerie, dancing shadows over her solemn features.

Rose moved quickly into the room, peeling the gloves from her hands. "Ah, Cat, you ninny, you needn't have waited up for me! We went to Willard's after the theater, and—"

"Bram was just here."

Rose halted in mid-step, as if a wall had suddenly been erected before her. A hundred fears shot through her mind all at once: he knew, and had come to arrest her . . . he was jealous because of her supposed midnight ride with Higgins . . . Nettie had been stopped on her return ride to Marble Alley and been interrogated. "Oh? Whatever could he want this time of night?" Rose seated herself and dropped her gloves into her reticule.

"Hollis was caught trying to sneak through a Union checkpoint at Indian Head tonight. He had stowed away aboard the ferry from Dumfries on the Virginia side."

Rose couldn't suppress a choked gasp. She started to speak, but Cat went on in a flat, emotionless voice.

"He was in civilian clothes, but he was recognized by one of his former classmates at the Point. When they searched him, they found a ciphered message in the heel of one of his boots."

"Oh, no . . ." Rose felt her knees quaking beneath her crinolines. She found it did little good to grip them, because her hands were also shaking.

Suddenly Cat's calm struck her. A man who had been her childhood friend, who had once been her beau, had been caught as a spy. And yet there was no hint of sadness in her face.

"Was he arrested, Cat? Where have they taken him?"

"To the E Street infirmary."

Rose leapt to her feet. "My God, he's hurt. What have they done to him, Cat?"

"He's dead, Rose. He tried to escape and was shot."

Rose shrieked as her legs gave way and she fell back into the chair. The tears came like a flood, soaking her hands where they covered her face.

Hollis dead!

How could it be? He was so young and so full of life.

The long minutes ticked by as Rose wept and rocked back and forth in the chair, seeing Hollis as he had looked during his "last fling" at Saratoga. Like a waterfall, grief washed over her, then finally subsided as her mind returned to the here and now.

And to the silk package secreted in her hair.

Who would take it to Beauregard?

There wasn't time to summon another courier, and Bennie, being a man, would never get across the river, much less through the Union lines.

Everything for the South, Rose.

Those were Mrs. Greenhow's words, and Hollis Johnson had often echoed them.

Resolutely she took a handkerchief from her bag and dabbed at her swollen eyes.

She would take the package to Beauregard herself.

"Rose . . . ?"

Cat was staring at her intently, much the same way she had looked in the kitchen before this night's adventure and catastrophe had begun.

"Yes, what is it?" Rose said crisply. Her sister's stoic acceptance of their old friend's death had begun to nettle her.

"Your bonnet. Why did you wear the sun bonnet after all?"

CHAPTER EIGHTEEN

WEARING the calico dress that by now had become her trademark for "visiting Virginia," Rose approached the Chain Bridge on the Potomac.

But on this sun-drenched July morning she did not make the crossing. Just before reaching the bridge, Rose turned left on the River Road and followed the Potomac on the Washington side toward Maryland.

To anyone passing her, Rose appeared to be a farmer's daughter driving a short one-hitch buggy to or from market. Anyone, that is, except the three Pinkerton men trailing the buggy's progress in one-man relays.

"Nettie?"

"Yessum," came the girl's reply from beneath

the horse blankets and baskets of produce in the bed beneath the rear seat of the buggy.

"Are they still following us?"

"Yessum, 'bout a mile back."

"Are you all right?"

"Yessum," the girl chirped. "I've *slept* on harder floors than this ole buggy bed."

Rose smiled at the girl's grit. It had been six hours since Bennie had spirited her into the stable and secreted her in the buggy. Now it would be at least another hour of jolting in the hard buggy beneath the smelly blankets before they reached John Harrison Surratt's tavern on the river about six miles below Washington City.

But not once had Nettie Corcoran protested.

To pass the time behind the slow-gaited horse, Rose ticked off each step of the plan she had so quickly conceived the previous night.

Poor Bennie. He had been up and riding the best part of the night, carrying messages to alert the many hands Rose would need this day to help her on the way.

The excuse she had given Cat was thin, but it would have to do. "Mrs. MacKall has asked me to sit with her little boy. I shall be late. Perhaps I'll stay the night."

It was not unusual for Rose to do this kind of favor for a friend. But Cat's expression as she left the house had been one of clear disbelief.

'Tis no matter now, Rose told herself. She had already decided to make a clean breast of everything to Cat when she returned from Virginia. If her intrigues built an insurmountable wall between herself and her sister, then so be it.

The most important thing now—more important than Rose's personal feelings, her personal life—was getting the tiny packet in her hair to General Beauregard. With Hollis gone and the time so short, Rose knew that she had the best chance of anyone to get through.

The road veered slightly away from the river and topped a commanding hill looking out over a wide valley, with Surratt's tavern in its center abutting the river.

The sight brought a smile to Rose's lips. Dear Bennie, she thought; how quickly and accurately he found a solid answer to every problem.

The ground, for long stretches on both sides of the tavern along the river, was swampy and thick with reeds and other heavy growth. Hidden somewhere in that swamp was the small boat that, come dark, would ferry Rose across the river to Virginia.

The tavern itself was on cleared land, but the road approaching it was heavily wooded. Rose was less than fifty yards from it when she lifted the buggy whip from its cradle and turned her head to speak to the girl. "Get ready, Nettie, only a minute or two now."

"Yessum, I'm ready. You jest yell out."

The horse's nose had barely passed into shadow

beneath the trees when Rose cracked the whip against its rump. The buggy lurched forward and Rose used the whip again, increasing the beast's pace from a trot to a canter that sent them flying into the semidarkness.

"They're over the hill, Miz Rose, and they've broke into a run," Nettie said, peering at the Pinkerton men from a slit in the blanket.

"Soon now . . . soon!" Rose cried, planting her feet wide apart for balance as the buggy lurched around one curve and then another.

The second curve was barely cleared when Rose began reining the old horse. "Now, Nettie—jump!"

"Yessum."

Like a young gazelle, the girl leapt from the side of the buggy and lit running. The instant the tiny figure in the baggy homespun trousers and brown jacket disappeared into the trees, Rose again used the whip. Minutes later, she turned the frothing horse into the tavern drive and drove into the rear yard.

R. V. Higgins had seen her emerge from the trees, and now stood awaiting her in the center of the yard. He raised his arms in greeting, and Rose waved a reply with her whip as she slowed and then halted the horse.

By the time she had stepped to the ground and run into his arms, two of the Pinkerton men had thundered up to the front of the tavern. Rose noted them, still sitting their saddles. They glared at her as Higgins' powerful, stubby arms wound about her.

His face was buried in her hair and his lips were pressed to her ear. "Nettie?"

"Safe in the woods," Rose whispered. "Kiss me!"

"What?"

"Kiss me. You're supposed to be meeting your love for an afternoon tryst!"

Higgins' face was flushed, and Rose almost laughed aloud when he lifted his head. His eyes were wide and she saw his lower lip quivering.

Instantly she went to her toes and wound her arms about his neck. In one motion she pulled his face down and clamped her lips to his.

Twice during the long kiss Higgins tried to back away, but Rose held him tight. Not only did she kiss him with all the fervor of a missed lover, she melted against him until their hips ground together.

At last she released him, but held his awestruck face in her hands to cover it from the two riders who studied them so carefully.

"Come, darling, hurry! I've missed you," Rose cooed. "I can hardly wait!"

Arm in arm they moved to the tavern door, passing within ten feet of the two Pinkertons.

"Wanton."

"Aye, a brazen tart she is!"

Rose heard their mumbled exchange, but

passed through the door with her back straight and her head held high.

Not for a second did she let her face reveal what her heart felt: what if they are reporting to Bram Darcy? What would he think of her now, riding the countryside to meet her newfound lover in secret?

They crossed the tavern's large room to a rough-hewn plank bar. Near it stood a tall raw-boned woman of about forty. She had a coarse but handsome face, and deep blue eyes that seemed to glow with admiration when they fell on Rose. But even at that, Rose detected a hardness in those eyes that chilled her.

"Well, Mary Surratt, a good day to ya."

"Mr. Higgins."

"Is my room ready?"

"It is. If you'll follow me?"

Rose followed the woman up narrow, rickety stairs, with Higgins close on her heels. They were nearly to the top when out of the corner of her eye she saw her two bloodhounds enter the room below. If her guess was right, the third rider would be outside, probably in back of the tavern, to be sure Rose didn't slip out that way.

"Dear God," Higgins said at her shoulder, "I hope this works!"

"It worked well once, Mr. Higgins," Rose replied. "I've no fear it shall a second time."

But deep in the back of her mind, she was praying.

*   *   *

Rose stood like a statue at the window. Through the mist rolling in off the river, she saw the couple, arms tenderly entwined about each other's waists, walk to the waiting buggy.

Nettie, dressed in the calico dress, with a heavy traveling shawl held tightly over her head and shoulders, allowed Higgins to hand her up into the buggy.

Higgins was barely seated beside her before a tall man in a dark frock coat, who had been idling near one of the outbuildings, walked briskly toward the tavern.

Rose knew him to be one of the Pinkertons, and guessed that he was heading inside to warn his two fellows that their hen had flown yet another coop with her lover.

Nettie snuggled close to Higgins in the seat and rested her head on his shoulder. Rose watched until the buggy disappeared, and then darted to a mirror to appraise her latest disguise.

The worn brown jacket fitted loosely over a boy's leather shirt, easily hiding her breasts. The womanly flow of her hips was also well covered by the baggy trews, and only a very close inspection would reveal how small her boots were.

She was just fitting a wide-brimmed straw over the dark coils of her hair when the door opened behind her and Mary Surratt stepped into the room.

In no time the woman had spun her around and run her own inspection. Again Rose felt a chill run through her body as the cold eyes appraised her.

"It'll do, at least by night, to get you into Virginia and to the Joneses', but it would never pass by daylight."

"Are they gone—did they follow the buggy?"

The woman nodded. "Like hounds to the scent. Come along, I'll take you down the back stairs, the same way I brought the girl up."

The mist became fog at ground level, and Rose was thankful for it.

"Wrap yer hand in my apron ties and follow close!"

Rose did as she was told, and still stumbled several times in the wake of the tall woman's long strides. There were night sounds all around her, but she could identify the river to her right.

"Watch yer step through here. One wrong move and ye'll go in to yer shoulders."

Rose froze her eyes on the woman's boots, doing her best to stretch her own stride and step in exactly the same places. So intent was she on the ground that she crashed into the woman's backside when she suddenly halted.

"It's a wee one," came a growl from the fog.

"No matter, jest get it to the other side," Mary Surratt replied, and stepped aside.

A great bear in black broadcloth topped by

whiskers and a broad-brimmed floppy hat sat huddled in the center of a small boat.

"In you go!" the woman said, practically lifting Rose with one free hand from the marshy path and depositing her in the stern of the boat. "Are ye armed?"

Rose shook her head.

"Can ye shoot if ye are?"

Rose nodded.

"Good." A tiny gun was pressed into her hand. " 'Tis only a one-shot, but if ye have need of it ye'll probably not get a second if ye don't hit with the first. God save the Confederacy!"

With that the woman faded into the fog and the bear put the boat in motion. In seconds they were clear of the marshy bank and Rose could feel the river's pull on the boat. The farther they went, the thicker the fog became, until Rose could not even see the water.

She could only pray that the huge faceless man before her knew where the other side of the river was.

It seemed an eternity, but at last the oars in his powerful hands rested and, seconds later, the boat came aground.

The man clambered over the bow and hissed for Rose to follow. She scrambled after him up a steep bank, and then across a bare meadow. Just inside a stand of trees, a horse whinnied a welcome.

The hunking man turned to face her. Fingers

of fog floated eerily around his shoulders, and the upper part of his face was totally obscured by the floppy brim of his hat.

"He's a good animal, a lot of heart. Just leave him with Mrs. Jones, he'll be picked up. The Ginnie River Road runs right beside these woods. 'Bout a mile on, they's a Y in the road. Take the left. A mile on, ye'll run outta fog, then ye can fly. Union patrols shouldn't be this far downriver, but watch fer 'em anyways."

Rose could only nod through the man's speech, delivered in a rapid, barely understandable drawl. He had barely finished the last word before he turned and was lost in the fog.

Rose wasted twenty minutes vainly trying to find a mounting stump, while cursing the big man for not even offering her a leg up. Thankfully the horse was docile and obedient, and he held his ground without twitching a muscle as Rose crawled laboriously up his side and finally found the saddle.

True to the bear's word, the mist and fog dissipated less than two miles from the river. But before it did, keeping the horse at a foot-picking walk, Rose found herself more lonely than she had ever been in her life.

Once she thought she heard voices behind her, near the river. She reined to a halt and clamped her hand over the beast's nostrils for a full five minutes before gaining the courage to ride on.

By the time she could make out the countryside in front of her, she had even begun to wish that the surly bear in the black greatcoat were still with her.

But now, with a clear road and a faint moon, she could ride. And ride she did, one with the powerful animal beneath her, the wind whipping the short tails of the boy's coat against her backside.

She guessed it was nearly two in the morning when she came up on the rails of a whitewashed fence and, eventually, the three-story house of her destination.

One light burned in an upper window. Other than that the house was completely dark, as was the entrance to the lane, which she nearly missed.

She passed under a double line of spreading oaks, and was only a few yards from the house when she suddenly cried out and yanked the horse's reins. From the darkness had suddenly appeared a dozen dark forms, quickly surrounding her, blocking the way.

Even in the faint light, Rose could see that every stern-faced man held a musket or pistol, and most of them were pointed directly at her.

She waited a few seconds, hoping that one of the men would identify himself first, in case she had blundered into the wrong plantation.

When no such identification was forthcoming, Rose swallowed deeply, reached very slowly with her right hand, and whipped the straw hat from her head. "I've come in search of Lieutenant Catesby Jones, late of the United States Navy and now a commander in the navy of Jeff Davis."

"B'Jesus, it *is* a woman!"

"Bring her closer!"

The second voice was a woman's, sounding clear and bell-like across the lawn, carrying a tone of authority and command.

The reins were taken from Rose's hands, and the horse was led to a wide set of wooden steps leading up to a veranda.

"From where do you come?"

"Washington City."

"By way of . . . ?"

"Mrs. Surratt."

"And who do you ride for this night?"

"A man named Fulton," Rose replied, surprised at the calm in her own voice.

The tiny flame of a lantern was turned up to reveal a striking auburn-haired woman of Rose's age. As she came down the steps, she lifted the lantern to reveal a sweet, serene face beaming with a broad smile. "You are welcome, my dear. My husband is not here. He has already left to join the fleet. I am Anne Jones."

"I am—"

"I know who you are, and no one else needs to know. Step down. There is food waiting, and your bed is ready." Anne Jones embraced her waist and guided her up the steps.

* * *

The morning was crisp, with a light breeze over the Virginia countryside that blew away not only the oppressive fog but also Rose's fears of the night before.

She rode sidesaddle now, dressed in a brown habit with flowing sleeves and large brass buttons. Beneath the jacket was a high-necked saffron blouse that matched the riding bonnet tied tightly over the coil of her dark hair.

Anne Jones's clothes fitted perfectly, down to gloves and doe-soft leather boots, so that riding along, a satin parasol jauntily spinning above her head, she looked every inch the Virginia belle out for a morning canter.

Anne Jones had proved to be a saint. After feeding Rose, she helped undress her and tucked her into a warm bed. That morning, a bath and hot breakfast had been waiting when the woman gently shook her awake.

" 'Tis time, Rose. You should be on your way before the sun is high."

The ride was uneventful, through fertile fields blossoming with summer crops. Several wagons and single riders had passed her with waves and smiles. Everything seemed so normal, it was hard for Rose to realize that within days this part of Virginia would be thrown into the chaos of war.

She had easily found the Fairfax road, and now approached the little village from the south.

Tents were pitched everywhere, and uniformed

men filled the road. But not a one attempted to halt her progress, nor did they communicate with her beyond an approving glance or an occasional smile.

Only when she reached the village itself did a sentry step forward and bar her way.

"Sorry, miss, no civilians allowed near headquarters."

"And where is headquarters?" Rose asked.

"The courthouse, ma'am."

"And is General Beauregard at the courthouse?"

"Yessum, but—"

"Sergeant . . . you *are* a sergeant, aren't you?"

"Yessum."

"Sergeant, I have a very important message for the general."

"I'm sorry, ma'am, my orders is—"

"Damn your orders, Sergeant, get me an officer!"

Rose's haughty, imperious tone sent the man back a step or two and brought a mask of doubt over his features. "But, ma'am—"

"I've no time to argue, Sergeant. Shoot me if you would!"

So saying, Rose thudded her heel into the horse's side and rode around the startled sentry. Halfway to the village square, the alarm was sounded. By the time she reached the courthouse steps, several whooping soldiers had caught the horse's bridle and brought it to a halt.

"What in the hell? . . . Rose, Rose Jacquard?"

A tall, swarthy officer had stepped from the doorway and now stood smiling down at her. Rose frowned, searched her memory, and then remembered.

"Tom Rosser!" she exclaimed, and then grinned. "Do you dance any better now than you did at West Point?"

"Not a bit." The tall Texan laughed. "What are you—?"

"I'll tell you inside," Rose replied, sliding easily and unaided from the saddle and casting her gaze around the street.

She sighed and uttered silent thanks when she saw no one within earshot dressed in civilian clothes. The last thing she wanted was a Northern sympathizer to hear her name spoken aloud on the steps of the Fairfax courthouse.

She accepted Rosser's hand and moved close to the tall Texan as they mounted the steps.

"Hollis Johnson has been shot," she murmured under her breath, still keeping her radiant smile in place. "I've brought urgent information for Beauregard."

The jaunty smile on the Texan's face disappeared instantly, and in its place was grave concern. "Come along, I'll take you to him right away." He grasped Rose's arm and called over his shoulder, "See to the lady's horse!"

Moments later, Rose was offering her hand to Brigadier General Pierre Gustave Toutant Beauregard, the Louisiana Frenchman who had been the hero of Fort Sumpter.

"Welcome, Mademoiselle Jacquard." He brushed his lips gallantly over Rose's hand as he bowed before her.

The man was as much the gallant and dandy as Rose had heard, but she knew that behind his twinkling eyes burned the fervor of a dedicated man.

"Mrs. Greenhow sends her regards and wishes you a speedy victory," Rose said.

"My condolences on your recent loss. We all held Major Johnson in high regard. I know he was your friend."

"Thank you," Rose replied. "I have come from Mrs. Greenhow in his stead."

Besides Rosser and Beauregard, there were four other officers in the room. All of them exchanged quizzical glances.

Without another word, Rose handed her parasol to Rosser and quickly followed it with her bonnet. Then she removed the tucking combs and pins from her hair and shook it free.

The men in the room shifted uncomfortably from one foot to another at this strange scene unfolding before them.

Rose ran her fingers through the cascading waves, then moved toward the bewildered Beauregard. "There you are, General." She handed him the tiny packet that had so suddenly appeared in her fingertips. "All you need to know of the Yankee advance."

Rose was provided with quarters for the rest of that day and the night. Early the following morning, before dawn, she was awakened. Shortly thereafter, Beauregard himself appeared before her. "I cannot thank you enough, mademoiselle. I am sure you know the value of what you bring to us."

"I know, General. I only hope it is enough."

"Let us pray it will be. Now, are you sure you wish to return to Washington?"

Rose nodded. "I can still be of use there, and . . ."

"Yes?"

"And there is really no place else for me to go."

Beauregard frowned. "Are you aware that, by coming to us, you might be compromised?"

"I am."

"And still you wish to return?"

"I do," Rose replied, not meeting his inquisitive stare.

He appraised her for a long moment, then finally shrugged. "Very well. Two of my officers will accompany you as far as possible."

By noon Rose was once again riding alone. Brazenly she rode around the Yankee encampment, noting that already the army was on the march.

Hardly anyone gave her a second look.

Twice she stopped and picked flowers along the roadside, until the basket she carried was overflowing.

At the Chain Bridge, she smiled at the sentries and threw them flowers. Shrugging, they waved her across.

At the Washington side, she was stopped. "Your business, ma'am?"

"I am just returning from saying a sad farewell to my husband, sir." The tears were flowing copiously from her red-rimmed eyes.

The sentries saluted, and Rose rode on to Washington City.

At Mrs. MacKall's, she dismounted and handed the horse over to a servant. In the house, she took tea and sandwiches, then freshened herself with a bath. She slipped into a new dress, a light green silk with narrow stripes of a shade darker green, and trimmed with lace and bugle ornaments.

She had ordered the dress weeks before from Madame Foshay, and Lily MacKall had taken delivery for her.

Only idle chitchat had passed between the women as they dined within earshot of the servants.

But as Rose prepared to leave, she paused on the stoop and turned to Mrs. MacKall. "Tell our friend that we had a very successful visit."

"I shall tell her this afternoon."

There was no sign of impending doom in Rose's

smile or her quick step as she began the short walk to H Street. She had accomplished her task: Beauregard was warned. But in her heart she knew that by now the Pinkerton men would have gotten inquisitive and secured a warrant to question Higgins. If they had, they would have found only the Higgins family and Nettie Corcoran in the house.

And of course R. V. Higgins would deny even knowing Rose Jacquard.

She rounded the corner of Thirteenth and H streets, looking like any high-bred Washington lady out for an afternoon stroll.

A half-block farther, she slowed her step.

There, standing on the front stoop of her home, were four men in dark frock coats.

Rose had no doubts about their identity or their mission. But without hesitation she squared her shoulders, took a deep breath, and with her crinolines swaying, continued on her way.

As she approached the front step, one of the men moved forward. "Rose Marie Jacquard?"

"Yes," Rose replied, lifting her chin to face him squarely. "Who are you and what do you want?"

"My name is Allan Pinkerton, and you are under arrest."

"Arrest? On what charge?" Rose said coolly.

"Treason."

"Preposterous."

"We shall see about that. Your bag, please."

Rose clutched her reticule, but it was roughly yanked from her hand.

"How dare you—"

"Rose."

Rose whirled. Bram Darcy moved around the corner of the stoop. "I'm sorry, Rose."

PART FOUR

1862

CHAPTER NINETEEN

Rose dressed to the usual accompaniment of marching feet, rattling drums, and reveling debauchery outside her cell window.

Old Capitol Prison was a converted boardinghouse a stone's throw from the Capitol building, in the center of newly erected brothels and gambling houses.

In the eight months since her arrest, the population of the city had swelled from seventy-five thousand to over two hundred thousand. And even with the limited view from the window of her makeshift cell, Rose could see that lowlifes made up a great deal of the new arrivals.

She spent her time reading or sitting at the window gazing out at the Washington that had become such a different city. Tents now ringed the whole city. Soldiers stood guard at every gateway and swarmed through the streets. An infantry brigade was stationed on Capitol Hill. Bands played and muskets cracked.

Saloons, gambling houses, and brothels flourished. Commission merchants appeared in the wake of the army. Pickpockets, crooks, tricksters, vendors, and adventurers of all kinds showed up. Circuses, bear shows, and other rowdy forms of entertainment were offered to the soldiers.

Rose took a dim view of it all. She observed thousands of drunken, demoralized soldiers in the streets, crowding women into the gutters, shouting obscenities. The public squares had become places of debauchery and crime.

Rose often wondered, with tears in her eyes, if Richmond, the capital of the genteel South, was the same.

When her crinolines were in place, she settled a green raw-silk dress over them and appraised herself in the tiny round mirror they had allowed her.

The dress was gaily decorated with pink ribbons and delicate lace and did much to soften the lines of worry that had crept into her face.

"Good," she whispered, "they might have me in jail, but they'll not have me mourning over it in black!"

A short cloak of sea-green velvet, white gloves, and a matching fur cap added to the lightness of her attire.

Her eye fell on the clock. It was near ten. They would be coming for her soon.

The clock was one of the few things they had allowed her to take from the house on H Street. Only after weeks of defiance and a storm of angry letters had she been allowed to add her desk to the few wooden chairs and straw-covered cot already in the room.

Her "sitting room," half as big, was adjacent, and as ill-equipped for comfort.

"Madam, you are in jail, not in the White House."

"Perhaps not," she had answered when first ushered into the squalid quarters, "but I hope to be by winter!"

But winter was at an end, and neither Rose nor the rebels were any nearer to dining in the executive mansion.

Tapping a few stray hairs under the fur of her hat, Rose moved across the ten-by-twelve room to the window. Though it was late March, there were snow flurries, and outside it was bitter cold.

Rose sighed and let her eyes flutter closed as she raised her hand and pressed her palm to the pane.

Eight long, weary months. Almost all of it spent in the dreary confines of these two dark, tiny rooms.

That day, eight months ago, on H Street, they had ruthlessly ransacked her rooms. And then, with Cat standing stoically by, they had gone through the entire house. Oddly, as Rose watched them tear the covers from her books and even sift through the ashes in the fireplace, she had felt sudden relief.

In many ways she was glad the charade was over. Now she could openly proclaim her true beliefs to the world. She could cast off the hypocrisy she had so hated but which had become such a necessity in her intrigues.

Eventually she was allowed to gather her clothing and told where she was being taken.

"Good!" she had replied. "A rebel should be in a rebel prison!"

She had walked from the house under guard with her head held high, assuming an air of indifference and scorn. Only when she had come face to face with Cat in the street had she let herself wilt the least bit.

"I want you to know, Rose, that you have probably ruined the one chance I have of happiness."

"If you mean Chance Flynn, Cat, you are better off without him."

Cat's hand across her face was like the bite of a striking snake. Rose tasted blood, and only then did she allow a tear to squeeze from her eye. "I am sorry, Cat, but what I have done, I had to do."

"So did I, Rose," she hissed, brushing by her sister and running into the house.

It was weeks later before Rose learned that Cat had been interrogated by Pinkerton, and had answered every one of the detective's questions to the best of her ability. Not once had she tried to shield her older sister.

But Rose also learned, almost from the moment of her arrival at the converted boardinghouse, that she was not without friends, or means of communication with them. She had barely unpacked her belongings when a message arrived from Mrs. Greenhow: "Keep your peace, Rose, for they would dare not harm you. And remember, the devil himself is no match for a clever woman!"

Within days the papers—North and South— were full of tales of Rose's bravery, without actually stating that she was a spy—a "secesh" woman, yes, but not a spy.

It was obvious to Rose that the stories portraying her as a Southern patriot and eliciting support for her cause flowed from Mrs. Greenhow's pen.

Soon, because of public opinion, the prospect of trying her for treason had become more and more difficult. She had never pledged allegiance to the Union, so although she was an adversary, the North had no desire to make her a Southern martyr.

Days became weeks, and still her fame grew. It was said that even in her prison cell, under the very noses of her guards, Rose was running a whole network of spies. Nothing could have been further from the truth; Rose was glad to be done with it.

But eight long months later, she still had not been brought to trial or released.

Only once in that time had there been an event that brought her grief: Cat's marriage to Chance Flynn.

Because of the furor swirling about Rose's head, the Washington wedding of her sister to a Yankee officer provided many days of gossipy columns for the papers.

Rose ignored these, but devoured the detailed description of the wedding itself. Only when Rose read the list of bridesmaids did she allow her tears to flow. Had she not been caught and sent to this wretched place, she would have been the maid of honor, but as it was, Cat did not even send Rose word of her nuptials.

Through a friendly guard Rose secured a copy of Mrs. Browning's poems, including "Whispers to a Bride," which she couriered to Cat, with a note wishing her sister all the happiness in the world. The book of poems and the letter were returned unopened.

Nevertheless, Rose prayed that she was wrong about Chance Flynn, that he did love Cat and would be a good and loving husband to her.

A rap came from the door of the adjoining room.

"Come in."

A key turned in the lock, and General John Dix entered, followed by two junior officers. One of them was her new brother-in-law, Chauncy Flynn. He was a major now, lately put in command of the Sturges Rifles, who made up the guards for the Old Capitol Prison.

Rose stared at him, at this man who had once been her friend, and very nearly her lover, and was now her sister's husband. But the man who stared back at her was no friend.

The desire that had once filled his eyes when he looked at Rose was now replaced with undisguised hate. He unrolled a paper, and as he began to read, Rose was sure she saw satisfaction faintly curl the corners of his lips.

"Rose Marie Jacquard, you are hereby summoned to appear before the United States Commissioners for the Trial of State Prisoners. You are charged with espionage in the following forms: aiding and abetting the enemy in time of war, spying for a rebel cause . . ."

Rose stood unmoving as the long list of charges was read against her. Her eyes moved from the paper in Flynn's hand to General Dix's face. His eyes were sad.

And Rose knew why.

How many dances had she whirled in the old man's arm in past years? How often had he sat at her table, laughing at her quick wit?

And now he was heading the committee that must decide if she should go on trial for her life.

How he must feel, she thought, to know that during all those gay times she was, in fact, betraying him.

When Flynn at last finished, the old general stepped forward. "Are you ready, Rose?"

"Of course, General, but it's a damnable day for it, don't you agree?"

Rose was elated when she saw the carriage in the prison yard. At least she would not have to trudge to her destiny this day on foot. But she could not suppress a laugh when she saw the troop of armed guards, both in front and to the rear of the vehicle.

"You think it funny, Rose?" Flynn whispered, handing her up.

"A bit. Am I such a dangerous prisoner?"

"Not at all," he replied with a snarl. "The guards are for your safety. There are those in Washington who would gladly rescue you from us so *they* could hang you."

Rose suppressed a shudder, not wanting to give Chance the satisfaction of seeing the fear she felt.

"How is Cat?"

"With child," he whispered. "And if it is a girl, you can be sure she'll not be named Rose."

She had to turn her face from his.

Flynn took the seat opposite her while General Dix huffed his way into the carriage, and they were off.

The heavy snow flying in the driver's face,

and the fact that the wheels sank so deeply in mud and slush, made the ride seem to last forever.

Rose leaned her head back against the cushioned seat and closed her eyes. Gloomily she thought of the day ahead of her, and even beyond, should they decide this day to take her to trial.

And then she remembered the days just following her imprisonment, and her heart lifted. Even though she was not allowed newspapers, the cries of newsboys on the street and what her own eyes could see told her everything.

How carefree and gay had been the congressmen and their wives as they crossed the Long Bridge and the Chain Bridge to witness for themselves the defeat of the rebels. Loaded with picnic baskets, their buggies and carriages had clogged the Long Bridge to Virginia for hours.

The battle would be fought under the eyes of Northern civilian merrymakers as if it were a monster military picnic. On every Northerner's lips leaving the Capital that day was the vow that they would be in Richmond two days hence. On the other side, secessionist sympathizers left in the Capital scoffed that Beauregard would knock their vow into a cocked hat.

The latter proved correct.

Almost hourly, word drifted back to the city that the Union Army had met much stiffer resistance than they had anticipated, that the rebels had been well-entrenched and were waiting for them.

Though she now had a better understanding of the chaos that was war, Rose still felt elated to know that she had played a large part in what appeared to be a rebel victory in the making. And then the dispatch came that the Yankees were in full retreat.

The following day, the two bridges were again glutted with people, coming back into Washington. This time they were beaten, footsore soldiers, along with all the debris of their army, slogging through mud and rain in defeat.

They appeared, Rose thought, looking from her window, more like woebegone rabble than an army. Many of the caissons lumbering through the streets were heavily loaded with dead or dying boys, and it was said that many more had been left to die on the battlefield itself. Those left staggered through the street, more dead than alive. Like sleepwalkers they were, many crumpling to the sidewalks and gutters when their legs could no longer carry them.

All that day they streamed into a city that had no place to house them. They collected in groups around fires made by ripping down fences and outhouses. And the feeling was that by morning the rebels would take Washington.

But morning arrived and the rebels never came. Two, and then four, days passed with still no invasion. No one realized that, even in victory,

WILD ROSE

the Confederate troops were in as great disarray
as their Union counterparts.

Slowly the city took heart and began to re-
group. Forts were quickly built to the north and
on the hilltops of Alexandria across the river.

McDowell resigned in disgrace, though none
of the debacle was his fault, and General George
McClellan was recalled to whip the army back
into a fighting force.

Slowly but surely, the Union Army fought back.

The Confederates were beaten at Mill Springs,
Kentucky, while the Tennessee forts Donelson and
Henry fell to the Union. Eventually the Confed-
erates abandoned Manassas and withdrew south.
Union victories all, but none that would com-
pletely turn the tide.

By March 1862, everyone, including Rose Jacquard in her prison apartment, conceded that it
looked to be a long and bloody war.

"Rose . . ."

The gentle hand on her shoulder brought her
awake with a start. "Wha . . . oh, yes, General."

"We're here."

Rose looked through the swirling snow at the
squat gray-stone building that housed the pro-
vost marshal's headquarters. The moment she
stepped from the carriage, she was mobbed by
reporters. Beyond them, crowds of people had
turned out to see the famous "Secesh Dame"
who had been such a vital cog in the Confed-

383

erate's Washington spy ring that was now known as "the pipeline to Richmond."

Rose was quickly surrounded by her guard, and as she passed through the crowd, she was relieved to note that there were as many smiling faces as stern ones.

The large third-floor hearing room was actually a courtroom, and would serve as such if, at the end of this day, the evidence against Rose was adjudged strong enough to bring her to trial.

Every seat was taken, and standers were packed three deep along the walls. All sound stopped when Rose stepped through the door.

A few steps down the aisle, Rose stopped and scanned the room. Then, with a flourish, she lifted the fur cap from her head and shrugged the cloak from her shoulders, handing them to a red-faced Chance Flynn. Again she swept the room with her gaze.

"If I had the ticket concession to this affair, I could hire the best lawyers in the land!"

Accompanied by shouts of approval, a few catcalls, and thunderous applause, Rose continued on to her seat.

Moments later, the eleven commissioners, led by General Dix, filed into the room and took their seats at the long table directly in front of her. Rose looked at each man in turn, and flashed them beguiling smiles. There was not a man among them who had not enjoyed her table or been her escort at one time or another to a prewar Washington function.

General Dix gaveled the room to order, and a bailiff stood with an inch-thick sheaf of papers in his hand.

Rose closed her ears to the litany of charges against her until, at last, they were read and General Dix recaptured her attention with his booming bass voice. "Rose Marie Jacquard, you are charged with treason, espionage, and holding communication with the enemy in the South, to the detriment of the United States of America. How say you?"

"I say, gentlemen, that these proceedings are a travesty, full of subterfuge and mendacity. I think that, since there is a war going on, your time would be much better spent fighting it."

Catcalls and laughter, accompanied by very audible groans from each of the commissioners. In Rose Jacquard they had a tricky tiger by the tail, and taming her would be no easy task.

"Miss Jacquard, are the charges against you true or untrue?" General Dix intoned, and then sighed. "In other words, Rose, do you plead guilty or not guilty?"

Rose thought for a moment, letting her arched brows come together in concentration. "I thought that this was a hearing, not a trial, General."

"It is a hearing. But if you agree with the evidence and declare yourself guilty, there is no need for a trial."

"And if I declare myself not guilty?"

"Then the evidence against you—which, I might add, is overwhelming—must be presented, and if deemed strong enough, you will be brought to trial."

"If my guilt were an established fact, I doubt that any of you would be surprised by it. Southerners are not my enemies, they are yours. I am a Southern woman, and I have never denied the fact."

As Rose spoke, several of the commissioners rolled their eyes to the heavens, and General Dix lowered his face into his hands. When she finished, he slowly spread his fingers and looked through them deeply into her eyes. "Does that mean, Rose, that you plead not guilty?"

"Most assuredly, General."

Down came the gavel, and the questioning began.

"Miss Jacquard, you have lived for some time in the North."

"I have lived in Washington, and for most of that time the Capital was a Southern city. Had it not been, I doubt I could have stood it."

"But you had become a Northerner?"

"I had not, and never will. There is not a drop of Yankee blood in my beins."

Another half-hour of such questioning went nowhere, and the tack was changed.

"When your house was searched—"

"Illegally, I might add, by a band of uncouth,

tasteless ruffians without a warrant. Why, they even ripped apart my underwear! Good God, what on earth could I hide in my underwear—unless, of course, I was wearing it!"

It took General Dix nearly ten minutes to quiet the response to these words before the interrogator could go on.

"When your house was searched, copies of Winfield Scott's *Infantry Tactics*, Mahan's *Treatise on Field Fortifications*, and several journals on the caliber and mobility of artillery weapons were found. How do you explain your taste in reading, Miss Jacquard?"

"I am an ardent admirer of General Scott," Rose replied with a perfectly straight face. "I have tried to read everything he has written, including his letters and dispatches to his field officers—"

The rest of her answer was lost in gales of laughter.

At this, General Dix gave up and recessed for lunch until one o'clock.

Rose was placed in a drafty room containing only a hard wooden bench. A piece of bread and a bowl of watery soup were her lunch, and if this weren't enough to anger her, the hearing did not reconvene until two, an hour late.

When they came for her, she dawdled with one excuse after another. By the time she entered the hearing room, even the commissioners were already seated.

"Gentlemen, please keep your seats," she said calmly. "Why stand and accord yourselves the hypocrisy of calling yourselves gentlemen, when you have kept me waiting nearly an hour in a cold and drafty room?"

On this note the afternoon questioning resumed, with Rose continuing to confound and, at times, ridicule her interrogators.

But her wit would carry her only so far when hard evidence was presented at last.

"Miss Jacquard, I ask you to examine this map."

The paper was held in front of Rose and she gave it a passing glance.

"Is that your hand, Miss Jacquard?"

"It is."

"Is that not a map, in detail, of the fortifications of Washington City just prior to the battle of Bull Run?"

"You may call it that. I drew it as a map to flee the city should it be overrun."

"By rebel troops? I would assume, Miss Jacquard, that you would have welcomed them with open arms."

From that moment on, Rose realized that, old friends or not, these men were out for blood. Her blood.

More papers were presented. Most of them had been obtained from the houses and apartments of others caught up in the same net with

Rose. Among them were several decoded ciphers containing her name.

"Miss Jacquard, are you familiar with a man called R. V. Higgins?"

"I know of the gentleman."

"Is he your lover?"

"Sir, how dare you ask—?"

"Just answer the question, Rose."

A rippling sensation raised the hair on the back of her neck. She longed to turn and sweep her gaze over the faces in the room. Was Bram Darcy's among them?

Her mind whirled back to that afternoon nearly a month after her arrest, when she had barked a loud "Go away!" in answer to a light rap on her door.

"Would that I could, Rose, for I have no taste for this duty they have given me."

She looked up quickly to see Bram's tall figure nearly blocking out the light from the door.

Usually immaculate, his uniform now looked in need of pressing. His mustache was untrimmed, and there were heavy lines of weariness about his eyes. The dark, handsome face that had once sported a constant smile of cocky self-assurance now was drawn in thought. "May I come in?"

"I assume you can do as you please, Colonel Darcy. You are my jailer."

The pain in his eyes made her want to quickly withdraw her words.

"Come in . . . sit down."

"Thank you."

He seated himself and opened a folder in his lap. "There will be a hearing to determine if there shall be a trial."

"Trial for what?" Rose cried. "I have done—"

"Rose!" Her name echoed like thunder in the small room. "Do you not realize the seriousness of what you have done? The Union Army suffered greatly at Manassas because of the information Beauregard was given! Information given by you!" He stopped, and sighed deeply. "Officially, I am here as your interrogator. But I am also here as . . ."

"As my . . . friend?" she said, suddenly mindful of the awkwardness between them.

"Yes, your friend. The evidence is mountainous against you, Rose. Should you be brought to trial and found guilty, the final verdict could be . . ."

Again he paused, lifting his eyes to hers. Rose bit her lower lip in dismay. If ever she had seen love in his eyes before, she saw it again now, and knew, in that moment, that her own look was a reflection of his. "The final verdict," she said, smiling, "could be . . . serious."

He nodded, allowing his own lips a faint smile. "That's putting it very nicely. But there is a way, I believe."

"A way?"

"The oath."

"Never!"

"Rose, I beg of you. Take the oath of allegiance to the Union, and they won't even prosecute you."

"No!"

"Damn! You can be the most stubborn, most resolute, most narrow-minded woman—"

"You've ever loved."

There, it was said, and no matter how many bricks and stones they had both added to the wall now between them, the love they felt for one another was still there.

Bram's eyes softened. "I want to save your life, Rose, and I am doing everything in my—"

"Don't, Bram, I beg of you. If it becomes known that you're helping me, it will only fuel the newspapers to bring up our . . . former life. Think of your career."

"Oh, Rose, how blind you can sometimes be. A military career is important to me, yes, but it is not the be-all and end-all of my life! The things I have done were to end the war, if possible, before it began, but I failed." Suddenly he laughed, a manic sound. "Whereas you, Rose, have succeeded."

"I . . . succeeded?"

"Oh, yes. Nearly twenty thousand men fell at Manassas, Rose, on both sides."

"Dear God," she murmured, dropping her head.

"Then that is your final word—you refuse to sign the oath of allegiance to the Union?"

She raised her head and looked at him steadily. "I refuse."

The fragile moment of love that had been between them was gone. When Bram spoke again, his voice was cold. "I have been assigned, for the moment, by the War Department as your interrogator. Now, do you know any of the following people?" One by one, he read off all the now-familiar names. Each one had been arrested in the wake of Rose's arrest. Among them was Mrs. Greenhow's name.

Rose knew them all and said so.

"How many of them aided and abetted you in your trip to Fairfax County?"

"None of them," she replied, managing a wan smile. "How could they? I have never been to Fairfax County."

"Oh? Never, Rose?"

Her face flushed a deep red. "You know the one time I was in Fairfax," she whispered.

"I wondered," he said dryly, "if you remembered."

Rose closed her eyes against the dizziness. How could she forget that afternoon on the riverbank, on the soft green grass of Virginia, writhing in Bram Darcy's powerful arms?

Behind her, his voice droned on with more questions.

Rose answered them all, mostly negatively, but her mind could think of only that afternoon.

He stood at last and moved to stand at her

shoulder. "I will ask you one more time, Rose. You're sure that you will not take the oath?"

"I'm sure."

"Very well, between now and the hearing and the trial—for there will surely be one—I will do what I can."

His hand came up, and Rose quivered as she felt it lightly sweep across her hair. Then he was moving toward the door.

"Bram?"

"Yes."

"Will you return?"

It seemed an eternity before he answered, and it took all the mettle Rose could summon not to whirl and run into his arms.

"I think it wise that I do not, Rose. For both of us."

"Yes . . . wise."

And then he spoke again, his voice calmer. "When this is over, I'm asking for a field command. Unlike you, my dear, I've no taste for this intrigue and deception."

The sound of the door closing and the lock turning had echoed in Rose's brain for weeks afterward.

She had been careful to answer his questions, and those of others, in such a way that Bram could never be implicated because of his past connection with her. She wondered what he would think when she answered the question now being put to her?

"Miss Jacquard."

"Yes?"

"Would you answer the question, please?"

"Would you repeat the question . . . please?"

"Miss Jacquard, was R. V. Higgins your lover?"

"Yes, he was."

The uproar was deafening. Three reporters lunged for the door to file this spicy bit of news on the Wild Rose.

General Dix adjourned the hearing until the following morning at ten.

"Miss Jacquard, on the evening of July 14 of last year, did you accompany R. V. Higgins to the drinking establishment of John and Mary Surratt?"

"I did not. I met him there."

"And what was the reason for this meeting?"

"Friendship."

Titters ran like wildfire through the room. Unlike the first day, fully half the hearing was now attended by women, many of them Northern wives anxious to see the brazen Southern belle Rose Jacquard brought down.

"Later that same evening, did you accompany Mr. Higgins to his home?"

"I did."

"And did you stay with Mr. Higgins until the afternoon of July 16?"

"I did."

"Then, Miss Jacquard, how do you account

for the fact that Mr. Pinkerton's men searched that house on the morning of the sixteenth and you were not there?"

"I was hidden, so that the Yankee hussies of Washington couldn't wag their tongues about my liaison."

General Dix's gavel quieted the uproar before it could get out of hand. He shouted above the clamor, calling one Archibald Harris to the stand.

A powerfully built youth in Union uniform walked with long strides down the aisle. In the front of the room he turned and removed his hat to release a mane of golden-blond hair. His eyes, flickering over Rose, were narrow and intent.

She was sure she had never seen him before.

"Lieutenant Harris, how long have you been in the army?"

"Seven months, sir."

"And before that?"

"I was a drover, supplying horses to the Confederate Army."

"Then you were a rebel?"

"No, sir. My real employment was with the Federal War Department, under the direct command of Colonel Bramfield Darcy."

"And where were you on the afternoon of July 15 last year?"

"I was in Fairfax County, Virginia, preparing to ride north with information to Colonel Darcy concerning the concentration of Confederate troops in Fairfax and Centerville."

General Dix nodded and pointed his gavel at Rose. "Have you ever seen this woman before, Lieutenant?"

"Yes, sir, I have, on the afternoon of July 15, last year."

"And where was that, Lieutenant?"

"On the steps of the Fairfax courthouse, speaking to a Confederate officer, Tom Rosser. He called her Rose Jacquard."

CHAPTER TWENTY

THE DAYS passed with agonizing slowness, and grew into weeks.

More and more Confederate spies were swooped up in the federal nets, without and within the confines of Washington City.

An extremely high percentage of them were women.

In the North, the strife that was ripping the country apart was called the Civil War. In the South it was termed the War of Secession or the War of States' Rights. But no matter its name, it had become a woman's war as a man's.

All over the North and South, women disguised themselves as men and joined the ranks. Others volunteered for duty as nurses near the front lines, many to be near their husbands.

But none were written about with more glee than the female spies, and most of these were Southern. They were called "Cleopatras," "seductive sirens," "downright courtesans," or blatantly "insane," once their deeds were uncovered.

Slowly Rose's name was pushed to the side by others; Belle Boyd, Ellie Poole, and Betty Hassler began to gain the headlines.

As the spring rains began, the army came out of winter quarters. Battles raged in Maryland, Tennessee, and Virginia. But by the end of summer, no side held any advantage.

And still Rose was not tried. It was as if the Justice Department preferred to punish her with the tension of waiting rather than try to sentence her.

Through smuggled messages Rose learned that Pinkerton and others in the War Department wanted her tried and, if possible, hung, as an example to other women who were so ardently pursuing her craft and prolonging the war. Seward and several congressmen were more attuned to public opinion and possible rebel retaliation against captured Union officers. They would have liked nothing better than to ship her South, through the rebel lines, and be done with her.

As the war of words raged on, it became clearer that no one knew exactly what to do with her.

Through it all, Rose remained undaunted.

Her interrogators came often, and always left

with their questions either unanswered or answered with riddles.

Not so the members of the press. They came in droves with each new rumor that her trial date was set. A few, with better connections, were allowed to interview her.

In many ways, Rose relished these times. She served tea and supplied them with copy they hardly needed to edit.

After one of these interviews, she received a visit from Chance Flynn. "You amaze me, Rose. The more you chatter, the more you hurt your cause."

"Perhaps, but thousands of women in the South take heart when they read my words."

"Mark me, Rose, one day you will go too far. You will ridicule me too much!"

"Then you shouldn't have become the brother-in-law of such an infamous woman."

"Do you care so little for Cat's happiness that you would hurt her by slandering me?"

Rose tossed her mane of raven hair and laughed. "You may fool poor Cat, Chance, but not me. One day the truth will reach her ears. Dear God, if it reaches mine here in this wretched prison, surely Cat will hear of it."

"Truth?"

"That you've used your father's influence to stay here in Washington, out of the fighting. At last count, you've been keeping two mistresses, and almost nightly you pass the evening hours with them or among the whores of Marble Alley. And all this while poor Cat has a belly full of your child."

The first blow, with the flat of his hand, did little more than send her flying against the wall. The second, with the back of his hand, cracked her jaw so badly that for several weeks she could take only soup for nourishment.

It was November, more than a year from the start of her imprisonment, when they decided to take Rose to trial at last.

It was Chance who brought the news. "Day after tomorrow, Rose," he said with a leer.

Rose was stunned. So much time had passed that she was sure they had decided not to risk a trial.

"By the way, Rose ..." Flynn was pausing near the door, one hand hooked in his pistol belt, the other resting on the hilt of his saber.

"Yes?"

"Catherine had a baby boy last night."

"Oh, my God," Rose cried. "Is she all right? Is the child—"

"The child is fine. Cat is weak, but still all right. We named the boy Abraham Lincoln Flynn."

The trial was a sham. The evidence against Rose was so overwhelming that she had no defense. It lasted only through the last week of

November, and the outcome was a foregone conclusion: Guilty as charged.

Sentencing was December 20, a bitter day with heavy snow that reminded her of the previous March and her trip to her initial hearing.

Rose was as proud and haughty as ever when she entered the courtroom, but there was a difference, and all who were present noticed it.

She was still a beauty, but the fire was gone from her eyes now, and no longer was she ready with the quips that had made her famous only a few months before. Now she was ready to accept her fate, and do so in silence.

"Rose Marie Jacquard?"

"Yes."

"Please rise."

Rose gathered the folds of dark brown empress cloth in her skirt and stood. She took two measured steps forward, and put as much iron in her spine as she could while drawing a waist-length green velvet wrap tightly over her heaving bosom.

"Rose Marie Jacquard, you have been found guilty of all the following charges. Will the bailiff please read the charges."

Once again, but thankfully for the last time, Rose was forced to listen to the long list of villainous acts she had been found guilty of committing.

"Do you have anything to say before sentence is passed?"

"I do."

"Be brief, please."

Rose swept her eyes about the courtroom and for the briefest of seconds flashed her old, familiar, jaunty smile. "Gentlemen of the North, and those true to the South—but who cannot afford to admit it in the present company—I have made no confession of treason, nor have I admitted to treasonable correspondence. In doing what I have done, I but claim the right that my forefathers had in the glorious year of 1776, the right to protest against tyranny and oppression—"

"Miss Jacquard—"

"I haven't finished yet. I think that I would be deemed the meekest, lowliest Christian on earth if, after being smitten on one cheek by this government, I should crouch like a craven female and turn the other for the same treatment. Therefore, gentlemen, whatever your sentence may be, I do not accept it."

A mixture of groans and chuckles filled the room. But all present, no matter their feelings toward this beautiful, willful woman, would agree that, no matter the sentence, the Wild Rose had the last word.

"Are you quite through, Miss Jacquard?"

"I am."

"Then, as the duly appointed judge in the case of the United States Government versus Rose Marie Jacquard, I pronounce you guilty as charged, and sentence you to twenty-five years in Mermount Prison in the state of New York."

The words had barely left the judge's lips when, from somewhere in the back of the room, a weighted Confederate flag sailed through the air to land on the table in front of Rose.

Without batting an eye, she picked it up, draped it about her shoulders, and strolled from the room.

It was a subdued, hardly merry Christmas in Washington City, but Rose barely noticed. She spent the week packing. One by one, she carefully folded her dresses, tissued them, and placed them in the waiting trunks.

She had been told that, once behind the walls of Mermount, she would be allowed to wear only homespun. But this did not deter her.

"No matter. I shall save them. Who knows, in twenty-five years they might be back in vogue!"

Her transfer to New York, via rail through Baltimore, was to take place on the fourth day of the new year. All through the last week of 1862, messages flowed into her quarters, hinting of plots to free her.

But not all the messages were in Rose's favor. Surviving families of the men killed at Bull Run expressed anger that she had not been hanged. Word flew around the Capital that she would never reach Mermount alive.

Rose paid little attention to any of it. Her

mind, for the first time since it had all begun, was on herself.

Twenty-five years. She would be almost fifty.

On the first morning of the new year, she received two messages, both through the legal mail of Old Capitol Prison.

The first was from Catherine:

My dearest sister:

Does that surprise you? I suppose it should. But you are still my dearest and only sister.

Though I have not had a change of heart, Rose, I have wanted to visit you many times. I dare not. Chance harbors such hatred for you in his heart that if he even knew I was writing this, I quake at what he might do. I have realized since my marriage that Chance, despite his charm and wit, is a quite violent man. And a great deal of his violence is against the South and those who would fight for her.

In other words, Rose, you.

I still do not condone you for the terrible things you have done, but I know now that you did them out of your convictions. I have done the same.

Your fate was in my hands, even though I did not know it at the time. It was I who mentioned to Chance your odd comings and goings, and the strange callers you received at all hours. Believe me when I tell you that I did not know Chance was relaying my every word to Mr. Pinkerton. Only Colonel Darcy has comforted me. He has told me that what happened would have happened had I never said a word. I hope with all my heart that this is true.

In any event, he has also told me that he is trying to secure your release. I pray every night, dear Rose, that this can be done. Twenty-five years seems such a great price to pay when one's only guilt was loving one's homeland.

I doubt, no matter either of our fates, dear sister, that we shall ever meet again. And that, really, is not so painful, for I think our paths in life split long ago and we failed too late to realize it.

For all that has happened, Rose, know that I forgive you, as I hope you do me. And know that I love you.

Cat

Tearfully, Rose picked up a pen to reply, and then put it down just as quickly. Cat had said everything that needed to be said, and she could add nothing to it.

The second message came from Bram Darcy:

I am in contact with Clay Fulton. Take heart. There is hope.

On the evening of January 3, Bram appeared at the door of her rooms like a specter, clad in black from head to boot.

"Dress in dark clothes," he hissed, "a riding habit if you have one, and take only what is most valuable and can fit in your reticule!"

"But why . . . what has happened?"

"More to the point, Rose, what *will* happen if you use reason instead of stubbornness with the man you are about to meet."

CHAPTER TWENTY-ONE

His suit, when he stood to greet Rose, was wrinkled, and the collar of his shirt splayed awkwardly over an ill-knotted tie. "We meet at last, Miz Rose."

The familiarity of his greeting took her aback, but not nearly as much as his awesome height when he stepped around the desk and stood before her. His lips, brushing the back of her hand, were as awkward as his straggling step.

"Good evening . . . Mr. President."

His taciturn face, with its dark, brooding eyes, heavy brows, and large nose, suddenly became animated. The full lower lip spread into a grin that sent his high, prominent cheekbones upward to meet his eyes.

"Do you find it so difficult—calling me President?"

"I . . ."

"No matter." His hand, like a great paw, settled around her arm and guided her toward a high-backed wing chair. "Come, sit! We shall talk."

Rose settled stiffly on the very edge of the soft leather and clutched her bag in gloved hands as if it alone would support her in the moments to come.

To her surprise, Lincoln sat on the desk before her, one foot resting on the floor, the other leg raised like that of a standing crane, the foot swinging like a pendulum. "Would you like a sherry . . . claret . . . brandy perhaps?"

"No, thank you."

"As you wish."

He looked at her intently for a long moment, and Rose felt herself drawn into the depths of those eyes that emanated such intelligence and, at the same time, compassion. For the first time she understood why so many people had followed this man, had elected him their leader. Her eyes dropped to study the dark blue merino of her riding habit.

Then he heaved a great sigh. "What am I to do with you?" he murmured.

Rose looked up in shock. "What?"

"What am I to do with you?" He wagged his head slowly from side to side. "You have played a deadly, dangerous game. You have lost, and by all rights, you should pay the price."

Rose sat up even straighter in the chair, her shoulders back and her chin lifted. "With all due respect, I think it's quite the opposite, Mr. President. I played the game, and I won."

The smile faded from his lips. The hollow eyes seemed to recede further into the gaunt skull, making his gaze so penetrating that Rose felt a chill ripple up her spine.

"Yes, in your mind, I suppose you have. Do you think your sentence just?"

Rose shrugged.

"You are young, and, I might add, as beautiful as the press says you are. Twenty-five years will be an eternity."

Rose nodded, unable to stop her chin from quivering. "I shall be nearly fifty by the time I am released. That is, unless . . ."

"Unless the South wins the war."

"Yes."

"And the way this war is going, that could well happen."

Again Rose's eyes grew wide. But before she could discern the full meaning of his words, he had turned away. He shuffled to the windows and stood, shoulders slumped, looking south over the houses of Washington, roofed in white.

A bitter laugh came from his lanky frame. "We have managed to construct a street railway system, with two tracks down the middle of

Pennsylvania Avenue, but we have only two horse-drawn cars running on it. Even I could not find space to ride on one yesterday."

Whether it was his words or his tone, Rose could not suppress a laugh of her own. "Just as you cannot put an army in Richmond."

"Exactly. Out there, somewhere, not far, Lee sits with his army. He could take Washington City, but he won't do it. Davis won't let him. The South is fighting a war of defense, upholding what they claim as their rights. We, on the other hand, must fight a war of offense, to retain the Constitution and keep the Union whole."

He turned again to face Rose. "In these past months we have, at last, discovered how to run a war. I pray that it is not too late and we may now find some way of winning it."

"Mr. President, I don't understand. Why are you . . . ?"

"Saying all this to you? Perhaps because I want you to repeat it to Jeff Davis . . . or perhaps, for a moment, I would rather talk to a pretty girl than to my generals!" His laugh was genuine this time, but then his eyes clouded with sad intensity once more. "War is the death of men's souls, Miz Rose. Perhaps you'll realize that when you see more of it."

Again Rose started to speak, but he silenced her with a wave.

"Mr. Seward is distressed at your sentence. He would have you serve a hundred years. My

Secretary of War, Mr. Stanton, lacks all sentiment when it comes to traitors. Indeed, I think Mr. Stanton is without any sentiment at all. Woman or not, he would dearly love to see you hang. For my part . . ."

Rose was sure she detected a sudden warmth in the stern eyes. "For your part, Mr. President . . . ?"

"Even if Lee were not at Washington's door and breathing down my neck, I would not want a Southern martyr—much less a female martyr—hanging over my head."

He returned to the desk and pushed a sheet of paper across it. "Read that, and if you agree, sign it."

Rose's eyes flew over the words. It was a simple statement pledging her word that, in consideration of her being set at liberty beyond the lines of the U.S. Army, she would never return north of the Potomac River during the present hostilities without the permission of the Secretary of War of the United States. "Free," she whispered.

"Yes, free," the President said, "but not without compensation. The South evidently thinks you a prize. They have agreed to exchange five Union officers for your release. You can thank your Colonel Darcy for that. He did the negotiations."

I'll never stop thanking him, Rose thought, signing the paper.

Lincoln stood, moved around the desk, and

walked with her to the door. "If it had been solely up to me, Miz Rose, could you have given me any good reason to free you?"

A slight smile curved Rose's lips. "None, I assure you."

Again he kissed her hand, and Rose thought she saw a bit of merriment in his eyes. "I admire your pluck, if not your politics . . . and I am relieved to have this burr removed from under my saddle."

He opened the door, and Bram Darcy spun toward them to stand at attention.

"Colonel Darcy, I assume the arrangements have been made?"

"Yes, Mr. President. A barouche and driver are waiting at the south portico. Mounts are waiting south of Alexandria. We'll ride from there to the post of exchange at the Rapidan River."

"Good. See that no one recognizes her until she is in rebel hands."

"I will, sir."

The towering figure turned to her and looked down from his great height. "Good-bye, Miz Rose," he said gently. "And Godspeed."

"Thank you, Mr. President." She started toward Bram, then turned. "And . . ."

"Yes?"

"In many ways, I shall miss Washington."

Without another word, Bram hurried her down two flights of steps and into the night. Gale winds whipped at the hood of her cloak as they ran across the courtyard to a waiting barouche.

"Ready, Sergeant?"

"Yes, sir!"

Bram handed her inside, quickly followed, and as they lurched forward, drew curtains over the windows.

"Why such secrecy?"

"Because the President's cabinet will not think five officers a big enough exchange for you. But once the deed is done and you're in the South, there's nothing they can do."

"Dear God," Rose asked, "am I so great a thorn in everyone's side?"

"Yes, Rose, you are," Bram replied quietly. "I even had to recruit a sergeant from outside my command so no word of this would leak out."

They were waved across the Chain Bridge without even a check for passes. On the other side, the horses were whipped up, and within the hour they were past Alexandria.

"We ride from here," Bram said, flinging open the door and helping Rose step down into the snow. "Sergeant!"

"Sir?"

"Help the lady mount. I'll check for patrols in the area."

"Yes, sir!"

The sergeant was a young lad, of small stature, with a serious face and gentle manner. He gave Rose a leg up to her mount, and then mounted

413

himself. "It's a cold night, ma'am. Will your cloak be enough?"

"I hope so, Sergeant. I'm sorry you've been taken from your warm quarters."

"That's all right, ma'am," he replied, his boyish face breaking into a grin. "I'm with the Twenty-third Ohio. We're posted on Upton's Hill. It's probably colder up there than it is here!"

"Have you . . . seen battle?"

"Yes, ma'am—Shiloh and the second Bull Run."

"Still playing the spy, Rose?" Bram had ridden up beside them without making a sound.

"Not at all," she replied. "I was just being civil."

Bram turned to the boy. "Sergeant, I'll take the lead. You ride with the prisoner—and stay close."

"Yes, sir."

For the first five miles, Rose was shocked into silence. Since leaving Washington, she had almost forgotten that she was still a prisoner.

"Ma'am?"

"Yes?"

"If you wrap this around your face under your hood, the wind won't burn so bad."

Gratefully Rose took a muffler from the young sergeant's extended hand and did as he suggested.

"How long is the ride to this place . . . Rapidan?"

"About four hours, ma'am."

"Well," she laughed, "it's going to be a long night. My name is Rose Jacquard."

"I know, ma'am, you're the Wild Rose."

"And what's your name, besides 'Sergeant'?"

"McKinley, ma'am. William McKinley."

The snow had stopped, and now a stark white moon made the landscape ghostly pale. The two-story clapboard house sat on a high hill about a mile north of the Rapidan River.

From where Rose stood in the second-floor window, she could clearly see the meandering stream. Far to her left she could just make out the village of the same name.

Somewhere near here the next morning she would cross over the river into the South. Leaving the North behind her meant little. Leaving Bram Darcy did. She knew now why she had insisted to General Beauregard, so many months before in the Fairfax courthouse, that she had to return to Washington. She had told herself then that it was only because there was more she could do for the South in the Capital.

Now she knew that to be a lie, a lie to herself. Even compromised, caught, and jailed, she would still rather be in the same city as Bram Darcy.

But no longer.

After this night, there would be little chance they would ever be in the same place again.

"Is there anything else you'll need for the night?"

Rose turned to see Bram filling the open door between their two bedrooms. "No, I don't need anything. Besides, there's not much of the night left."

He shrugged his massive shoulders. His hair, still damp from the ride, curled over his forehead and nearly obscured his ears. His breeches, too, were still wet, making them cling like a layer of skin to his long, powerful legs. Rose thought that she had never seen him so handsome.

He frowned and took a few steps into the room, his eyes raking the sudden paleness in her face. "Rose . . ."

"Yes."

"I . . ." His eyes darkened, and when he spoke again, his voice was husky and his words hurried. "It was Bennie McAdam who carried my messages to Richmond and Fulton's back to Washington. He's waiting now across the Rapidan River."

"Dear, sweet Bennie," Rose whispered.

"He will signal Sergeant McKinley when they are ready. That should be just before dawn—three hours away. There are lady's things there in the armoire. You should get some sleep, Rose."

"I doubt I could sleep a wink this night."

"It will still be a long ride for you in the morning—to Richmond."

"Richmond." She whirled back to the window to hide the sudden mist that had filled her eyes. Home, to the South, at last. But at the cost of never seeing Bram again.

"Rose . . ." He was at her side, his hands turning her to him, his arms engulfing her quivering body. At his first touch she felt her body come alive. She wanted to melt against his strength and scream out the terror that suddenly filled her heart.

"Tears, Rose, at such a time, when you are free at last?"

"Free, yes, but . . ."

The flood spewed forth. She could no longer hold it back. At the same time, she threw her arms about him and buried her head against his chest.

His hands came up to stroke her hair, and she heard his voice, quiet, soothing. He spoke her name over and over again, as if she were a child just awakened from a horrible nightmare.

But, Rose thought, the real nightmare was just beginning.

"How many times before have we said goodbye?" she whispered. "But this time . . ."

"I know, my darling," he sighed, "oh, dear God, how I know." His eyes devoured her face, and then his lips lowered to take hers. The kiss quickly turned into many kisses that covered her eyes, her cheeks, her throat, only to return and find her mouth.

His lips parted and his tongue teased hers in a dizzying, overwhelming sensation. Her legs gave way, but she no longer had need of them, for her feet were inches from the floor, her body caught up in the powerful vise of his arms.

And then he was nuzzling into the damp, fresh scent of her free-flowing hair. "I promised myself, my darling, that this wouldn't happen."

"I dared to hope that it would." Her voice, speaking as she caressed his cheeks, was soft and warm. "Put me down, Bram, and let me undress."

Her boots touched the floor, and almost reluctantly he released her. She was a few steps toward the fire, with her back to him, when he spoke.

"You're sure, Rose?"

Without turning, she reached for the top button of her riding habit. "I'm sure that I want you now more than ever before. I thought I sensed the same feeling from you. Was I wrong?"

"No."

"Then, what is it?"

"It will be a long war, Rose, and we may never—"

"I know," she cried, not wanting reality put into words. "All the more reason for this night."

With quaking fingers she removed her riding habit, her blouse, and her pantalets. She was about to reach for the laces of her chemise when she felt the wiry hair of his bare chest against her shoulders.

"Let me."

In seconds his deft fingers had removed the

last garment between them and she was turned, pulled by his demanding arms into his embrace.

His need was all too evident, throbbing against her. She responded to it, pressing her pliant body willingly against him, pleading with her every move and sobbing groan for him to take her.

She had never felt so aroused as she did at that moment. Their tongues dueled, sending fire through her loins as his hands sought out every nerve under her skin.

With his lips still locked to hers, he swept her into the air. The lumpy straw-filled mattress felt like a cloud beneath her back as he settled her and moved to her side.

"You're so alive," he moaned. "Every nerve, every pore in your skin responds to my touch."

"I know," she gasped, curling her fingers in his thick black hair and guiding his lips to her breast as his hands wandered over her thighs.

She gasped when his fingers found and parted her. His own gasp told her what she already knew—that she was ready, that her body exuded the strength of her desire.

His lips left her breast and trailed white-hot flame down over her belly and thighs.

"Yes, oh my God, yes!"

Her body arched as he plunged his seeking tongue inside her. Stars exploded behind her tightly clenched lids as his tongue withdrew, only to thrust again. And the tip was teasing her, throwing her whole being into spasms of abandoned passion.

Her arms flailed until her hand found him and folded around his rigid thickness.

This only inflamed her all the more, and she was writhing beyond control, tugging and urging him to cover her body with his. Her legs parted and lifted, finding their way about his hips. At the same time, his hands crept beneath her, finding the tautness of her buttocks.

She knew that his need was as great as hers, for she could feel the pounding and pulsing of him in her hand. He began to enter her slowly, but Rose threw herself onto his thrust. "Take me, my darling! Take all of me!" she cried.

He gave up, entering her to the full, groaning out his pleasure.

Rose cried out in joy as she felt the steady throb of him fill her again and again. From somewhere far away she heard his voice gasping out her name, and her own cries answering him.

He whispered of the ecstasy he felt inside her, his breath hot on her face, his mouth covering hers with fire.

Rose arched her body, taking him fully, crying out for more, and his hands slid beneath her buttocks, forcing her up to meet his hungry plunges. His movements were sure, his thrust deep, and she could feel the passion in her belly mount higher and higher.

A strangled cry escaped her lips as exquisite pleasure flooded her body then cried out again as their passion for each other culminated.

Rose clung to him for many long moments, struggling to regain her breath, as Bram murmured continuous words of endearment into the damp softness of her hair.

Finally, as the passion ebbed from her body, her mind returned to reality. What they had just shared would never be enough, Rose told herself, but it would have to do.

"We shall never forget this night," he said, moving his hands in loving circles over her back.

"I know."

"And maybe—"

Rose quickly placed a finger over his lips, stopping his words as she snuggled closer into his arms, letting them hold and cherish her for the few minutes they had left.

Rose sat rigidly in the saddle, the dark jacket of her riding habit and cloak intensifying the paleness of her face. She had drawn her long black hair tightly away from her face and tied it with a ribbon at the nape of her neck. Only the wayward curls toppling over her forehead softened the bleakness of her features.

Bram sat, equally stoic, beside her, his eyes piercing the predawn mist toward the bridge below them and the hill he knew was somewhere beyond the river.

They had been roused, not from slumber, but
from the bliss they had found in each other's
arms, by a light rap on Bram's door. He had slid
quietly from the bed and padded into the adjoining room, closing the door behind him.

Seconds later he was back, gazing down at
her. "The signal has come. First dawn."

Just inside the front door of the house, Bram
had leaned down and pressed his lips to hers.
There would be no good-byes possible under the
eyes of the men outside.

"I shall always love you, Bram," she murmured into his lips.

"And I you. More than life itself." With that,
he had swept her out the door to the waiting
mounts.

Now they sat waiting at the rise of the hill. As
they watched, the sun rose like a majestic orange ball. Its rays soon penetrated the gray pall
and cast a shimmering glow over the white fields
and swift-flowing river.

"It shall be a beautiful day," Rose whispered.

He didn't reply, only nodded, keeping his face
forward. Rose did the same. Then she saw the
bridge, and beyond it, the group of dark-coated
mounted men. She could not discern the colors,
but she knew that five of them would be wearing blue.

And then her eye fell on the ugly snout of an
abandoned cannon protruding from the snow.
"Was there a battle here?" she asked.

"Yes, all through this area."

"How many men died here?" she asked quietly.

"Too many," he replied. "I don't know how many, exactly. After a battle, one shouldn't count how many men died, but thank God for the number who lived."

Before she could reply, the youthful sergeant had ridden up the hill and skidded his horse to a halt beside her. "They've started, sir."

Bram turned in his saddle, and his black eyes locked with Rose's. "Miss Jacquard, the sergeant will escort you as far as this side of the bridge. You will cross alone, passing our officers in the center. Do you understand?"

"Yes."

"Good-bye . . . Miss Jacquard."

"Good-bye . . . Colonel."

They rode side by side to the bridge. Just before reaching it, Rose handed the sergeant his muffler. "Thank you for the loan. It was very thoughtful of you."

" 'Twas nothin'. S'long, Miss Jacquard. Don't tell them rebels, but it's been a pleasure meetin' ya. Somethin' I can tell my gran'kids."

Rose reached over and touched his hand briefly. "Make sure you come out of this war alive so you can have some. Good-bye, Sergeant McKinley."

The five Union officers didn't give her a glance, nor did Rose look at them when they passed.

Just over the bridge she paused, partially

turned, and raised two gloved fingers to her lips and held them there for several seconds.

She saw Bram's head nod, and then she turned her mount toward the group of waiting riders.

A single tear formed in the corner of one eye, but by the time she had reached them, she had managed to blink it away and force a smile to her lips.

You're going South now, Rose—home—and whatever was in the North, you'll just have to leave there.

Bennie McAdam awaited her with a grin from ear to ear on his ruddy face and a flask in his hand. "Jeff Davis, meself, and the whole damn Confederacy welcome ya to Virginia, Miz Rose."

"Thank you, Bennie. What's this?"

"It ain't in a fancy glass, Miz Rose, but it's champagne—the real French stuff!"

Rose added a laugh to her smile and raised the flask. "Gentlemen, to Jefferson Davis, Robert E. Lee, and the Confederate States of America!"

The men cheered. As she brought the flask from her lips, a young captain spurred his horse forward. "And where does the lady wish to go?"

"To the capital of the Confederacy, Captain, wherever that might be."

"It's still Richmond, ma'am, although the

Yankees are giving us hell. It might even be in Northern hands by the time we get there."

"I shall take my chance on that, Captain, for I'm no amateur at being in Northern hands!"

PART FIVE

1864

CHAPTER TWENTY-TWO

As THE WAR rolled on through 1863, it became more and more like a bad play that seemed to go on forever, never coming near a third act.

Richmond itself had been threatened for seven bloody days in the early spring of 1863. Through the summer, the death toll on both sides mounted, with no conclusive battles. The armies see-sawed back and forth between Richmond and Washington in the east, and up and down the Shenandoah Valley to the west.

But slowly, as the steamy days and nights of the Southern summer turned into fall, the tide began to change. Routs in the Shenandoah Valley culminated in the Union's bloody victory at Gettysburg. Soon after that, Lee retreated deep into Virginia, and Grant secured Vicksburg at last.

Rose took each day's news in stride.

By her own wish, she had arrived quietly in Richmond. She took lodgings at Ballard's Hotel and spent the first few weeks putting her new life in order.

Most of her estate in the North had been confiscated, but through Bennie she was able to sell the jewelry her jailers had left her. This, coupled with a gift from the Confederate war chest of Colonel Clay Fulton, allowed her to live as well as she considered she needed to.

Her anonymity was short-lived, however. Reporters from the Richmond *Dispatch* and other newspapers learned that the Wild Rose of Washington was in Richmond, and for weeks her name and picture were emblazoned on front pages nearly every day. Rose could only hope that it would soon die down.

And it finally did, for with the spring of 1864 came new battles and a new threat to Richmond. By May the Union armies of the Potomac had crossed the Rapidan and were again driving relentlessly south. Few in the Confederate capital had any illusions now about the outcome of the war. But no one, certainly not Rose, would speak of defeat aloud.

As the siege continued, Richmond changed from a city of leisurely strollers into a fortified garrison of young men laughing to hide their fear and young belles unable to hide it in their wide eyes.

The ethereal blue sky above the James River was filled with smoke from the battles in the rolling countryside nearby. The city's days were given over to hard work and calming shattered nerves from the sounds of Yankee artillery. But in a desperate attempt to ignore the chaos, the nights were filled with dancing, music, and romance.

Rose, now without servants, learned to cook and sew. Seeing the rows upon rows of wounded in the makeshift hospitals, she also took up nursing. She learned to pick lint to fashion bandages, as well as the technique of applying them. Barely controlling her nausea, she mastered the skill of applying hot tar to the stump of a severed leg after the surgeon had applied his saw.

Each day she trudged her way to the hospital to give aid to the wounded and dying, Union and Confederate alike, always fearing that one day she would see a familiar face among them.

Rose did her part, but never was her heart completely in it. She could see that behind the eyes of the men in brass buttons, epaulets, and sword belts was the knowledge that the South was losing.

The young belles of Richmond did everything in their power to look beautiful and gay for the soldiers who would spend the following days in the trenches. Rose herself went through the motions and said the things expected of her, but she began to brood more and more as her thoughts returned to that last night of love with Bram.

Where was he? Was he still alive?

Each day, she felt more alone and heartsick than she had ever felt in her Washington cell, but like everyone around her, she carried on.

And she watched.

She watched the wounded carried in, and the dead buried. She watched young men vomit with fear when they thought of the next day's battle. And she watched the young girls with the light of love in their eyes turn away until their escorts were ready to dance again.

She watched until she could watch no longer.

And always, like a specter haunting her every thought by day, her every dream by night, was the face of Bram Darcy.

One morning she ran toward a buckskin-clad rider stepping from his horse, only to realize as the amazed man turned toward her that it was not Bram, after all. Another time, she thought she saw him emerge from a tavern near Libby Prison. "Bram, what are—?"

"Ma'am, I don't know your name, but I'd be mighty proud to learn it."

Red-faced, she ran on down the block, only to have the same thing happen the following day.

Once, while having dinner with two of her

nursing comrades in the America Hotal, she looked up to see a Confederate captain in the adjoining hotel bar. The size was perfect, the profile almost right. Then he turned, and Rose's wrist went limp, spilling her cup of tea across the table.

It was he. She knew it. This time there could be no doubt of it. He wore a beard, and his mustache was wider and curled, but it was he, she knew it!

"Rose, what is it?"

"Yes, Rose, you look as if you've seen a ghost."

"Excuse me!" But as she stood, he merged into the crowd near the door and quickly disappeared.

"Are you all right, Rose?"

"Yes, yes, it's . . . nothing."

A week later, Clay Fulton called on her. In his high, reed-thin voice, he told her that he needed her help urgently.

"But how?" Rose asked. "What can I do?"

"It's actually your memory I need, Rose—your recollections."

"I don't understand . . ."

"Pinkerton and the Union War Department have sent a few infiltrators South. Some we catch, some we don't. But there's one in particular we'd like to get our hands on. We've had an artist put together a sketch of him. I thought you might just recognize him from Washington, or you might have seen him during your time in the Old Capitol Prison."

"I'll do what I can."

Fulton sorted through his folder and laid three sketches on the table before her. Each looked slightly different, but they were all of one man: Bram Darcy.

Rose felt her cheeks grow hot and her breath catch in her throat.

"This one's a character, he is, sneaky as a snake," Fulton growled, "and a damned good actor. He's been an English blockade runner in Charleston, a riverboat captain in Vicksburg, and a Creole trader in New Orleans. We think he had a lot to do with the Yankee wins in those cities. We even think he was in Richmond not long ago, posing as a Confederate captain."

Dear God, Rose thought, hoping that the perspiration beading her forehead wouldn't give her away. Now she knew that, at least once, she *had* seen Bram!

"The man's like a chameleon, Rose, he pops up everywhere, always in a different disguise. Does the sketch remind you of anyone?"

Her lower lip curled between her teeth and she steadied herself by clasping her trembling knees.

"Well, Rose?"

"No," she managed, "no, he's not familiar at all. I . . . I'm sorry."

If Fulton heard the hesitation in her voice, he

gave no indication. Rose breathed a deep sigh of relief when he finally left.

After that, the nights grew longer and the days more miserable. As fall approached, she could stand it no longer. She asked for and received a pass for Charleston. Hopefully, she could visit Belle Erin and the places in the city she had known as a child. Perhaps seeing them would make her less bitter about the present, and more sure of the future.

It didn't.

She learned from strangers that Belle Erin had gone to seed, and anyway it was overrun with Yankees.

Charleston itself was under siege, and conditions were even worse there than in Richmond. People no longer had leather for shoes, so wooden footwear was fashioned. Food was scarce, and what could be found was too expensive to buy. Even the soldiers were no longer in gray. Their uniforms were worn out and the Confederate treasury had no funds to replace them. Now they wore anything they could find—mostly patched rags, nothing that vaguely resembled a uniform.

Only the very rich—and only the rich who had gold, at that, for the blockade runners had lost faith in the paper money of the Confederacy—were able to maintain their life-styles of handsome carriages, fine silk, and liveried servants.

Rose returned in despair to Richmond.

In early September Clay Fulton came again to Rose's rooms at Ballard's Hotel. "The President would like to see you, Rose."

"Me? When?"

"At your convenience, but now if possible."

"I'll get a wrap."

Jefferson and Varina Davis had taken up residence in the old Brochenbrough house. It was a lovely plantation-style manor with a wide, pillared veranda and terraced gardens full of flowering fruit trees.

Clay Fulton escorted her into the parlor, and then retired to inform President Davis of her arrival.

Rose sighed as she looked around the tastefully furnished room, with its marble mantel, its tapestries and raw-silk draperies, and carpeted floors. It had been a long time since she had seen such style.

"Hello, Rose."

Even in the midst of war, Varina Davis was dressed in the height of fashion. She wore a pink satin breakfast dress, with an ivory sash at her waist and matching ribbons laced through the entire bell of the skirt.

Rose felt her face flush when she thought of her own calico and muslin. And because of her work at the hospital, she wore but one crinoline, and had long ago cast aside her hoops during the day.

Self-consciously Rose looked down, and then back up at the elegantly attired woman, a slight flush reddening her cheeks.

The war-weary lines of Varina's face instantly disappeared, to be replaced by an elfin smile. She lifted her arms in welcome, and Rose flew into them.

"I'm so sorry, Rose, about that day so long ago."

"Day . . . ?"

"When I thought you had snubbed me in the Senate chamber, just before Jeff's speech. I didn't know then what you would one day do for us, or I would never have called you a Yankee sympathizer in the Southern press."

"I know," Rose replied, stepping back. "Colonel Fulton thought it best that no one outside his own circle know the truth."

"I only wish that I had been here, at Jefferson's side, when you first arrived in Richmond."

"It doesn't matter," Rose said, smiling herself now. "I'm only glad to see you again at last."

"Good day, Rose."

Rose looked up over the woman's shoulder, and barely suppressed a gasp at the tall, thin figure of the President of the Confederacy. He had so changed. His chin was now adorned with a wispy Imperial that was swiftly turning gray. The aristocratic nostrils no longer flared, and the defiant gleam was now gone from his sunken, hollow eyes. The cheekbones had always been prominent, but now they stood out like bony wings from the starkness of his face.

Rose had been welcomed by him upon her initial arrival in Richmond. Then he had looked weary and unwell. But in the intervening months he had become a skeleton of his former self.

"Good afternoon, Mr. President."

"Varina," he said, lightly kissing his wife's cheek, "some *cafe au lait*, or perhaps tea. Or would you like something stronger, Rose?"

"No, no, tea would be fine."

"Please sit, I'll only be a moment," Varina said.

As soon as the doors closed behind his wife, Davis turned to Rose with a hollow chuckle. "She shall be longer than a moment. I have already told her we have much to discuss. Come, let us sit on the porch. I like the smell of the trees."

His grip was like a feather on her elbow as he guided her through the tall French doors and seated her on the rear veranda.

"I thank you again, Rose, for all you have done, and ask your forgiveness for what you have had to endure because of it."

" 'Tis nothing to what I have seen others endure since I have been in Richmond, Mr. President."

"Oh, it's bleak, yes, but not over. No, Rose, it's far from over. We shall defeat them yet!

But we shall need help ... new help. That is why I have asked you to come, Rose."

In her breast, Rose felt a tinge of anger. How could he say this? His soldiers were in rags, ill-fed, their eyes opaque marbles looking out on a desecrated world.

How could he still believe?

But then, didn't she? Of course she did. They all did. They had to. It was all they had left.

As if to amplify her thoughts, there was a sudden boom of artillery from the hills north of the city. Davis seemed not to hear it, or chose to ignore it, as he poured tea from a silver service held by a Negro servant.

Will the ironies never cease? Rose thought, watching the colored woman's smiling face and adoring eyes. A few miles away, men in blue were fighting and dying to secure freedom for this woman, and she was gladly serving tea to one of the men most responsible for keeping her in servitude.

"There you are, Rose."

Rose accepted the bone-china cup and saucer, and watched Davis settle back in his chair. When the servant was gone, he leveled his gaze on her face and began to speak. "Rose, I shall not lie to you, it would be foolish. What you have already done, and the work in the hospitals you do now, is far more than could be expected of any one person. But I must ask more of you."

Rose brought the cup and saucer closer to her

lips, partially to hide her face, for she knew that she was allowing a cloud of doubt at that moment to pass across her features.

"You know, Mr. President, of the promise I signed for Lincoln?"

"Oh, yes. You yourself told me, in fact. But what I have in mind would not involve crossing north of the Potomac. No indeed, Rose, if you agree to what I propose, there would be a much greater distance traveled than that from here to Washington."

"You know I will do anything I can."

"The clouds of defeat gather daily over the South. But there are ways to stave them off. The Union blockade of Southern ports has begun to take its toll. Food is scarce, and military supplies grow dangerously lower each day."

"I . . . I can see that."

His smile in reply was enigmatic. "We need money, Rose, and my agents in London tell me it can be obtained. They are very close to securing a loan, partially from France, partially from England. They tell me that just a gentle shove, a little convincing, will secure that loan for us."

"I don't understand."

"Don't you, Rose? You have education, manners, resourcefulness, and most important, you have unsurpassed beauty. All of England and the Continent know of your imprisonment in Washington City by the Yankees. You would be a great hit in England, Rose, a most influential agent for the Southern cause."

She was awed. The magnitude of his words set her hands to shaking so much that she had to place the china cup on the table between them.

"I understand you are also fluent in the French language," he continued. "That, too, would be a great advantage, should we be able to secure you an audience with Napoleon the Third."

"The emperor?"

Jefferson Davis nodded. "He has always sympathized with our cause, and still does, even now when the war goes badly for us. You, of all people, might sway France to actively come to our aid."

Now Rose was even more fearful. London? Paris? Charleston, Washington City, and a few trips to New York and Philadelphia had been the extent of her travels. To sail across a vast ocean and confer with kings and emperors?

"We would consider it a great boon, Rose, if you would go to London. If anyone in the South can stir up sympathy for our cause, it is you. We would be hard put to find a more appealing agent."

Slowly, as the initial shock receded, Rose realized the truth of his words. She knew that her fame had reached London; William Howard Russell had written several stories about her in the London *Times*.

She knew that if such a mission were successful, if she could gain some help and barter cotton futures for ships and supplies, it would buy the South time. The war would still be lost—she was not such a fool to think that it wouldn't—but time might buy a better peace when the end came.

But she paused.

Bram Darcy was in the South . . . somewhere. It was unlikely he would try to contact her, unless . . .

The end came.

When that happened, he would seek her out, and he would never find her if she were in London or Paris.

"You pause, Rose. Do you have doubts?"

"No, Mr. President, not doubts. It's just that all of this is so very sudden. It's a bit beyond me."

"And a bit frightening, perhaps?"

"Yes, yes, that's it."

"I understand." He stood, moved around the small tea table, and took her hands in his. "Take a day or two to decide. But I must know in that time. A week from today, a sleek new packet, a sidewheeler called the *Defiance*, sails from Wilmington. To do any good, Rose, you must be on board."

"I understand, Mr. President, you shall have my answer by day after tomorrow."

"Excellent, Rose . . . and I pray your answer is yes."

She nodded and took her leave.

Each step she took back to Ballard's Hotel brought another wave of indecision. The night made her more miserable. She tossed and turned, her perspiration soaking the sheet.

By morning she was still far from a solution.

The events of the following day would make Rose's decision for her.

Bennie McAdam had prospered; since his return to the South he had begun to trade in cotton, and a considerable amount of his business was dealing with the blockade runners of Charleston and Wilmington.

This afternoon, in the dining room of Ballard's, he looked, from head to toe, the successful trader. A tailored black frock coat fitted snugly across his broad shoulders, and new Spanish leather boots were on his feet. A gold watch chain spread across his brocaded vest, and his cravat was topped with real Irish lace.

"Bennie, you've come up in the world," Rose laughed, accepting a bear hug from his powerful arms and slipping into a velvet-covered chair.

"Aye, that I have," he replied, taking her hands in his and seating himself directly opposite. Then he leaned forward with such a conspiratorial expression in his normally twinkling eyes that Rose knew something was wrong.

"Bennie, what is it?"

He shook his head and dropped his voice to a low whisper. "Ah, Miz Rose, 'tis heartsick I am to tell ya. This news won't be out to the papers until early tomorrow morning. They don't want anyone to know until they're safely in Castle Thunder prison."

"Until who . . .?"

"A Pinkerton man named Timothy Webster . . . and yer Colonel Darcy."

"Oh, dear God, no!" Rose cried. "How . . . where?"

"Near Wilmington. They were caught posin' as traders, like meself. They've already been tried as spies, and now they're bringin' 'em here to Castle Thunder."

Rose's face paled. There could be only one reason they would be incarcerated in Castle Thunder instead of Libby Prison, but she still heard her voice asking Bennie the inevitable question.

"They were both caught in civilian clothes, o' course, and when they tried to escape, a Confederate officer was killed. Webster was wounded in the thigh and Darcy in the arm."

"What is the sentence, Bennie?"

"The Confederates are gonna hang both of 'em in one week's time."

"No . . . dear God, no . . ."

Rose reared back in the wide wings of the chair and covered her face with her hands.

"Miz Rose . . . ?"

"Yes?" Slowly she lowered her hands to see that Bennie had pulled his chair so close that their knees were almost touching.

"As far as this Webster is concerned, I don't give a tinker's damn if Major Alexander over at Castle Thunder hangs him. But I know yer feelings fer Darcy."

"We have Bram Darcy to thank for our own freedom, Bennie, you know that."

"Aye."

"And perhaps our lives."

"Aye, I know that as well, and that's why I've already come up with a bit of a plan. I know a guard at Thunder who can be bribed. If I can get a message to Darcy through him . . ."

Rose listened intently, and nodded each time Bennie paused, urging him to go on.

"But Bram is not Catholic."

"Then"—Bennie smiled—"he'll have to become one fer a while!"

He went on, again with Rose digesting every word.

"It's a bold plan," she said at last, "but it might work!"

"Oh, it'll work, Miz Rose, I've no doubt of it."

"Bless you, Bennie," she said, life having returned to her features now. "We'll do it. Even if I didn't love him so, we owe him this much."

"There's a bit of a drawback to it."

"What is that?"

"Even if we get him out of Thunder, there's slim chance we can get him North."

Rose thought for a moment, then smiled. "There's a way, Bennie, to get him clear out of the country—by sea."

CHAPTER TWENTY-THREE

NEARLY all prisons in the South were made up of old, unused buildings converted from barns or tobacco warehouses. For acres around them, walls or high fences were built.

Castle Thunder was no different.

Enlisted men and noncommissioned officers were housed in tents under the open sky. Officers were interned in a separate building. Spies, wealthier civilians, and condemned men were housed in the second story of the same building.

"Can I help you, Father?"

"I have a pass fer meself and the sister to give succor to the Catholic prisoners who have requested it."

The sleepy-eyed guard took the pass from Bennie McAdam, examined it with a cursory glance,

447

and consulted a sheet tacked to the wall. "We only got one, Father, name of Darcy."

"That would be the one."

"This way."

Rose shriveled her body into the habit she wore and used her hands to fold the wide white wings of the hood over the sides of her face. She kept her head bowed, so she could see only the back of Bennie's legs as they moved down the dark corridor.

The guard stopped at one of the rooms and unlocked the door. "You wouldn't be bringing a Gatling gun or anything like that to the prisoner, would ya, Father?" He chuckled.

"Hardly, my son." Bennie moved into the room, and Rose slithered sideways in behind him, her face averted from the guard.

"Call me when you're done."

"I will, I will," Bennie replied.

Rose rolled her eyes up, blinking in the dimness of the room. It was a hovel, barely ten by ten, with one wooden chair, a table, and a straw-covered cot. There was straw strewn on the floor, and the only light came from the moon through a paneless barred window. She could barely see the figure on the cot trying to rise. She started to move forward, but Bennie's hand caught her.

"Wait," he whispered, bending his ear toward the guard's retreating footsteps.

Rose held her breath until she felt Bennie's hand release her.

"Who . . . is it?"

Rose bolted forward just as the figure struggled from the cot. "Bram . . . it's Rose."

"Rose . . ."

"Yes, my darling, yes!" And then her arms slid around his neck and she was planting kisses on his nose, his eyes, his bearded cheeks, any part of his face and neck she could reach.

"Good God, girl, are you mad?"

"Yes, for you," she cried, and quickly released him as an agonizing groan erupted from his throat. "Bram, what is it?"

"My arm, the left one. They've done what they could, but it's not been much."

"Keep yer voices down!" Bennie hushed from the door.

"Is that you, Bennie?"

"Aye, Colonel."

"I figured the message was from you, but I didn't really expect you to come."

Rose managed to hold back her tears when he turned toward her and the moonlight fell across his face. He looked like a wild thing. His face was covered with many days of stubbled growth. Dark hollows were edged like soot under his vacantly staring eyes, and his clothes were ragged and filthy.

"I'm glad you came, Rose. I've thought about you, always. Once, right here in Richmond—"

"I know, I recognized you in the America."

He nodded. "It took all the will I had not to bolt across the room and take you in my arms."

Rose went to her toes and gently brushed his bruised, chapped lips with the softness of her own.

"Miz Rose . . ."

"Yes, yes," she whispered toward the door, and looked back up into Bram's weary eyes. "We're going to free you."

"Impossible."

"It is not."

"I won't have you involved—"

"I am involved, my darling, and you have nothing to say about it."

"They hung Timothy Webster this morning."

"Oh, no . . ."

"Yes. I think I'm to go day after tomorrow."

"All the more reason, then," Rose whispered, her voice suddenly full of steel, "that we get you out of here tomorrow night."

"Rose, you can't! I'm guarded night and day. They check every prisoner in this wing, every hour."

"You won't be here."

"What?"

Rose found the pocket in her habit and withdrew a tiny vial containing three pills. "Here." She pressed them into his hand. "Tomorrow, around noon, take these. They will make you violently ill. The effect should wear off within an hour or two after they take you to the infirmary, but don't let them know that."

"But, what then?"

"Bennie will take care of that. Say that you'll do this, Bram, please."

"But what will you do with me, once—"

"That has been taken care of as well. President Davis has requested that I go to England to help raise money for the cause. I have agreed to go, as long as Bennie goes with me."

"Bennie?"

"*You* will be Bennie, Bram. We sail in two days' time, aboard the *Defiance*, from Wilmington."

"Rose," Bram sighed, encircling her with his good arm, "you never cease to amaze me!"

"Nor love you, Bram."

Again she pressed her lips to his, and thrilled to the feel of his heart beating against her breast.

England, she thought, with Bram. At last, just the two of them, with the war a world away.

Rose watched with bated breath as Bennie drew the canvas-covered wagon up to the loading dock. She waited just inside the ward area until he stepped from the wagon to the dock and approached the duty sergeant.

Rose got there seconds ahead of him. "Good evening, Sergeant Bowen."

"Evenin', Miz Rose," he replied, touching the

bill of his hat with two fingers. "Through for the night?"

"Not quite, I—"

"Excuse me ... name's Crow, Martin Crow. Got papers here to pick up my brother, Clyde ... passed on."

"I'm so sorry, Mr. Crow," Rose said, lifting the papers from his hand and passing them quickly under the sergeant's nose. "Yes, they are in order. I'll take care of it, Sergeant. Please follow me, Mr. Crow."

"Yessum."

Rose moved quickly away, with Bennie at her side.

"Where is the Colonel?"

"In the prisoners' ward, but it should be all right. We can take a shortcut through there with the dead man. There shouldn't be any suspicion. We do it all the time. How did you get the papers to release Clyde Crow?"

"The forms are real," Bennie said. "I forged the signatures meself."

"Down here," Rose said, guiding him by the elbow down a dim hall that would lead to the morgue room. "This is the one. Wait here!"

Clutching the papers, Rose entered the room and steeled herself to the odor of death that pervaded it. Narrow tables lined the walls and the center of the room. Each of the tables held a body beneath a rumpled sheet.

The orderly's desk was just inside the door.

When he saw her, he set aside the paper he was reading and stood. "What brings you down here, Miz Rose?"

"Just lending a helping hand." She passed him the papers. "The name is Clyde Crow. His brother has come to take him. He's right outside."

She hid her quivering hands in the folds of her skirt as the orderly scanned the paper. And then she sighed when he looked quickly up. From past experience, she knew that he had looked no further than the name of the deceased, and had not bothered to check the signature of the releasing military physician.

"Crow, Crow . . . yessum, I think I know which one."

Rose followed him through the maze of tables until he halted and slipped up the sheet on one of them to reveal a pair of stark white feet.

She felt ill, but forced herself to stand steady. She had done this same thing—delivered a dead soldier to his family—often before, but she had never gotten used to seeing the bare feet uncovered, with a stark white tag attached to one of the big toes.

"Nope, not this one," the orderly said, squinting at the name on the tag, then dropping the sheet. He shuffled over to another table and repeated the process. "Maybe . . . yep, here he is, Miz Rose, Clyde Crow. I'll get a gurney."

Moments later, she and Bennie were wheeling

the body of Clyde Crow toward the prisoners' ward.

"Have you talked to Darcy . . . told him what to do?" Bennie whispered out of the side of his mouth.

She nodded. "Get ready!"

Ahead she could see the open doors of Ward B. Beyond them, the ward itself was nearly pitch dark, lighted by dim candles in wall sconces, one on the wall at each end. Near the door, leaning idly back in a chair, barely noticing them, was a guard.

"Private, we're taking the deceased out to the loading dock. I hate to go through one of our wards—the other men don't like to see . . ."

"I know, Miz Rose, go ahead."

"Thank you, Private." She smiled, wheeling the gurney through the door. Then she turned to Bennie. "Go ahead, Bennie, hurry!"

Bennie struck off down the ward at a brisk pace, fishing a cigar from the inside pocket of his duster. At the other end of the ward, he would obtain a light for it from the second guard and engage him in conversation.

Rose moved along slowly, counting the beds. At the tenth bed she stopped and peered into the darkness.

"Nurse . . ." came the familiar voice.

"Yes," she sighed.

"I wonder if you could get me some water. The pitcher is here, on my left."

That meant the bed to Bram's left was empty. Quickly she slid the gurney into the slot between the two beds and hurried around the empty one. She could already see movement from Bram and feel that he was pushing the body toward her.

Taking a deep breath and biting her lower lip, she grasped the sheet and heaved with all the strength in her arms. The body came over onto the empty bed with ease, and she saw Bram settling the sheet over his face on the gurney.

She leaned forward and gently pulled the sheet from Clyde Crow's stark white face just enough so his hair would show, then rushed around to the foot of the gurney.

"Ah, here we are. My thanks for the light, lad."

" 'S all right, sir. 'Evenin', Miss Rose."

"Good evening."

Near the loading dock, Bennie moved to the head of the gurney while Rose squeezed Bram's foot and whispered, "Don't breathe!"

The sergeant only nodded and waved as they went by. When Bram was safely in the wagon and the gurney pushed back, Rose spoke in an overly loud voice to Bennie. "I am through for the night, Mr. Crow. I wonder if you could give me a ride as far as the square?"

"Be proud to, ma'am."

"Good night, Sergeant."

" 'Night, Miss Rose."

"Hurry, Bennie," she whispered as the wagon lurched forward, "or I know I shall faint!"

The following evening, just past dusk, they boarded the British packet *Defiance* at the Wilmington dock.

Rose was dressed in a traveling skirt and jacket of green crushed velvet, with a white underblouse patterned with muted rose stripes. The traveling garb, along with a trunk of clothes, were compliments of the Confederate government.

Bram, shaved and barbered now, was clothed in a gray velvet frock coat, a white-on-white linen shirt with a red cravat, and sparkling new breeches and boots. He even carried a walking stick, all compliments of Bennie McAdam.

But as handsome as he looked to Rose, she knew that he was not well. His face was ashen and his eyes were racked with the pain of his wound. Twice during the wild flight from Richmond they had stopped and Rose had redressed it. He needed medical attention, and probably hospitalization, but they couldn't stay in Wilmington, neither of them. Bram would be recaptured, and she would most likely be imprisoned herself for her part in his escape. All around Richmond the authorities would be looking for Rose Jacquard, who had helped the Yankee colonel Bramfield Darcy escape the hangman's noose.

She had written a long letter of explanation to Clay Fulton. In it she had begged him to explain her act and the reasons for it to President Davis. She knew he would, and was sure she would be forgiven for what she had done, particularly if she carried out this one last duty for the Confederacy in England.

But now, as they handed their papers to the stern-faced British captain, Rose wanted only one thing: to get Bram out of the South.

"Mr. and Mrs. Benjamin McAdam," he said with a wry twist to his smile.

Rose gripped Bram's good arm and flashed the captain her most engaging smile. She knew that *he* knew they were not who they professed to be. The captain probably knew who she really was, even if he didn't know who the tall, swaying, pale-faced man on her arm was.

But he would never admit it. If they were stopped after heading into open sea from the mouth of the Cape Fear River, he would have enough trouble explaining the seven hundred or more bales of cotton on his decks to the Yankees.

"My mate will show you to your cabin. We'll be casting off within the hour. Kindly stay below until you've been told we're through the blockade."

"Thank you, Captain," Bram murmured. He did his best to walk on an even keel behind the officer who led them belowdecks.

The man had barely left their quarters before Bram collapsed into a berth.

Rose was at his side in an instant. "Bram, darling, what is it?"

But she knew. She had seen too much suffering, too many wounds and their aftermath, not to know what was wrong.

His face was devoid of color now, almost the stark whiteness she had seen so often in death. And his eyes were growing more fixed by the second.

Gently, but as quickly as possible, she divested him of his coat and vest. The left shoulder of his linen shirt was damp with blood, and the bandage beneath it was a livid crimson.

"The wound has reopened," she whispered, as much to herself as to him. "I'll have to redress it."

As she rummaged in her bag, she felt the powerful engines below her feet begin their throb. By the time she returned to Bram's side with fresh makings for a poultice, bandages, quinine, and water, the ship had begun to move.

"We're moving."

"Yes," she replied, forcing back the tears that stung her eyes as she swabbed at the ugly, raw wound.

"How odd it is," Bram said. "I'm running my own blockade with the heroine of the Confederacy, and praying to God that we make it."

"We'll make it. We will!" she gasped, pressing the poultice to his fevered flesh and beginning the bind. "It is but three days to Bermuda. Once there, I'll get fresh bandages and medicines. And then it's on to England."

"England," he murmured, rolling his head toward her. "The war will be over for me then."

"Yes," she said, trying to keep the relief out of her voice. "Here, take this."

"What is it?"

"Quinine."

He swallowed, and was quickly racked by a cough as Rose held him tightly in her arms. When it subsided she gently rocked him, blotting the perspiration on his face with a cool, damp cloth.

"England, my darling," she murmured. "We'll be together at last, the two of us, with a vast ocean between us and this damnable war. I must do what I can for President Davis and the Confederacy. I promised, and I know that you won't deny me that. But with Sherman in Savannah and Grant near Richmond from the North, it will soon be over. Then, my dearest, there will be no obstacles between us—nothing."

He was limp in her arms, and for a moment alarm raced through her mind. "Bram . . ."

But he was only asleep.

Carefully, she leaned down and brushed her lips over his closed eyes. She held him tighter and let the swelling throb of the engines relay what was happening in the night outside.

Many an evening she had sat in the dining room of Willard's and heard tales of running the blockade from the very men who had done it so often.

By closing her own eyes now, she could practically chart their progress. They would steam quickly down the Cape Fear River to the cape itself, where they would slow to a crawl.

Somewhere outside Cape Fear there would be Union gunboats, perhaps four or more of them, lying in wait.

The *Defiance* would wait until the nightly bank of fog rolled in. Then, with all lights out and all the chains aboard muffled to ensure complete silence, they would slip out to sea.

Where were they now? Had they steamed the seventeen miles from Wilmington to the cape yet? Rose could stand the suspense no longer. Gently she stretched Bram in the bunk and covered him with a quilt. Then she eased from the cabin and mounted a ladder to the deck.

The night was inky black as she stole forward to the wheelhouse. When she could hear muted voices from just above her, she found a place among the bales of cotton and crouched down to pray. "Dear Lord, the months and years of terror and heartache have been so long. Please—"

"Flare!"

"Gunboats port and starboard, sir!"

"Full speed ahead!"

Rose raised to her knees. The black of night around them had turned a dull orange, and directly in front of them she could see two Union gunboats steaming to intercept the *Defiance*.

"Dear God!" Rose gasped when she saw the captain's intent. He meant to sail right between them!

There were bright flashes from both the Union boats, and then she heard the rolling boom of the guns. Shells shrieked over the bow and then over the stern as the long, sleek hull of the packet sailed through.

Another flare illuminated the sky, and more shells whined overhead, falling harmlessly into the sea.

But they were through, and beneath her Rose could feel the powerful engines giving them more speed with each passing second.

A half-hour later, they were again engulfed in inky blackness, and safe.

Rose retreated to the ladder and fairly flew back down to their cabin. "Bram, Bram, we've made it! We're through the blockade, darling—we're on our way to Bermuda and England!"

But Bram didn't hear her. He was unconscious and delirious. And when she took him in her arms, the quilt around him was soaking wet.

The first day out of port, Bram was able to take a little water and food. He had moments of clarity, but by evening they grew fewer and farther between.

By afternoon of the second day, Rose had to

force water down his throat by working his muscles with her fingers. The wound was red and raw now, and as he thrashed more in his fever, it became impossible to stop the bleeding.

By noon of the third day, Rose reluctantly made her decision. Shredding a sheet in strips, she tied him securely to the bunk and went in search of the captain.

"I am sorry to disturb you, Captain, but I would like to know when we will reach port in Bermuda."

"Sometime around dusk today, I would imagine."

"My husband is very ill. Since you carry no skilled surgeon on board, I think it best that we go ashore there."

"I suspected as much, missus, when I saw neither of you on deck these past three days. I'll see to it."

Darkness was just falling over the island paradise when Bram was placed in an ambulance caisson and Rose climbed up to sit beside him. In the last hour he had become somewhat rational, and now gazed up at her with the first sign of recognition she had seen since they had run the blockade.

"Rose . . ."

"Yes, my darling."

"Where are we?"

"Bermuda. They are putting you in a hospital here. I have already informed the Union consul of your real identity. He promises me that you will get the best of care."

Bram nodded feebly and made an attempt to squeeze her hand. "So I don't reach England after all."

"No," she whispered, turning her own haunted eyes from his. "No, not yet."

"Go on, Rose. I know you must."

For two days she stayed at his side, nursing him. Both doctors in attendance assured her that, barring any complications, he would recover from the infection.

And then the captain of the *Defiance* informed her that he would be sailing the following morning.

Winter was moving in on the North, bringing heavy gales and high seas to the North Atlantic. If she didn't sail on the *Defiance*, it might well be March, months away, before she could reach England.

Once again, as it had so many times before, duty and her pledge fell in the way of her love.

"Go, Rose," Bram urged. "For if you don't, it will haunt us both for the rest of our lives."

Rose gazed down at his handsome, pale face on the pillow. "It can't last much longer," she sighed. "And when it is over we can both say that we gave our all—we did everything we could, to the very end."

"England, Rose. I'll come for you, I promise."

She sat by his side the entire night as he slept

fitfully. In the morning she sought and received more assurances from the doctors. And then she returned to his room. "Why are we always saying good-bye?" she whispered.

He managed a weak smile. "This is not good-bye, my love. Merely a slight . . . interruption in our plans."

She pressed her lips to his and slipped away from the bed with a last squeeze from his hand.

The *Defiance* lifted anchor at noon, bound for England. Rose Jacquard was aboard.

CHAPTER TWENTY-FOUR

ROSE secured quarters in Chelsea and went about the task assigned her. She received aid from other delegates of the Confederacy in London, as well as from Englishmen sympathetic to the Southern cause. But even Rose could see that it was a *lost* cause as she prepared in February to depart for France and plead her case to Napoleon III.

Before leaving, she sent a request to Lady Camilla Fontaine, asking for an audience.

A note came back within the hour:

> *Dear Rose:*
>
> *I have been angered that, in the two whole months you have been in England, you have not once contacted me. No matter what there has been between us, I hope we are not enemies.*

Yes, please come. My coach will wait at your door until you do.

Camilla

The Kensington town house was beautiful, four stories of comfort and wealth. Camilla Fontaine met her at the door with open arms. "Rose, you are still so beautiful." She smiled, and then her delicate brows formed a frown. "But you look weary. Come, sit, we shall talk."

Camilla had not aged a day. If anything, she was more lovely than ever. In minutes, Rose felt herself warming to this woman whom for so long she had considered an enemy.

"I read about you daily in the papers, Rose. It seems that you have charmed all of London!"

"Have I? It appears that my charm doesn't extend to anyone's pocketbooks, I'm afraid."

Camilla shook her head slowly from side to side. "Rose, give up, I beg of you—for your own good. Damp London and the exhaustion I see in your eyes will put you in bed. It's over, Rose. Save yourself."

"I will, soon. But first I'm going to France. I must, Camilla."

Camilla shrugged. "I understand. I think you are a fool, but I do understand."

"There is something . . ."

Rose felt awkward, but finally, urged by Camilla, the real reason for her visit poured from her lips.

She wanted news of Bram. There was no way she could write or contact him. Had Camilla heard anything?

"Yes, I have had word," Camilla said, averting her eyes.

Rose leaned forward eagerly. "How is he? Is he well?"

"He is . . . well."

"Then he returned to Washington from Bermuda?"

"Yes. He is no longer in the Army, but has obtained a very high post in the State Department."

"Camilla, would you forward my letters, please?"

"Perhaps it would be better, Rose if . . ." She hesitated, searching Rose's eyes.

"What is it?"

"Nothing," she sighed. "I will forward your letters. And if there is any answer, I shall hold it until you return from France."

Rose thought Camilla's reticence odd, but didn't press the matter when it became obvious to her that Camilla Fontaine would say no more.

Two days later, she embarked for Paris, only to discover upon her arrival that Napoleon was out of the city and would not return for a month.

France was the last chip Rose could play. Already the British government had held up the ironclad rams the South had requested before they could sail from Liverpool to the Confederate states.

She was determined to wait and face the head of France in person.

Exiled Southerners and interned Confederate naval officers made her stay at least pleasant. She was distraught over the delay, but took heart as she began to enjoy the sights and wonders of Paris. The shops were filled with goods and the leading salons alight with charm and laughter.

How wonderful it would be, she thought as the days passed, to share Paris with Bram. How joyful to put the past behind them and just be lovers in Paris.

Almost daily she wrote to Bram and Lady Fontaine. Gossipy, newsy little notes came back from Camilla, but they contained no word about Bram.

And no reply came from him to any of her letters.

She followed the war in America through the papers in the reading room of the Grand Hotel. It was obviously progressing no better. But still Rose persisted. If the South was defeated, it would not be because she had not tried to the end.

While still awaiting Napoleon's return, she spoke persuasively to French bankers and diplomats, urging them to grant credits on cotton certificates from the Confederate treasury. She met with some success, but most refused her, adding to her sense of impending doom for the land she so loved.

But slowly, without realizing it, she began to regain the zest for life she had once known as the Wild Rose of Washington. The lines of worry fell away from her face. As the war seemed more and more distant, she smiled more often, becoming almost as gay as the Paris around her.

At last word came, and on a cold and rainy day in March, Rose entered the anteroom of the Tuileries Palace and waited to be received by the emperor of France.

Her hopes were high, but they were soon dashed. She pleaded her case eloquently and, as usual, she charmed him with her wit and beauty. The emperor was courteous, but she had come too late. The door between France and the Confederacy was closed, and it would not open again.

Rose walked the distance from the palace back to her hotel with a heavy step, knowing in her heart that her beloved South was doomed.

Two weeks later it was over.

Rose devoured the newspaper accounts of the final days.

General Sherman, the odd little man with the mane of red hair who had escorted her home from an Independence Day parade in Washington so long ago, had become one of the North's most brilliant generals. He had taken Savannah and slashed north across the Carolinas to lay seige to Petersburg and join the Northern armies of Grant.

Lee's dwindling and starving army was finally forced to retreat from Petersburg on April 2, and Richmond had fallen the following day.

On April 9, in a tiny courthouse at a place called Appomattox, Lee had surrendered.

The war was over, the Union was restored, and Rose felt empty, drained.

With a heavy yet hopeful heart she returned to England and her tiny Chelsea room to wait for Bram, as they had agreed.

For days she sent messages to Camilla Fontaine. None were answered.

At last she could stand it no longer. Hiring a hack, she journeyed to Kensington without an invitation. "Camilla, you must have some word ... you must!" she exclaimed, as the other woman led her into the drawing room. "And if you do, I beg of you, tell me! Is he coming to London? And if so, *when*?"

Rose was so distraught she bordered on hysteria. But through her own tears, she looked into Camilla's eyes and saw tears forming there as well.

"I swore, Rose, that I would not tell you."

"Tell me what?" Rose cried. "Please ... please, Camilla, I *must* know."

"All right."

In that moment, Rose knew that her first thought so many years before was true. "You love him too, don't you?" she whispered.

Camilla nodded, the tears now slipping from her eyes to form rivulets down her cheeks. "Like you, I always have. But unlike you, Rose, my love was never returned. I am afraid, however, that we have both lost him."

"No, I don't believe that!" Rose cried. "He promised. He vowed that he would come to England. And he will come! I know he will!"

"He's here, Rose. He has been here since just after you left for France."

Rose was thunderstruck. "He's . . . here? And he has not contacted me?"

Camilla bit her lower lip. "He doesn't want to see you, Rose. He made me promise not to tell you."

"I don't believe you!" Rose cried. "Bram would never say such a thing!"

"Rose," Camilla said, her eyes welling with tears, "Bram is . . . different now from when you last saw him."

"I don't care, I must see him! Where? Oh, my God, tell me where he is! I *must* see him!"

"You'll be surprised, Rose, and . . . dismayed."

"What on earth do you mean?"

"He's changed—a great deal."

Rose struggled to control the emotions raging

within her. "No amount of change could alter how I've felt and always will feel."

Camilla looked at her for a long moment, and then nodded. "Then I should let you try. Go to him, Rose. Take my coach. He sails for America on the morning tide from Southampton."

"The ship, Camilla—what is the name of the ship?"

"The *Dover*. Godspeed, Rose, and God forgive me if I have done the wrong thing."

Rose clasped her arms around the other woman. "You haven't. Believe me, you haven't." Minutes later she was urging Camilla's coachman to drive faster, and yet faster, through the mist and drizzling rain toward Southampton.

Dawn's first light barely creased the blanket of mist rolling over Southampton port from the sea.

Frantically, accompanied by the eerie blast of foghorns, Rose searched from pier to pier until she found the *Dover*.

"Darcy . . . Darcy—aye, he is on the passenger list, miss, but he's not aboard yet. He might be seeing to his luggage, there, at pier's end."

Rose could see nothing but yellow lights vainly trying to pierce the mist as she raced down the gangway and the pier with her skirts flying.

I've missed him! her mind screamed. He's bound for another port because of the fog . . .

He's laying over until there's another ship ...
He's decided to go by way of France.

All those fears and a hundred more raced
through her mind faster than her slippered feet
flew over the pier's rough planks.

And then a tall, wide-shouldered figure loomed
before her, clad all in black, a voluminous greatcoat thrown rakishly over his shoulders. Even
though thick fingers of fog clawed at his face,
partially obscuring the rugged features, Rose
knew it was he.

"Bram!" she cried. "Bram!"

The figure whirled. "Rose ..."

She slowed to a walk, her fevered brain trying
to comprehend the sudden fear and pain in his
eyes as they met hers.

"Bram ... why?"

"Go back, Rose."

"Go back?" she cried. "Dear God, I can't go
back. I've been running away from you since the
day we met. I'll do it no longer!"

"Rose, I beg of you ..."

She was close enough to touch him now. She
raised her hand and gently ran her fingertips
along the strong line of his jaw. "It's over, Bram,
at last it's over," she whispered, and then, with
a whimper, threw her arms about his neck.

So violently did she throw herself against him
that the heavy greatcoat fell from his shoulders
to puddle on the pier.

Rose's eyes raked his shoulders, and instinctively she recoiled. The left sleeve of his frock coat hung empty, the velvet sleeve rolled, the cuff pinned to his shoulder.

"Now will you go back?" he said, retrieving the cloak and clumsily throwing it back around his shoulders.

"I will not. When . . . where?"

"Bermuda."

"But they told me—"

"What I told them to tell you. Good-bye, Rose."

She looked up into his eyes and saw all the pain she herself had felt through the long trial that had kept them apart. "There will never be another good-bye between us again."

"Please, Rose, go."

"No, and don't ask me again. Do you think that that empty sleeve makes you less a man . . . makes me love you less? Too long I've given you only half of myself. I've made you share my love with a cause that you said was lost from the beginning. Well, now it is lost, it is over. But not between us. Don't you love me?"

His lips quivered. "You know I do, Rose. I've always loved you."

"And you always will," she replied, moving against his chest. "For I'll never again give you reason not to. Now, hold me, Bram, with your good right arm. And don't fear to do it, for one of your arms is worth ten of any other man's."

His right arm spanned her waist, and when his lips met hers, it thrilled Rose as if it were the first time.

"No more good-byes," she whispered into his lips. "This time it's forever."

About the Author

A professional actress for many years, Mary Canon embarked on a writing career five years ago. Ms. Canon, who shares a passion for travel with her husband and fellow author, Jack Canon, makes her home in North Carolina.

Great Reading from SIGNET

**Buy them at your local
bookstore or use coupon
on next page for ordering.**

Ø

Romantic Reading from SIGNET